THE ZOYA FACTOR

Anuja Chauhan

westland ltd

61, II Floor, Silverline Building, Alapakkam Main Road, Maduravoyal, Chennai 600095

93, 1 Floor, Sham Lal Road, Daryaganj, New Delhi 110002

First published by HarperCollins India Publishers 2008

Published by westland ltd 2016

Copyright © Anuja Chauhan 2008

All rights reserved

10 9 8 7 6 5 4 3 2 1

ISBN: 978-93-85724-83-1

Typeset in Electra LT Regular by SÜRYA, New Delhi

Printed at HT Media Ltd., Noida

The prequel 'Here's what was happening in Zoya's life exactly two years ago' was first published in *HT Brunch* and was commissioned exclusively by and for *HT Brunch*

The author asserts her moral right to be identified as the author of this work.

For Niret, Niharika, Niranjan and Daivik John.
You are my world.

1

'Zoya, *chal*, it's time to go.' Monita's husky voice had an edge to it. She sounded both totally wired and hugely relieved. I told her I'd be down in twenty minutes and jumped to my feet, smiling excitedly at my reflection in the mirrored wardrobe.

The two of us had been chafing in the luxurious embrace of the Taj Mumbai for the last three days. We'd demolished tinfuls of salted cashews and trayfuls of fancy chocolate, sweated in the sauna, primped in the parlour, and watched television mindlessly. All with one eye on the massive bay windows, down which smooth sheets of snot-coloured water had been pouring for thirty-six hours straight.

'It could be an award-winning ad for Coldarin or something,' Mon had said, gloomily surveying the rain that morning, lying on her tummy with her chin propped up in her hands. 'One of those intense, Cannes-Lion-winning type of ads, made on a million-dollar budget. God has a thunderous phlegmy cough and a rainy runny nose. The mortals, drowning in celestial snot, spray the skies with Coldarin mist. The satanic streptococci flee, the Almighty recovers and a huge double rainbow forms in the sky and morphs into the Coldarin logo. Slow fade out.'

I'd shot her a concerned look – it wouldn't do for my creative director to have a nervous breakdown bang at the beginning of the biggest cola ad-shoot of the year – and quickly handed her the Room Service menu for some light eating. 'It'll stop today, Mon,' I said soothingly, after she'd ordered two Prawns-Pepper-Salt platters and a Triple Hot-Choc-Fudge in a tearful voice. 'We'll shoot tonight. You'll see.'

Sure enough, by seven in the evening the rain had reduced to a slow snivel and an apologetic-looking sun had put in a cameo appearance before drowning itself in the Arabian Sea, leaving behind a clear, star-studded sky.

And now Monita had called.

The *Zing!* Cola shoot was finally on!

Humming happily to myself, I dived into the shower cubicle at seven forty-five, and emerged in a cloud of steam at five past eight. Then I wiped the steamed-up mirror and examined my face critically.

People are always saying *so cute!* when they see me and grabbing my cheeks and squeezing them with gusto, which is okay when you're a moppet in red corduroy dungarees but not so good when you are a working woman armed with a degree from a lesser business school, frantic to project a mature image in your job as a mid-level client-servicing executive in India's largest ad agency and twenty-seven years old to boot. By that age, people should be more interested in squeezing your butt, right?

Wrong.

'I don't know *what* it is, Zoya,' Sanks, my boss, (a forty-three-year-old, hardened adman, not some cheeky, empty-nester auntieji, okay) once told me, 'but just looking at your cheeks makes my thumb and index finger sort of *spasm* – I want to squeeze 'em and squeeze 'em and squeeze 'em till they pop.' He got a manic gleam in his protuberent eyes when he said this and I backed away from him hurriedly, thinking, *Okay, here's conclusive proof that the CAT and IIT JEE exam formats totally suck.*

Oh well, at least I'm not hideously deformed in any other way. I mean, my skin's okay, and my hair's actually quite nice – it's dark and shiny and cascades halfway down my back in a mass of bouncy ringlets. I never tie it up.

Now I shook it out and yanked open my duffel bag. It wouldn't do to be late.

The call time for the shoot was nine p.m. and it was only a short drive from where I was to the location, Ballard Estate. We'd cordoned off the whole ilaka and got police permission and protection for the entire week. We needed both because we were blocking busy roads *and* because we were shooting with one of the biggest stars in the country. Which brought me back to the all-important question of what cool outfit I was going to wear.

I obsess a little about being 'cool', because, hello, when people ask me where I stay I have to look them in the eye, smile brightly and say 'Karol Bagh' with casual unconcern. Which is *agony* in advertising because when all the snooty ad-people think Karol-Bagh-type, they imagine a pushy wannnabe in a chamkeela salwar-kameez with everything matching-matching. Someone who says 'anyways' instead of anyway, 'grands' instead of grand and 'butts' instead of butt. (As in: She has no *butts*, earns twenty *grands* a month and lives in Karol Bagh. Who does she think she is, *anyways?*)

Of course they don't know anything. They have no clue that the fancy south Delhi movie halls where they all throng to see the latest Hollywood films are owned by an enterprising Karol

Bagh boy who lives down my road, *still*, even though he now owns houses all over Delhi, *including* one in Golf Links, the poshest quarter in the capital.

Because Karol Bagh has Soul.

It may be a loud, expansive, *dhik-chik dhik-chik* music-loving soul that died and became a soul because its arteries were clogged with too much high-cholestrol, ghee-laden Punjabi food, but it's a soul nonetheless.

Think lousy old Golf Links has Soul? Naah.

I finally settled on loose khaki cargos and a skinny black ganji. Then I fluffed out my hair, yanked on my red sneakers, grabbed my matching-matching red rucksack (fully uncool I know, but what to do – control *nahi hota*) and slammed out of the room, hugely excited.

Monita was waiting for me in the lobby, grinning happily, tall, helmet-haired, strong-featured (*her* cheekbones are fully out there) and strong-minded too. She's nursed me through not one but two major heartbreaks that I don't like to talk about. She wears fusionish clothes and writes some pretty zany scripts. She's very cranky nowadays though, being fully nicotine-deprived. Her younger son (twenty-six months old) is refusing to relinquish his rights to her Goddess-like breasts. 'I swear, Zoya,' she'd said on the flight in from Delhi, 'seven whole days away from him, this time I'm going to pull the plug for good.'

Anyway, she said I looked nice and made some cheapie remark about how I'd duded up to meet movie stars. I beamed like a besharam and shamelessly admitted that I had as we stepped out jauntily into the dripping world, hailed a cab and told the driver to take us to Ballard Pier.

'*Wahan* barrier *laga hai*, shooting *chaalu hai*,' he said dourly and I got major thrills out of replying, '*Pata hai*, it's *our* shooting only!'

Monita rolled her eyes at me, but I just giggled. Hey, she'd shot a million films but this was my first! I was allowed to chirp a little.

We wove our way through the crowd, holding our official CREW tags before us like talismans. The 'sikorty' was very tight, guards were everywhere, prodding a million curious people to stay behind the cordons. Finally, we reached the crossroads, the location for the night, and Monita waved to the director, PPK – fifty-ish, with a bushy beard, hat and ponytail – who signalled to the guards to let us through. 'Hi girls,' he said, grinning. 'What do you think?'

I looked around, totally awestruck. The chowraha was at the centre of four massive roads, black, gleaming and (rare for Bombay) pothole free, because the crew had doused them all with water from huge pipes as far as the eye could see. Noble colonial buildings loomed behind huge lattice-leaved neem trees, their pillared corridors and Gothic balconies shining white in the moonlight. Bang in the middle of the crossroads was an old fountain and a statue of a crouching gargoyle that the art department had mocked up to exactly match the architecture of the period.

'Gotham City,' grinned PPK. 'Just as I promised!'

'How come I've never seen this place before?' Monita asked as he led us to a semicircle of blue plastic chairs placed next to an open garbage dump. I wrinkled my nose at the stench but no one else seemed to care.

'You have,' he said in answer to Mon's question. 'It's just that it's always choc-a-bloc with traffic so you've never noticed how pretty it is.'

'Uh, why are we sitting here?' I indicated the trash heaps behind us.

'So that, along with the garbage, we're not in the frame,' said PPK.

'And what's this little TV thing?' I asked, pointing to a set in front of us.

'A video-assist,' PPK said sweetly. 'Exactly how long have you been in advertising?'

'Two-and-a-half years,' I said defensively. 'But this is my first big film shoot.'

'That, my dear, is obvious,' he said, breathing heavily. 'Kenny, come and give young…uh…Zoya here a crash course in film-making while I discuss the storyboard with Monita.'

An earnest-looking boy in a red baseball cap hurried up and led me away even as Mon said, 'PPK, get off my bachcha's case. She's a good kid.' I wasn't too hassled, though. I've figured out that if you wander around looking smart and never ask any questions – stupid or otherwise – you don't learn much in life.

Kenny walked me around the location. He introduced me to the cameraman, who lay flat on his stomach on the road, peering rather macho-ly down into a camera eyepiece like it was the barrel of a sub-machine gun. 'He's framing for the shot,' said Kenny. 'Anything he shoots there, PPK can see on the assist where you guys were sitting.' Next, he pointed to a guy sitting hunched over some equipment, with earphones on. 'There's a sound system too, it'll play the track so everybody can lip-sync the words. And these,' he stopped and indicated with his arm, 'are the make-up vans.'

I looked up to see three big white vans the size of minibuses, lined up next to each other. A huge fourth van – a generator van, Kenny said – was parked alongside. Each van had a sheet of paper stuck to the door: DIRECTOR, AGENCY and a third that made my heart race a little faster.

SRK.

'Is he here yet?' I asked Kenny eagerly.

He nodded. 'That's his car,' he said, reverentially eyeing the vehicle, but apart from noticing that it was silver-coloured and longish-looking I didn't give it much attention. I just don't *get* it with guys and cars.

Then Mon was hurrying up to me. 'Zo, I'm going in to check out Shah Rukh's costume. Wanna come?'

I nodded, giggling idiotically, and she looked at me in disgust. 'Do you know, Young Zoya,' she said, 'that Truly Spiritually Arrived People behave *exactly* the same way when they meet kings as they do when they meet beggars? They don't go all pink and sweaty-palmed and fuss with their hair and they *definitely don't giggle.*'

'You mean to say your heart doesn't beat faster when you talk to Shah Rukh Khan, Mon?' I asked disbelievingly as I skipped along behind her.

She gave me this really superior look. 'No,' she said baldly.

'How about when you talk to Amitabh Bachchan?' I asked slyly.

She went a little pink and snapped, 'Come along now,' and striding up to the door of the van marked SRK, turned the handle authoritatively and stepped in.

There was no one there. 'He's in the other half,' Mon whispered.

I nodded, stifling more nervous giggles, and looked around curiously. It looked a bit like an AC-first coupé, only bigger. There were flowery curtains in the windows, a folding bed along one wall with matching flowery bolsters, and a little folding table, on which were placed a thermosy-looking black and steel coffee mug and a pack of cigarettes. There was a music system built into one wall, and a TV too, but the major part of the 'room' was taken up by a dressing table. The mirror had all these yellow bulbs stuck along its frame. Our shirt options for the shoot, draped on hangers, hung from the clothes-hooks on the wall. Monita looked at each of them critically, debating which to pick. 'All these are crap,' she muttered. 'But this plain white one might do, don't you think, Zo?'

I was muttering something idiotic in reply when the connecting door opened and SRK emerged, saying 'Heyyy!' to Monita. They hugged and then he smiled at me, quite sweetly, and said hi.

It was pretty unreal. Shah Rukh Khan saying hi to me. And I behaved all grown up too, like I was on autopilot, or something. I shook his hand, smiled into his baby-browns and sat down again. Like I met superstars every day of my life. Monita and he made some small talk about his recent movies (she vowed she loved 'em all) and the Knight Riders' performance at the last IPL. Then they discussed what he should wear for tonight's shoot while he smoked a cigarette and sipped his coffee. Monita looked wistful when he lit up, and sidled a little closer to him, but all she said was, 'Why don't you try on these three shirts and we'll pick one.' He nodded, and reached down to pull off the navy-blue sweatshirt he had on – right there, *outside* the bathroom. *Wowie!* I thought, and perked up and paid attention.

I had just got my first glimpse of the toasty brown midriff when my phone rang. Shah Rukh said, his shirt still only half off, 'The signal's better outside,' and I nodded maturely and exited the van.

'This had better be good,' I snarled as I punched the answer key.

'Um…Zoya, how are you? Hope there's no rain tonight?' It

was Sanks. Now I know why Monita calls him old coitus interruptus. He was talking to me in this mild, nice way, which of course set all my alarm bells ringing. 'Nope,' I said cautiously, 'though we haven't really started yet. They're setting up for the truck shot.'

Sanks made little clicking noises as I spoke, like he couldn't wait for me to finish. It's one of his most irritating little traits, right up there with his tendency to come in to work at eight a.m., and then go *Good Afternoon, Good Afternoon* smirkily from behind his bristly moustache when we stagger in at half past nine. The moment I finished, he said, still in that nicey-nice voice, 'Well, Zoya, I'm sorry but you'll have to come back to Delhi right now.'

You're kidding, right?

'It's the ICC Champion's Trophy in Dhaka and I need someone I can trust to go shoot the team. Ishaan's dad is in the ICU so it's going to have to be you.'

The ICU! I knew Ishaan (my one and only flunkie) had trouble at home but I hadn't realized it was so bad.

But the even worse news was that *Zing!* Co. had obviously gone and signed the cricketers *again*. I mean, when were these people ever going to learn? Wasn't the last World Cup – where our 'best batting line-up in the world on paper' had got out right at the very first stage itself – enough of a lesson for them? They'd sunk seriously obscene amounts of money into an intensely patriotic *Zing! Together Now, India* campaign, and then they'd had to scramble to take it off air before the irate public burnt down their trucks and hoardings and totalled their factories.

All of us at the agency had had to scurry around, creating new ads for them to run on the World Cup slots they'd paid so much money for. Whole consignments of *Zing! Together Now,*

India armbands, wristbands, bandannas and tee shirts had had to be pretty much thrown away. It wasn't safe to wear them any more. Really. You could get beaten up if you were foolhardy enough to wear one and walk the streets.

The whole sorry circus had turned me into a cricket cynic for life.

The cricket team had slunk back to India, under cover of darkness, police jeeps trailing behind their BMWs, protecting them from the wrath of the people. The IBCC called a council and there had been massive amounts of name-calling and buck-passing. And a little bit of soul-searching. With the result that about eighteen months later the 'greatest batsman in the world', the 'wall' and the 'comeback kid' had called it quits from ODI cricket. A new Australian coach was produced from somewhere and India had gone about building a whole new cricket team, pretty much from scratch.

It was a team of rookies and wild card IPL discoveries, with a couple of leftovers from the old order. The board had rotated the captaincy till it had become a bit of a joke, but about six months ago, the Aussie coach had thrown a stink and the Board had finally plumped for one particular candidate. Since then, things had steadied a bit. Still, nobody was expecting the ill-assorted team to exactly cover itself with glory at the mini World Cup. Except, it seemed, eternally optimistic *Zing!* Co., who had gone and signed them on all over again!

'They got them cheap, I suppose?' I said snidely.

'Kind of.' Sanks was evasive.

I sighed. 'What's the tack we're taking this time?' I asked. 'Or is it too early to ask?'

'Oh, it's a campaign celebrating the spirit of cricket,' he said glibly. 'The Joy of the Game, as it were. No narrow jingoistic side-taking. It's not about winning or losing but how you play the game.'

That figured.

'So when can you get on a plane, Zoya?' Sanks said again. 'We've been working on getting your visa done here.'

'Sanks, can't it wait a couple of days? I've really been looking forward to this shoot,' I said feebly, thinking of Shirtless Shah Rukh in the make-up van.

I had to hold the phone away from my ear. 'Have you any idea how *difficult* it is to get a window to shoot with these guys? One day later and they'll go into *training camp*. And if we disturb them *then*, the media will *crucify* us!'

'But I don't know anything about cricket!' I wailed desperately. 'I don't even know who the captain is, for heaven's sake.'

'Of course you do,' said Sanks irascibly. 'It's that guy you like, the one'– he made his voice all squeaky and produced what he fondly assumed was an imitation of *my* voice – "'with the cute butt."'

Oh, *that* guy.

Well, he did have a point, the new skipper looked pretty good when he leapt about fielding, all lithe and leonine, which is a huge thing to pull off if you're wearing those awful light-blue track pants... And I could shop for pretty saris in Dhaka. Also, there was no way I couldn't do what Sankar Menon wanted and survive. The man is a butcher, an absolute kasai.

Sanks was still talking. 'Besides, didn't you once have lunch with the whole team in Bombay, Zoya? You *know* these guys.'

'Breakfast,' I corrected him automatically. 'Right before some big match. But that doesn't really count. You sent me there to get some No Objection Certificate signed and they just let me sit at their table for, like, fifteen minutes. No one talked to me or anything.'

'See?' said Sanks, happily ignoring what I'd just said. 'You know them! You're going. It's just a two-day thing. And might I remind you that a lot of people would give an arm and a leg for an opportunity to observe world-class cricket up-close.'

Ya-ya, people who lived, ate and dreamed cricket. I wouldn't cut off any body part for the dumb game, except maybe the extra two inches of subcutaneous fat on my cheeks.

'Okay, Sanks,' I shrugged, bowing to the inevitable. 'I'll go.'

I hung up and gloomily retraced my steps to Shah Rukh's make-up van. I tried the handle Monita style (i.e., authoritatively), but it didn't budge. Then one of the spot-boys loitering outside the van dug out this little strand of dried snot from his nose, rolled it between forefinger and thumb and flicked it in the direction in which Shah Rukh had (presumably) gone. I looked that way and managed to spot him in the distance, atop a giant *Zing!* Cola truck parked in the middle of the square, practising dance steps with the choreographer.

A crowd of about a thousand extras milled below him.

I sighed.

So much for Veer–Zoya.

2

The next day I caught an insane flight back to Delhi and hired a kali-peeli to take me home, rattling up to the gates of Tera Numbar around midnight. The cabbie and I bickered amicably over the fare and parted friends. I swung open the rusty iron-sheeted front gate, lugged my bag through the garden and up the veranda and peered through the fly-screen door into the drawing room.

The room was dark but the TV was on, and Eppa, our severe, fifty-plus maid, who's looked after me and my brother since we were born, was catching some late-night television with Meeku, my mother's aging-but-feisty, one-eyed hairball. Eppa rules our house and has been with the family since '79 when my dad was posted in Cochin Cantt and my harassed Ma took her on to help cope with my horrible older brother, Zoravar. 'Hoo's dyuere?' she called.

'Bhooooot,' I said in my best spooky voice.

Eppa snorted as she unlatched the door. 'Zoyaaa!' she said. 'Why yu are skaring me, notty gul?' I gave her a hug as Meeku yipped eagerly around my heels and then collapsed right in front of the AC again, his duty done. '*Kaisa tha* Shah Rukh Khan?'

'He was hot, Eppa!' I told her. 'I saw him shirtless, can you imagine?'

She leaned forward excitedly. '*Photu liya?*' she asked, and I had to sheepishly confess that I hadn't managed any photographs. She sniffed in disgust; she'd really been looking forward to showing off a photo of me in a clinch with SRK to her entire social circle.

I collapsed on the sofa and scratched Meeku behind the ears. 'What are you watching, Eppa?' I asked her placatingly.

'*Paap Ka Ant,*' she said, a little sulkily.

The End of Sin. 'Cool! What's it about?'

I really like watching TV with Eppa because it's something she does only late at night, after her work for the day is done – the dishes washed, the kitchen swept, the copper gas burners meticulously cleaned with a skinny number 18 knitting needle and the glass lid firmly closed over them for the night. It's the only time she relaxes, squats before the TV, combs out her wiry grey hair and giggles girlishly over WWF wrestling matches, high-level politics in the Viraani and Aggarwal dynasties and the occasional sex-and-violence movie. Now she spoke in her gentle late-night voice, so different from her shrill quarrelsome day voice: 'The hero, no, he is loving rich girl, and her family is not happy, so her vicked brother, what he doos, he takes the hero sister and spoils her. Now she will have to kill herself...'

I choked on the glass of water she'd handed me. 'Excuse me? What d'you mean, Eppa, if he spoi – uh – rapes her, why should she kill herself?'

'She have to! That is the only way... Spoilt girls have to kill themselves. Or become nun. They can take badla on him first if they want.'

'Revenge?' I asked. 'You mean they should *kill* him or something? Why can't she file a case, win it, then meet some nice man and marry him?'

Eppa shook her head vigorously. 'That is not the way, Zoya Moya! She *havtu* die!' She looked at my appalled expression and added charitably, 'And go to heaven, of course.'

I woke up around eight and came out to have my tea in the garden. Our house is on this very busy main road that links Delhi to the industrial town of Rohtak. Huge, smoke-belching trucks, illegally overloaded with mysterious merchandise, trundle up and down it daily. But my grandfather's house has a huge wall all around it and masses of bougainvillea and bamboo thickets that muffle the sound and create this really cool secret-garden feel.

I watched Eppa watering the flowerbeds, humming to herself. 'Good morning, sex bomb!' I said cheerily and flashed a benign smile as Meeku hurtled into the lawn and started digging vigorously in the purple masses of verbena blossoms. 'Where's Dad?'

Eppa sniffed, 'Dyuere!' and I turned and saw my father walking up, the sun gleaming on his smooth bald head, his moustache bristling. He was still in his pajamas and looked really worked up about something. 'It's that damn Gajju again,' he grumbled, without looking at me. 'He keeps parking in my spot all the time.'

Eppa made soothing noises and poured out the tea.

My grandfather built this house in the early thirties and I've often wondered why he bothered because all he does is hide in his village and avoid it like the plague. Of course, according to my grandmother, Karol Bagh was a happening address back then. 'It was all the Punjabis coming in post-Partition,' she'd told me once with a disdainful sniff, 'who ruined the neighbourhood.'

I don't really see her point. I love the Punjabi-ness of Karol Bagh. It's chock-full of colourful fabric markets and sinful, ghee-drenched sweet stalls and peopled with rocking Punju auntiejis with flashing eyes and massive shelf-like uniboob bosoms. *My* theory is that my grandmother 'who's a little – uh – *girlish* in the chest department' found them hugely intimidating. That's why she beat a prudent retreat to the haveli in the village some twenty years ago, hauling my granddad off with her.

When he left, my granddad divided the house among his four sons. My father, Vijayendra Singh Solanki, is the eldest, followed closely by my trio of Chachas: Mohindra, Gajendra and Yogendra. 13, New Rohtak Road or Tera Numbar, as we call it, is an ungainly white two-storeyed bungalow with pillared verandas and overgrown lawns in the back and front, and we all live in different bits of it. We cousins love it, because the division created some really eccentric architecture, like a kitchen in a garage, a dining room you enter through a loo, a perfectly circular drawing room or gol kamra, various secret passages, and a bathroom window through which members of all four families can talk and lend and borrow stuff.

Dad moved in here when he retired from the army because he felt that motherless kids like Zoravar and me needed all the family we could get. His relationship with his brothers was tempestuous, to say the least. Like, these days Gajju was totally pissing off my dad by parking his crappy old car in Dad's parking spot in the drive. 'He's just doing it because I bought a new car,' Dad grumbled. 'I've a good mind to go upstairs and pull his nose.'

I used to stress about this internecine warring among the brothers when I was younger, till Eppa explained that my dad and his brothers were actually quite fond of each other. 'Your mummy alvayz said they shows their loves by fighting, Zoya,' she told me once after Yogu Chacha had torn into our house like a guided missile and ripped the shirt off my dad's back, claiming it was his and that we'd flicked it off his washing line. 'Actually, they verrri close family. See how they all sees the cricket matches together!'

She had a point.

The ICC World Cup is a huge family event in our house. Everybody huddles around one TV and cheers like crazy. They curse and kiss and chest-bang and stuff. All is forgiven. Total bonding happens. In fact, my dad and three Chachas were all thrown out of the maternity ward of the Military Hospital by the irate Mallu nurses the day I was born because they were cheering the Indian team so loudly. It was the Prudential World Cup final that day and their lusty yelling had put all the delivering mommies on the floor off their *breathe-in breathe-out* rhythm.

Apparently, I only very narrowly escaped being named Kapila Devi Solanki.

Sometimes I can't help thinking that the fact that the last World Cup had been such a washout as far as India was concerned, was one big reason why our family bonding had taken such a nosedive.

Dad sipped his tea moodily, finally spotted me and did a double take. '*Arrey*, Zoya! When did you come?'

I told him about the change in plan at work and he beamed happily. 'That's more like it!' he said. 'Flying to Dhaka to see some top-class cricket! Much better than shooting with hero-sheros.'

I was in office by eleven. I signed the register, greeted Totaram, our amiable security guard, and drifted in only to suffer everybody going, 'Zoya? Why aren't you at the shoot? What happened?' It was full *jale pe namak.*

AWB is the biggest ad agency in the country. Its Delhi office churns out TV, print, radio and outdoor ads for a huge number of multinational clients, one of the biggest of which is the cola company *Zing! Co.* An agency basically has three departments: Servicing (that's me), whose job it is to suck up to the clients and help them work out what kind of strategy they need; Creative (that's Mon), whose job it is to actually *create* the campaign based on that strategy; and Media, whose job it is to decide where the campaign should appear (as in TV channels, radio channels, newspapers, magazines, the Internet, and street hoardings) so that the maximum number of people of the type the client wants to target end up seeing it. It's a fascinating, unabashedly shallow world, and I fell madly in love with it when I came here as a summer trainee two years ago.

I snuck into Sanks's cabin and hung around waiting for him to look at me. But he was leaning back in his armchair, both eyes closed, listening to a script that Neelo Basu (a lean, mean cadaverous machine, in a SICK MY DUCK tee shirt who lives to smoke joints and download south Indian sleaze off the Net) was narrating with full feeling. I had no option but to hang around near the cabin door and hear it too.

'Film opens on this sexy fucking highway, okay? There's this biker dude riding the Terminator, and as he cruises by, these massive fucking gates open for him, all by themselves, like magically. The dude grins a crooked grin and rides through and then he comes up to this high mountain pass in fucking Ladakh, okay? And these massive boulders roll aside magically too. He grins, again, like this happens every day for him, you know? And then he passes this green meadow where these babes are doing yoga, okay? They're all really hot, stacked types. Solid mutton-*shutton* happening, in skin-tight leotards, okay. And as he approaches them, they do this fucking *mandook aasan*, the *frog position*, okay, basically all hundred of them go up on their hands, raise their butts in the air and spread their legs out, like *fully*, man. Then this Hollywood-trailer type voice-over says: "THE WORLD OPENS WIDE FOR THE NERO–TASHA TERMINATOR."'

Neelo dropped the dramatic pose he'd frozen in, looked eagerly at Sanks and asked, 'What d'yu think?'

Sanks, eyes still closed, said mildly, 'Comments, gentlemen?'

One brave little servicing guy spoke up. 'I like it,' he said stoutly. 'It's different. It'll get us noticed.'

Neelo beamed at him, but Sanks said, eyes still closed, 'Why don't you come *naked* to work tomorrow, fucker? You'll be different and you'll get noticed.' The servicing guy shrank backward as Sanks opened dangerously glittering eyes and glared at Neelo. 'It's the Nero-Tasha *Terminator*, you fuck,' he spat out balefully. 'Not the Nero-Tasha *Fornicator*. When are you going to get your mind out of the gutter?'

But Neelo stood his ground. 'Don't be so one-track-minded, Sankar,' he said loftily. 'I'm showing how much *respect* this bike commands. Gates and shit open for it. Ladakhi boulders! And I did *research*, man! I went on the Net and found out the names of yoga aasans and all. This is a *real* aasan, by the way, in case you think I've made it up. Actually, if you think about it, it's quite a subtle script...'

Sanks got to his feet. 'Subtle, my ass,' he said rudely and then, spotting me, said, 'Aah, Zoya, take Subtle Bihari Vajpayee here and hit the airport. Your flight leaves at one.'

So then Neelo took me home in his rattling car to pick up my things for the trip. On the way he went on about how cool his script was and how he was a creative giant reporting to pygmies-in-suits and how the only way to sell bikes was to tell the consumer he would get laid big time if he bought the Nero-Tasha bike.

'In fact,' said Neelo, fully warming to his theme, 'that's the only way to sell *anything*, man! Bikes, televisions, insurance, cold drinks... Buy *this*, get laid! Buy *that*, get laid! Buy fucking *anything*, get laid! Hey, maybe I can sell my script to *Zing!* whatdyuthink, Zoya? "The World Opens Wide For The *Zing!* Drinker". Cool, huh?'

3

Dhaka isn't that popular a destination but that day the lines snaking in front of the Biman Air counters were the longest in the terminal. Malayalis, Manipuris, Sardars, old, young, pierced or vibhooti-smeared, they were all in the queue.

That's cricket fever for you.

It's the Great Indian Disease, I tell you. Worse than dengue or polio or tuberculosis. They should vaccinate us against it when we're born, I thought gloomily as I queued up behind the long line of Dhaka-bound cricket freaks. One shot at birth, a couple of boosters over the years and you're immune to cricket for life. No heartache, no ulcers, no plunge in productivity during the cricket season and no stupid bets that make you lose money and lead you to commit suicide.

The queue was over forty people long, but luckily we spotted the still photographer on the project, Vishaal Sequiera, more than halfway up the line. He waved to us and we strutted up to join him, moving up some twenty places in the process.

Vishaal was all excited about the trip. His artily untidy hair (in which orange gulmohar petals were scattered like confetti) stood up like it was electrically charged and his eyes had the manic gleam of a cameraman-with-a-plan. '*Kaafi* intense type *ke* shots *lenge*,' he told Neelo, puffing on a Navy Cut. 'You know, Reebok, Nike types…sweaty, focused, looking right into camera. Attitude, you know? Besides, we'll get to see some matches, it'll be cool.'

As cool as clandestine glimpses of Shah Rukh Khan's chest? I don't think so. But that reminded me... 'What's the captain's name again, Neelo?'

'Nikhil Khoda,' Neelo said, rolling his eyes. 'Really, Zoya, you're pathetic. Please do read up on all these guys or you will fully cut off our noses in Dhaka.'

Vishaal said, 'How can you not know *Khoda?* He's a *God*, dude, he's a *King!*'

'Plays that well, huh?' I asked as we all moved up a place in the line.

Vishaal shook his head impatiently. 'Never mind *that!* Do you know who he's *dating?*'

'Some Bollywood heroine?' I hazarded, not very interested.

'No, no,' Vishaal shook his head again. 'Nothing so mundane! He's dating' – he clasped his hands together, lowered his voice and breathed reverentially – 'the girl in the *yeh toh bada toinnngg hai* ad!'

Both Neelo and he let out a long low moan. Oh, please.

The ad in question is an extremely raunchy spot for men's underpants. It features this ripe-'n'-tight village babe in a choli-sari who sashays really proudly down to the river panghat to wash her husband's chaddis. All the village women gather around to watch as she soaks, scrubs and rinses the garment in the sudsy river water, getting more and more turned on in the process. There's a one-line song-track that sighs steamily, *'Yeh toh bada toinnngg hai'* right through the ad, seeking to inform us that the wearer of the underpants, which the proud village babe is washing so slavishly, is very *toinnngg*, whatever *toinnngg* may mean. It is seriously the most sexist piece of advertising I've seen in my life. But no one can deny that the babe is a scorcher...

'Big deal,' I muttered. 'What does *toinnngg* mean anyway?'

Neelo cleared his throat. 'I think it means' – he held up his hand with his index finger hanging downwards limply and then slowly raised it till it stood fully erect – '*TOINNNGG*, you know?'

I choked, but was saved from having to answer because we'd finally reached the check-in counter. I hitched my bag higher on my shoulder, handed our tickets over and resigned myself to a really educational trip.

We got into Dhaka by six in the evening. The airport had this air of smug self-importance and a big banner over the arrival gate. 'WELCOME ALL THE CRICKET PLAYING NATIONS FOR THE ZING! MINI WORLD CUP!'

A chubby boyish type was standing holding a placard with our names on it when we finally staggered out. He smiled and grabbed the trolley and bundled us into an Ambassador car with 'Sonargaon' emblazoned across the door. Apparently, all the teams were shacked up in either the Sonargaon or the Sheraton.

As we drove through the city I saw all these awesome trees ('What are they called,' I asked Neelo and he answered, 'Uh, *Bong* trees?') strung up with banners and buntings and stuff. It was very festive. Neelo was busy commenting on the hoardings along the road. There were lots of *Zing!* and Niceday Biscuits (the other big sponsor) hoardings with the Bangladesh team looking all resolute and focused. We even saw one for 7-Up, a still our agency had shot five years ago. Yana Gupta sizzling in a green qawaali outfit. Only, while ours had her in just a teeny-weeny kurti and juttis, flashing smooth bare legs at the grateful public, this version wore a demure green churidar. Well, this was an Islamic country.

'Imagine the poor choot who must have sat and painted on that churidar, man,' Neelo cackled. 'Must've taken him three whole days at least!' He sounded a little wistful, though. Ever since he'd heard about this guy who actually held a highly paid job as Hollywood's official nipple-tweaker (apparently, he pinches famous pairs with just the correct amount of pressure before every shot to make them look all perky), Neelo had been fantasizing about a similar job, one that 'would totally fulfil my creative soul'.

When we arrived at the Sonargaon we discovered that the Indian, Sri Lankan and Australian teams were staying there as well. Of course, lots of teams had already packed up and gone home. My client Ranjeet, brand manager of Zing! Cricket and Promos, was checked in there too, which was pretty painful. (He got in on the Idiot Quota; everybody else at Zing! Co. is pretty savvy.) The commentators and umpires were lodged there as well, which meant we would be running into them in the elevators. The hotel was totally buzzing. OB vans from practically every news channel were parked outside. The guy in the coffee shop (called Coffee Shoppee) confided that this was the biggest thing to happen in Dhaka for like, forever.

Well, I guess it *was* pretty cool. Unfortunately, I know next to nothing about cricket and knew I wouldn't be able to make any intelligent conversation with the sports-celeb types we were sure to meet. Anyway, we were going to be there only for two days. I figured we'd just herd the cricketers together and get our shots and grab the next plane out – I to Bombay for the Shah Rukh shoot and the boys to Delhi, to develop all the stuff we'd got. Posters and shop signage had to roll out within the week. The only catch was, in case our team made the final, we three would have to careen back to Dhaka to shoot them with the trophy, slap on the rah rah song we'd already recorded, and send it out via satellite just before the awards ceremony on TV.

Uh, that's *if* they won the final.

Not much chance of that happening, I thought, though Vishaal and Neelo felt this was the best India team we'd had after a long, long time.

We walked into the Coffee Shoppee and I took in the decor bemusedly. It was a peculiar blend of Mediterranean and Shantiniketan.

'That dude's cool,' Vishaal declared, still thinking of Khoda as we pored over the menu. 'He's only been captain for six months but he's the best this country has ever seen.'

'How can you say that, Vishaal?' I asked. 'We lost the last four finals we played! The papers say this team can snatch defeat out of the jaws of victory any time, anywhere! Your Nikhil Khoda's hoardings were smeared with gobar from Rajkot to Calcutta!' (This is a sacred Indian ritual. People gather in hoards to chant bitter breast-beating slogans and smear fresh, still-warm cow droppings on the faces of cricket players on advertising billboards all over the country. It happens every time the headline 'INDIAN CHALLENGE ENDS' appears in the sports page, which is often.)

Vishaal shook his head in a sage manner I found really irritating. 'Keep the faith, Zoya,' he said. 'It's a team in transition. Khoda has made it shed all its baggage, like a snake sheds its skin. Now,' he said, cupping both hands and waving them in front of me, Sridevi-style, 'he's going to strike like a cobra!'

I am so surrounded by weirdos.

'The Board seems to be behind him,' Neelo said matter-of-factly. 'Or else they're giving him a long rope hoping he'll hang himself.'

Vishaal snorted: 'He won't. He's too damn smart. I'm telling you, *agar* Khoda can't bring home the World Cup, no one can!'

I didn't say anything.

I still bear the scars of One Who Has Done Cricket-Based Advertising. And I know it can completely backfire on you. You spend like half your annual advertising budget on a cricket campaign and then they go in there and play abysmally and the public says it's because they do too many ads and they start hating your product. It happens without fail after every major tournament. Even after our *best* performance in recent times, when our team managed to make it to the finals (and then lost miserably, but why go there?), this chain sms did the rounds saying: *On this shameful day, we hereby promise to boycott every product the team endorses, Jai Hind*. It doesn't help that the channel guys seem to get a sadistic pleasure out of running a player's ad right after he gets out for a duck. One moment he's *out*, and the next he's *in* the ad break, receiving phone calls from his mother telling him, *Beta, karlo duniya mutthi mein…* That's why I say, give me movie stars any time. I mean, a lot of people say Shah Rukh can't act but at least he's never given a performance so bad that it incited people to climb up ladders and put gobar on his hoardings.

I put down my Sonargaon Super Club Sandwich. 'So what's the plan for the shoot, guys?'

'We'll be all set up by eight a.m.,' said Vishaal who's pretty put together in spite of the moron-on-marijuana image he projects. 'I booked the banquet hall when we checked in.'

'I'll take them through the shots as we've visualized them, once they arrive,' said Neelo, putting down his (already?) empty glass. 'All you have to do is make sure they reach on time, Zoya.'

'Okay,' I said, trying to look unconcerned, though I groaned inwardly at the thought of waking up a bunch of starry-type cricketers and getting them to the banquet hall by eight in the morning. Still, I couldn't let these two veterans think I was nervous. So I nodded all confidently as I got up to go to my room and said: 'I'll call Lokendar and coordinate...'

But it wasn't just Lokendar Chugh I had to call. His company, Entel Sports, handled just Hharviindar (Harry) Singh, Shivnath, Zahid Pathan, and Nikhil Khoda. Another firm called Telstar handled the rest of the guys. The Telstar guys are all very young and sporty-looking themselves – sharp dressers with fancy phones and haircuts straight out of the latest Farhan Akhtar film. They always carry books like *The Seven Habits of Highly Effective People* with Business-Class boarding pass stubs as bookmarks.

There's nothing so spiffy about Lokendar Chugh's Entel Sports though. Lokey's the main man there. Chubby, fair, balding, sporting a million rings on his stubby fingers, he prefers to fly Economy unless someone else is paying. He says 'thee' instead of 'the', calls me 'Joya' instead of 'Zoya' and is constantly eating pistas, scattering the shells around like some kind of organic confetti.

The agents answered their phones at the first ring (they always do). Both lots promised me their boys would be in the banquet hall by eight o'clock sharp. I put down the phone, raided the minibar, and stepped out on my balcony to see if I could spot any sportstars.

Right below my balcony was a cobbled courtyard, pretty deserted to begin with, but after about ten minutes a couple of the Coffee Shoppee guys shuffled out and, much to my delight, started setting up a fireworks display.

I'm a fireworks freak. Rockets, shooting stars, flowerpots,

one-million-ladi-bombs, and even the wimpy phuljhadi – I love them all. As a child nothing thrilled me more than strutting down to the brightly decorated fireworks stalls on Ajmal Khan Road, all my Diwali money balled up in my hot little fist, to discuss the merits of Cock brand versus Lantern brand with the old kohl-eyed men who sold them. It used to be delicious agony deciding what to buy – the humongous gold-and-silver cascade rocket with the skimpily dressed babe on the box, or the pink-paper-covered earthen flowerpot anaars? The dotted, silvery pencils or the jazzy, diagonally striped, large-as-your-face chakrees? To say nothing of the tantalizing, red-and-gold-foil-covered, latest-latest, imported-from-China 'Laughing Dragon' bombs, which promised three minutes of non-stop pyrotechnics and the admiration of the entire neighbourhood. They cost a lot of money, sure, but think how much bang I'd be getting for my buck!

The old men would give me some sweet crumbly batashas to suck on and let me put together my arsenal at leisure. And then, of course, I'd have a huge blow-up in the evening, capering amongst the sparks as chakris and bombs swirled and spat around me, feeling reckless and hugely powerful somehow.

My brother Zoravar calls my pataka obsession 'unladylike and unnatural'. But, hello, he's just sore because I've lit the fuse of bombs he's been too scared to even approach.

Anyway, I ran downstairs, out onto the cobbled courtyard, to see the Sonargaon arsenal up-close. It was pretty impressive and fully made-in-China. The smiling guy from the Coffee Shoppee asked me if I'd like to set off the first cylinder packed with 'Golden Dragon Fire Breath' and I grabbed the fancy fuselighter from him before he could change his mind, asking him what the occasion was.

'We're celebrating Bangladesh's win over New Zealand today,' he told me.

'Congratulations!' I said bending down to light the cylinder he placed in the centre of the courtyard. The fuse spluttered and caught and I stepped back nimbly as the tongue of flame raced towards the open mouth of the dragon on the cylinder. The whole cylinder glowed a deep red and then with a confident *wfffooooft* sort of accompanying sound, rockets started shooting out of the dragon's mouth in a steady stream. *Wfffooooft! Wfffooooft! Wfffooooft!*

It was awesome.

I craned my neck back to see them rise high up and bloom into spectaular golden starbursts in the inky blue sky. Then, with a sort of a *chimmering* sound, they died out, some of their spent sparks floating down to fall benignly all around us.

I inhaled the gun smoke deeply and turned to smile ingratiatingly at the Coffee Shoppee guys. 'Can I light some more, please?'

I arrived at the banquet hall at seven-thirty the next morning, to find it had been transformed into a huge, green, limbo background overnight. Vishaal's crew was setting up their lights, working smoothly and noiselessly, all of them grooving to different music on their iPods.

They looked a little startled to see me and I didn't blame them. I was having a big-hair day. I could, of course, have tied it up neatly but then, hello, my cheeks would have looked huge. Still, I'd darkened my kajal, worn sensible cargos and a dark grey ganji and the many mirrors in the banquet hall reflected an image that was pretty much as good as I could get in work clothes.

Anyway, the crew kept shooting me dirty looks, like I was in their way or something, so I found this giant Plaster of Paris *Zing!* Cola can, one of the props from Neelo's shots, and sat down on it to wait. The boys had to arrive within the next fifteen minutes or we'd never wrap this shoot today. And then of course Sankar Menon would have our blood. Neelo and Vishaal were already looking a little worried, huddled in a far corner, squinting down at their reference layouts spread out on the floor. It was half past eight.

Suddenly, there they were. A boisterous, back-slapping gaggle of strapping young men, all scruffy and unshaven (Neelo wanted them rugged and stubbly for the shoot), dressed casually in tee shirts and track bottoms. They looked around the transformed, lit-up banquet hall curiously, and – I was reassured to see – a little apprehensively. Their eyes swept past the camera crew, past Neelo and Vishaal conferring in their corner puffing on their fags, and then settled on me on my *Zing!* Cola can.

There was a little silence.

Heart beating fast, I reminded myself that this was a bunch of total *losers* and I hopped off the can as elegantly as I could and walked over to them. 'Hi,' I said brightly, sticking my hand out at the one closest to me. He had a Sanjay-Dutt-in-*Saajan* hairdo and a gold earring. 'I'm Zoya from AWB.'

'I'm Harry,' he said, brandy-brown eyes smiling down at me obligingly. He pronounced it 'Hairy', and being at eye level with his chest, I agreed wholeheartedly. 'Where's Ishaan?'

'His father's unwell,' I said. 'So they sent me instead.'

'Oh, no, what happened?' Hairy said with what sounded like genuine concern. He tucked one bleached lock of hair behind his earringed ear and said earnestly, 'Please message me his number, I'll call him…'

Wow, he was a nice guy then, this Hairy, I thought, and was pulling out my phone when Lokendar bustled up, expansive as always, and introduced me to everybody. They all shook hands politely enough and then shuffled off to the make-up area to change into their *Zing!* India tee shirts and I sat down to chat with Lokey. He told me that this was the youngest team India had ever had. 'Only three of them – Nikhil, Laakhi and Robin – are above twenty-four. The youngest of them – our newest signing, Zahid, is only nineteen.'

It made me feel pretty old.

I sneaked a look at the boys as they were changing. Not very fit looking, considering they were supposed to be sportsmen. A couple of them were very skinny and one of them, Balaji, was positively roly-poly. None of them rated anywhere close to Shah Rukh in the vital stripped-down-to-the-waist-and-looking-biteable test. Actually, Laakhi and Robin were just very Uncleji-looking, and the younger lot, well, they were too *cocky*-looking – hairy and zitty and in-your-face. But this was just my first impression.

The younger bunch were all single and, according to Lokey, very, very ready to mingle. 'Don't let thee bhola faces fool you, Joyaji!' Lokey said, splitting open pistas and popping them into his mouth while shells fell all around him. 'They are a bunch of haramis.'

The spiffy banker-like guy from Telstar looked appalled at Lokey's language. He opened his book and started leafing through it, his back very straight. Lokey continued shelling pistas unconcernedly. '*Arrey*, most of them come from very humble backgrounds and then' – he waved a pudgy arm at the green-swathed banquet hall like it was the height of debauched living – 'this! Their *Standing* goes up so much in thee *Society*, it turns their heads. Thee kind of messes they get into…you will not believe…' He looked at me expectantly, all puffed with importance.

I figured he was waiting for me to ask, 'What kind of messes?' I did want to know, but I decided to get my cheap thrills by looking totally incurious instead.

Lokey deflated a little. 'Sorry Khoda isn't here yet,' he said, returning to his businesslike manner. 'He had to go for some official debriefing.'

Of course, we were missing Nikhil Khoda, the leader of the eleven yoddhas.

'That's why all these fellows are so jolly,' Lokey said, raising one pudgy shoulder and indicating the players behind him. 'See them! When he gets here they will all pipe down…'

I turned around and looked at the boys. They *were* looking pretty chirpy. They were quibbling about what music to play while we shot – everybody wanted something different, but finally they settled for Ricky Martin's *Cup of Life*. Vishaal's assistant pumped up the volume and they all sat around and lip-synced the lyrics while the make-up and hair people buzzed around them, making them look all grim and sweaty by squirting water from spray guns all over their faces, hair and chest.

One of them, a floridly good-looking type called Nivi, was a bit of a player. He slunk up to me and asked if I was a model. I said no and he acted all surprised. '*Par* you are so beautiful!' he exclaimed in a loud, fake voice. 'So' – he looked me up and down – 'slim-trim also!'

I got seriously embarrassed, sneaking looks at Vishaal who shoots with supermodels every day of his life and must think this remark was a bit of a joke. Luckily, I don't think he heard.

'He's always like this,' Neelo said dampeningly, after Nivi

had walked away. 'He always asks all the models what school they go to, and then when they say they finished college two years ago, he goes all fake-ily, *"No way, you look like schoolgirls!"* It's all for show anyway, he's shit scared of his girlfriend. She was Miss Universe, you know.'

Uh, thanks, Neelo.

The openers came up then, to check the shots on Vishaal's laptop. They seemed nice – earthy and engaging in spite of their fancy cellphones and the sunglasses (hello, inside a *banquet* hall?) perched on their noses. They made some basic PC with me: where are you from, how long have you been working, and Shivnath even asked me what my sun sign was (which means he was officially flirting, right?).

I was just about to tell him when Robin Rawal came up and whinged to me: 'I don't like these shoes,' he announced baldly. *Huh? So?*

But Neelo said smoothly, 'No problem Rawal-sir, the shoes won't be in the frame, look...' He showed Rawal the shot we were framing for on Vishaal's laptop. Sure enough, it showed all of them only up to their knees.

Rawal grunted. 'But they're uncomfortable to wear. I won't be able to smile properly.'

Hairy and Shivnath started sniggering at this and Vishaal shot them a dirty look. I wondered if I should tell Rawal that we didn't want smiling shots and the grimmer he looked the better, but before I could, Neelo said pleasantly, 'We can shoot you in your socks, sir.'

But Rawal wasn't falling for that. 'Then I'll look short,' he said.

So Vishaal said, somewhat ill-advisedly, that we could give him a little stool to stand on. Hairy and Shivee sniggered even more loudly at this and Rawal started to look thunderous. So I got into my in-charge mode and hurriedly asked him, as politely as I could: 'So what do you want us to do, Rawal-sir?'

He looked at me like I was super-dumb or something. 'Get me new shoes, obviously. A UK nine-and-a-half. These are UK nines.'

Man, this was an all-time low. This is why I'd gone to management school, apparently. So I could scurry around buying a pair of *shoes* for some dumb-ass whose only claim to fame was that when he hit a small round object with a stump of wood it travelled very far indeed.

'Okay,' I told him, smiling through gritted teeth. 'I'll go get you a new pair of shoes.'

'Nike,' he called after me. 'I can't wear anything else. I'm on contract.'

I nodded and ran for the door. 'Keep shooting,' I told Vishaal as I left. 'I'll *jugado* something.'

Luckily there was some kind of shopping arcade in the hotel so I hurtled in there and told the guy behind the counter the size I wanted. He was showing this lean dark dude some shoes but looked up long enough to shake his head and say in a singsong manner, 'No UK-nine-and-half-in-Nike-madum.'

Shit! Should I buy some other brand? Or appeal to Lokey for help? But Lokey'd probably just say Rawal's Standing-in-thee-Society would go down if he wore anything less than a genuine pair of UK nine-and-a-half Nikes.

'Okay,' I told him rapidly. 'D'you have one in *any* other brand?'

He waved to an underling, who came up and started showing me the size in lots of other brands. I grabbed a pair of Montu shoes (very-good-local-brand-madum-very-cheap-madum!), whipped out a black permanent marker and blacked out the logo. Then I asked the dark guy (who was signing a credit card receipt at the counter) for his blue ballpoint pen and made an artistic little Nike swoosh on the side of both shoes.

Then I dashed back to the banquet hall and presented the UK nine-and-a-half Montu-Nikes to dumb-ass Rawal, panting slightly.

He nodded regally and cracked a constipated kind of smile. *Get a move on, you lid.* I thought. We're losing *time* here. Man, did he expect me to put his shoes on for him or something?

'They're Nike, *na?*' he asked, one fat foot sliding reluctantly into the right shoe.

'Sure,' I said heartily as I turned away. 'They're Ni...'

And found myself face to face with the dark dude whose pen I'd just borrowed. And then Lokey hurried up, puffing a little, and said, 'Joya! Meet Nikhil. Nikhil Khoda. Thee skipper, you know.'

I squared my shoulders, took a deep breath and looked thee skipper in the eye. I mean, what else could I do? 'Hi,' I said, shaking his hand firmly and praying he wouldn't squeal on me. 'Nice to meet you.'

Nikhil Khoda was tall. His shoulders were broad under his navy-blue India blazer, and his slightly overlong hair was very black against his creamy white shirt. His brown eyes were warm in a strong, bronzed face. As his lean fingers gripped mine an insane little voice in my head instantly started warbling, *Yeh toh bada toinnngg hai...*

I shook my head to clear it.

'Joya's from servicing, Nikhil,' Lokey was saying. 'She's here to keep everything running smoothly.'

'And I'm sure she does a good job of it,' Khoda said to Lokey in a deep easy voice. Then he turned to me, 'I've seen you before.'

'Yes, I know,' I responded hurriedly, my heart sinking. I sneaked a look in Rawal's direction, lowered my voice and said, 'Look, I'm sorry but it was an *emergency*...'

'Oh, not when you were buying those *genuine* Nikes,' Khoda said, his mouth twitching just a little. 'Earlier.'

'When?' I asked blankly.

'Yesterday. It was you, wasn't it? The pyromaniac who was letting off all those mini-Scud Missiles on the parapet last night?'

I flushed a little and Vishaal said, 'She can't help it, dude, it's in her genes. These Rajputs smell baarood and their nostrils flare. They start rolling their eyes, tossing their heads and pawing the ground, frantic to rush out into war.'

'Brave but stupid,' Neelo said, chiming in happily.

'Definitely the latter,' Nikhil Khoda said dryly. 'You could've hurt yourself, you know.'

Great. This was going *so* well. The captain of India's loser cricket team had just called me *stupid* in front of a whole bunch of people. What made it worse was that right away *everybody* – including Vishaal and Neelo who'd been with me last night – started nodding sycophantically and murmuring, *Yes-yes-very-unsafe-very-risky-not-good-very-bad-small-children-make-them-in-Sivakasi-causes-pollution-also*.

I wanted to tell them that, hello, Truly Spiritually Evolved persons behave exactly the same in front of a king as they do in front of a beggar, and that they didn't have to slavishly agree with everything Nikhil Khoda said, but all I managed was a defensive, 'Oh no, I've been lighting crackers in my colony for *years*. I've got loads of experience,' which made Khoda raise a disapproving eyebrow. And then Neelo said jovially, fully putting the chopped green coriander on the bharta of my mortification, 'You can take the girl out of Karol Bagh but you can't take Karol Bagh out of the girl.'

It was awful. I was *this* close to tears.

So, of course, I squared my shoulders and smiled so brightly my cheeks hurt. There was an awkward little pause as everyone stood around grinning foolishly at *famous* Nikhil Khoda and then he said, 'Would you like me to change?'

'Sure,' I nodded, quickly giving the fully professional ones. 'The make-up room's through there.'

He nodded, hitched his kitbag a little higher onto his shoulder and walked away. Automatically, my eyes strayed towards his fabled butt, but just then, he turned and smiled at me, in a very no-hard-feelings sort of way, and his eyes were suddenly so warm that my stupid Non-Truly-Spiritually-Evolved heartbeat zoomed to about a thousand beats per minute and I couldn't help smiling back.

I was still smiling idiotically when Hairy came up, a full two minutes later. 'What's this about you being a fireworks freak, Zenia?' he demanded as the make-up man touched up his face.

'It's Zoya,' I told him. 'And yes, I *am* a bit into fireworks, but that's just because the day I was born so many crackers went off it kind of got internalized into my DNA.'

'You were born on Diwali?' Shivee asked.

'No,' I said laughing. 'I was born the day India won the World Cup. You know, in '83.'

'Twenty-fifth of June,' said Hairy promptly.

I nodded and then Vishaal said testily, 'Harry, if you've finished your touch-up can I have you two back in the frame, please?'

I don't think they liked the way he said it, because right away, the two of them started messing around. They got hold of the *phuss phuss* sprayer the make-up people were using and started spraying serious amounts of water onto Zahid Pathan's face, chortling happily.

I think they were picking on Pathan just because they'd spotted he was a total heart-throb in the making. A simple boy from Sangrur district in Punjab, with tousled copper curls, fair Greek god looks (except for a delightfully snub nose), and big brown eyes. The most attractive thing about him was that he didn't have a clue how hot he was, though I'm sure there were a billion girls out there who'd be happy to enlighten him. And I think that's what was getting Hairy and Shivee's goat.

Pathan was being good-natured about all the kidding around. I could see Vishaal was getting hassled though, but was too intimidated to protest. Damn, I hoped I wouldn't have to go over and intervene. I nudged Lokey: 'Do something, *na.*'

'I don't have to,' he whispered back. 'Look, Khoda's coming now.'

And sure enough, the moment Nikhil Khoda took his place between them they got all sober and cooperative.

The rest of the shoot was pretty orderly. Zahid went off for a bit to read his namaz while Saif hung around guiltily, but didn't go. Neelo was looking more relaxed now, as one by one he ticked off all the shots on his list. I studied Khoda while we shot him because I was curious to see how he would react in front of the camera. Most cricketers freeze when the lights come on, they smile this stiff, too-wide smile and their eyes get a panicked deer-in-the-headlights look. You have to shoot reams of film just to get *one* decent shot where they don't look like halfwits. Or they make their eyes all *big-big*, as Eppa would say, and end up looking idiotically startled. Or they get that cocky grin that Hairy and Shivnath had perfected. The one with that cheapie *meet-me-outside-baby-I'll-show-you-my-quick-middle-wicket* quality to it.

Nikhil Khoda did square his shoulders just a little when the camera came on, but he didn't turn into a halfwit. I was pretty impressed, till I remembered that he probably had a lot of experience doing this kind of stuff. I mean, he's done so many ads for Vodafone that people have started calling it Khodafone. The only telltale sign that he wasn't absolutely comfortable facing the lights was the way he sort of narrowed his eyes down to slits before every shot. Luckily for us, though, that ended up looking good.

The players seemed to like Neelo. He'd shot with them tons of times and they were all fairly matey. Over tea he told me that some of them, specially Hairy, were curious about me. 'They asked me who that little girl was and I told them you're this major executive who only does the Bollywood shoots,' he grinned. 'Now they all want to know if you'll go out with them.'

I knew he was pulling my leg of course, but he'd definitely created some trouble in my life, because the next thing I knew, Shivee and Bala were on my case demanding to know why I didn't make an ad featuring them and Deepika Padukone. '*Arrey*, we'll never be able to get three big stars like you together on the same dates,' is all I could come up with. 'But it's a great idea, all the same. We'll get our creative team to work on it.'

They went off gratified and I slumped back in relief, only to notice Nikhil Khoda looking at me with amusement in his eyes. 'Nice save,' he said quietly.

'Save?' I replied, widening my eyes as innocently as I could.

He nodded unconvinced, and then leaned forward suddenly and touched my knee. 'Look, I'm sorry, but we have to leave now.'

'Huh?' I said, a little wildly. 'Neelo, d'you have any shots left...?'

He did. Three vital shots with Shivee and Hairy for a promo we were going to run called OPEN YOUR ZING! COLA WITH THESE TWO OPENERS. I whispered to him what Khoda was saying and he said all he needed was the openers for forty-five minutes more.

'Sorry,' said Khoda, when I told him this as nicely as I could. He got to his feet and suddenly loomed hugely above me. 'The boys have to leave now – practice. And Harry has an appointment with the physio.'

And that was it!

In spite of the obscene amount of money we put into this stupid sport, they all just grabbed their kitbags, muttered goodbye, and left! Lokey, the snake, who pockets this huge commission from Zing! Co. as well, didn't say a word! And of course my idiot client Ranjeet just smiled weakly and thanked them in a servile way. The best part was, remember that dumbass Rawal? The one who'd caused us to lose a good half an hour at least? He took away three pairs of shoes with him! His own, the Montu-Nikes, and the pair *he claimed didn't fit!* What kind of cheapskate was he, anyway?

Now I was stuck in bloody Dhaka, with a bunch of shots left to shoot and a deadline staring me in the face.

Damn! I thought wildly. What the hell am I going to tell Sanks?

4

Neelo, Vishaal and I had a distress meeting after the players left and tried to figure out if we could manage without the opener shots. 'I could do some Photoshop, I guess,' Neelo said dubiously. 'Shoot some guys in office and stick Harry's and Shiv's heads on their torsos, but it'll look fake.'

'Besides,' I reminded him, 'we cost separately for those shots and if we don't get them *Zing!* won't cough up that money.'

That made Vishaal sit up and take notice. 'Fuck, do something, Zoya!' he pleaded. 'You're in servicing. This is your thing! You didn't just come to Dhaka to meet a lot of hot cricketers, you know.'

Hello, that was so uncalled for! I had done nothing but concentrate on work the whole day. Okay, except for one quick peek at Nikhil Khoda's chest as he'd switched shirts (totally biteable, sculpted toffee, *awe*some). Still, these creative types panic easily, so I didn't take offence. Just looked into his wild staring eyes, patted his arm and told him reassuringly, with more confidence than I felt, 'Chill, okay? I'm on it.'

That evening I took a long walk past the hotel property and down a tree-lined lane. I even did some jogging, and each time my feet hit the ground a voice in my brain went *'don't panic, don't panic'* in an insanely martial rhythm. But it was useless. I was completely and totally panicked. The shots I'd missed were actually *vital*. We needed them for a promo that was breaking ten days from now. Two litre and 600ml *Zing!* bottle labels had to go in for printing in three days' time.

I collapsed onto a conveniently placed wooden bench as little pulse points twitched all the way up and down my legs. I twisted my sweaty hair, curling wildly in the humidity, into a knot at the nape of my neck and sighed. What was an unsporty person like me doing taking all this exercise, anyway?

'Excuse me, is this seat empty?'

The inane question was uttered in a smoothly sing-song voice, which I recognized instantly. Sure enough, I looked up to see Hairy the opener smiling down at me. 'No, it's cool,' I managed to answer and he promptly folded up beside me. He'd obviously been out jogging too; he was all sweaty and smelly. He pulled out a bottle of Gatorade and chugged it down while I looked at him warily, not quite knowing what to make of the situation.

'The batti went in the Sonargaon,' he announced eventually. 'Instead of waiting for it to come back, I decided *ki, chalo,* ditch the treadmill and hit the road!'

'Oh,' I said inadequately.

Then, Hairy Harry started jerking one leg *up* and *down, up* and *down, up* and *down.* It is a very irritating habit. My brother Zoravar used to do it a lot when he was younger, but he stopped when one of his Military Academy instructors told him that it was a habit that betrayed extreme sexual frustration. (He didn't put it quite so elegantly, though; his actual words had been, 'It reveals you're tharki, Solanki.')

'So...how long have you been a custard?' I finally heard myself say.

'*Hain?*' He looked at me in surprise.

God, what was *wrong* with me? 'I meant a –' I cut myself off abruptly. I had been about to say 'cut-surd' but then I thought maybe it wasn't a politically correct question. 'Damn these machchars,' I said quickly, slapping at the mosquitoes on my bare arms. 'Are they biting you too?'

'No,' he said, brightening up. 'But, *pata hai*, I know this really cool joke about machchars. There was this one machchar, okay, and he got married to a makkhi, okay? On his wedding night all his buddies pushed him into the wedding suite for his suhaag raat but he kept coming out into the corridor instead. They sent him back in again, but again he came out. Again they sent him in, again he came out. So then they asked him *ki* why do you keep coming out of the room? And he said, "What to do, the makkhi has put Odomos and slept!"'

Oh my God, how old was this guy? He was looking at me, expecting me to crack up. So I did. He nodded at me happily and then – with rather obvious cunning – draped one arm over the back of the bench. 'You know, Zeeta,' he said, one leg twitching madly, 'there's a very nice nightclub at the Sheraton, do you want to go check it out tonight?'

'No, thanks,' I managed, 'and it's Zoya. I have a lot of work to do. But if you're so free' – I tried some obvious cunning myself – 'why don't you just shoot my three shots tonight?'

His handsome face clouded over. 'Nikhil-sir won't let us –'

I didn't let him finish. I could see Sankar Menon's big bulging eyes before me, telling me to go for the jugular or he'd dock huge chunks off my measly salary. 'Hairy,' I said, sidling closer, 'isn't there *any* way we could shoot those shots we missed today? They are *very* important. I can't *manage* without them. Because you and Shivnath are the…uh…*biggest* stars in the team.'

'Really? he asked eagerly. 'And how do you measure that, Zoya?'

'We do research,' I told him smoothly, lying through my teeth. 'Among teenage boys and young men. Across five metros, twelve mini-metros, and thirty small towns. They rate celebrities on a scale of one to ten. You are nine, Shiv is eight, and Shah Rukh Khan is seven.'

'What about Nikhil-sir?'

'We didn't bother to research him,' I said dismissively. 'We only did big stars.'

'Oh?' he said softly, like a man in a happy dream. Then something struck him. 'But why have the boys rated me so highly?' he asked worriedly. 'They don't think I'm a chhakka, you know, a *homo* or something?'

'No-no!' I assured him, 'they rated you nine on the...uh...I-wish-I-was-him-o-meter.'

'Wowji!' said Hairy happily. Then he turned to me and said, 'Why don't you speak to Lokendar, Zoya? He'll work out something for your bacha-kucha, leftover shots.'

It was a 'beautiful-day-at-the-Shere-e-Bangla-Stadium-in-Dhaka' as the sportscasters say, but there was nothing sportsmanlike about what I was trying to do. Basically, I snuck around the nets trying to get Lokendar Chugh to catch my eye so I could spirit the openers away for a quick photo-shoot. Of course, it was totally unethical and unpatriotic and nobody in Delhi knew what I was trying to pull. But it's not like I had a *choice* here. I'd dreamt they were lobbing massive sums from my cost-to-company, all of last night.

Lokey was nowhere in sight. His portly form and many flashing rings would've been easy to spot in this drab landscape;

so I guessed he was inside somewhere. I looked on the ground for a telltale pista shell trail but I didn't spot anything. The boys waved to me once or twice, and I waved back sunnily, but the man I needed to see was Chugh. After many tries – mobile signals sucked out there – I got through on Lokey's cellphone number. His phone played *Ek baar aajaa aajaa aajaa aajaa aa-aaja* for a long time and then Lokendar's voice suddenly cut off the tinny, nasal Himesh Reshammiya track, sounding surprisingly deep by sheer contrast. 'Hello?'

'Hi,' I said fluffing my hair out nervously as I spoke. 'This is Zoya from AWB. What's the scene on sneaking Shivee and Harry out for a half-an-hour photo-shoot tonight?'

A little pause. God, the man was slow. 'Where are you?'

'Right by the OB vans…' I waved up at the players' balcony, where I imagined him to be. 'Can you come down here and talk to me?'

'On my way,' he said in a low strangled sort of voice.

I lurked around the OB van and waited for him, my face feeling warmer and pinker with every passing moment in the hot Dhaka sun. The sporty-looking journalist boys smiled at me perfunctorily, and then looked beyond me, got all excited, and started adjusting their cameras frantically.

I turned.

Nikhil Khoda, dishevelled but dishy in white tracks and tee, was heading straight towards me with long loping strides. He looked like a sleep-deprived superhero who'd been up all night saving the planet. His jaw was set and his brown eyes had that steely killer light that's been patented by the Boost ads. You know, the ones where the bowler tosses the ball up in the air in slow-mo and then catches it again, all the while glaring menacingly at the poor non-Boost-drinking batsman at the other end of the pitch, before stumping the hell out of him and winning the match for India. As I watched him stride up, a female chorus singing *yeh toh bada toinnngg hai* wiped Himesh's sonorous singing clean from my brain. I gave myself a little shake. And moved out and away so he could take the OB van guys apart for showing up and destroying his team's concentration.

Instead, he swung in right beside me. 'Zoya?' he said, politely enough.

Wow, I didn't think he'd remember my name and everything. I smiled a bright smile and said, 'Yes! From AWB.' I held out my hand, oozing professional charm.

He didn't take it. Instead, he slowly held up his own hand, which held a cellphone. I looked at him blankly. 'Lokey happened to leave his phone with me...'

Nice one, Zoya. You are so up excreta creek.

I couldn't think of one single thing to say, so I continued to stare at him, the smile frozen stupidly on my face.

Khoda took a deep breath, swept a look at the journalists looking on curiously from the OB vans and then reached out and grabbed my hand. He walked me away from there to a spot behind a big Bong tree and then glowered down at me. This close to him, I observed that not only were his eyes agleam with that Boost-ad gleam, they were also the exact chunky brown colour of Boost powder with Advanced Energy Boosters.

'Do you have any idea how sacred the evening before a match is, Zoya from AWB? It's not the time for holding a product so that the logo faces the camera, or for striking smiling poses. A good player prepares for a big match in the way a warrior prepares for war.'

Okay, so this man took himself seriously. I mean, I knew I was in the wrong here but there was no need for him to start talking like a Nike poster. Besides, I'd seen how his openers had behaved in the restaurant the previous night. They'd been singing Hindi film songs and dabaoing tandoori chicken, and though I'm no expert, I'm pretty sure that's not what warriors do before a war. So I chinned up and looked him in the eye.

'I'm really sorry, Nikhil-sir, it was just an outside possibility I wanted to put to Lokendar. Because we *had* been promised three clean hours with the boys yesterday, but all we got was two-and-a-half.'

He shook his head and smiled a little at that, his brown eyes grim. 'You think you're so smooth, don't you, Little Miss Fix-It? Creating fake Nike logos, saving the day. The – what d'you guys call it? – the *servicing* girl. Well, do me a *service* and stay away from my team.'

It was nasty. He made me feel incredibly small. Especially by reminding me about how he'd covered for me with Rawal yesterday. And the worst part was that I *knew* he was in the right. 'Look, I'm sorry,' I said contritely. 'I wouldn't dream of upsetting your players' focus.' And then – I *swear* I didn't mean for it to come out sounding the way it did – I added, 'I know how badly they need it!'

He'd relaxed a little but that unfortunate remark got him pissed-off again. I saw something *smoulder* in his eyes. And it wasn't, you know, a *sexy* smoulder (like how hunky heroes smoulder in wet white shirts in Mahesh Bhatt movies). It was more of a *nasty* smoulder (like how housewives smoulder before zapping cockroaches to death in pesticide spray commercials). God, I couldn't believe this was how badly my first conversation with a guy who could get me fired with one phone call to my boss's boss's boss was going. He was the captain of the Indian team, after all. I had paranoid visions of him calling the *Zing!* CEO and getting me sacked. Or saying he wouldn't endorse the product any more, because we were commercializing the sport. Or, even worse, calling Coke and endorsing *them* instead. How hideous was that?

But then the pissed-off look left his eyes, the shutters went down, and he just looked bored. Like I wasn't worth his time or something. He let go my hand, pushed back his hair and said dismissively, 'Just lay off my boys, okay? Or I'll treat you to a fireworks display you'll never forget.'

I scurried back to the hotel, called Vishaal and unloaded the bad news. He started moaning celebrity-photographer moans about how he had to be in Bombay tomorrow. I called my idiot client Ranjeet and told him what had happened and he had a major cardiac because I'd been 'rude' to Nikhil and had 'over-exceeded my brief'. Then Neelo called me and started hyperventilating about how we would all three be sacked. 'Because they always hang you in threes, Zoya, you know? No one ever gets executed alone. Bhagat Singh hanged with Sukhdev and Rajguru, Ravana burns with Meghnad and that glutton Kumbhkaran...even Jesus took two guys with him, hanging right and left. You, Zoya, are going to take me and Vishaal...'

I hung up on him too and decided to take a long shower to calm myself down. When I emerged, the afternoon paper had been slid under the door. I grabbed a Diet *Zing!* from the mini-bar and sat down to read it.

Only to come face to face with an article on Nikhil Khoda in *Sonali's Gupshup* column.

There was a hot-looking picture of him in his India blazer, pushing an airport trolley with an abstracted look on his face.

Nothing abstracted about the headline though. It screamed
KHODA THE COLDHEART! in 40 point:

Apparently, Nikhil Khoda doesn't believe in love, darlings!
He's got this distressing scientific theory that love is...just
hormones. A little society bird tells us that he sat next to
Yash Chopra at a gala dinner last week. And guess what
the two of them ended up talking about, sweeties? Love.
Well, Nikhil did the talking mostly. When prodded by the
Love Guru about his love life, he opined that he found
Ishq, Pyaar and Mohabbat to be highly overrated. He said
that he thought love was just a messy glob of hormones
running amuck. A mixture of 'glandular imbalances,
adrenalin surges and spring fever'. Aren't your hearts just
shattered, sweethearts? Mine was. And that's when Mr
Chopra told him that he should be called not Nikhil
Khoda but Nikhil Coldheart! Wasn't that too, too witty of
him, girls? So even if your hearts skip a beat when you see
the skipper, I suggest you give him a skip, darlings.
He may drink *Zing*! but his Dil is Thanda!

Hah! Can you imagine?

This Nikhil Khoda was either a completely cold fish or had
a very, very wicked sense of humour. Oh, and Sonali added that
he also told Mr Chopra that the only things he revered were
honesty, discipline and courage. Which are values I can totally
respect, except for the fact that she went on to reveal that he
(Nikhil Khoda, not Yash Chopra) had been a 'messy glob of
hormoning it out' with two NRI supermodels on the fringes of
Bollywood, one sports journalist and, of course, the girl in the
yeh toh bada toinnngg hai ad, all in the last one year, and would
be 'pursuing his penchant for beautiful damsels by judging the
Miss India pageant later this month'.

All of which led me to think that he sounded way too busy to make phone calls to CEOs to have me sacked. Hopefully, I'd be able to fly below his radar for the rest of this trip, scurry back to Bombay for my glamorous shoot and never have to meet him again.

But my happy mood didn't last too long. I realized pretty soon that even if Nikhil Khoda didn't get me sacked, the fact that I *still* didn't have the openers shots might do the job for him. I tossed and turned all night and woke up obscenely early. Too stressed to just lie in bed, I took a long shower, pulled on some clothes and shaking out my hair, zipped down to the Coffee Shoppee at half past seven in the morning.

The Coffee Shoppee guys were clearly taken by surprise because all the tables had chairs upended on them as three skinny dudes in Hawaiian shirts scurried around swabbing the floor. The chubby restaurant manager smiled at me extra-chirpily. 'Miss Solanki! A table for one?' Like he had piping hot breakfast all ready to serve or something.

But maybe he had. Because as he flipped over a chair for me to sit on, I spied all our Men in Blue, and their coach, tucking into a lavish breakfast at a table at the far end of the room.

Uh oh…

I looked away quickly but it was too late. Hairy was waving happily: 'Hey, Zoya!'

I waved back weakly. Then made a big deal of reading the menu card. The last thing I wanted was for Captain Coldheart to read me the Riot Act about how my crass commercial presence was going to corrupt his pure little performers. Hairy looked a little disappointed. Out of the corner of my eye I could see him half rising in his seat but then Shivnath said something to him that made him sit down again. Meanwhile, Khoda just sat there, stolidly eating his way through an entire watermelon.

As I fiddled with the cutlery and waited for my order, bits of their conversation drifted over to me. They were discussing what to do if they won the toss. Fat chance. Nikhil Khoda hadn't won a toss for seventeen one-dayers running. Even a cricketing ignoramus like me knew that.

'Ma'am, your breakfast…' One of the sweet skinny boys was back with my order, which he placed carefully before me. I picked up my fork and dug into the bhurji with gusto. Just then, a tardy arrival to the team table, smelling strongly of aftershave, swung past me in a hurry and his entire kitbag, loaded with bats or dumbbells – or maybe, just bulk-building, protein-shake powders – slammed into my table and collapsed it totally. In one moment I went from a poised, put-together working girl breakfasting alone, to this total *lid*, sitting there, mouth agape, a tiny triangle of toast and bhurji speared on my fork and the rest of it scattered all around me.

The dude and the kitbag swung back at once and started apologizing profusely. It was Zahid, the I-don't-know-I'm-good-looking-yet one. 'So sorry,' he was going. 'So sorry, Zoyaji!'

The entire team – showing the kind of synchronicity it seldom showed on the field – leapt to its feet as one. They hadn't seen what had happened, just heard the crash, and I think at first they thought the place had been *bombed*, a likely possibility given the amount of hate mail they'd been getting lately. Hairy rushed over at once, going: 'Zenia? *Tussi theek ho?*'

Of course I jumped up and said I was fine. And I was, really.

But Zahid, very contrite, totally ignored my frantic protests and scooped up the remains of my breakfast and carried it to the team table.

I trotted along behind him, feeling completely idiotic. I mean, they must think I'm a super klutz or something. Or, even worse, some kind of desperate groupie who throws her bhurji-eating self into the flight path of hot-looking bowlers at seven a.m. to swing breakfast with them and their team-mates.

Shivee set my plate down on the team table with a flourish. Hairy pulled up a chair. Everybody had a go at poor Zahid for knocking me down. And even Nikhil Khoda, who'd glanced up swiftly when the table crashed to check that I wasn't dead or something, was content to just ignore me. Which was really quite excellent behaviour, given his attitude yesterday. In fact, halfway through the meal, I think he even passed me the butter...

Anyway, I ended up eating breakfast with what the commentators are always calling the 'youngsters' on the team. After they were satisfied there was nothing wrong with me they started kidding around like crazy. The match didn't start till twelve-thirty and they were pretty chilled. Nikhil Khoda was in his own private huddle with Wes, their bald Aussie coach, the boyish-looking physio, Dieter Rund, Laakhi, and that shoe-flicker Rawal at the other end of the table, but down here the mood was definitely lighter.

'Zoyaji,' asked Hairy, doing this really bad Charu Sharma imitation as Shivee waved a banana in my face, 'what do you think India should do in order to win today?'

Like I had the foggiest idea. 'Uh,' I said, into the banana mike, 'they should eat a good breakfast, focus hard and just play their natural game.' *Not bad*, I told myself, relaxing a little. *Pretty cool of you to use that phrase 'natural game', Zoya, it sounds like you know what you're talking about...*

'Good advice,' said Hairy, one leg jerking the table up and down.

The other boys nodded.

Hairy looked set to hit me with another question but I had no intention of playing interviewee any more. My lack of cricket knowledge would be totally revealed. After all, yesterday, on the bench, I'd told him that I was a *huge* fan of the game and watched *every* India match, always. So I quickly grabbed the banana from Hairy's hand and asked a question of my own. 'Tell me, boys, do you guys always eat breakfast together like this before a match?'

It worked. They all started talking at once.

They did always eat together before a match. It was Wes's idea, apparently a bonding exercise of sorts. Some of the guys didn't like doing it, it made them feel like kids, but everybody fell in line because Nikhil backed Wes on it.

So, of course, I started stressing that Khoda must be really hassled that I'd gatecrashed their exclusive team-only breakfast but then I realized it wasn't the first time I'd done so. I said, 'Hey, I've had breakfast with all you guys once before too! Don't you remember?'

They all looked blankly at me. And I suddenly felt very stupid. Because I'm not exactly a supermodel, or an actress, or a two-headed freak, or anything. There was no reason for them to remember a nobody in a baseball cap and jeans who had sat at their table for fifteen minutes or so, a year and a half ago. I looked down at my bhurji and tried to look like I hadn't said anything.

But Hairy was all excited. 'Really? When, Zoya?'

I said sheepishly, 'In Bombay, ages ago. At the Wank...Wankhede Stadium...I think it's called. It's no big deal. I bet lots of people share breakfast with you now and then. Agents and family and stuff...' I trailed off self-consciously.

But Hairy was shaking his head impatiently. 'In Feb?' he demanded. 'Or September?'

'Feb,' I muttered, wishing I hadn't brought it up. 'At some unearthly hour in the morning. Actually, we needed an NOC from somebody – *you*, as a matter-of-fact,' I nodded at Balaji, who nodded right back, going '*Ya ya, of course, of course,*' doing a terrible job of pretending that he remembered me. 'I had to get your signature on a lot of papers so you guys let me sit at your table and I grabbed a toast or two.'

There was a little silence around the table. Everybody chewed their high-fibre cereal moodily. Then Hairy said, 'That was our first big win, wasn't it, guys?'

'First and last,' Khoda said dryly, spearing a pineapple chunk.

'Hey, maybe I bring you guys good luck!' I said brightly, for no better reason than that I wanted to show him I was unaffected by his presence.

'I don't think it was *luck* that won us the match that day,' Khoda said witheringly.

'No, no,' I replied in a rush, worried I'd made him mad at me again. 'Of course not. It was just a bad joke. There's no such thing as luck!'

He didn't say anything, just made a kind of grunting noise.

But Shivee spoke up, a little defiantly: 'By the way, skipper, do you know when Zoya's birthday is?'

'When?' Khoda said, looking bored.

'Twenty-fifth of June, 1983,' Shivee said, and Hairy chimed in with: '*Now* say *ki* she's not a good-luck charm!'

Nikhil Khoda didn't look too impressed. 'Is that a fact?' he asked me, his tone sceptical, almost like he was insinuating I'd made it up.

'Yes, actually it is,' I said quietly.

He half-shrugged in an ungracious sort of way and looked away.

There was a long uncomfortable silence and then the coach said, 'Well, we all know what Shivee and Harry are thinking, Nikhil! If these blokes win today, it won't be because we played well, or because we had a good strategy or because the other buggers screwed up. It'll be all because we broke bread with born-at-the-auspicious-hour Zoya!'

The boys all laughed at that and I gave a nervous little giggle too, but I couldn't help feeling uneasy. Because even though his eyes were twinkling, I somehow sensed that the new coach was hassled.

It was like he was this First-World-type gora stuck with a bunch of superstitious Indians or something. I went back to eating the debris of my bhurji, cursing myself silently for making that idiotic 'lucky' remark and even more for backtracking on it so hastily. I must've sounded like such a suck-up. *Yes sir no sir three bagsful sir...*

Really, when was I going to become a Truly Spiritually Evolved Person?

5

Neelo, Vishaal and I bagged (what we thought were) really good seats, at the orchard end of the stadium. We had a clear view of the skippers coming out for the toss, Khoda's loping stride contrasting oddly with the England captain's stocky shuffle. The crowd was pretty much expecting him to lose as usual, and there were many surprised gasps when India won the toss, and even more when we heard *'and has decided to field'*. People started debating the wisdom of this decision in excited Bangla all around me. It was apparently a fairly controversial thing Nikhil Khoda had done. Not that it seemed to bother him. He sauntered back in with his players, slapping a back here and there, clapping his hands together and doing whatever it is cricket captains do out in the field.

Vishaal and Neelo were all excited. They'd put all their work-time woes behind them, spiked their *Zing!* cans generously with Bacardi and were ready to rock all day. I wasn't feeling so bubbly, though. Last morning's events had freaked me out totally. My idiot client Ranjeet was on my case, whining about the 'opener' shots. The sun was hot. *Upar se*, the players looked so far away and the scoreboard looked all hazy at this distance. And there was this weird echo, so you couldn't really understand what the commentators were saying up there in the press box. And then, when the Indians came out to field, half the people in front of me leapt to their feet, effectively blocking our view of the match.

'Damn,' went Neelo, as we clambered on to the benches. '*Agli baar*, we'll insist on passes to the VIP box.'

Poor Neelo. Being a creative type he doesn't have a clue about how low the ad agency is in the *Zing!* Pecking Order of Passes for Concerts and Matches. I, of course, know it by heart. It's Celebrity Endorsers and Their Families first, Pesticide Levels Testing NGOs second, Bottlers and Families third, Press People fourth, Contest Winners next, then the *Zing!* people themselves and, bringing up the rear, us poor agency sods. Oh, and that's only if nobody at *Zing!* has a kid looking for admission to a hip school. Because then the principal and staff get the Celebrity Endorser passes and it all moves down one slot and we get none.

Anyway, when the two of them started hurling abuses at the guys in front of us in robust Bangla, I decided I'd had enough. I decided to sneak back to the Sonargaon and watch the match in peace in the Coffee Shoppee. I yanked at the back of Vishaal's jeans and told him I was off. He nodded bye, his eyes on the action on the field and Neelo yelled over the din: 'Come back for the second half in case we seem to be winning.'

Honestly, what touching faith we had in the team.

Uh, we won.

I'd decided to do a bit of sightseeing, after watching the first few overs in my room. So I missed all the action. Not that I minded too much. I find ODIs really boring, and during the twentieth over it occurred to my wandering mind that today would be a great day to shop. The markets were sure to be deserted.

So I hailed one of those bumblebee autos with gold 'n' white conical crowns upon their heads, and took a tour of the city. It was fun, it took my mind off the opener shots. And Sanks. And Nikhil Khoda's mean *do-me-a-service* crack. I got back by six, weighed down with all this stuff I would probably never use.

That's when I met Neelo and Vishaal who told me that the match had been *awe*some. Bala, Zahid and gang got the English all out for 210. After lunch, when Shivee and Harry came out to bat, everybody was hailing Khoda's decision to chase as the smartest, most far-sighted thing any captain had ever done. From being foolhardy and downright stupid, he'd risen all the way to a fabulous judge of pitches, a captain who leads from the front, and a master of psychology.

Wow, what a rollercoaster that man's life must be!

They finished it off in thirty-seven overs, with five wickets still in hand. Harry was Man of the Match, but apparently it had been a close thing between him and Bala. In fact, Vishaal was very indignant about the whole thing, insisting Harry's was a crowd-pleaser innings and that it was Bala's stint that had really broken the back of the English attack.

Whatever.

Meanwhile, Neelo was already looking glassy-eyed and muttering under his breath. He had to sms lines to Delhi tonight so *Zing!* could string up banners all over the country tomorrow, crowing things like *Men in Blue Eat an English Breakfast* or *Barmy Army ki Khattam Kahani*, or even ruder ones in which London was spelt 'lundon', you get the picture…

I must say I felt pretty deflated about missing all the action, even though the boys assured me the stadium had not been a good place for anyone of the female sex to be in, by the time the match got over. Apparently, all the Indians, Bangladeshis, Pakistanis and Sri Lankans in the crowd had got into a *Mera*

Subcontinent Mahaan mood after India knocked the stuffing out of the common enemy. They'd lurched around the stands hugging all brown-skinned girls in sight and boozily saying, 'Congratulations, sister!'

'Why don't we catch the highlights on ESPN?' Vishaal suggested, as though he couldn't have enough. 'C'mon, let's hit the Coffee Shoppee.'

The restaurant was deserted. The only person there was Shanta Kalra, a slim, sporty-looking sports journalist with very short silver-grey hair framing a surprisingly young face. She was tapping away quietly on her laptop when we entered but waved and called out: 'Looking for the gang? Most of them are over at the Sheraton, celebrating.'

Already? I thought crankily. *Surely it was early days yet?*

'Racing towards a deadline?' I asked her.

'No, not really, just working on my questions for an interview.' It turned out she'd got an exclusive deal on interviews with Nikhil Khoda after every India match. 'He should be here soon,' she said. 'He said eight-thirty and he's usually very punctual.'

'Then we should leave you alone at your table!' I exclaimed, quickly leaping up and rushing towards the buffet.

Vishaal followed me bemusedly. 'And what was all that about?' he murmured into my ear as I stared blankly at the fish (Rohu, Hilsa, Pomfret, Sole) selection.

'Nothing,' I said, smiling brightly. 'Lovely fish, huh?'

'You're vegetarian,' he reminded me mildly.

I didn't bother to reply and instead carried my loaded plate to the TV area and dropped down there. If I crouched low I would be (almost) invisible from where Shanta was sitting. I sneaked a look. Khoda was there...the two of them seemed totally engrossed, and so I thought it was safe to sneak back to the buffet and pick up something I could actually eat. I grabbed a naan and daal and started skulking back to my spot. Out of the corner of my eye I saw that both interviewer and 'viewee had left. Great! I thought, they've got a three-day break before the next match, I'll speak to Lokendar, get the shots tomorrow evening and catch the first flight out day after...

So engrossed was I in my little plan that I didn't see Shanta and Khoda till I was almost on top of them. They'd moved right in front of the TV, obviously having decided to watch the highlights too.

'Zoya!' said Shanta pleasantly. 'Have you congratulated Nikhil?'

'Uh, no – actually.' I swung my gaze up to meet his and said, as composedly as I could, 'Congratulations. Great performance.'

'Hey, I should be saying that to you,' his mouth curled into a smile I thought was distinctly unfriendly.

'*Matlab*?' Shanta looked from him to me in an interested, smelling-a-story sort of way.

'Oh, Zoya knows what I mean,' said Khoda dismissively. 'Thanks for your time, Shanta. I think I'll watch the rest of the highlights in my own room. Goodnight.' He shook her hand, nodded politely at Vishaal and me and made to leave.

But Vishaal was on him before he made the door. 'Hey, Nikhil, I was wondering if we could shoot Shiv and Harry tomorrow...if it's cool with Wes and you? We really need those shots, dude...'

Khoda nodded, pretty curtly, I thought. I was pissed off that Vishaal had even asked him. I mean, the boys don't really need the skipper's permission to shoot – not officially, at any rate, but clearly there was nothing official about the hold he had on them.

Vishaal came back grinning. 'It's in the bag, Zoya, we'll be patli galli-ing out of here by day after morning.'

I smiled back at him hoping he was right. Somehow I had a feeling it wasn't going to be that simple.

It wasn't.

Shivee and Harry – those crafty little kids – had something up their Men-in-Blue sleeves. They started by acting really elusive the next day. 'Zoyaji,' groaned Harry down the phone to me the next morning. '*Mere* groin *mein* strain *hai.* I have been advised full rest and cannot do your shoot today.' *Bullshit. If the Man of the Match's groin was critically strained it would've been in the papers today.* 'Why don't you stay back a few days…have breakfast with us day after and over breakfast only we can discuss when to shoot…'

Like that, was it?

I called Lokey and told him to read Harry the small print in his contract.

But Lokey had news for me: 'Shivee can't shoot either, Joyaji!' he said. 'His groin is strained too. He wants you to have breakfast with them day after and discuss the situation.'

God, who did they think they were kidding?

'Lokey,' I said slowly and carefully, 'Harry is delaying things because he thinks I'm some kind of good-luck bringer.'

'I know, Joyaji,' he said in this oily, fakely concerned voice. 'But can't you just humour him and stay? He may get rattled and throw his wicket away in the match if you leave now. Why risk it?'

I couldn't believe this! Even my Rinku Chachi in Karol Bagh was a bigger rationalist than this Hairy dude. 'But how come he's so superstitious?' I demanded of Lokey. 'He's so modern and with-it types.'

62 ANUJA CHAUHAN

Lokey sighed gustily. 'He's insecure, Joyaji. All stars are insecure. They have so much Standing in thee Society, so much to lose...not like you and me...' (Excuse me, Lokendar, I wanted to say, *you* are so not like *me*! *You* are raking it in, while I'm on some bullshit slave-labour two-lakhs-per-annum package.) 'Harry's very vehmi,' Lokey continued. 'He has even changed the spelling of his name to Hharviinder Singh...'

'And he wears a neelam on his middle finger,' I added and sighed. This guy Hairy was obviously a fruitcake. (A neelam-wearing fruitcake with a strained groin. How gross is that?) 'Look, Lokendar,' I said, 'the bottom line is that I need those shots fast – I have to print bottle labels *and* roll out posters within a week.'

'Okay, okay,' he huffed and puffed. '*Mein kuchh karta hoon...*'

But of course he couldn't do a thing. The whole day went by chasing those idiots. My idiot client Ranjeet called Sanks who called me and freaked out totally. 'Why are you not on top of things, Zoya?' he ranted. Do you want me to pull Ishaan out of the ICU and send him there to show you how it's done?'

Please. I'd trained Ishaan from scratch. Did he really think he could get under my skin with that pathetic ploy? 'I *am* on top of things, Sanks,' I said soothingly. 'And don't insult me by going on about Ishaan all the time. I also have some Standing in thee Society, you know...'

The next morning I pulled on my cargos and a tee shirt I'd borrowed from Neelo (I was fast running out of clothes) and hit the ground running. Time was running out. Vishaal was piling up an unimaginable food and beverage bill and my much looked-forward-to Bombay shoot was almost over. I had to nail those bastards today.

THE ZOYA FACTOR   63

I got into the elevator to find Khoda on board, looking
freshly showered and riding downwards in his grey Gold's-Gym
tracks. 'Good morning,' he said pleasantly. 'Aren't you late for
your flight?'

'No, actually,' I said sweetly. 'My boss says I can't leave till I
get *all* my shots.'

He looked a little taken aback. 'What d'you mean? Don't
tell me your photographer couldn't finish all the shots *yesterday*
either!'

That made my hackles rise. I mean, Vishaal would've finished
all the shots on the *first* day itself if Khoda hadn't rushed his
boys for practice. And now, he was insinuating *we* were slow
when it was the boys who were dragging their feet! 'He didn't
get a chance to shoot yesterday, at all,' I said, feeling my nostrils
beginning to flare. 'Your openers are suffering from strained
groins and so are unavailable to shoot.'

He looked surprised, and not un-amused. 'Harry's strained
his groin?' he grinned. 'First I've heard of it.'

'Well, he says he has,' I said as neutrally as I could. I mean,
I couldn't call Hairy a liar to his skipper's face. 'And so has
Shivnath, apparently.'

Nikhil nodded, his smile getting wider.

'And so my shoot' – my voice wobbled a little but I couldn't
help that – 'is off.'

Khoda was grinning unabashedly now. 'So Little Miss Fix-It
has run up against something she can't fix!' he crowed in a not
very captain-like manner.

Then, as I looked up at him, practically teary-eyed with
frustration, he said, in a nicer voice, 'Tell me, do you think
they're faking it?'

Well, he'd asked for it. 'Yes!' I nodded, vigorously. 'Harry and Shiv are playing hide-and-seek with me. They're thinking that maybe they won the other day because of me and so they want me to stay here for the next match-breakfast to test the theory! I can't – obviously! Because I have a *life* too, you know. So now they're trying to delay my departure as long as possible by lidding around with my shoot...'

'But *you're* the one who put the idea into their heads,' Khoda pointed out, infuriatingly logical. 'Didn't you go, all chirpily, *"Hey, maybe I bring you guys good luck!"*'

I winced. He'd mimicked my voice perfectly. 'It was a *joke*,' I said defensively. 'I never thought they'd take it seriously.'

He was quiet for almost a whole minute. Then he said, 'Look, why don't you just do what the boys want? Stay till tomorrow, eat breakfast with us, get your shots in the evening, and leave?'

I was surprised. 'But, you said, that day...' I started and then stopped.

'...that I don't think you're a good-luck charm?' he said calmly enough. 'Of course, I don't. But the next match is against Australia, so I don't want to take any risks. If it gives some of the lads more spunk, I'm all for it.'

'But suppose you win that one?' I protested. 'Harry's quite capable of insisting I stay on for the match after that too!'

Khoda smiled enigmatically. 'Let's cross that bridge when we come to it. You set up your patchwork shoot for the evening after the next match and get yourself a seat on the morning flight.'

I nodded back at him doubtfully and he reached out and tousled my hair in a nice, elder-brotherly sort of way. 'Now smile,' he said.

I smiled.

The elevator *pinggged* open. He stood aside to let me exit first, in this very cheesy mock-chivalrous way.

'By the way, Zoya?'

I turned.

He grinned at me, white teeth flashing in his brown face, 'Nice life philosophy.'

Huh?

He glanced down at my tee shirt quizzically and then walked away.

Puzzled, I yanked it away from me and squinted at the lettering. There, in bright firoza blue on a purple background were emblazoned three words I'd failed to read when I'd slipped on Neelo's tee shirt in the morning: DRINK. HUMP. DIE.

I aimed a woman-of-the-world-ish shrug in the general direction of where he'd gone. 'Yeah...heh, heh,' I said weakly, 'pretty nice, huh?'

Later that day when the three of us went down to the lobby we saw this big *Zing!* banner strung up outside one of the banquet halls. It said 'A SODA WITH KHODA' in big blue letters and underneath was a message in Bangla which Neelo translated for us, '*Welcome Little Winners of the Share-a-Zing! with Nikhil Khoda Contest!*'

There was a scrum of dark-eyed, excited-looking kids at the door, most of them looking no older than twelve, escorted by some event management people in *Zing!* tee shirts. A perspiring Lokey was standing by the door, talking on the same cellphone Nikhil Khoda had shaken threateningly under my nose a couple of days ago.

'Hey, hey stop!' Neelo said, grabbing the back of my, well actually *his*, stupid tee shirt (which I was now wearing inside out). 'Let's go in and watch. It should be a blast, man!'

Lokey said it was cool if we watched, so we went in and found some chairs in the back row and settled down. There was a little stage up front and lots and lots of kids, some of them with bats and balls and pads, *all* of them with Zing! bottles in their hands.

'Where are these bachchas from?' I asked Lokey as he came in and collapsed on a chair next to me.

'From all over the subcontinent, they are thirty-five in all,' he puffed.

'What did they have to do to win, dude?' Neelo asked curiously. 'Some of them look really small.'

It was an under-the-crown-cap scheme, the event management guy explained. They all got to have a Q and A session with Khoda, and one of them (the first Indian kid to have found the A SODA WITH KHODA crown cap) would get to read out a special message that he wrote himself (well, with a little help from his dad or his elocution teacher or whatever) for the Indian team. He pointed out the winner kid to us, very small and brown, but with spiky hair and eyes as bright as buttons. He was wearing a shiny suit with a ready-made tie on an elastic band and had a very purposeful expression on his face. He held a thick sheaf of papers in his hand.

'Khoda had better watch out,' Vishaal snorted. 'That kid means business, dude!'

'Where's he, anyway?' I asked, hoping Khoda wouldn't be starry and show up late or not at all and fully break the children's hearts.

'He's here, Joyaji!' Lokey puffed. 'Look, he's walking in now.'

Sure enough, Nikhil had just emerged from behind the stage in a blue Zing! tee shirt and grey tracks, grinning happily, waving with both hands.

The kids all jumped up and cheered, '*Khoda! Khoda! Khoda!*'
It was infectious. I found I'd leapt up too, clapping madly.

Khoda pulled the mike out of the upright stand, walked
forward casually, collapsed cross-legged right at the edge of the
stage and started talking to the kids in a babble of English,
Hindi and broken Bangla. They asked him a million questions
on training, muscle building, diet, stroke play, team management
and strategy, all of which he answered solemnly and without a
hint of being patronizing. The kids were nodding seriously and
some even took notes (which Neelo found hysterically funny
for some reason).

And then it was the little winner's moment in the sun.

His name was announced with a flourish of trumpets.

A spotlight followed his small figure as he strutted forward,
plucked the mike from Khoda's hands and waited for silence
with quiet confidence. There was a little whispering and
shushing and Khoda had to put his finger to his lips and glare at
the kids mock-threateningly a couple of times, but finally silence
fell and the little dude started to speak. (Vishaal pulled out his
camcorder at once.)

His voice was in that just-about-to-break, sometimes-hoarse-
sometimes-girlish zone, but confident, with just a tiny betraying
quiver to it.

'It was sunny days in thee jungal,' he began impressively.

'Oh cool, the lateral approach!' Neelo guffawed. I kicked
him hard in the shin.

'It was sunny days in thee jungal,' the little boy repeated.
'Guru Drona was giving his dissy-pills an arching lesson. Thee
guru strung up a clay...a...uh...a clay-birdd on a tree and
baded the princes to come forward and aim on it, one by one.
As each prince stood before him, closing one eye, thee guru

asked *ki* "Whatcanyousee, O prince?" And each prince said, "Thee birdd, O teacher, thee tree, a little piss of sky and thee jungal's behind." And the guru was very much waxed and bid them to move on. Till it was Arjun's turn. "Whatcanyousee O prince?" "The eye of the birdd, O teacher," little Arjun replied. "What else?" asked teacher craftily. "Canyounot see thee tree, a little piss of sky and thee jungal's behind?" But little Arjun said stud-fastly, "The eye of the birdd is *all* I see O teacher." Much happy, Drona bid him shoot, shoot! and little Arjun's arrow flied straight and pierced the eye of the birdd, falling it to thee ground.' The little boy stopped here for a sip of *Zing!* and looked Khoda straight in the eye. 'I am sure, Mr Nikhil Khoda,' he said, very man to man, 'that you are knowing this story.'

Nikhil inclined his head gravely and said that yes, he did know it.

'I am no Drona-achaar,' the little fellow said shaking his head modestly. 'Australia' (he gave a light laugh), 'is not a tree, and the ICC World Cup is not a *birdd*, but is a *cup!*' He raised one dramatic finger to the sky, 'A cup-birrd! And if you want to win it you must' – he turned and bored his burning eyes into Khoda's face – 'see only thee eye of thee cupboard, Mr Nikhil Khoda!'

He swung around to face all of us, speaking in ringing accents, 'See only thee eye of thee cup-birrd, Team India! See only,' concluded the little thespian, his voice dropping to a whisper that could be heard in every corner of the hall, 'only...*only* thee eye of thee cupboard.'

Huge applause rang out from every corner of the hall. Vishaal and Neelo got to their feet whistling enthusiastically. I blinked back tears and blew my nose vigorously as I watched the upright little figure accept the standing ovation with a grave bow.

And then it was Nikhil's turn to speak. 'That was an excellent speech, sir,' he said and he sounded like he meant it. 'You're absolutely right. Just like when the exams come around you must focus totally and concentrate only on your studies and *nothing* else, in the same way when you wear the blue uniform you must stop thinking about internal politics, or personal records or *Zing!* ads or' – this with a rueful grin that made all the little boys laugh out loud – 'girls, and see only the eye of the bird. I promise you guys today, that till the ICC World Cup is over, I will see only the eye of the cupboard. Only' – he gave the same dramatic pause the little boy had done, but in the *nicest* way possible – 'the eye of the cupboard. Thank you.'

What a cheerful little gang we were at breakfast the next day. The boys looked disgustingly triumphant about getting me to stay. It was Hairy's birthday and everybody was wishing him. Wes, Laakhi and Nikhil looked pretty upbeat at their end of the table too. 'Wait and see, Zoya,' Shivee chortled. 'We'll fix those Aussies good – you are our secret weapon!'

'Isn't that totally insulting to all the talent on this team, Shivee,' I asked him, irritated. '*Matlab*, according to you, if I eat breakfast with *monkeys* even they can go out and beat the best team in the world!'

'Zoya, these fellows are also *monkeys* only!' Laakhi boomed down the table at me, his big shoulders shaking as he laughed.

The 'monkeys', instead of being offended, looked mighty tickled. Hairy even went as far as to scratch his armpits. Really, what had got into them?

'It's nerves,' Khoda said to me as I walked back to the buffet to pick up more papaya. He was there, shovelling all the watermelon the Sonargaon had to offer onto his plate. 'They'll be fine once we're on the field.'

'Best of luck,' I said. And then felt pretty stupid. He'd probably think I was being oversmart or playful or something...

But he didn't seem to mind. 'Thanks,' he said simply.

Back at the table the boys were planning a little party afterwards for Hairy. (Obviously, Nikhil hadn't told them about seeing only thee eye of thee cupboard yet.) Navneet's Miss India-Universe had shown up to watch the semis with some hot southern actresses in tow and the boys wanted to let down their hair a bit. 'The three of you must come too, Zoyaji,' Zahid said enthusiastically. 'We'll do something cool.'

'Okay,' I said, thinking how pathetically grateful Neelo and Vishaal would be. Hot southern actresses were really their thing. But only after my shoot with these two was over. I pointed at Shiv and Harry who appeared to have made miraculous recoveries, 'Groins feeling good, guys?'

They nodded solemnly. 'Yes, Dieter-sir is a *miracle* worker. He has massaged us *personally* all night.'

Dieter looked up startled, but said nothing (he never did), and then Wes looked up and said they had to board their team bus now.

'Give 'em hell, boys,' I said as they trooped out, feeling a bit like Bharat Mata Incarnate. And in spite of the casual matey way in which they treated me, I had an uncomfortable feeling that's how they perceived me. I mean, Zahid even asked me to give him my blessings! I felt so dumb – like I should have said *'Vijayee Bhava'* the way Durga Khote does in the old movies. Instead, I just leaned in and kissed him on the cheek.

I didn't have the stomach to watch the match in the stands. Though my Standing-in-thee-Society had moved up a lot since the last match (VVIP enclosure passes lay on my dressing table now!), I didn't fancy seeing my Lucky Charm status being ground to dust live in the Sher-e-Bangla Stadium. Because 'Australia is by far the stronger side and their best boys are playing today' is what I'd overheard the commentators say when they'd got into the elevator.

So, what I did was, I got into the Miss India-Universe's room (her name was Ritu Raina, and she was heart-stoppingly beautiful: glossy ironed hair, high cheekbones and all) and watched it there with her. She was nervous as hell too – 'I never see Nivi playing live,' she confided. 'It makes me nauseous.'

I did kind of wonder why she'd risked her life and flown Biman Air to Dhaka then. But she said her hot actress friends were keen to see the cricketers close up. Besides, she liked being with him when the match was over. 'Because it's another whole trip when he comes back to me all sweaty and flushed with victory,' she said, her eyes shining. 'I feel like a prize then.'

Okay, that was a pretty corny thing to say, but she was only nineteen, after all, and probably didn't know any better. So I forgave her. Also, I needed to borrow clothes from her for tonight, so I needed to keep liking her. (Besides, deep down, in the most unemancipated Mills and Boon reading part of my soul, I kind of knew what she meant.) We got out her manicure kit and a flask of strong coffee and settled down to watch.

Khoda sauntered in on the telly (after an ad break saying the toss was sponsored by Niceday Cramjams) and asked for heads. The Aussie captain said he'd settle for tails, and some dude in a FLY EMIRATES coat tossed the coin. It landed heads up. Khoda said he wanted to bat first and then Aamir Khan traipsed out dressed as a Malayali massage lady and exhorted us to *lagao thande ka tadka*.

And then Hairy and Shivee walked on, stretching and hopping, and the match began.

It moved pretty slowly in the beginning, so we put the TV on mute and chatted and stuff. Ritu pulled out a deep purple nail varnish for me and said it would go well with my 'kohl girl' look. She also laid out lots of sexy black halters, saying I could wear them with my jeans and black cork-soled clogs. I went into the loo to try them on and was fluffing out my hair and pouting vampishly into the mirror in what I fondly believed was a Ritu-Raina-ish way when she screamed loudly.

I came out to see that the Aussies had struck not once but twice and that Laakhi and Khoda were the new men in. They steadied things up a little. The score didn't move much for a while, but that was okay, because the openers had been doing full maar-dhaarh when they got out. We were 79 for 2 in 15 overs when the drinks came on. I looked at the drinks trolley critically. It was a design Neelo and the studio guys had slaved over last month. A giant *Zing!* two-litre bottle (we were pushing large packs this year) mounted on a tiny Dhaka-style autorickshaw. It toot-tooted on to the pitch happily and then an ad break came on.

When the match came back on, I started feeling pretty damn sick. Especially when the Aussies jumped up and appealed manically and the red light flashed and Laakhi walked. Ritu went a delicate shade of green when Navneet came out to bat. He seemed cool and was chatting easily with Khoda, nodding repeatedly and tapping the pitch with the end of his bat. Then some Aussie dude with sunscreen slathered all over his face raced down the pitch towards him and...the TV went off. I looked up, thinking it must be the batti again, but then saw Ritu clutching the remote, looking very white around the gills. 'I can't watch,' she said. 'Let's go out.'

So we went to the hotel parlour for a full body massage,

shampoo and blow dry. I sneaked a peek at the TV from under the blower and saw we were 220 for 7 in 40 overs and felt fully deflated. Because even though I knew it was idiotic I *had* been getting a bit of a cheap thrill out of maybe being a lucky charm. Still, it was good I hadn't said anything to Vishaal and Neelo. I could quietly leave Dhaka and forget this had ever happened…

By the time we got out of the parlour the Indian innings were over. We'd finished at a decent 267 for 9 – Zahid had come in and hit some big ones and Khoda had carried his bat right through – but the commentators were saying we were still short by some thirty runs and didn't have much of a chance. Still, they did say we couldn't be ruled out altogether, cricket being a game of glorious uncertainties, and all that usual crap.

Ritu looked a little chirpier now that Navneet's part in the game was mostly over. She walked through the lobby, hair swinging, looking every bit the beauty queen she was. 'See you in the evening, Zo,' she beamed at me suddenly and vanished into her room. I nodded, went to my room and crashed.

I don't know how much later it was when the phone woke me up. It was Neelo – 'Put on the TV, Zoya,' he yelled. 'We're going to win, Zahid's on a hat-trick!'

I turned on the TV and saw Zahid streaking down the pitch, long locks flying. He looked like a young god – the crowd was screaming – there was a thrilling *thwacckk!* and I saw the ball making contact with the stumps and the bales flying, and then the cockney-accented commentator was yelling: 'And he's done it! The Sangrur Express has derailed the opposition! The young India team has won and what a win…!'

He went on and on. They replayed the shot from every possible angle. Then he started rhapsodizing about how cool Khoda was too. And then the two commentators pounced on Khoda and Zahid as the team came walking back to the pavilion.

'Congratulations...what an innings...fabulous... How do you feel?'

'Good,' said Khoda, with a quick grin. He looked happy, sweaty and relieved. 'We started well but then we lost a couple of wickets but then we steadied and Zahid played a very useful knock and then we managed to restrict them and it all worked out in the end...the boys did great.'

'Was there some point where you lost the faith at all, Nikhil? Or were you confident right through?'

'Well, I did start to worry in the last five overs because it was so very close but then we changed the field around and Zahid did a great job and the boys took some incredible catches...'

'I was wondering, why did you play only Zahid in those last four overs? Because Bala and Thind had a couple of overs still in their kitty too. And Zahid didn't seem to be doing too well against them initially.'

Khoda had screwed up his face thoughtfully halfway through this question and now he just shrugged and said: 'Well, he was a little expensive at first but I felt he was the right guy to get those wickets – it was close, too close for comfort, but it did end well.' A boyish grin lit up his face. 'Thankfully!' he said.

The commentator turned to Zahid.

'And how do you feel, Zahid? Thirty-three runs, five wickets and a hat-trick, you've had a big day.'

'Yes,' Zahid agreed happily. 'It was all a team effort and God has blessed me greatly and also I was just really really lucky.'

'That's really modest of you,' the commentator said, clapping him on the back. 'You were great out there today. You've made a record, by the way, all that can't just be luck!'

I watched Zahid, my heart hammering against my chest.

A cheap little part of me wanted him to say something about

me, after all I'd given him a lucky kiss, hadn't I? And I imagined my dad falling off his chair in KB, Sanks doing a double take in Delhi, Ritu Raina freaking out in Dhaka. But another part of me cringed at these idiotic groupie-type fantasies.

Zahid looked like he wanted to say something but before he could, Nikhil patted him on the back and said cryptically: 'Great job, Zahid! *Chalo*, let's go in now!'

Then this little presentation ceremony came on after another ad break. (Aamir for Coke again, those guys have such *obscene* budgets.) My idiot client Ranjeet presented a fifty thousand taka cheque to Zahid, a few speeches were made and it was all over for the day.

Harry and Shivnath were really excited when they came in to do our patchwork shoot. Both of them insisted they'd won the match because of me, which defied all logic of course, but was very flattering. And then Zahid called up and gushed, insisting I was a farishta. I was dumb enough to put it on speaker phone and then had to endure Neelo and Vishaal singing *Farishta sabun mera naam, mail bhagaana mera kaam, mein hoon kapdon ki shaan* for the rest of the shoot.

Well, at least we got our shots pretty quickly. Harry and Shiv were in high spirits and they posed happily for Vishaal – *I Believe I Can Fly* alternating with *We Are the Champions* on the speakers. Neelo was hugely relieved. He'd quickly sent off his jingoistic *Zing!* banner lines to Delhi – ('Australia's easy,' he confided to me. 'We can always use "*Assi jeetey, Aussies haarey*".') Lokey bustled about in the background while we shot, tripping over the cables and wires, taking calls from Corporates who wanted to sign up Zahid immediately. 'Thee price just went up, Joyaji!' he said chuckling fatly, his face ashine with sweat and happiness. 'You people got him cheap!'

By ten o'clock I was back in my room. I'd messaged Sanks the moment we clicked the last shot and now I was in the mood to party. Ritu had phoned a while ago. 'Meet you in the lobby in twenty, Zo,' she'd crooned. 'Or d'you want me to come fix your make-up?'

I assured her that I was fine and then got all nervous about the evening. Because the truth of the matter was that I didn't have too much experience in going to clubs with international-level cricketers.

I showered quickly, then sunk onto the bed and slathered on huge amounts of moisturizer. Then I combed out my hair (always a long painful process) and got it semi-dry with the hairdryer in the loo. I'd sent my jeans to be washed and ironed and so I dialled Housekeeping and asked them to hurry it up. I was just worrying about getting late and getting left behind by the beautiful people when the doorbell rang and I ran to get it, tripping over the stupid extra large Sonargaon bathroom robe. 'About time!' I said. I put one hand out for the laundry and then froze.

Yeh to bada toinnngg hai...

Nikhil Khoda was standing in the doorway, looking sombre. 'Can I come in?' he asked.

'Sure,' I somehow managed to say, like cricket captains called on me on a regular basis.

He came into the room and then just stood around silently for a bit while I eyed him, totally flummoxed. What was he doing here? Had he come to *thank* me or something?

Finally, he spoke. 'I hope you're leaving tomorrow,' he said abruptly.

Slightly taken aback at this unfriendly tone (he'd been so nice to me in the elevator), all I could come up with was a puzzled, 'Sorry?'

He raised his voice a little and said, like he was talking to an idiot, 'You're leaving tomorrow?'

I was. Of course I was. But he was being so mean, I didn't feel like saying so. What I *felt* like saying, and so what I said was, 'Why?'

He shrugged. 'Because it's better that way.'

Feeling a little monosyllabic, I repeated, 'Why?'

'Because the boys' attention is very flattering and you must be feeling very important' – I looked at him, a little irritated – 'and you've probably decided to stay on and win the series for us' – sarci as hell – 'but, here's the thing' – Boost-brown eyes glittering – 'I won't let you.'

I opened my mouth to answer, but he didn't give me the chance. 'The only reason we're winning is because we've all trained with single-minded determination for the last six months. This team is slowly learning to have faith in itself. I can't have them putting that new-found faith in you instead.'

He was doing it again. Talking like a Nike ad.

But, hello, did the guy have amnesia, or something?

I said, as reasonably as I could, 'But *you* only asked me to stay, Nikhil-sir. I would have been happy to leave that day itself. You said it was a good idea to stay and support the team against Australia.'

He made a little impatient gesture with his hand and I had a sudden flash of insight into his twisted mind. 'You thought we'd lose today, didn't you?' I demanded. 'Are you *allowed* to think like that?'

He shrugged. 'I'm a realist.' Then he looked me right in the eye and said, 'But we won. A fact I'm proud of. And it wasn't because of you.'

God, what an insecure guy he was. Running up here and

going *Mine! Mine! Mine!* The victory is only *mine*. And to think I'd liked him! 'So it was because of *you*?' I asked as neutrally as I could.

He nodded doggedly. 'Yes. And because of Zahid, and because we won the toss and everybody kept their heads.'

Well, that was fair enough, really. They'd played a fantastic match. Every man had done his bit. Only a fatalistic, uneducated, superstitious person would think their fabulous performance had anything to do with *me*.

Then Khoda said, clearly proving he thought I was all of the above, 'So I don't want you to start believing *you* had anything to do with it, okay?'

I nodded, keeping calm, just about. 'Okay.'

'Because there's no way you're going to get any mileage out of it!'

That's when I saw red. I'd been holding myself in, thinking about my job and how much I loved it, about how he was such a *famous* guy, and a *captain* and everything, but now I couldn't help myself. 'Mileage?' I said, in what I'd intended to be a mature, dry voice, but what may have just come out sounding like an outraged squeak. '*Mileage?* That is so uncool! You know, not to be rude or anything, but I don't even *like* cricket! The last thing in the world I would want to do is become some kind of glorified cricket-groupie!'

That surprised him. I guess his trio of Bollywood starlets didn't talk back to him like that. But then he came back at me with a really nasty one. 'Really? You seemed to be enjoying yourself so much this morning. A gracious kiss on the cheek, that got us a world record? What have you got planned to win us the World Cup, Zoya? How far are you willing to go for your country?'

I felt my cheeks go red hot with embarrassment at what he was implying. But I played it pretty cool. 'Oh, I might just have to go all the way...' I said musingly. 'It's probably the only thing that could win us the World Cup with a clown like you in charge.'

His eyes blazed. 'You're pretty cocky for a lucky charm who's only three matches old!'

'And you're pretty cocky for a skipper who's lost every final he's ever played,' I said and shut the door in his face, already appalled at the mess I was in.

6

Of course I missed the Shah Rukh shoot. But I did manage to have a long, lazy weekend at home, licking my wounds and being coddled by Eppa and Dad, with no calls from office at all. They were all excited because my horrible brother Zoravar was back for a break after some kind of commando training course, looking completely hideous. He'd been catching and eating snakes cooked in hollowed-out bamboo stems, was tanned deep purple and had these really wiry muscles everywhere. Of course Eppa thought he looked really great. 'Just like soldier shud luk,' she said fondly, as she ladled a third serving of her Balls curry (as she insists on calling her famous, cooked-only-on-special-occasions mutton kofta curry) onto his plate at dinner time.

He wolfed it all down, gnawed on a particularly chewy bit of mutton and grinned at me manically. 'So how are you, Gaalu?' he asked. 'Sunk the company's fortunes yet?'

Basically, Zoravar's thing in life is to make fun of me.

His face is shaped like a cashew nut, all long with a protruding chin, and he has the gall to think *my* cheeks are a hideous deformity. When I was little he was always letting out this loud scream and going, 'Ma! Ma! Zoya *got stung by a bee!*' And when my mother came running, he'd go, 'Oh no, sorry, her face is like that only.'

The other really painful thing about growing up with Zoravar is that ever since he was like five months old or something, he knew he wanted to join the army. He never wavered. Any time an auntie at a party asked him, 'Beta, vot you wantu be ven you grow up, *hain*?' He'd chirp, 'I'm-going-to-be-a-soldier-and-fight-for-India!' And then everybody would go all moist-eyed and sigh, '*So cute.*' While I spent my childhood and adolescence dithering over lawyer/banker/fashion designer/nurse, he remained committed to playing with his tanks and singing *Chal chal re naujavan.*

No wonder he thinks my job is a joke. Even after three-and-a-half years, he finds it hugely funny that people are paying me money to work for them. So then my dad told him: 'No, Zoravar, Zoya is doing well, she was even sent abroad on company work.'

'Dhaka isn't really abroad,' Zoravar said snidely but did ask me, in quite a civilized way, how the experience had been.

I gave him a carefully edited version of events, sans any mention of my brawl with Khoda. Even thinking about it now, three whole days later, the aftershock was huge. Because, of course, the moment I'd said it, I had been appalled. What had I been *thinking*? How could I have been so *rude* to somebody so *important*? I kept imagining he'd get me sacked or blackballed from advertising or just command the universe to stop liking me or something...

Both Zoravar and Dad were disgusted to learn that I had gone all the way to Dhaka and watched the matches in my hotel room. 'Oh well,' Dad sighed. 'When has she ever been interested in sports? Zoya, I hope they will pay you more from this April. You are working so hard – these people take you for granted – at least they should give you overtime.'

'Dad, I'm not a *driver*,' I said, rolling my eyes at him. 'They don't give overtime in management jobs…and anyway they pay me enough to get you guys presents from Dhaka!'

I'd got shirts for him and Zoravar and a pale pink-and-white Dhakai sari for Eppa, which had softened her face and given a halo-like glow to her iron-grey curls. 'Too much money you spent, Zoya Moya,' she'd grumbled happily. 'You shud hav got presents for your Chachis, not me.' (Yeah right, like she would have let me *live* if I'd come back from Abroad without a present for her.)

And then my dad said, 'Run along upstairs, the two of you. Rinku Chachi wants a couple of guinea pigs. She's bought a new grill and is testing it out making pizzas.'

Awesome! Rinku Chachi's pizzas were legendary. They were loaded with tandoori chicken, achaari paneer, Amul cheese and hara dhaniya and no Italian would ever recognize them, but they rocked. So both of us got into our pajamas and trooped up the rather steep and narrow staircase, Meeku at our heels, tail held jauntily high.

Rinku Chachi had opened the door even before we banged on it. There was a yummy wafting smell of masalas and her hearty, happy voice going: '*Arrey*, Zoya! Zoravar! G. Singh, the children are here!'

Gajju Chacha was inside, pottering about his study. We chorused a formal, 'Namaste, Chacha' and happily ignored him after that. He is one *strange* little man and safest left alone. He's some kind of fancy educationist and looks like a peaceable old turtle with his bald, egg-shaped head and skinny neck. But once, when he was fourteen, he'd grabbed a heavy copper ladle out of the daal ka donga and hurled it across the table at his brother Yogu with such ferocity that it had embedded itself into his scalp, standing upright for forty-five seconds before teetering and falling off. Yogu Chacha got seventeen stitches, and was permanently brain-damaged as a result, according to my dad.

Rinku Chachi is a little lonely now because Gajju has dispatched both their kids (our cousins Monya and Montu) to boarding school in Ajmer. Which is why she loves having Zoravar and me around.

Zoravar started on the pizza with ecstatic moans, all the while grossing Rinku Chachi out by flashing the pus-encrusted blisters he'd got at the commando course, his appetite amazingly unaffected by the three kilos of Balls curry he'd polished off downstairs.

Then Gajju sidled up to me: 'So how was your cricket experience, Zoya?'

'Uh, good, Chacha,' I said, realizing with a sinking heart that he must want to talk cricket. The last thing I wanted to do was chat with him.

'Did you have the opportunity,' Gajju asked in hushed, awed tones, 'of meeting Mr Jogpal Lohia?'

'Um...who's he, Chacha?' I asked. 'I don't think I've ever heard of him.'

Gajju smiled enigmatically. 'He's the president of the IBCC, child,' he told me. 'A most powerful man, a *good* man. Discerning. Intuitive.'

'Uh, no,' I said. 'I just met the Indian team, really.'

'The new captain's not bad,' Gajju conceded grudgingly.

'Not bad at all. Not in the same league as earlier skippers, of course.'

'Oh?' I said. 'But I thought, statistically speaking, that Nikhil Khoda is the most successful Twenty20 captain of his age, and has already led India to more One-day tournament finals than any other skipper and also has thirteen ODI centuries in international cricket to his credit?'

Gajju just nodded tolerantly in a little-knowledge-is-a-dangerous-thing way, but Zoravar's jaw dropped. '*Arrey*, not bad, Gaalu! Never thought I'd hear *you* spouting cricket stats!'

I went pink. Okay, so I'd been, as Monita would say 'ogling and Googling' Nikhil Khoda a bit. I'd checked out all his stats on the Net, proving myself to be a masochistic loser who obsessed about people who were super rude to them.

'Tell me,' Gajju asked in his pedantic voice, 'do you think they could win this tournament?'

I said I didn't know enough about cricket to comment, but Zoravar looked up and said, with his mouth full of pizza, 'What win-shin, Chacha? Don't you know what happened today?'

Gajju's face went all self-righteously pious. 'How can I know? Yogu cut my cable wire, it only got repaired half an hour ago…' he said in a martyred voice.

There was a full story in there but I didn't want to know it. Hurriedly I turned to face my brother. 'Zoravar, what happened today?'

'We lost,' he replied resignedly. 'Dad and I watched the whole match while you were sleeping off your' – he made sarcastic little inverted commas in the air – '"transcontinental" jetlag.'

'Not to – ?'

'Bermuda!' Zoravar nodded.

'That's impossible,' I said weakly, reaching for the remote.

'Nothing is impossible for India,' said Gajju quietly and shuffled away to his study, a broken man.

I couldn't believe it! A match whose outcome had seemed

so totally obvious had turned the Champions Trophy around! The Aussie-tamer India was out and the minnow Bermuda was in.

I reached for a slice of pizza in a stunned kind of way.

'It was a complete rout, Gaalu,' Zoravar said, nicking it away from under my nose sombrely. 'Painful to watch. The entire team, scurrying around like headless chickens, calling wildly, getting each other out. Total disaster. And the umpire was a jerk. Okayed some very dicey appeals.'

'But they're still in the reckoning, right?' I asked. 'Isn't there a point system or something?'

'It's a knock-out tournament,' Zoravar shook his head, digging little meat bits out of his teeth morosely. 'Not league. You lose one match, you have to go home.'

Still not wanting to believe him, telling myself it was some twisted joke he was playing on me, I sat back and switched on the TV. Sure enough, the news was showing the Indians coming back, blazers on, pushing their trolleys through Calcutta Customs. It was a strange feeling, watching them all on Rinku Chachi's twenty-one inch telly in Tera Numbar. It gave me some perspective on what big stars those boys really were.

Of course my mind was in a whirl. A smug little part of me was going 'Hah! Serve the Khoda-thing right. He was so full of himself that night.' But my heart beat for India enough for me to feel bad about yet another crappy end to our cricketing dream.

I sat there, staring at the TV, watching Nikhil Khoda have microphones thrust into his face, and thought about what he'd told me. That I could do a lot of damage to all the hard work he'd done, if the guys started to *believe* I was lucky. 'I can't have them putting their faith in *you* instead of *themselves*,' he'd said.

At that point I'd thought he was just being insecure. I'd thought he'd meant: 'I can't have them putting their faith in *you* instead of in *me*.'

I wasn't that sure any more.

Then I thought about what Lokey had told me. About how most of the players were pretty immature. 'They cling to straws,' he'd said. 'Harry and Zahid really believe you're lucky, Joyaji.'

Harry hadn't exactly covered himself in glory at the Bermuda match. He'd got out for a duck, to be exact.

Zahid hadn't taken a single wicket.

'It's the glorious uncertainties of the game, Gaalu,' said Zoravar, licking his fingers clean. 'And anyway, there's still the World Cup. Don't look so stricken.'

But I couldn't help feeling guilty. I wanted to punish myself. So I pushed the last cheese-and-pineapple-laden slice of pizza at a surprised Zoravar and said, 'Here, you can have this.'

I hit office just a little after nine-forty a.m. on Monday. Zoravar dropped me, and was even intuitive enough to ask, halfway through the drive, if I was quite all right. Of course I said I was absolutely fine.

'Hey! Zoya!' beamed Monita, flashing her usual ear-to-ear smile, both arms held out in welcome. 'Give, girl, give! How *were* the Men in Blue?'

I smiled. Our shoot at Ballard Estate seemed so very long ago. 'Unbelievable!' I assured her. 'Tell you all about it soon!'

'Right after you report to Sanks!' she said. 'I'll order us both a cold coffee in my cabin. And there are Greasy Crispy Breadrolls for breakfast, you want?'

I walked to Sanks's cabin and looked in. He was busy stuffing himself full of GCBs (Greasy Crispy Breadrolls) while talking on the phone, so I bobbed my head in and mimed *hi, I'm back.*

He looked up, grunted and gestured for me to sit.

I sat, looking around, fiddling with stuff on his desk till he wound up the call and banged down the receiver. 'You look like shit,' he barked.

Thanks, Sanks, you don't exactly look like a branch of blooming bougainvillea yourself.

'What the hell have you been up to in Dhaka?'

'Huh? Nothing!' I told him. 'Just been working very hard. Getting you shots of every possible cricketer from every possible angle! Don't tell me there's something I missed?' I knew the images would have come in on Thursday. Neelo would have worked all weekend getting the prints and making poster layouts.

Sanks waved the shots aside like he hadn't been haranguing me about them for the last week. 'That's not what I mean. What have you done that Zing! wants you off the account?'

Oh no. This reeked of Nikhil Khoda. And to think I'd been defending him to Gajju last night. 'I haven't been up to anything, Sanks,' I said stiffly. 'But I have no problems working on some other account if there's any issue.'

'Shut up, Zoya,' he said crankily. '*I* have a problem with you working on some other account! Fat lot of work I'd get done around here if I started listening to everything the clients say!'

'But what *did* they say?' I asked, a sick feeling in my stomach. I mean, I love my job. (In fact, according to my friends and family, I *was* my job.)

'That you're a loose cannon, you overstepped your boundaries, or something. What have you been up to, kiddo?'

So I told him the whole story.

Sanks's (slightly bulging) brown eyes got even bulgier as he listened. 'But you haven't done anything unethical,' he said finally. 'Nothing at all.'

'Yeah, but I'm in trouble,' I said miserably. 'And the client knows it. Khoda must've called them and complained. After all, I did call him a loser.'

'Now, that wasn't exactly a scintillatingly intelligent move, was it?' Sanks grumbled. He looked up at me, his eyes almost sympathetic, and said, 'I really don't know if I'll be able to save your sorry ass, kiddo.'

I nodded miserably.

'I'll work out something,' he said. 'Now, get out of here. There's tons of work to do!'

I crawled out and staggered into Mon's room.

'What happened?' she exclaimed. 'What'd he say to knock the stuffing out of you like that?'

I told her. It was a very long story that got longer with every retelling.

Mon was hugely concerned. She stopped me now and then to ask me some very Mon-like questions: What did the team eat for breakfast? Did you wear perfume in the elevator? Is it true that Laakhi's gay?

I told her everything and then wanted to kill someone when Shiven rushed in going: 'Hey! How was Dhaka?' He was followed by the other office kids asking the same question.

'It was good, okay?' I stood up. 'I've already told the story twice. Ask Mon for the details!'

Shiven (a creepo who'd filled in for me at the Shah Rukh shoot) puffed out his chest importantly. 'I know, it's crazy, *everybody* keeps asking for all the dope when you come back from a shoot. Yours was just cricketer stills in Dhaka, Zoya! Imagine *my* plight, after a theme film with SRK!'

Mon rolled her eyes. 'Please! You've told Totaram and your Bijnaur-waali mausi and the canteen guy. That's three people. Who else asked?'

I gave Mon a reproachful look as Shiven slunk away, crestfallen, but she just grinned. 'If I can't have GCBs for breakfast I have to sink my teeth into *something*,' she pointed out. 'So when will Sanks tell you if you have to shift to another account, Zo?'

'Soon, I guess,' I said. 'Mon, not a word about this part of it to anyone, okay?'

She nodded. 'Don't worry, Zoya,' she said gently. 'It'll all work out great.'

Fighting back a sudden rush of tears, I walked over to my cabin and switched on my comp.

It didn't. Work out great, I mean. Basically, my Standing in thee Society fully plummeted, because Sanks had to take me off *Zing!* and put me on Maximilk. *But just for three months, Zoya, after that you're fully on again.*

I got a lot of curious looks from the Maximilk gang, who are a committed and down-to-earth bunch. They do wholesome, non-celebrity ads and look down on cola advertising for being basically shallow and relying too heavily on celebrities to make it look good.

They didn't know me too well and now I seriously regretted being so snooty with all of them while I had been working on *Zing!* This earnest bespectacled guy, Animesh, took me through an orientation on Maximilk. 'There are basically five brands in one. Like in *Zing!* you have cola, orange, lime and clear-lime variants? Here in MSK we have Maximilk, Chocolate Maximilk, Woman's Maximilk, Junior Maximilk and Maximilk Lite which is for diabetics…'

I nodded intelligently, trying not to look too depressed.

'Our target audience is Moms twenty-eight to forty-five years. Bullseye thirty-five. Middle class, usually with two kids or more with some elderly people, in-laws usually, whom they have to look after too.'

Man, was this a far cry from Boys, fifteen to twenty-five years. Bullseye eighteen. The tribe Neelo had once grossed me out by describing as 'young, dumb and full of cum'. What was I doing here?

'We have to walk a fine line between appealing to the mom by being nutritious and caring, and appealing to the kid by being fun and cool. We need to have both on our side. I'll give you a CD of all our ads so far as well as the ones the competition has done. Bournvita and Complan, you know. And I think it would be a good idea for you to come along for this housewife research we're having soon. You'll get to see the consumer up close.'

'Great,' I said. 'Thanks, Animesh.' And under my breath added, 'And, thanks, Khoda, you bastard.'

I was painting my toenails a hot orange on Wednesday evening when Eppa rushed into my bedroom screaming, 'Zoya, Zoya, *tumhara photu paper mein aayyaa hai!*'

She rushed into the room brandishing *Sonali's Gupshup* column in her hand. With a sinking heart I saw an image of me dancing with Zahid at that club in Dhaka. Across our fronts the headline screamed, 'KHODA PAHAAD, NIKLI ZOYA'.

Damn.

I grabbed it and read:

Did you wonder why our cricket team's been acting so erratic lately, darlings? At least earlier they lost predictably

to everyone! Then they managed two big wins and got us all excited only to break our nazuk little hearts by losing to Bermuda! Well, I've got a scoop for you, sweeties. A triple scoop with a cherry on top! Apparently, the two victories (and one defeat) have nothing to do with our almost brand-new Captain's leadership abilities. And have everything to do with one sweet lil' thing (pictured above) called Zoya. Zoya – jiske liye Zahid Pathan ne dil khoya! Zoya, it seems, is blessed by the Great Batsman in the Sky. She was born at the very moment India won the '83 World Cup twenty-seven years ago and if she nibbles her morning naashta with the Boys in Blue on the day of the match, they win! If she doesn't, they lose. It's as simple as that. But after she clinched two big matches for his team, Khoda ordered her home! Being the big strong man he is, he felt he could take on Bermuda without Zoya's help! Bet he's really sorry now, girls...

My first instinct was to roll the paper, shove it into my mouth and chew it down to destroy the evidence. But I couldn't do that with Eppa watching. She was looking at me, all bright-eyed and tremulous, waiting for me to read it out to her.

I cleared my throat and said, 'You're paagal or what? That's not me in the picture! You know I don't have a shirt like that.'

Eppa looked unconvinced so I tried to stare her down. It didn't do a bit of good. She peered down at the picture again, gave a disdainful sniff and went: 'Kucch ghapla kiya hai tumne, I know! You can't bluff me, Zoya Moya...' She flounced out, but she let me grab the paper from her as she left.

I read it again.

It was nasty all right. This Sonali babe obviously had it in for Khoda. She didn't really say anything mean about me, though. All she'd done was make that lucky charm theory public.

Thankfully, it sounded pretty stupid in print. Oh, and she'd called me Zahid's lady-love, to which I could only say *I wish!*

Of course I was worried about what they'd say at work. But far more scary was what the reaction of the gang at Tera Numbar might be. What *would* Dad do when the Chacha-Chachis descended in a chattering horde?

When I was a kid, I would get really awful one-on-twenty scores in English dictation. The teacher always told me to get them signed by Dad. I'd spend the whole weekend making myself sick with apprehension about what his reaction would be and finally slide it shamefacedly next to his teacup on Monday morning. Till he explained to me that it was far more painless to get it over with on Friday afternoon itself.

So that evening at the dining table, I slid Sonali's article under Dad's nose right after Zoravar and he had finished eating. 'I'm in the news,' I said lightly.

Eppa snorted in the background but I ignored her.

Dad and Zoravar pored over the paper together, Dad's lips moving slightly as his bifocals travelled slowly past the luridly coloured picture to the catty copy below.

I waited, heart in my mouth. God, they were *slow* readers!

Finally, Dad put the paper down on the table with a little *tchai!* sound and Zoravar fished out his red Swiss knife and started cutting some bright-orange Dussheri mangoes with it, whistling tunelessly between his teeth.

'What?' I demanded. 'Hello, you guys, say something!'

Dad just shook his head but Zoravar said simply, 'We know you're lucky, Gaalu.'

Huh? They *knew?* I *was?*

'I used to take you with me to all the mohalla and inter-school matches I ever played,' he continued. 'We never lost a single one.'

I gaped at him, open-mouthed. 'What? Why didn't you ever tell me?'

He looked at me as if I were nuts. 'Obviously, because you'd have got all pricey or asked me to give you money so you could save up to buy firecrackers.'

What? I couldn't believe this!

'Your Ma knitted you a V-necked white cricket sweater with cables down the front,' Dad said reminiscently. 'You won us a lot of inter-regiment matches too.'

'And why didn't *you* tell me, Dad?' I demanded.

He shrugged, removing his glasses and rubbing his eyes. 'By the time you were old enough to understand, my cricket playing days were over...and after your Ma died...I guess, I just forgot.'

There was a little silence, broken only by the sound of Zoravar sucking noisily on the Dussheri. I just sat there and stared at them. I couldn't process what they were telling me – that I really could make people win matches with my very *presence*. 'So, Dad, how many cricket matches have I attended in my life?' I ventured hesitantly.

He shrugged, 'Nothing pukka, but about...twenty?'

'More,' said Zoravar. 'Many more, if you count all the ones I took her to.'

'And the team I supported always won?' I asked disbelievingly.

Zoravar nodded blithely. 'Always. You didn't even have to stay for the match. I'd bring you in, make you have a Campa Cola or a snack with the boys, and then Eppa would take you home before the match began. That's because you were a real pain to have about the place, you always wanted to pee or puke or something.'

I ignored that last crack and said, 'So you never lost a cricket match in your life?'

He shook his head. 'I did. Lots of times, whenever Ma said I couldn't take you. In the cold weather in Kalimpong. And of course, at the IMA. But I never lost a match *you* came to, Gaalu.'

'Your mummy did not like it, Zoya!' Eppa said loudly all of a sudden. 'She allvayz saying *ki* if this girl uses up all her good-luck vinning matches then no good-luck vil be left-over for her ownself only! Only bad-luck.'

Oh my God, *Ma* said that? What a scary thought. And strangely logical somehow. Almost karmic. I started feeling slightly ill.

'What rubbish you're talking, Eppa,' Dad said dismissively. 'Anyway, I just hope this whole thing doesn't get out of hand. People mustn't take it too seriously. I don't remember you ever losing a match for us, Zoya, but of course there will be a first time, someday.' He had put on his glasses and was frowning down at Zahid's picture. 'And what about this Pathan fellow?' he finally asked. 'If he's so rich why doesn't he get a haircut? Don't tell me you like him?'

I shook my head, 'No, Dad, I don't,' I said firmly and quite truthfully.

'Of course not, Dad,' Zoravar said as he got to his feet and stretched luxuriously. '*He's* not the one you have to worry about!' He sneaked a beady, knowing glance at me and then stuck out one sticky-with-mango hand, grabbed my dupatta from the back of my chair and started skipping with it. '*One, two, three, four…*' he went, bouncing up and down, his stupid bathroom chappals slapping against the floor.

'*Kya kar rahe ho*, Zoravar?' Dad asked mildly. 'Don't exercise after eating, you'll feel ill…'

'*Arrey nahi*, Dad,' my worm of a brother sniggered, skipping madly. 'I'm doing it for Gaalu. She likes *skippers*, you know!'

The Asian Age **Sports page**

CHARMING TALES FROM HERE AND THERE

More strange things have been done in the World of Sport to woo Lady Luck than have ever been done between the sheets in a Jackie Collins novel, or for that matter, between the sheets of a bed at a downtown Bangkok motel. Because Luck, and its close companion, Superstition, definitely have had a hold on the mind of competing athletes since time immemorial.

Lucky underwear, lucky songs, lucky pets (worn to the field under helmets and damn the RSPCA), lucky bed-mates the night before (specially popular on the Formula One circuit), lucky wads of chewing gum carefully tucked away in cling-wrap match after match, they're all part of Great Sporting tradition.

The Mojo derived from powdered bull testes has powered many a 100-metre dash at the Olympics and is supposed to confer an amazing 'spurt' of speed to the performer. It may be harder to get hold of than the more usual performance-enhancing steroids but has the advantage of being virtually undetectable in your urine sample. And while on the subject, here's what Argentine goal-keeper Sergio Goycochea used to do before facing a penalty shoot-out: he'd step aside and urinate on the pitch. He was convinced this was the lucky charm that helped him save goals ever since he survived a penalty shoot-out (post a quick pitch-urination) against Italy in the semi-final of the FIFA World Cup 1990.

Luckily, the increasing level of television coverage (more than twenty-six cameras and counting) means that Goycochea had to ultimately desist from his 'charming' habit of treating the pitch to his 'golden showers'.

Talking of body-waste disposal, ex-Australia cricket

captain Steve Waugh has a lucky snot-rag that he always carries on to the field with him. The 'good medicine' in the hanky (a present from his grandmother) played a vital part in making Waugh the most successful Test captain in history with forty-one victories from fifty-seven Tests. (Of course, other teams have tried repeatedly to steal it, but their attempts have been foiled by the fact that Waugh never sends it to the laundry.)

In fact, cricket, so tied with tradition and history, has an amazing list of definitely odd superstitions. The entire Indian cricket team once sat frozen in their respective positions in the dressing room at Lords, for the duration of an entire match (the Final of the Natwest Trophy 2002). And we all know what a long game cricket is. One wonders if they were tempted to test the efficacy of a quick dressing-room urination while they were at it. Incidentally, they won.

There are opening batsmen (Sunil Gavaskar) who always walk in to the right side of their partner or they can't contribute much to the scoreboard; batsmen who have to touch the bales before taking strike or they can't perform well (Alan Knott) and fielders who have to raise their collars or they drop the easiest of catches (Mohammad Azharuddin).

At any time during a cricket game, you may be treated to the peculiar sight of a portly cricket umpire (David Shepherd) hopping from foot to foot, if a team is stuck at the Nelson scores of 111, 222, 333 (and, of course, the dreaded but seldom achieved number of the beast, 666). If he stops hopping before the score changes, so the superstition goes, he may precipitate a collapse, an injury, freak weather or any other calamity that could possibly strike a cricket side.

Sadistic batsmen, or those with a grouse against the umpire must be sorely tempted to let the score stand for a bit and watch the umpire hop.

Or maybe they're as anxious to get off the unlucky Nelson as he is. Because, no matter how good the preparation, no matter how talented the sportsmen, there is an unknown, unpredictable variable to all sport.

That variable kicks in for some and not for some others. That variable is the difference between winning and losing.

That ingredient X, which sportstars alternately swear by and scoff at, is Luck.

I just couldn't get over what Dad and Zoravar had said to me that night. It was so weird, it was like I'd discovered I had a third eye or a second nose or something. You know, another whole organ I didn't know about.

I could make people win cricket matches.

Not a great power to have, one would think. Not quite up there with making the lame walk or the blind see. But, hello, we're talking twenty-first century India here. People who can win cricket matches are just about the richest people in the country today.

The thing is, could it actually be true?

Could I really do it?

Why *me*?

Because, there's nothing very special about me – is there? I mean, okay, I was born on 25 June 1983 but isn't there one Indian baby born *every second*? That means there were 86,400 kids out there with the same birthdate as mine, if I was doing the math right. That's hardly a Unique Selling Proposition!

Dad of course swears that I was born at the very *second* the last wicket fell and therein lies my luckiness. He says the gynaecologist was hovering in wicket-keeper stance before my mom, shouting encouragement, shifting her weight from foot to foot, gloved hands spread out to catch me, and that I plopped out just as India clinched the last wicket.

And the other thing that Eppa had come up with? That was just plain spooky. But so *fair*, somehow. Like a natural progression of *lucky at cards, unlucky in love.*

And if you stopped to think about it, nothing good had happened to me since I started breakfasting with the team, had it? Khoda had bawled me out, I'd practically lost a job I loved, nasty gossip had come out in the press about me…hey, it was a miracle my bumpy plane back to Delhi hadn't crashed, scattering my remains across rural Bihar…

And things got worse the next day. The office gang told me that *Sonali's Gupshup* article wasn't the only one. *Lots* of channels had covered the story on the news. Zoravar called at work and told me he'd seen Khoda fielding questions on Star News. Then the Aaj Tak guys gheraoed Zahid somewhere and he tried to pull a no-comments but then suddenly broke and told them all about my 'lucky' kiss and the hat-trick that followed. Then they dug up some old army uncle who said he remembered how some inter-regiment five-dayer had turned totally after I up-chucked a mixture of apple juice and Cerelac on the captain's shirt over breakfast on the last day's play.

And while I was stuffing GCBs into my face in office the next afternoon, my cellphone rang and some clipped-sounding dude said he was from NDTV and wanted to ask me to come on his chat show panel tonight. I panicked completely, said *no thanks* and switched off my phone.

Sankar, of course, was totally ballistic on the subject. 'The problem with you girls,' he yelled at Monita and me as we cowered in her room, 'is that you can't keep your mouth shut. How the hell did this get out?'

Of course I was asking myself the same question. I played back the whole set up in Dhaka in my mind...the team, Wes, Lokey, Vishaal... It could've been anybody.

Anyway, I figured it would die a natural death soon. I just had to pretend I lived in a circus for a little while.

That evening Nikhil Khoda was on the news. We all watched it together. It was some sporty show and Khoda was being interviewed by one of those guys who sound eerily like Prannoy Roy. They discussed all kinds of other stuff and then the guy asked Khoda about me. Well, actually, what he said was: 'So what's this about a lucky charm, Nikhil?'

Khoda, looking darkly dishy in a white-collared shirt open at the throat, said easily: 'Well, I don't believe in luck, Raghav. I feel the only way we achieve anything is by working hard, focusing, and keeping a cool head on our shoulders. Good luck is a short cut. I don't believe in short cuts. Bad luck is an excuse. I don't believe in excuses.'

Wow. He looked hot saying that. I felt a peculiar mix of Lust and Loathing as I looked at him, wondering if he'd made that dialogue up right there or rehearsed it.

'But what *about* the loss to Bermuda *then*, Nikhil?' asked the Prannoy clone, steepling his fingers and stressing all the wrong words, just like his boss.

'Well, there were a lot of reasons. Bermuda played extremely well, the crowd was backing the underdog, we lost the toss and certainly the boys were starting to place their faith in something other than their own abilities.'

'And Zahid's hat-trick?'

Nikhil's face hardened. 'Zahid Pathan got five wickets including a hat-trick because he is an extremely talented bowler. He insults himself if he believes otherwise.'

Raghav nodded several times and shuffled some papers around on his desk. Then he asked, 'A lot of cricket fans want Zoya Solanki' – Eppa gave a little scream hearing my name on TV – 'to be given some *kind* of an official designation and be allowed to *travel* with the team. What's your view?'

Nikhil wrinkled his brow thoughtfully – the Lust and Loathing mix sloshing around inside me intensified a little – and shrugged. 'Well, I think it would be detrimental in the long run. Ours is a superstitious country and a precedent like this could lead to chaos in the future.' Then he added lightly, 'Besides, a very busy career girl like Zoya,' – he shook his head and smiled a little and I got the oddest little goosebumps watching his lips curve around the syllables of my name – 'may not be willing to travel all year round with us.'

'Well, thank you very *much*, Nikhil. And best of luck to the Indian team for the benefit match then.' The clone giggled a little and pumped his puny fist into the air: 'Go Indians!'

After the initial rush of hearing myself discussed on TV wore off, I started feeling really pissed off with the guy. (It didn't help that the *yeh toh bada toinnngg hai* ad came on in the ad break right after.)

I mean, this guy had lost me the *Zing!* assignment I loved because of which my promotion was pretty much nixed this year. He had made nasty insinuating remarks about me. And it was all his fault that every time his mug came up on TV, my moronic brother made idiotic baboon-like gestures. And now he was sitting there on the news and being all gracious while the truth of it was that he didn't want *anybody* to get the credit for his stupid team's victories besides himself.

I decided I hated his handsome guts and went to bed in a state of total indignation.

7

I attended a Junior Maximilk research session the next day. It was an interactive session, held in the little drawing room of a tiny second floor flat in Lajpat Nagar. These sessions have to happen in an unintimidating sort of setting, kind of like what the subject's own house is like, otherwise the data gets skewed. So our twelve carefully selected subjects, from the Socio-economic Category B+ (education: graduation, family income: Rs 30,000 per month or less, language of choice: Hindi) had gathered in a room with one three-seater and two one-seater sofas, with a twenty-one inch TV in one corner, printed polyester curtains, an oil painting of a babe in a ghagra with a matka on her head, and a small carpet down the middle with a low table topped with a brass vase with plastic flowers. We had just played them a recorded script narration when my phone rang.

I flushed bright red, muttered an apology and hurried out of the drawing room, bumping into one of the two one-seaters as I did so. My phone didn't recognize the number, but I recognized the voice that went, 'Zoyaji? Hello, Zoyaji?'

I stepped out onto a shady-looking balcony where a massive water cooler rumbled noisily. 'Zahid?'

'Zoyaji? Are you on a motorboat?'

'No, on a balcony,' I said waspishly. 'Why are you ji-ing me, Zahid? I'm supposed to be your girlfriend.'

He cleared his throat nervously. '*Arrey nahi*, these newspaper people are crazy. Zoyaji, you have to do something for me, something very, very important.'

'What?' I snapped, but half-heartedly.

'I don't want to discuss over phone like this,' he said. 'Let's meet somewhere and talk.'

'Okay,' I said hurriedly. 'Message me. I can't talk right now.'

Zahid's message said: *bed@7*. I stared at it in complete incomprehension for a while till I decoded it to mean that I was to meet him at The Bed Lounge, a desperately trying-to-be-in nightclub in Gurgaon.

I entered the nightclub at seven sharp and looked around. It really *was* shady. The kind of place where Dawood and Monica would have partied in the good old days. There were all these huge four-poster beds everywhere, with curtains drawn around them, so you couldn't see what the hell was going on inside. It was very, very dodgy.

'Psssst, Zoyaji!'

I turned around to see Zahid lurking behind the curtains of a 'bed'. With relief I noted that it wasn't really a bed – there was a cosy table for two inside the bed frame, with plates all laid out for dinner.

I clambered over the bed frame and took a chair. 'Isn't this a great place?' Zahid asked, enthusiastically. 'My close friend from school owns it. He's asked me to drop in whenever I can. *Kehta hai* it's,' he pushed his hair back, self-consciously, 'good for business.'

'It's straight out of *Shantaram*,' I told him, giggling a little as I sat down.

'What's that?' he asked, puzzled.

'A book,' I replied. 'A bestseller, actually.'

'I don't read books,' he said.

Okay, so much for that line of conversation. 'So what's up, Zahid?' I asked him resignedly. '*Kaise ho?*'

He flashed his gorgeous smile. 'Fine. And you? *Sab khairiat?*'

He was kidding, right? I laughed ironically, but I don't think he got it. 'Yeah, everything's just great. So why did you want to meet me?'

He rumpled his copper curls in an uneasy kind of way and then said, 'I want to invite you to eat breakfast with ten of my friends.'

No subtlety about our Pathan. No beating about the bush. He was seeing only thee eye of thee cupbirrd, wasn't he, just like his captain. 'No way,' I said.

'Please, Zoyaji,' he went, 'just one last time. It's very, very important to me.'

'Listen, it's very sweet of you guys to have so much faith in me, but my job and my privacy are very important to me. You guys have band bajaoed both.'

'Zoyaji!' Zahid made a dismissive gesture with a large calloused hand. 'What is privacy? *Arrey,* where's your patriotism? You have been specially blessed so that you can serve your country!'

I shook my head. 'Zahid, I'm sorry. I wish you'd told me what you wanted over the phone. I would have said no then itself.'

He hadn't heard a word I said. Instead, he just started shredding his paper napkin efficiently to bits. 'What is this about your post?' he asked. 'What has happened?'

I told him.

He looked totally shocked. 'Skipper complained to your client? I don't believe it.'

Yeah, of course he would think the sun shone out of the (admittedly cute) Khoda posterior. I sighed tiredly: 'It's all true, Zahid.'

'*Phir toh* you have to meet him!' Zahid said animatedly. 'Ask him why he did it. Demand your old job back. Sort it out,' he urged, and then added with a subtlety that surprised me, 'over breakfast.'

'Does Nikhil-sir know that you're inviting me?' I asked him. He nodded.

'And he's okay with it?'

'Then what!' said Zahid roundly. 'In fact, he said it was an excellent idea and that he was "all for it".'

Amazing huh? The mighty sure had fallen, if not on TV, in private at least. 'Okay, then I'll come,' I nodded, feeling an absurd upswing in my mood. I didn't dare analyse why the thought of meeting that horrible Nikhil Khoda again was so oddly invigorating...

Zahid had said he'd send a car to take me to the match, which was being played at the Feroz Shah Kotla on Wednesday. I'd been in too much of a hurry to get home that night to even ask him who our team was playing against. And it wasn't till I was in a huddle with Mon, sipping coffee in the office, that I wondered what this match was about.

'Is anybody touring India right now, Mon?' I asked her.

She shrugged, 'I don't know,' she said. 'Let's ask the boys. Neelo!'

His head stuck out, giraffe-like, over the cubicle dividers. 'What?' he asked in a distracted way.

'What's this match on Wednesday? Who's India playing?'

'There's no India match on Wednesday,' he answered. 'Use

your brain, Mon, if there was a match, we'd have been deluged with requests for passes by now.'

Hmmm, valid point. So what was Zahid up to? I called him, but got his voicemail.

I hung up without leaving a message. And then decided to call Lokey.

'Joya!' went Lokey. 'Joyaji! *Arrey aap toh bade aadmi ban gaye ho!* How are you, madam Lucky Charm?'

'I'm fine, Lokey, listen…'

'If you want an agent, give me a ring! I'll get you a contract from Mohun's Cornflakes.' His voice went all announcer-like suddenly, 'Breakfast with Joya. Victory guaranteed! Get Set Jo!' He chuckled fatly, '*Aisa kuchh*, you know.'

'Ha ha,' I laughed weakly. 'Lokey, listen, what is this match day after at the Kotla?'

'*Parson?*' He thought for a bit, then went, '*Arrey, voh* IPL *ka* exhibition *match hai* – for thee flood victims, you know. Champions Mumbai Indians are playing runners-up Kings XI Punjab.'

He kept talking after that, going on about how I could endorse Natraj HB pencils too ('best of luck for your exams') but I wasn't really listening. I was thinking of that Raghav guy on NDTV going *Go Indians* (he'd meant the Mumbai Indians obviously), and Zahid, that snake, they called him the Sangrur Express, which made him Punjabi, right? No prizes for figuring that one out. In a moment of total revelation, I could see into both their minds clearly. Zahid was planning to get kissed on both cheeks by me, make a double hat-trick or something, win the exhibition match and pressurize Khoda into making me the national *animal* or whatever of Indian cricket. Khoda (far from wanting me to cheer his side on like I'd naively assumed) was planning to pulverize Zahid's side and discredit me as a lucky charm once and for all. *That's* why he'd said inviting me to the Kotla – to eat with the Kings XI Punjab team, of course – was a great idea.

God, he must really hate me.

Oh, well, the feeling was mutual.

I sat with Eppa in the garden the next morning. My dad and she had been doing a great job keeping the Chacha/Chachis off my case over the last few days. I don't know what they had threatened them with but they'd all given me a lot of space.

Eppa was spraying water on the cannas as I sat there thinking about what a messy situation I was in. It made a lovely soothing sound as it spattered the dark green leaves and a smell of first rain filled the air.

When she'd finished she said, echoing Zoravar really: 'Zoya Moya, everything okay, no?'

Boy, if only she knew. I just shrugged and bent to gather all the freshly fallen harshingar blossoms from the grass, and went: '*Haan* gorgeous, *sab theek hai.*' I handed her the flowers and she went in to say her morning prayers, humming the first lines of a hymn under her breath.

I wandered around feeling unwanted at work. The Maximilk team didn't really know what to make of me with all this stupid press coverage happening. In my super-sensitive state I was convinced that even my pals in the *Zing!* group resented me. Because junior servicing people don't really end up getting talked about on NDTV. Animesh was nice to my face but I was convinced he was moaning behind my back about having a freak like me in his group. I heard that jerk Shiven say that there was no wonder that true love had blossomed between me and Zahid Pathan, because he was a small-town, non-MBA-holding, sports-quota type and his English *sucked*; just like mine, apparently. 'They'll be so matching-matching,' he was saying to the guys in Research and Planning, 'they're from the same SEC, after all! D minus minus!' Then he cackled his stupid, shrill cackle.

I wanted to shove my ballpoint pen up his nose. Instead, I said snootily that I was expecting a call from Barkha Dutt, went into my cabin, and tried to write a new Chocolate Maximilk brief.

Which is when Zahid finally called me. 'Sorry, Zoyaji,' he said breezily. 'Team meetings you know.'

I didn't want to talk to him. I said, as shortly as I could, 'Zahid, you *snake*, I'm not coming to your match.'

He got very upset. He tried to persuade me for a while, and then infuriatingly, just when I was weakening and about to give in, he suddenly caved in, said 'Okay,' and hung up, leaving me feeling really KLPDed.

I slammed the phone down, a crushing feeling of anticlimax sweeping over me. My innings as an *important* person, as a national lucky charm, was going to be over before it ever really began.

I sank low into my chair, shook my hair forward so it obscured half my face, kicked my cabin door shut and did this really dumb thing.

I cried.

Bawled my eyes out, if you want to know the truth.

I know, I know. It's really uncool to cry in office. But, hello, I was really messed up.

Firstly, there was this whole Good Luck thing. It was totally seductive. I mean, who wouldn't want to believe that they're special? Maybe God *had* blessed me specially, to make up for my motherless, chubby-cheeked, twice-jilted, not-smart-enough-to-crack-the-CATs status. Maybe I really was a Goddess of the Pitch. I was born at the stroke of the auspicious hour and so my very *pores* breathed propitiousness for men in badly-fitting, light-blue, microfibre, cotton-blend tracksuits. Maybe this was my ticket out of the boring, safe, middle-class life I'd lived so far. Maybe this was how I'd become rich and famous, appear on magazine covers, and have lean mean cricketers grovelling at my feet.

Yeah right, I thought, and blew my nose vigorously. *Like that'll happen.*

All I'd be doing, by allowing myself to get drawn into the international cricket circuit, would be setting myself up for the inevitable fall. Because one day, they'd lose after eating with me. And the later it happened, the worse it'd be.

All the Zoya fan club guys would swarm up ladders and put gobar on my hoardings…The rejection would probably *kill* me.

That's why going to the Kotla breakfast was not an option.

I mean, I'd probably just end up watching my team of choice be ass-whipped by an angst-ridden, smarting-from-losing-to-Bermuda Nikhil Khoda, who was obviously out on a mission to crush me under his foot like he would an ant.

No way was I going to give him that satisfaction.

When I got home that evening my dad was all jumpy because Anita Chachi's nephew, Kattu, was visiting from Bikaner and had dropped in to our part of the house and formally asked Dad if he could take me out to dinner. Dad, instead of calling me and asking first, had happily told him, of course young man, by all means. Now, he told me, with a wink, to make a good meal of it.

I groaned to myself.

Dad has recently become a real bore on the subject of marriage. My two Chachis – Rinku and Anita – have been at him ever since my eighteenth birthday and now that my twenty-eighth was approaching, he'd finally begun to sit up and pay attention. After I broke up with my second boyfriend, the three of them even got together and put an ad in *The Times of India*... *Beautiful, fair, convented, Rajput, retired colonel's daughter, 5.4 feet, 27 years, seeks handsome kshatriya match, boy must be tall, highly qualified professional, 26-30 years*...

It's all lies of course, I'm neither fair nor 5.4 (more like five three-and-a-quarter inch actually).

Anyway, thanks to that ad, I'd spent some hairy Saturday mornings at the DSOI (the army club), meeting fair, moustachioed, ghee-fed Raju boys who all looked like they had surma in their eyes even though they didn't. Some of them were even *nice*, but just the thought that they were uncool enough to reply to a matrimonial ad put me off them completely. Which was totally hypocritical of me because, hello, I was the one who was uncool enough to *take out* a matrimonial ad.

Still, I didn't say *haan* to any of them. For that matter, some of them didn't say *haan* to me.

Actually, my dad is too sweet to tell me this, but the fact of the matter is that I don't exactly *shine* on the arranged marriage circuit. I have to tie up my hair, so I look all moon-faced. I have to wear salwar kameezes, which do nothing for my body type. And, of course, I have no accomplishments whatsoever. I don't play the piano/sitar, I don't know any classical Indian dances, I can't sing, I can't paint and I'm a lousy cook. I'm not a doctor.

I'm not a professor. I *do* have an MBA but from a dodgy business school. And because I have this idiotic involuntary tendency to check out guys from what my Rinku Chachi euphemistically calls the 'marriage point of view' as I talk to them (basically I keep imagining them naked) my conversation is far from scintillating. I end up looking slightly nauseous and totally tongue-tied.

Anyway, the fact that Kattu had raised his ugly head meant that Dad was really scraping the bottom of the barrel. I remembered him as a snively little kid whom Zoravar and Montu were mean to when we were growing up.

Still, at least because our families knew each other I'd been spared the morning-tea-at-the-club routine. We could cut straight ahead to step two: the dinner-date-with-the-eleven-p.m.-deadline.

Kattu called me on my cell a short while later. 'Hi, Zoya,' he breathed heavily down the line. 'Remember me?'

I rolled my eyes. I hate people who call me up and say arch things like, *Remember me.* (It could've been worse, though. He could've said, *Guess who?*) 'Hi Kattu,' I said, cautiously. 'I believe we have a date tomorrow night?'

'Ya! So tell me!' he said expansively. 'Where would you like to go?'

I told him to pick me up from work the next day and hung up as fast as I could.

Still, in a way I almost welcomed the Kattu development. I told myself severely that my head was too full of romantic Bollywood nonsense. Real life wasn't all about *Zing!* shoots and Shah Rukh Khan's torso and sparring sessions with Indian skippers. Level-headed twenty-seven-year-old women didn't dwell on such facile non-encounters. They laughed them off and kept their feet on the ground.

So I made a special effort with my grooming the next day. I wore a 'good girl' salwar kameez, shampooed my hair and applied my make-up with care.

Kattu was lurking near the sidewalk in a fat yellow car when I came down from office in the evening. Totaram was giving him dirty looks. 'Hi, Kattu,' I said as I opened the door of the car and recoiled at the blast. He'd really overdone the aftershave. The mature twenty-seven-year-old woman in me wanted to turn tail and scurry for an auto.

'Hi, Zoya,' he goggled at my get-up, glasses gleaming.

I inhaled cautiously and internalized the fact that the years had been kind to Kattu. He looked okay, nice even, in the usual Rajput butterball-with-a-moustache Raj Kiran-ish kind of way. Then he put on music, which was good because we didn't have to talk, and I directed him to the Carmic Cat, a nice cosy pub nearby. They serve drinks and dinner and it's pretty brightly lit, so I could examine Kattu minutely for flaws and he could do the same to me. I ordered a *Zing!*, took a sip and immediately an unbidden image of Kattu's face, contorted with passion right above mine in a dimly lit room, rose before my eyes.

'D'you have stomach ache, Zoya?' Kattu asked, concerned.

'No!' I said, smiling brightly, wondering if his cheeks would droop in that position. His lower lip definitely would. And I couldn't shake the creepy feeling that he would drool. 'I'm fine, what's up?'

'Nothing,' he said, making this expansive gesture with his hands. Mon says a man's hands are a good guide to his... uh...*equipment*. Kattu's were very thick, fair, hairy and bejewelled. I almost gagged.

'Are you *sure* you're all right?'

'I'm fine,' I managed to say.

He looked unconvinced but continued, 'I'm here for a sales

conference, though Ma and Babuji want me to meet some girls, too, and then it's just work, work, work.'

'How nice,' I said. 'How many girls have you met?'

He shrugged, 'I've lost count actually. Some of them were very nice, but you know, I'm looking for something magical....You know, a *connection?*'

I nodded, warming to him a little. 'I know exactly what you mean,' I said, and meant it too. *Really.* I liked the fact that he was romantic, that he was looking for true love. I tilted my head to one side and tried to imagine how his face would look *below* mine, say if I was on top. Bad mistake.

'Why are you squinting?' he asked.

'I'm not,' I said brightly, thinking sinkingly that the inside of his mouth was *pink*, and that his tongue looked like it would *wag*. 'Could I get another drink?'

He nodded and snapped his fingers at the waiter in an authoritative (some might say obnoxious) way.

'You've grown up a lot since we last met,' he said rakishly. 'I like it!' Then he started elaborating on his romantic theme. 'I dream of meeting an unspoiled girl, Zoya!' he said, his eyes locking into mine. 'A shy, unopened *bud*, a *kali* you know, whom I will then, slowly, slowly,' – he exhaled deeply and opened his hairy hand out daintily in a classical Indian dance mudra – 'turn into a *flower.*'

I choked on my drink.

He beamed at me and said, 'Please excuse me, I have to relieve myself.'

I nodded, hiding my face in my napkin and he sped away to the loo, his shoes squeaking a little. I sipped my drink gloomily as the *chwing chwong chwing chwong* of Kattu's shoes faded away. Had I gone through two heartbreaks to end up with this? *This* was the hero of the movie of my life?

Because, hello, I've grown up thinking I'm starring in DDLJ. Or *Titanic*. Or at least *Bride and Prejudice*. And all the time it's actually been *Dunston Checks In*.

I had a sudden vision of Kattu and me at a honeymoon hotel in Goa, him all cocky and expansive in swimming trunks, with a towel hanging around his neck, snapping his fingers at the waiter. And me, with sindoor in my hair, a mangalsutra dangling demurely between my recently-pawed-by-Kattu breasts, modestly encased in a prim salwar kameez of course, smiling bravely in spite of suffering a raging case of honeymooners' syndrome a.k.a. urinary tract infection. Later, we would live in an apartment with stiff cream curtains that you pull open with a cord, in a gated community in Gurgaon, and make a couple of Kattu-like kids. I would feed them every single meal by hand, like a good mother should. Naturally, I would have to give up my job, start wearing long kurtis to hide my flabby, scarred-by-a-million-stretch-marks tummy, learn to do a million clever things with leftovers and bread crumbs, and have to ask Kattu for money to buy sanitary napkins every month. In the holidays we would go on long car trips where the kids would drink Mango Frooti and throw up in my lap. We would spend every weekend with our in-laws, including horrible Anita Chachi. The kids would leave home and then bald, pot-bellied Kattu would get diabetes, without losing his appetite for sex. I would have to take his urine samples in warm little jam jars to the doctors' every day.

Then I would die.

By the time Kattu came back from the loo and sat down again, the mature twenty-seven-year-old woman in me had been completely vanquished.

I wanted excitement.

I wanted adventure. I wanted *out*.

Come Friday, I was going to the Kotla.

8

I decided to be as lucky as I knew how. So the next morning, I went to the Punjab Emporium opposite Hanuman Mandir and picked up this hardcore salwar kameez, a little phulkari jacket, juttis and a pink parandi. I wore the whole ensemble and drove to the Kotla stadium in the car Zahid had sent for me, Daler Mehndi blaring from the speakers.

The team was already at the table when I reached. I knew Zahid, of course. Hairy was the captain of the Kings XI side, apparently, so I met him, and Shivee and a couple of hulky, vaguely familiar looking goras.

'They are Australia's best bowlers,' Zahid whispered when I dug him in the ribs questioningly. 'You should know that much, Zoyaji!'

I muttered something about them looking so different in the Punjab uniform and he nodded, mollified, and introduced me around. Then Nivi Singh rushed in, falling all over himself to say hi to me. But that was just because he'd thought I was Preity Zinta, come to wish him in person.

'She really wanted to be here,' Hairy told me wistfully, once Nivi had slunk away disappointed. 'But she is shooting some big film in Prague and cannot make it.' He then showed me this long bloodthirsty sms from Preity, telling him to go out and basically kill the Mumbai team.

I admired it dutifully, suddenly feeling very small-time. After that the boys pretty much left me alone. They got into this strategic-sounding conversation. Not that there's much strategy involved in a Twenty20 match. Seems to me you just go in there and hit the hell out of the ball. Still, Hairy seemed to have some kind of a plan. Which is good because everybody was kind of expecting this match to be a replay of last year's IPL final in which Nikhil's side had trounced Hairy's soundly.

After a rather quick breakfast, I got up and went out on to the terraced balcony adjoining the dining hall. It had a great view of the maidan below, where the groundsmen were scurrying around doing stuff. I thought I recognized one of the umpires from Dhaka and was leaning out to get a better look when I heard footsteps approaching and turned to see Nikhil Khoda, lean and keen in the spiffy Mumbai Indians uniform, looking right down at me.

'Hi,' I said, stupidly. Loathing 80%. Lust 20%.

'Hi, yourself,' he smiled back. 'You look sweet. Thanks for coming.' Was this guy for real? He'd got me off my favourite brand, was out to disprove my lucky status, and he was now being *nice*? The outrage must've showed on my face because he said quickly, 'Look, none of this is personal, you know. It's just that we're all keen to settle this luck thing before we get into the run-up for the big one next year.'

'How civilized. So you've decided to test my luckiness out in simulated test conditions,' I said sweetly.

His teeth flashed in a very white grin. 'Yeah.'

I leaned back a little and opened my eyes wide. 'You think I'm going to be a flop today, don't you?'

He grinned again. 'Pretty much,' he drawled.

'And your side's going to win?'

He lifted the collar of his striped shirt and eyeballed me with his Boost-browns, 'Yeah.'

'*Great*,' I cooed. 'That should make a nice change for you.'

His eyes glittered but all he said, pretty neutrally, was, 'Are you so nice to everybody or is it just me?'

'Just you, actually,' I said, 'because *you've* been so nice and gone out of your way to have me practically sacked.'

He had been looking over my shoulder at the pitch, hardly listening to what I was saying but at this his eyes snapped back to me. '*Matlab?*' he asked.

'*Matlab*, thanks to you, they took me off *Zing!*. I'm working on Maximilk now.'

'Thanks to me?' he repeated, puzzled. 'What'd I do?' Then his brow cleared. 'But it's the same company right? What's the problem?'

I gave a tight little laugh, 'Oh, just that I hate the job,' I said.

Khoda shrugged and went back to looking out at the field again. 'Oops,' he said indifferently. Then he added, 'Much as I'm enjoying this conversation, I really have to get onto that field now.' And with a curt nod he clambered onto the balcony railing, leapt lithely onto the grass, and got into a chat with some guy in a Fly Kingfisher coat below.

I glowered at him for a while, then shrugged and went downstairs in search of Zahid and the other boys.

The stadium was decently full, but it lacked the hysteria of a proper *India* match. Speakers were blaring the Kings XI Punjab anthem and there was a sprinkle of vaguely famous looking people with their sunglasses on, but there was no one I actually recognized.

I looked down and saw Zahid chatting cosily with Khoda,

like they weren't set to disembowel each other later at all. Guys are *so* weird…

I walked up to them. 'Best of luck, Zahid,' I said and he turned around, unruly copper curls falling into his eyes, a little surprised at the intensity in my voice.

'Thanks, Zoyaji,' he said formally, going pink as always. As I smiled up into his serious brown eyes, something about the bored smirky grin on Khoda's face behind him got to me.

And that's when I did a rather silly, filmi kind of thing.

I reached out for Zahid's hand as he turned to walk away, yanked him back, and kissed him full on the mouth.

He was surprised. I could tell from the way his eyes widened just before our lips made contact. Obviously his 133 female fan club members had not pulled this stunt on him – yet. Still, he stopped being surprised pretty quick and it ended up being a nice kiss, toe-curlingly tingly and smelling of CK One and some minty brand of chewing gum. But the nicest part was that Nikhil Khoda wasn't smirking any more. He wasn't *there* any more actually. He'd walked away, to be exact.

And then Zahid pulled back and looked at me, a little confused, a little unfocused. Then he smiled. '*Mein abhi aataa hoon, haan?*' he said quite gently and walked off to join Khoda who was waiting for him with the umpire on the pitch, hands deep in his pockets.

'*Arrey wah*, Joyaji, you have made him forget his English even!' I heard a voice booming behind me and turned around to see Lokendar Chugh, chomping pistas as usual and looking rather hideous in a Kings XI tee shirt.

'I didn't know you support Punjab, Lokey,' I said.

'*Lai*, I am Punjabi only!' he said. 'And you are looking so *soni kudi!* Come in and watch the match with me.'

'No way,' I said, shaking my head, my idiotic parandi swinging from side to side. 'I have to go to work now.'

Well, I left on a high all right. But as I rattled towards office in an auto, it suddenly occurred to me that a picture of me smooching Zahid might make it to the papers. Which made me feel totally nauseous – because, hello, my dad would totally freak.

And what would Zahid think?

He'd think I was some total despo, fully nuts about him.

God, how humiliating.

Of course, all I'd been seeing was Khoda's smirky face so confident of victory.

I'd wanted to lash out at him in any way possible. (Don't ask me why. All I can say in my defence is that when I'm around him, I'm rendered unstable by a thick rush of Loathing tempered with Lust.)

But now, my miraculously clear mind told me, I'd pretty much ended up lashing out at myself.

Because Nikhil Khoda didn't give a damn who I kissed. Why should he? What went of *his* father's?

But something sure went of mine.

My father likes to believe he's 'broad-minded'. He's kept the same standards for Zoravar and me right through school and college. He's cool with the fact that I'm still not married. He's proud that I'm working. I think he knows I've had boyfriends and stuff, and the policy we've been following since I was about seventeen is that he doesn't ask me about it and I don't tell him about it. Of course, Eppa knows exactly what Zoravar and I are up to and I have a sneaking suspicion that she spills the beans to my dad and then he goes around fully clued in but pretending he doesn't know a thing. But it's pretty hard to play that game if your daughter's picture is in the paper, kissing some cricketer on the mouth. If that picture *does* come out, I will have put my dad in quite an intolerable position. His Standing-in-thee-Society will totally plummet. He'll be like the dad of that sixteen-year-old girl from DPS, whose jerk of a boyfriend released a raunchy mms of her.

Shit.

He won't be able to go to the club for a drink, even.

I sat around in office, a bundle of nerves till noon, when Monita came to me with two cups of coffee. 'Are you all right, Zo?' she asked me gently. 'And what are you wearing to work nowadays? Suits? Parandis? *Kya baat hai?*'

I grabbed the coffee cup, gulped it, and gave her the whole story. Halfway through, she got up and yelled to Neelo to join us. He ran in and sat around blinking, shaking his head in disbelief when Monita told him I had taken over where Emraan Hashmi had left off. 'You chicks, man,' he said finally, 'you're something else. Why the hell d'you kiss him if you don't like him?'

'So that he would win,' I said miserably, 'and so that bastard Khoda would lose.'

'This,' said Neelo with unnatural calm, 'is what is called becoming a victim of your own hype. So now you've started believing that whoever you kiss can win a cricket match, have you?'

'Of course not, you *moron*,' snapped Mon nastily. 'She just wanted Khoda to see her kissing somebody else!'

I jerked my head up. 'I don't give a damn about Nikhil Khoda!'

'Course you don't, baby,' said Mon pushing my parandi

back neatly. 'Neelo, phone *lagana*, call Lokendar and find out
what's happening there in the Kotla.'

Neelo nodded. He put his phone on loudspeaker and dialled.
Aashiq banaya aapne played full blast in my cabin for a whole
minute till Lokey finally picked up.

'*Haan*, Lokey?' Neelo spoke loudly. 'Match *kaisa chal raha
hai?*'

I snatched the phone from him and heard Lokey squawk,
'*Kaun*, Neelakhshi? It got over little while ago. You won't
believe it but Punjab have won, it's a *historic* win, a...'

I put down the phone slowly, saying nothing. My mind was
churning crazily, cataclysmic music from saas-bahu serials was
playing in my ears. So the *Zoya ka* magic *chalega kya* question
had been answered decidedly. There was no question about it.
For whatever reason, I was lucky for whomsoever I chose to
support. Why, even Neelo and Monita were looking at me with
something approaching awe.

And I had chosen to support Zahid Pathan, a yummy but
too-young-for-me boy, from whom I had nothing but 'brotherly'
vibes. A *Mid-day* picture of me kissing him was about to land on
my desk any minute now.

And I had not chosen to support Nikhil Khoda, a man I was
almost certainly obsessed with.

Thank God I am not the prime minister of the nation. With
my powerful strategic mind, I would have totally band-bajaoed
the country...

The Mid-day page 1
Shanta Kalra

NEMESIS IN PIGTAILS?

Any doubts that Nikhil Khoda may have had about the
efficacy of Zoya Solanki, a junior advertising executive at

AWB, Delhi, who was born on June 25th 1983, the day India won the Cricket World Cup at Lords, as a lucky charm for whichever team she breakfasts with, were dispelled today at the Feroz Shah Kotla.

The odds were decidedly stacked against Punjab when Zoya arrived, pigtailed and peppy, to eat breakfast with them early this morning. She wished the Kings XI Captain Hharviindar Singh and his Aussie vice-cap, Kevin Astle, before they went in to play. And seemed especially fond of Sangrur speedster, Zahid Pathan.

Punjab won the toss and decided to field first. And what a field day they had. Bullabaroo Butch Astle got South African opener Graeme Watson on the first ball itself – and Mumbai never really recovered from that scalping. Zahid Pathan took three quick wickets in the next 4 overs, and at the end of 10 overs Mumbai were 73 for 4. Skipper Nikhil Khoda stuck it as best as he could, hitting an incredible 63 off 14 deliveries, but he eventually ran out of partners at the other end. The IPL champions scraped together a sorry 133 all out at the end of 17 overs.

Punjab easily totted that much in 12 overs, with a sparkling 89 by skipper Hharviindar Singh, and a truly stupendous cameo by Pathan who hit three consecutive sixes in the last over.

Khoda, who has come out fairly strongly against the superstitious belief that Zoya brings 'luck' to the team, looked visibly frustrated when questioned and said he had no comments to make about his nemesis in pigtails. Instead he said that he would 'much rather take the opportunity to congratulate Harry and the Kings XI squad for pulling off a truly amazing win'. 'Gritty, gutsy cricket like this is oxygen for the domestic game,' he said.

Zoya's track record as a lucky charm is turning out to be both consistent and impressive, and is gaining attention in IBCC circles. It is clearly no longer being dismissed as sheer coincidence, as it was earlier even by this correspondent. 'We believe in her,' said Mumbai spinner Balaji, a player who has felt both the benign and blighting effects of Zoya's charm. 'She is specially blessed. The Board should give her some official status.'

Even coach Wes Harden who had said in an earlier statement that he didn't believe in lucky charms, as he'd never come across one that actually worked, admitted that the Zoya Factor was 'pretty damn astonishing'. He even said he wouldn't rule out Balaji's suggestion out of hand.

IBCC president Jogpal Lohia was present at the Kotla today, but was unavailable for comment.

There was a picture of me right in the middle of the article, with my face looking unbelievably chubby, and my hair all pulled back in that wretched parandi. I had this really nasty expression on my face and I seemed to be glowering at a figure wearing a Mumbai Indians uniform in the background.

Well, at least I'm not smooching Zahid! My father can still go to his club and drink with his cronies.

Thank you, God.

At office Sankar forwarded a mail to me. It was from the *Zing!* client (not idiot Ranjeet, but his boss Vaishali Paul, the top honcho at *Zing!* Co.).

Regarding your little miracle worker. Have just got off the phone with Nikhil who called to demand why Zoya's been taken off the account. I told him that it was because

Ranjeet said she mishandled the situation in Dhaka.
He said quite nicely, but firmly that there was no
mishandling and Ranjeet must've got hold of the wrong
end of the stick. He wants her reinstated. Though no
cricketer – even one as cute as this one – tells me how to
do my stuff, I'm all for it. Zoya's good at her job and I
don't know what Ranjeet was thinking letting her go in
the first place.

He says she exceeded her brief but I think, by having
her removed, that he exceeded his.

So we want her back, if she'll have us back.

And by the way, Sanks…

I think I smell a romance…

Hee hee hee

Vaishali

Honestly. This woman is a forty-year-old mother of two, a gold medallist from FMS and top Indian business person of the year, for the last three years in a row. Why is she talking like some *Stardust* junkie? (I was acting cool, but of course I was totally flattered, I thought Vaishali Paul didn't even know my *name*.)

And wasn't it decent of Khoda to call her and get me my job back? And he did it today, which meant he couldn't be mad at me about how the match turned out today. Which in turn could mean:

a) that he was nursing a grand passion for me in his extremely hunky chest and was trying to woo me back from Zahid (ha ha ha);

b) that he was a decent guy doing a decent thing and had, maybe, a certain tepid concern for lesser beings like myself (pretty possible);

c) that he was scared of angering me, the High Priestess of Indian Cricket (somehow I didn't think so).

Whatever the reason, I was pretty grateful to have my old job back! No more housewife research – yippee! And then a new and daring plan entered my brain, fuelled by Vaishali's crack about smelling a romance. (*Matlab*, she's so clever and all, maybe she's right!)

I thought it might be a good idea to phone Khoda and thank him personally.

Hello, it's not like I was making up excuses. I had a legit reason to call and everything. And his voice was so warm and deep, my toes curled just imagining him say *Hello*…

Loathing 10%. Lust 90%.

'Hello?'

It wasn't Nikihil's deep drawl. It was a female voice. Husky and all. And it sounded familiar.

I said, my voice sounding high and unnatural even to my own ears, 'Uh, hello, can I speak to Nikhil-sir?'

'Can I take a message?'

And somehow, I was instantly convinced that the voice belonged to a certain supermodel from the Kingfisher calendar, whose legs the Bangladeshis had painted over, because they were too sexy to be seen. Not that I had any proof or anything. And I certainly didn't go, *Excuse me, you are April and October, na?* But I was just sure it was *her*.

'No,' I said. 'There's no message as such.'

And hung up.

And went home to my SEC D minus minus house in Karol Bagh.

9

Well, that was it for a bit really. I was a celebrity in the colony and at Tera Numbar but office life pretty much returned to normal. Zahid called me a couple of times but I felt too embarrassed to take his calls. Besides, I figured that if I didn't take his calls he'd understand I wasn't really in love with him after all and he could relax. A couple of days later, he messaged me saying he was off to Bombay to shoot for some bicycle he endorses. And that was the end of that.

A week later, Mon and I boarded an early morning flight and headed for Bombay. We took a cab to the Famous Studio at Mahalaxmi to check out the edit of her Shah Rukh film. (It was too long as usual, ninety seconds instead of seventy-five, and she was very worried about it.) As we inched by Worli Naka Monita screamed and pointed to a hoarding above us. I peered out of the window, almost bumping my head against the roof of the cab. It showed a chubby girl cartoon with wildly curling black hair standing nose to nose with a dark, scowling boy cartoon in India cricket blues. The girl was smilingly offering a slice of buttered bread to the boy. The line on top advised, 'Don't skip her breakfast, Skipper,' and underneath it a legend read, 'LUCKILY, BUTTERLY DELICIOUS – AMUL!'

I can't say I wasn't thrilled. Even though they'd painted me chubbier than I was, it sure beat obscurity, didn't it?

At Famous, Mon and I walked into the edit suite where PPK's boy, Kenny, was halfway through dubbing Shah Rukh.

'*Shhh*,' he said as we walked in, and from the darkness behind the mixer board Shah Rukh's trademark voice floated out: 'Heyy, Monita! Hey, Chubby Cheeks! Aren't you the new Lucky Charm, huh?'

'*Shah Rukh's* here?' I squeaked, wildly excited, whipping my head round to look at Mon with such force that I almost snapped my neck off.

'Well, his *voice* is here,' she said wryly, throwing open the door to the dubbing room to reveal a large, brown, man-mountain with little twinkling eyes and a bristly moustache, a headphone perched like an absurd hairband upon his balding head. 'Hi, Sohan!'

'Good afternoon, Monitaji!' said Sohan in a ringing Amitabh Bachchan baritone. Then he turned to me and said in perfectly flat, nasal Saif Ali Khan accents, 'And how are you m'dear?'

I clapped my hands in delight. 'Awesome! Who-who can you do?'

Sohan grinned. 'The question is *not* who-who I can do,' he said suavely, Pierce Brosnan's Bond voice sounding completely bizarre coming out of his benign Ravana face, 'but who-who I *cannot* do!' Then he took off his headphone, thrust out one meaty paw and said, in a completely ordinary slightly Marathi voice: 'Hello, I'm Sohan. You're Zoya, no?'

I nodded.

He grinned again. 'Very good, very good, like me, you have been blessed with a God-given gift!' Then he switched to an eerie Darth-Vader-talking-through-a-metal-box voice and bent almost double to rasp into my ear, 'Make sure you use it for evil, not good!'

'Uh...okay,' I said, somewhat bemusedly as he winked and said, 'Keep it up!' Then he turned to Kenny and started discussing how much he was planning to charge to dub the Shah Rukh voice.

Leaving Mon and Kenny to haggle with Sohan, I wandered out and skulked around in the seedy corridor, hoping to bang into people I knew.

Because that's the beauty of Famous Studio.

If you hang around there long enough, you will meet every possible person in the advertising industry in India. Its three dingy floors are lined with dirt-encrusted, paan-streaked corridors – with not *one* non-fused bulb in their AC-exhaust-filled passageways – that lead into swanky edit suites, designer animation houses, music studios and film production units. The permanent residents here are the post-production types: editors, sound engineers, animators. These unkempt insomniacs live on an unhealthy diet of Britannia Jimjam and Bourbon biscuits and cigarettes bummed off each other. They discuss the music of Led Zeppelin, the poetry of Rumi and the films of Tarantino – even as they cut thirty-second spots for Nirma detergent, Nestlé Funbar and Tobu cycles. Occasionally they swap horror stories about insane deadlines, moron clients, turncoat agency types and tragically butchered would've-been-a-Cannes-finalist-if-they'd-let-it-alone films. When they're really bored, they even hit on visitors in a half-hearted kind of way. Because everybody else is, basically, only visiting. Film-makers, musicians, singers, agency people (and sometimes movie stars) come to Famous to direct/record/approve/dub on a project-to-project basis.

There are tonnes of studios all over Bombay now, Monita had told me, really fancy, plush ones where you don't need to ask for the key before going to the loo, but Famous is Famous! 'It's the mother ship of Indian advertising,' Mon had declared.

I met nobody I knew in the corridors, so I came down to the ground floor and sat in the café (not as hip as it sounds, it's really a plants nursery that serves coffee and a lousy pizza) where I finally spotted a famliar face. Vishaal, our photographer from Dhaka, smoking a cigarette and managing to look intellectual as he gazed pensively upon a plate of rapidly congealing omelette-toast.

I waved at him through the smoke and he came alive. 'Farishta Sabun!' he went, sweeping me a bow. 'Zoya! Good to see you, yaar!'

'What you up to, Vishaal?' I asked after he'd made all the usual noises about my talisman status and so on.

'New Nike film,' he grinned. 'You're the brief for it, you know! It features Nikhil Khoda.'

'Oh?' I said. 'Cool. Big one for you, no? Celebrity film and all! Can I see it?'

'Sure!' he went. 'We're in Galactica B. C'mon, tell me what you think!'

So I went with him to Galactica B and saw the Nike film.

It was pretty cool.

He'd shot Nikhil against surreal backdrops. Burning, battlefield-like cricket pitches that dissolved into janam-patri parchment, that sort of thing. Nikhil looked totally hot, in a grey, distressed-fabric sweatshirt, very Neo from the *Matrix,* and was playing some big dramatic shots, wielding his bat like a broadsword. There was this voice-over, all echo-ey they'd made it, and what it was saying was:

You can believe in lucky charms
A Goddess to keep you from harm.
A lucky number on your shirt.
Some extra vowels in your name.
You can believe in luck…
Or you can believe in yourself.
And just play your game.
Nike.
Just do it.

It was really goosebumpy. And I don't think it was just because I'm fully Lustful and Loathing-ful about the guy.

'I got it from that NDTV interview Khoda gave recently. We're going to run it after they win their next big match. I thought it would be pretty topical,' said Vishaal.

'It's cool, I said. 'Only the voice….Who's done it?'

'Ignore the voice,' Vishaal said quickly. 'It's mine. I wanted Sohan, but the bugger's too expensive. He makes a fortune dubbing for stars who're too busy to show up for recordings.'

'Can't you get Nikhil?' I asked and added, a little snidely, it must be admitted, 'this film should be really close to his heart!'

Vishaal nodded. 'Oh, he loved it,' he said. 'In fact,' he pushed his hair off his face and cleared his throat modestly, 'I'm waiting for him to come dub it right now.'

I froze. 'Now?' I squeaked. 'He's coming here?'

'Yeah.'

I turned to flee Galactica B but it was too late. Nikhil Khoda, casual in worn jeans and a navy blue tee, had just strolled in.

His eyes lit up when he saw me (*they did! they did!*) and he went: 'Zoya!'

'Hi,' I said, wishing wretchedly that I'd had time to primp before banging into him. I was all bedraggled from my morning flight, dressed in a baggy red shirt of my dad's and loose unflattering jeans. I fluffed out my hair self-consciously with one hand and tried not to think about the fact that he'd probably spent the night with a Kingfisher calendar model.

'Hey, man!' Khoda was saying to Vishaal as they slapped hands. 'How's everything?'

Vishaal smiled a little nervously, 'Great! Why don't you go right in?'

Nikhil went in, slipped on a pair of headphones and started skimming through his lines. I decided to slink away and was heading for the door when Khoda's voice, sounding deep and growly and amplified by the dubbing mikes, said: 'Zoya? Don't go too far. I have to talk to you.'

I nodded, muttered something, and fled.

He found me.

And why wouldn't he? After all, I wanted to be found.

I was sitting in the Famous café, freshly moisturized and kajal-ed, hair all bright and black. Of course my clothes still sucked but there wasn't much I could do about that. He waved to me and I waved back, pretty casually too. 'Are you free for a bit?' he asked.

'Sure,' I shrugged casually.

'Then let's go out somewhere nice and grab a coffee.'

I nodded and hitched my red rucksack a little higher onto my shoulder, trying not to look too overwhelmed.

He took the bag from me, ignoring my protests and said, 'Come on, let's go.'

He drove us to Gallops, at the race course, which was just a short distance away. We didn't talk much. A little street urchin peered into the car at a red light, recognized Khoda and did a double take. Face splitting into a large grin, he mimed hitting a big six into the air with an imaginary bat. Then he shaded his eyes with his hand and pretended to be looking for the ball in the sky, scratching his head in a puzzled sort of way. I laughed, and Khoda looked at me and laughed too.

Lust 98%. Loathing 2%.

Actually, who am I kidding? Lust 100%.

At Gallops, we ordered coffee and then smiled across the table at each other. 'Hi,' he said.

'Hi,' I replied and then quickly added, 'Thank you for speaking to Vaishali. It meant a lot to me.'

'You're welcome.' He looked embarrassed. A silence followed, where he just looked at me. Then, he asked abruptly, 'How are *you*? I mean, *really*. With this whole lucky charm thing hanging over your head?'

'Uh, okay, I guess,' I said with a shrug.

'You're looking thinner.'

I beamed, 'That's good, isn't it?'

'Not really,' he said slowly. 'You look stressed.' He frowned, 'That's why I wanted you to stay out of this whole damn cricket circus.'

'What d'you mean?'

'I mean, now you're in. Say hello to uncertainty, pressure, fear, and insecurity.'

'What d'you mean I'm *in*?'

He looked at me, amused. 'Don't you know, Zoya? Jogpal Lohia was at the IPL match. He was really impressed by the way Harry's lot played with you around. I think he was even more impressed by the way my team crumbled. He's convinced you're going to give us a major psychological edge. He's found some legal loophole that allows him to give you some kind of official status. You're going with us to the World Cup.'

'What?'

'I didn't want to break your friend Vishaal's heart in there, but the chances of his Nike film running are zero. The Board's made me bite the Lucky Charm bullet.' Khoda stopped and smiled at me. 'Close your mouth, Zoya,' he said, not unkindly.

I couldn't. I just stared at him round-eyed and horrified. I could totally see the gobar on my hoardings, I *totally* could!

Khoda grinned. 'Should've thought of that before you smooched Zahid on the mouth,' he said mockingly. Just to piss me off.

That really *was* a cocky thing to say, wasn't it? I decided to be a little cocky myself. 'Oh, were you there? Did you see us?' I said demurely. 'I couldn't help myself. I'm so fond of Zahid.'

'Really?' Khoda remarked. 'And if you're so fond of him, how come you've been dodging his phone calls?'

(I had no answer to that, though, of course, I noticed – and filed away for later gloating over the fact – that Nikhil Khoda was keeping track of whom I was *not* talking to on the phone.)

'Anyway,' Khoda continued, 'I guess you'll be dining with him – and all of us – a lot in Australia.'

'But I don't want to go for the World Cup,' I wailed, a sense of complete panic gripping my belly.

'No choice,' Khoda shrugged as he poured out the coffee for both of us. Then he flourished the teaspoon about and said grandiloquently, 'Ask not what your country can do for you, ask what you can do for your country!'

'I won't go,' I muttered mutinously.

'Say hello to emotional blackmail too. Do you know you've sprouted almost as many fan-clubs as Harry and Shivee?'

'Really?' I brightened up, just a little.

Khoda sighed, 'C'mon, Zoya, don't you want to be famous for something *worthwhile?* Instead of just being famous for being *lucky?*'

He had a point. 'But, you're famous for playing a *game*,' I pointed out defensively. 'That isn't exactly up there with finding a cure for cancer, you know.'

He shook his head in exasperation. 'I know, but in this country, if we did a poll, people would probably be happier if we won a World Cup than if we found a cure for cancer! If *they* give it that much importance, I have to, too!'

'Still, you're famous, you should set a good example,' I muttered. 'Indians are fatalistic enough as it is.'

He sighed. 'Look, you know I tried. But your record's quite impressive and as a humble rookie captain, I have to adopt all means, no matter how unorthodox, to win a match.'

'So, is this official status what you wanted to talk to me about?' I asked, my voice trembling just a little (I'd been hoping he had something more personal in mind, of course).

'Yes,' he said gently. 'And also to tell you, that in case your luckiness, or whatever it is, runs out, right in the middle of the World Cup, I'll be there for you.'

Shit, he really was a nice guy. No wonder his stupid team liked him so much.

I nodded, and smiled up at him brightly. 'Thank you,' I said formally. 'I appreciate that.'

He smiled back at me, the sunlight slanting across his face and lighting up his Boost-brown eyes. And at that moment I found another emotion sloshing around in the mixture of lust and loathing he usually aroused in me.

Another 'L' word.

Liking.

And even though I knew he'd fought tooth and nail to keep me out and that he despised everything I was supposed to be representing, I found myself believing that it had been nothing personal, that he wasn't *against* me or anything and that he liked me too.

Zing! had obviously exhausted their budget for this ad film because Mon and I had to share a room at the Taj Land's End. Which was okay, because I like her, even though she takes ages in the loo and coos lullabies to her boys on the phone for hours at night. Tonight, after she'd put both her kids to sleep and argued amicably with her husband for a while, we ordered Salt and Pepper Prawns from Ming Yang and broke open the complimentary bottle of wine. Monita was clearly in a mood to party. She was pretty relaxed now because the film was looking good. The music recording was tomorrow and that meant a late start 'cos the music guys never got to work before noon.

'So,' she grinned, dipping a prawn into the chilli sauce with gusto, 'how was the coffee session with El Khoda?'

I shrugged. 'Okay. I told you about the IBCC thingie, didn't I?'

Mon rolled her eyes. 'Not that!' she said. 'I mean how was the *vibe*, the *mood*, the, y'know, *connection?*'

'Monita,' I said, 'there is no *vibe* as such. He was just being nice, okay?'

'Yeah, but why?' Mon sat up a little straighter and yanked her plunging neckline back upward. 'There's no need for him to be nice to you. Or buy you coffee or anything.'

'Please,' I said, 'supermodels answer his phone, for heaven's sake.'

Mon clambered off the bed, picked up a magazine from the

coffee table and chucked it at me. 'Take a look at this!' she said
smugly, and clicked her tongue impatiently, the way she does
on the phone, when her five-year-old keeps asking her when
she's coming home. 'The favourite things page, Zo! Read it!'

I found it. Khoda was in there, laughing into the camera,
These are a few of my favourite things was written across his front
in a curly-whorly font:

> *Fav food:* Paranthas. Sorry, not oysters or filet mignon
> or anything expensive like that.
> *Fav one-liner:* Just Do It!
> *Fav bedroom line:* Just Do Me!
> *Fav fantasy:* Very basic actually, slanting sunshine, a
> bottle of wine, masses of long dark curls upon a creamy
> white pillow...
> *Fav perfume:* None. Don't use any. Not a big fan of it
> on women either.
> *Fav place:* A cricket pitch.
> *Fav trait in a woman:* Courage. I like gutsy women.
> *Fav drink:* Zing! Obviously!
> *Fav band:* Dire Straits
> *Fav person:* Mom
> *Fav dream:* The World Cup in my hands.

I read it through and looked up all innocently, even though I
knew what was coming: 'What?'

'The *hair*,' Mon chortled. '*Your* hair, Zo! It's unmistakable!
He is *so* in love with you!'

'Monita,' I said, 'you of all people should know that guys
don't fall for me. They just *use* me – and not even for sex!'

She wasn't listening to me, just shaking her head and giggling
and doing this ridiculous dance around the room, 'No, no, no,

it's *you!* I can just picture it, first you'll make him paranthas in the slanting morning sunshine, then he'll put on Dire Straits while opening a bottle of wine and phoning his mom and then you'll courageously break all the perfume bottles with your bare hands and throw them out onto the cricket pitch and pour a *Zing!* into the World Cup and offer it to him and fall back upon the creamy white pillows with your glorious hair all a tumble and then' – she looked down at *Stardust* to see if she'd forgotten anything and gurgled in delight at the perfect fit she'd found – 'you can Just Do It!'

'Mon, stop yelling!' I hissed. 'You'll wake up everybody on the floor.'

She calmed down a bit after a look at my face and muttered, 'Okay, okay, *fine*, you never used to mind when I teased you about Shah Rukh…'

We carried the presentation material back to Delhi with us that day. The flight landed at some ten minutes to noon and we staggered out feeling spent. Both Monita's cherubic little Bong boys were hopping up and down behind the rails in the reception area, screaming 'Mummee! Mummee!'

Mon promptly dropped her bags and scooped them both up for big smacking kisses while I stood around behind her foolishly. I don't dislike kids, but I mostly don't know what to say to them. Little girls are still okay, but little boys are quite a mystery to me.

The younger one, Aman, was already sneaking a hand down Mon's shirt front and she was slapping it away as subtly as she could, but the five-year-old, Armaan, looked at me intently and then said solemnly. 'Zo – ya!'

'Ar – maan,' I nodded back at him politely.

He had a Dinky toy car in his hand which he suddenly let fall and then went, all round-eyed contrition, 'Oh! I dropped something!' before swooping down and scrabbling about near my feet.

'Armaan, no!' Mon said sharply and I looked at her in surprise.

Armaan straightened finally, grinning and flushed, his Dinky car in his hands.

'Pink,' he announced happily. I looked at him: 'What?'

Monita shook her head in exasperation as she wheeled our trolley out to the car, the boys and their young didi running merrily through the parking lot in front of us. 'Armaan is turning into a complete sex maniac,' she muttered.

'What are you saying, Mon?' I protested. 'He's an innocent baby, only five years old!'

'Yeah, right,' she sighed. 'And what colour panties are you wearing under that skirt, Zoya?'

There were cars parked all along the drive at Tera Numbar when I reached home, feeling tired and exhausted. I looked at the line-up blankly as I paid off my auto guy and then remembered. Lunch in the hag's part of the house.

I took the stairs two at a time, wondering if I'd forgotten a birthday or something. Mohindar Chacha is the most painful of my uncles. He's a retired air force officer, a red-nosed, have-a-drink-beta type, who picked up a Mahavir Chakra in the '71 war and never lets anybody forget it. Gajju Chacha once sourly told a starry-eyed Zoravar that it was less about bravery and more about being in the right place at the right time. He's very hairy, Mohindar. Zoravar and I once saw him casually dab shaving foam on his nose and earlobes as he shaved, which led us to speculate about what he would do if he were marooned on an island; end up looking like Meeku, we concluded.

Anita Chachi's hot in a middle-aged, skimpy-choli-ed way. She's into Fengshui and horse riding (Zoravar insists she takes a whip to Mohindar on full moon nights) and is the undisputed 'classy' bahu of the family, who can barely conceal her mortification at having to live in KB. She's all for selling the kothi, splitting the moolah and moving 'south'. Thankfully, nobody listens to her.

Anyway, I made my way towards her crystal and ikebana drawing room, with Meeku at my heels. There was nobody in what Anita Chachi likes to call the 'foyer' and that's when a little decorative card on a brass stand caught my eye. A cheesy little heart made of entwined pink roses. *'Congratulations Kartik and Neha.'*

Huh? Who *were* Kartik and Neha? And why was Anita Chachi having a lunch for them?

I walked slowly up to the door, feeling like those guys on Eppa's favourite investigative show *CID*, who sneak up on empty houses with their guns held high, ready for anything... And sighted Kattu, a horrid sight in a too tight, white bandgala with a red carnation in his buttonhole. He was holding hands with an incredibly beautiful girl in a silver halter and white sari. She was gorgeous. Seriously. I should've dropped dead. That's how gorgeous she was.

Total consternation swept over me as I realized that Kattu had 'rejected' *me* even before I'd had the chance to reject *him*. This was his engagement party which I was apparently going to attend in a transparent kurti crumpled from the flight, outlining my oldest, shabbiest bra.

I crossed my arms across my front, thinking, *Lucky girl, she really hit the mother lode, Kattu's gonna turn her from a bud into a flower.* I took two steps back, hoping I could sneak out without being spotted, and collided right into Anita Chachi.

'Zoya! Beta, come in, meet the lovebirds,' she cooed, her eyes shining with a horrid triumphant gleam. As she led me towards them she murmured to me, 'I'm sorry, I should have informed you, *par* you were so busy with your cricket-shiket. In fact, Kattu's mummy said *ki aapki* Zoya *toh* cricket team *ki* Draupadi *hi ban gayee hai.*' She gave a horrid tinkling laugh and said, 'Neha, meet Kattu's friend Zoya.'

I soon found myself seated between Dad and Gajju at Anita Chachi's monstrously carved dining table. Some lady I didn't know was seated across from us. My mind was still in a whirl with all this Indian-team-*ki*-Draupadi thing when the auntie opposite me asked, '*Toh*, Zoya, you have become a national lucky charm, *hain?*'

I looked up, blinked, and sneaked a look at my dad. He looked pretty serene.

'*Arrey nahi*, auntie, nothing like that,' I started to say, when Gajju snorted beside me, '*Arrey* Zoya is born lucky!' He looked at my dad, '*Yaad hai, bhaisaab*, the day she was born? *Wahi*, Prudential Cup *ke din*, I told you *ki* this baby is the reason we have won.' He looked at the auntie and said confidingly, 'I wanted them to name her Nike. The Greek goddess of victory, you know…'

This was the first I'd heard of it. Thank you, Dad and Ma, for not naming me after a shoe.

My dad said, 'Yes, yes, Gajju,' and looked like he wanted to change the subject, but then Kattu piped up, 'Zoya's very friendly with all the team, she was mentioning it when we went out for a' – he looked here and there and actually had the grace to blush – '*friendly* dinner the other day…'

I choked at that, but it got worse, because Anita Chachi joined in the conversation. Adjusting her pallu so it showed a little more cleavage, she murmured, '*Arrey*, the whole world knows that it's Zoya, *jisko* Zahid Pathan *ne dil khoya…*'

Ouch.

I tried a casual laugh. But before I could speak, Yogu said smoothly, 'What terrible rhyming. Is that original-Anita, or are you quoting someone?'

Chachi flushed, but stuck to her guns. 'It's from *Mid-day*. Where Zoya's being featured regularly. I'm surprised you allow it, bhaisaab.'

'I'm surprised you read that rag,' Yogu started to say, but my dad cut in with, 'Zoya's life is her own.' He spoke calmly, though his nostrils did flare, just a little: 'She showed me the article in question herself, by the way, Anita. Sorry if she stole your fire.'

Then Mohindar got up and raised a toast to Neha and Kattu and everybody started cheering. I cheered the loudest, a fake smile plastered on my face, hating Anita Chachi's guts.

I know my dad, and I knew there was trouble ahead.

Monita dispatched Neelo to Bombay the next day to carry out all the changes on the Shah Rukh film. She was full of guilt for not going herself, but she was also full of guilt because her older son, Armaan, the panty-peeker, was going through a weird phase where he wouldn't leave the house without carefully arranging a dupatta around his shoulders. This had totally horrified her homophobic husband. And Aman, the just-turned-two-year-old, had apparently kept her up the whole night, insisting that if he was too big to be allowed a snack at the maternal bosom, he could at least be allowed to keep a firm hold on it all night.

'On top of *everything*, Zoya,' she sighed into her coffee cup on Monday morning, 'Armaan stumbled into my room in a blind panic at five this morning and announced that he had to go to school dressed as a Polluting Chimney.' I nodded sympathetically, not really listening. 'So then I had to run around rolling him up in chart paper and making smoke out of bathroom tissue because he *always* wins the fancy dress contests. He'll be totally traumatized if he doesn't....' She suddenly realized I wasn't listening and demanded: 'Why are you looking like such a bheegi billi today, anyway?'

I told her about the lunch yesterday, the cocky Kattu, the beauteous Neha and what my cow of an aunt had said.

'What a kutiya,' said Mon matter-of-factly. 'Don't worry, Zo, she probably has all these kinky Men in Blue fantasies herself. Hey, maybe she makes Mohindar dress up in cricket blues and then beats him up with a Sahni Sports *groin* guard.'

I laughed, feeling a little better, 'So you don't think that's what everybody in office thinks too, do you?'

'Naah,' said Mon comfortingly. 'Besides, why would you care? You should just care about what your dad thinks.'

We started talking about work after that. Sanks had handed me a new HotCrust brief for Mon and I quickly filled her in on it. 'They want to do a big awareness-building campaign on fast deliveries. Presently, Benito's Pizza owns that turf with their promise of half an hour for delivery or the pizza is free.'

'So why can't HotCrust make a twenty-nine-minute promise or something?'

I shook my head. 'That was the first question I asked. They won't. Too me-too. Besides, they don't have the infrastructure to make that promise come good. Too few kitchens. Also, there was a spate of accident cases in the US involving pizza delivery guys who mowed down a lot of pedestrians because they were speeding to meet the half-hour deadline. It made a big stink. We'll never get approvals from the head office in the US.'

'But you're saying *fastest* deliveries,' Mon pointed out. 'How can you say that if it isn't true?'

'Don't *say* it,' I told her. 'The legal people say if you just *imply* it, very strongly, our ass is covered.'

Mon rolled her eyes. She hates the legal guys with a passion. They keep ruining her taglines with their quibbling. (Once, just because there's no actual *nimbu* juice in Belinda Lemon, they made her change, *Belinda Lemon, Made in Heaven* to *Belinda Lemon Flavour, Made in Heaven* and couldn't understand what she was mad about.)

'Okay,' she said, 'anything else you want to tell me?'

'Well, we do have this one thought starter,' I told her eagerly. 'How about if we promise Hot deliveries? That will imply fast, because they're still hot when you get them, see?'

Mon didn't look too impressed. 'When do you want this?'

'This evening,' I told her.

'Balls,' she said, without rancour. 'Day after tomorrow, second half. Now run along, okay?'

I ran along. And sat, totally at a loose end, at my table. There was nothing much for me to do on *Zing!* because all they were doing was cricket. As I fiddled with the Dealer Board layouts lying around the servicing area and looked wistfully at close-ups of Khoda's face smiling out at me with GOLA RESTAURANT ZING! RS 10 ONLY emblazoned across his front, the phone rang.

It was some dude from IBCC. He wanted to meet me to hammer out the details and 'firm up' my contract with the Board! I bit back my panic, acted as savvy as I could, asked him to call me again in the evening, and rushed into Sanks's room screaming Help!

Sanks has this spondylosis problem that acts up now and then and basically makes him even more cranky than usual. 'What?' he snapped, as I burst in.

I told him.

He rolled his eyes at me. 'Just tell the guy you'll meet him tomorrow with your lawyers.'

My lawyers? Hello, I'm a lowly account executive, drawing a twenty grand basic every month! I don't *have* any lawyers! I tried to say as much to Sanks but he just waved a hand dismissively. 'Now get that HotCrust thing done, will you? Those guys are really on my case.'

I told him what Mon had said, that we'd get nothing before day after tomorrow, second half. He snorted, muttered *totally unacceptable*, hauled himself out of his chair and headed for her room, the tuft of hair on the back of his head bristling dangerously.

Five minutes later, the door of her cabin opened and Sanks emerged. He looked at me and said, 'Day after tomorrow, second half.'

Okay, I nodded, totally straight-faced.

'What're you grinning about?' he snarled. 'Go call up that IBCC guy and get your meeting organized.'

I ducked into Mon's room again.

She was on the phone with Neelo, discussing the Shah Rukh film changes, bloody but unbowed. 'I don't care what the post guy says,' she was raving, 'we can't have any flab around the girl's navel! Clean it up, frame by frame if you have to! And don't lose that list of seventeen changes I gave you. Bye!' She slammed down the phone and pulled out a cigarette. I eyed her warily as she lit up with shaking hands, exhaled a long stream of smoke, and said, in a very mild voice, 'I told Sanks I can't give you HotCrust earlier.'

'I know,' I said. 'D'you want to brainstorm on it?'

She glowered at me for a bit. These creative types hate it when they feel the servicing people are *managing* them. Then she shrugged. 'Okay,' she said. 'What we need is a symbol, something that cues speed and swiftness without our having to say it.'

'Cheetahs?'

She gave me an impatient look. 'No, Zo! Like Formula One racing.'

'But the delivery guys ride bikes...'

'That's true. So we can't do cowboys drawing their guns at lightning speed either. Hey, maybe we should get Abhishek Bachchan and do something *Dhoom*-ish?'

'Too expensive,' I said gloomily. 'These guys bust the bank getting Javed Jaffrey to endorse them.'

Mon scowled. She hates working on stuff that doesn't have a huge budget. She's quite a snob about it.

'What about our Hot delivery idea?' I asked her tentatively. 'Nothing there?'

She shook her head emphatically. 'Nope. It's too layered. The other guys are saying *fast*. We have to say fast too...'

I didn't expect her to come up with anything till day after, so I was surprised when she came and folded up on the chair next to me while I was talking to the IBCC dude on the phone that evening. 'I've cracked your HotCrust thingie,' she said smugly, exhaling a long stream of smoke into the air. 'What do you think of when I say fastest deliveries?'

I shrugged. 'What?'

'Zahid Pathan!' Mon said grandly. 'The world's fastest delivery record holder. 169 kmph!' Then she added, in a more prosaic voice, 'Actually, that's second-fastest but who cares?'

Huh?

Basically, she wanted HotCrust to tie up with Zahid. And get him to deliver HotCrust pizza for a week. On a *Dhoom*-type bike, or something. It was strange, but it could work. Except that Zahid wasn't on contract with HotCrust... But if HotCrust gave some free *Zing!* away with the pizzas, *Zing!* Co. might be willing to let HotCrust have him free. Of course, the bike idea may be unfeasible because of security reasons but I'd voice that concern later. Right now, I had an insane deadline to meet and also, I had a feeling that if I said anything negative Monita Mukherjee might start bawling. She looked pretty pushed to the edge to me...

Sanks liked Mon's HotCrust concept. We took it along and got approvals from both *Zing!* and HotCrust the next day. Now the next crisis was, of course, Zahid's dates. So I called Lokey.

'Where are you, Joyaji?' he demanded. 'And who's looking after your legal affairs?'

I told him what Sanks had told me. That the head of *Zing!* Legal would come along for the meeting with the IBCC guys today at five.

'That buffoon Saldhana?' Lokey snorted. 'Take me, Joyaji! In advisory capacity only if you like. No charges.'

I told him he was welcome to come along. The whole conversation felt totally unreal. 'But what about Zahid's dates?' I said, remembering why I'd called him in the first place. 'We'll need to take him through the scripts.'

Lokey chuckled fatly. 'He and Nikhil are in Delhi only, to

judge the Miss India Contest. You know he will make himself free, Joyaji. He thinks of you very highly.'

I muttered something non-committal.

Lokey said he'd see me at the IBCC meeting and hung up.

We rolled in to the Taj Mansingh business centre at a quarter to five. Me, Sanks, Joel Saldhana from *Zing!* Co., Lokey, trailing pista shells behind him like an overfed Hansel, and, looking a little bewildered by it all, my dad.

A smiling lady showed us into a long conference room where four guys in dark suits and one bulbous dude in bright orange robes, sporting Jimi Hendrix dreadlocks, were seated. We all did some hello-helloing, and then they handed us the contract they wanted me to sign:

This is a contract between ZOYA SINGH SOLANKI (henceforth referred to as the Undersigned) and the INDIAN BOARD OF CRICKET CONTROL (henceforth referred to as the Board). It pertains to a six-month contract of employment by the Board of the Undersigned in the position of third additional coach to the Indian Board of Cricket Control Team (henceforth referred to as the Team). The Undersigned is bound to EAT EVERY MEAL with the Team for the time period of the World Cup 2011 if the Team so wish it. The term 'meals' pertains to breakfast, lunch, dinner, and any snacks at any other time of day.

The Undersigned is EXPRESSLY FORBIDDEN FROM EATING ANY SOLID FOOD WHATSOEVER WITH THE MEMBERS OF ANY OTHER TEAM, participating in any Cricket World Cup whatsoever.

The Undersigned is to REFRAIN FROM FASTING OF ANY

KIND at all mealtimes for the duration of the World Cup 2011 in spite of any religious injunctions or reasons of health.

The Undersigned is to REFRAIN FROM ANY BODILY CONTACT with any members of the Team, except from a kiss on the facial cheek or a comradely pat on the back.

The Undersigned is to KISS AT LEAST ONE TEAM MEMBER on the facial cheek directly after breakfast on the day of every India match.

The Undersigned is expressly forbidden from engaging in any physical contact with any member of any other cricket team whatsoever.

The Undersigned is forbidden from the Team locker room, the Team strategy and coaching meetings and training sessions.

The Undersigned is to defer at all times to the team leadership and chain of command.

The Undersigned is to refrain from endorsing any product that may be in conflict with the products or companies sponsoring the Cricket World Cup 2011.

The Undersigned is to MAINTAIN HER SPINSTER STATUS till the 22nd of May 2011.

The Undersigned is to treat every conversation with the Team or any or every of its members as TOTALLY CONFIDENTIAL.

The Undersigned is to divulge no information regarding the workings and strategies of the team, that she may be privy to either intentionally or unintentionally.

The Undersigned is to give NO INTERVIEWS OR QUOTES

to any member of the print, TV, email or radio press. The Undersigned is to travel and stay at any five-star hotel of the Board's choice in the continent of Australia for the period of the World Cup 2011.

For this the Undersigned will receive from the Board, all expenses paid, and a sum of RUPEES TEN LAKHS in cash, on the 23rd of May 2011.

This sum will be paid out irrespective of how the team performs in the Cricket World Cup 2011. IF HOWEVER, THE TEAM WINS THE ICC CRICKET WORLD CUP 2011 TOURNAMENT, THE SUM PAID OUT TO THE UNDERSIGNED WILL DOUBLE EXACTLY.

The Undersigned will be, for the period till the 22nd of May 2011, a bonafide employee of the Board and will be subject to all its rules and policies as such.

If the Undersigned violates any terms of this contract, it shall be declared instantly null and void.

It took me forty minutes to read through the whole thing and to kind of grasp what it meant. I read the ten lakhs bit right in the beginning though, because they'd written it in big type and it kind of jumped out of the page at you. It was good money for someone like me who hadn't ten thousand in the bank. But some of the clauses in the contract worried me.

Like, where had they picked up the phrase *facial cheek*? What was all that stuff about kisses? Why couldn't I get married? Why couldn't I endorse brands? And why did I have to defer to the 'team leadership and chain of command'? That sounded like Khoda and Wes Hardin could really push me around!

As I read the thing through, I felt my (facial) cheeks getting hotter and hotter. When I reached the end of the page, I looked up and asked, in a voice that was shaking slightly, 'Is this some kind of a joke?'

At the other end of the table, my dad snorted loudly in agreement.

None of the IBCC guys said a word.

And then Lokey burst in, breathing heavily, 'Ten lakhs? That's *it*? You are expecting my young client here to disrupt her professional life, experience, her...um...distasteful physical contacts and go through so much ups and downs psychologically for this' – he paused, tried to find an English word that fitted and then gave up – '*chawanni* sum?'

'And why can't *my* client get married if she likes?' Joel Saldhana demanded (stressing the *my* for Lokey's benefit I think).

The IBCC contingent, obviously taken aback at this onslaught, turned to look at the godman-type dude in mute appeal.

He inhaled deeply, put his palms face down on the polished table top and said calmly, 'We fear marriage may affect her propitiousness.' He turned towards me, locked his hypnotic, boiled-looking eyeballs with my indignant ones and said in a kindly voice that sent a shiver down my spine, 'You see, your propitiousness is directly proportional to your purity, Devi.'

I almost choked. How humiliating. Now this entire room knew that at the grand old age of twenty-seven I had still not been relieved of my 'purity'. And how did the old godman variety know anyway? It wasn't like I was walking around with a STILL-A-VIRGIN glow-sign on my forehead. So it had to be total guesswork on his part.

Whatever. He was seriously intruding on my personal space. 'Listen, you're seriously intruding on my personal space,' I told him.

The godman said nothing, but all the legal types leapt up and started making a lot of soothing noises, saying nothing was *final*, it was all very rough, just a first draft, and so on.

My dad held up one hand, and such was the impact of his flaring nostrils that they all backed off one by one.

When the room had gone quiet, he said, 'Gentlemen, I will be honest with you. The money is tempting. Besides, my daughter is dutiful and would like to be of service to her country. But she is not a minor. Even *I* cannot tell her to wed or not to wed, to fast or not to fast. How can *you* people do so? There are too many conditions to this contract. And forgive me, but I have to add that it's also extremely crassly worded. So I'm sorry, your offer, as it stands, is unacceptable.' He turned to look at me. 'Right, beta?'

I nodded back gratefully. 'Right, Dad.'

10

The next day, Mon, Neelo and I drove down to the Taj to take Zahid through the HotCrust Fastest Deliveries concept. Monita grinned knowingly at me as I got into the car. 'Nice lipgloss,' she said slyly. 'I hear Khoda's staying in the same hotel as Zahid.'

Zahid was already in the lobby, studiously ignoring a gaggle of about ten giggly Miss India contestants, when we breezed in through the revolving doors. 'Look at them,' Mon said as they sashayed past us, trailing shiny re-bonded hair and flowery perfume. 'Armaan would've died and gone to heaven!'

Zahid smiled up through his tousled curls and bounced to his feet when he spotted our little party. 'Aadaab,' he said to Monita, who looked instantly charmed. 'I'm Zahid.'

'Oh we *know* that!' she gushed, while I, frantic to show I wasn't in love with him, limited myself to a cursory 'hi'.

But he was fully enthu. 'Hey, Zoya!' he went, all booming and beaming. He came forward like he was going to give me a hug and then for some reason, didn't. 'How are you? *Maine suna* you're coming with us to Australia?'

'Nothing's certain yet,' I said, wondering if he had any idea about the idiotic contract I'd been asked to sign. Who knows, maybe he was the one who'd put in the 'facial cheek' caveat. Trying to look all professional, I asked him in a business-like way: 'It'll take a little while. Shall we go to the coffee shop?'

He nodded and stood up again, bouncing slightly on the balls of his feet, his hands in his pockets. The girls behind us gave out little hysterical screams. I heard one of them shriek, 'He did aadaab! He's too yum, ya!'

Zahid looked at us, an expression of comic alarm on his face and asked, 'Can we go up to my room instead? Coffee shop *mein kaafi* crowd *hai!*'

Monita laughed and nodded. 'Lead the way,' she said, and he walked us to the elevators.

Going up, Neelo explained to Zahid that Mon was his boss and responsible for most of the *Zing!* stuff he saw on TV.

An awkward little silence followed.

I cleared my throat and said, 'Um, this is quite a unique concept she's thought up, it's been tailor-made for you.'

'Great,' he said, as we exited the lift. 'Only, I hope it won't take up too much time. We have only got three weeks off and I want to go home for a while.'

'Where do you live, Zahid?' Mon asked, looking at him all maternally.

He smiled and tossed his curls back a little. 'In Sangrur district *ji*,' he said easily. 'Family home *wahin hai.*'

Then Neelo and Monita explained the HotCrust Fastest Deliveries concept to him as I looked about the suite. It was pretty plush. Would the IBCC put me up in a room half as nice as this if I promised to 'maintain my spinster status' and went to Australia with the team, I wondered.

'Zoya?' Mon was saying.

I snapped back to the here and now and looked at her guiltily.

'Zahid was asking how many houses we'd be visiting every day and what the security arrangements would be like.'

'Oh!' I nodded and pulled out my notes.

'I like the concept,' Zahid said finally. 'It will be very fun. Also, reality shows are very nice. But the dates you'll have to discuss with Lokendar.'

'No problem,' Neelo said easily. 'We'll get it done.' Then he grinned and asked, 'So when does the judging start?'

Zahid went a little pink. 'Now. I have to go down to the poolside. I do not do these things usually,' he explained, 'but Harry sir has phasaaoed me. He was supposed to do it but cancelled last minute.'

Neelo looked at him enviously. 'Swimsuit round!' he breathed, his voice all thick with saliva bubbles. 'What's the judging procedure, exactly?'

Zahid grinned weakly and stole a look at Mon and me, obviously embarrassed at having this conversation in front of us. 'I think *ki* you just look at them as they walk past you and give them marks out of ten,' he ventured finally.

'Uh huh?' Neelo said, opening and shutting one hand with a distracted air. 'But then how can you check for *firmness*? and –' he made little caressing movements in the air – '*smoothness*? Surely those are vital criteria?'

Zahid looked completely stumped at this. 'You think so?' he said doubtfully.

Neelo nodded. 'Absolutely! You'd better feel them up thoroughly, dude,' he said. 'I mean, it's your *responsibility*. This is a Miss India pageant after all – it's a matter of national *honour*. Tell you what, I've shot supermodels many times. If you like I can stay back and…'

'Neelo!' Mon groaned. 'Shut it! Zahid, nice meeting you, catch you at the event launch, ya?'

Rinku Chachi and I watched the Miss India final that night on her TV. She'd made hamburgers for dinner – spicy aalu tikki really – and cold coffee in big glasses. We chatted during the commercial breaks, which were extremely long and full of Fair and Lovely ads, and played at being judges when the girls came back on the screen. She was very excited about the fact that I knew not one but two people in the contest. Nikhil Khoda, of course, and Ritu Raina, who was going to come in at the end of the show to crown the new Miss India Universe.

Rinku Chachi thought Nivi was a real loser for caving in to his mom and dumping Ritu – it had been in all the papers recently. '*Arrey*, he has no guts only, Zoya! He's a mouse, a fat, darpok chooha! I hope she snares Rahul Gandhi now and shows him!'

That's Rinku Chachi's philosophy. If a guy breaks up with you, find someone higher in the pecking order and go out with him instead. She suggests Rahul Gandhi as a get-over-your-ex remedy for every girl who ever gets dumped – from Princess Diana to all the former Mrs Khans.

'Shhh, Chachi,' I said. 'Look, they're asking the questions now.'

The five final contestants were all lined up and pulling judges' names out of a hat. The first babe drew a card with Shah Rukh Khan's name on it and almost died of happiness.

He dimpled at her charmingly and went, 'Good evening, Urvashi,' or whatever her name was, and then came out with this really convoluted question: 'If you could marry a film star like me, or a business mogul like Andre here, or a cricketer like Nikhil, which one of us would you marry and why?'

I waited for her to say that she would marry the man she happened to love, regardless of his profession, of course. Duh!

But she didn't! She simpered and said that while she appreciated his acting and Andre's contribution to the nation's economy, she would marry Nikhil because she was a patriotic girl and he was a soldier who fought for the country.

And she got a standing ovation!

They cut to Nikhil and he smiled at her and everything! It was so cheesy!

And Rinku Chachi clapped too. 'Bhai, ten out of ten!' she declared. '*Kitna* good answer *diya na*, Zoya?'

I looked at her, completely disgusted. I wanted to tell her, remember your ugly nephew, Zoravar? *He* was a soldier who fought for his country. Nikhil Khoda was just some overpaid, over-hyped pretender. But she wasn't even looking at me. She was looking at the TV where the next babe had drawn a card with the name of the spurious soldier, Captain Coldheart himself. Well, I knew what was on his mind when he pinned his Boost-brown eyes on her. 'Do you believe in luck?'

Poor girl, it was an out-of-syllabus question and she got really rattled. She started off by saying that we make our own luck, then changed her mind and said luck was another name for blessings from God, and wound up by looking very confused and wretched and said that she wasn't sure.

There was a strained silence and then Khoda leaned in and said into the mike, 'My sentiments exactly.'

That got a laugh. The other judges and the large-toothed compere all applauded madly.

Nikhil said, 'Well done, Deepika,' quite kindly, and then they cut to an ad break.

Rinku Chachi went to the kitchen to fry some more tikkis for Gajju while I sipped my cold coffee thoughtfully and wondered if Khoda knew about my dad's blow-up with the IBCC yet. I didn't think he did because I had bumped into him in the hotel lobby after our meeting with Zahid. He'd been wrestling grimly for his kitbag with an overenthu bellboy who wanted to carry it for him. He'd spotted me, said a surprised *hi* and suddenly let go of the bag. The bellboy had almost fallen over backwards.

Maybe he thinks I'm following him around, I thought gloomily. First Famous Studio, now the Taj lobby. And before that the elevator in the Sonargaon! Oh God, that's it! He probably thinks I'm a total stalker! Maybe I should call him and tell him I'm not. I fished out my cellphone and looked at it dementedly.

And then it rang.

I almost dropped it in surprise but recovered and hit the answer button.

'Hello?'

'Zoya?' A toe-curlingly deep, warm voice. 'It's Nikhil.'

'Nikhil,' I said like a witless person. 'Uh...Nikhil, who?'

'Nikhil Khoda. You know, from Dhaka?' he said dryly. My eyes swivelled to the TV instantly. 'But you're on TV!' I said stupidly.

He *tched* impatiently. 'The show got over an hour ago. It's not really live, you know.'

'Oh,' I said idiotically. 'Who won?'

'Urvashi, I think...Listen, I know it's very short notice but is it okay with your dad if I take the two of you out for dinner tonight?'

Huh? Nikhil Khoda wants to take Rinku Chachi and me out for dinner? Then I realized he meant Dad and me. He must've been briefed on the IBCC meeting. Before I could stop myself, I blurted, 'My dad's out of town. But I'm available!'

He sounded a bit like he was laughing as he said, 'Okay. Message me the address. Pick you up in half an hour.'

I told a confused Rinku Chachi that I was going out for dinner. 'Oh, and by the way,' I said as I kissed her goodbye to go downstairs and dress, 'bet you a thousand bucks Urvashi wins.'

The moment I was downstairs I got cold feet. Damn, I'd been overeager, hadn't I? I'd yelped and squealed and actually said I was available. I wondered if I should call Nikhil back and say that I was actually at a rocking party and had somehow managed to forget that while talking to him. But then I decided he might see through the ploy. I would just have to be extra cool when we met, I figured.

Still, at least getting ready was a no-brainer. After seeing all those hot Miss India contestants on TV, I decided the smartest thing to do was to not try at all. So I showered quickly and yanked on a faded-to-threadbare pair of jeans along with a rather bravely pink little kurti. I rubbed on some carefully careless kaajal, pulled on my chunky red sneakers, fluffed out my hair and sat around breathlessly, wondering if I'd *dreamt* the phone call.

Clearly not, for in a while my phone rang again.

'I'm here,' Nikhil said. 'Are you going to open the gate?'

'No, no, I'm coming out,' I said hurriedly and made a dash for the door, leaving Eppa flummoxed, watching *Kyunki* in the drawing room, with Meeku snoozing by her side.

I slipped out of the gate, and peered about. Then Nikhil stuck his head out of the driver's window of a long white Taj car and waved to me.

I dove in through the other door. 'Hi,' I went breathlessly.

He pushed his dark hair off his forehead. 'New Rohtak Road? You live on New Rohtak Road? I've never heard of New Rohtak Road in my life!' He looked perfectly edible. And perfectly exasperated.

'Well, it's Karol Bagh technically,' I admitted, as I fastened my seat belt and flicked my hair back. 'But that sounds uncool, so I say New Rohtak Road.'

'But that's deliberate misdirection!' he exclaimed, throwing up his hands and sitting back in the driver's seat. 'Zoya, you're nuts, you know that, *na*?'

About you, I thought idiotically, fiddling unnecessarily with the seat belt clasp. I was finding it hard to look at him, because, hello, he was just sitting back and *looking* at me.

Like he was really happy to see me.

Like he thought I was nice…

More than nice. Maybe even…pretty?

I managed to look up at him and say, 'No, I'm not.'

He looked at me like he wanted to argue the point, but all he said was, 'Hey, is that your dog barking?'

'Yes,' I said brightly, 'that's Meeku. He's a mix between a Lhasa Apso, a Bhutanese Peke, and an Indian Hound.'

'You mean he's a mongrel,' Khoda said, grinning.

'No, he's not,' I said indignantly. 'He's a mix between a Lhasa Apso, a Bhutanese Peke, and an Indian Hound.'

'He's a *mongrel*, Zoya,' Khoda repeated, grinning even wider, that warm look in his eyes again.

'Mix,' I said idiotically.

'Mongrel,' he said, very softly, leaning in and looking me right in the eye.

My cheeks felt hot. I was not sure why. It wasn't like what he was saying was terribly intimate or anything. But the effect it was having on me was as if he had leaned in and softly said, *Take off your shirt*.

I somehow managed to keep my voice steady, 'Well, yes, actually, but that sounds so…'

'Uncool,' he said, drawing away much to my relief. 'I get it.'

He turned his head to look out of the car window then, so I looked out too. I examined the gate of my own house with great concentration, as if I didn't see the stupid, rusty, decrepit thing fifty times a day. It was a pretty unremarkable gate, with an embarrassing number of nameplates nailed onto its brick gateposts.

COL. VIJAYENDRA SOLANKI (RETD)

WING CO. MOHINDRA SOLANKI (RETD)

DR GAJENDRA SOLANKI (PHD, EDUCATIONIST)

MRS ANITA SOLANKI (TAROT READINGS, DESIGNER SUITS, MONDAY CLOSED)

YOGENDRA SOLANKI (FINANCIAL CONSULTANT)

I was thinking gloomily that he probably lived in a house with a beautiful wrought iron gate with no nameplate at all when he said, making me jump a little, 'What smells so nice?'

'Huh?…Oh *that*,' I pointed at the creeper growing in a thick flowering arch above the gateposts. 'Madhumalati,' I said. 'Honeysuckle. My mum planted it.'

'Madhumalati,' he said carefully. 'It's lovely. Wild, but sweet.'

I nodded, wondering if he could smell the putrefying dead-cat odour underlying the madhumalati that was wafting up from the drain under the gaps in the pavement slabs. That was the reason my mum had planted the creeper in the first place. But he didn't mention it. Instead he said, 'So, where d'you want to eat dinner?'

'Actually, I've already eaten,' I confided.

'Oh great!' he answered, rather surprisingly. 'Listen, I haven't been able to hit the treadmill today, d'you think we could take a walk someplace?'

'But what if people recognize you?' I exclaimed, genuinely concerned. 'They may beat you up!'

His face darkened immediately and I almost bit my tongue off. 'Sorry,' I said quickly. 'Stupid thing to say.'

He nodded. 'Yeah.' His tone went very dry. 'Contrary to what you may think, people don't hate me just because we lost a couple of matches.'

Keep telling yourself that, I thought, but what I said, rather fervently, was: 'I know, I know. You're a great player; you're the hope of India, you're –'

'– ready to walk,' he interrupted impatiently. 'Can we hit the road or something?'

So I ducked in through the gate and got him a hooded sweatshirt of Zoravar's from off the washing line. He wore it instead of his fancy jacket, and with the hood pulled way down low, he did look pretty much like everybody else, only taller.

Then he parked the hotel car in Gajju's spot (with me hoping to get back from this walk before Gajju returned or there'd be a huge family crisis which could escalate into Gajju going on a daal-ladle-hurling spree) and set off for a long walk down the main Ajmal Khan Road.

This road – made famous through a million radio ads for saris, jewellery, suiting-shirting and pressure cooker shops that all sign off with a sing-song *Ajmal Khan Road, Karol Bagh, Nai Dilli* – starts off, all whisperingly, as a wide boulevard lined with old neem trees. Then, after you cross rows of parked cycle-rickshaws with their drivers slumbering all curled up below the trees, oblivious to, or maybe knocked unconscious by, the susu smell of a hundred stray dogs that hangs over that particular stretch, the action begins to heat up. You spot peanut sellers and machine-*ka*-cold-water carts. And once you cross the first red light, Ajmal Khan Road turns into a bright, spangled gypsy's ribbon, unrolling blithely before you in a gay street carnival, with vendors selling every conceivable food and toys on carts lit with cheerily hissing hurricane lamps. Fairy lights twinkle above, a reminder that the Nauratra and Dussehra holidays are just round the corner and rocking Hindi film music blares from speakers strung up on street lamps.

'I thought this place was closed on Monday!' Khoda said, pulling his hood lower in a bemused sort of way as we emerged from under the trees and into the thick of the action.

'It is,' I told him. 'This is the famous all-night Monday cart-market. Pedestrians only. These guys come from all over Delhi to sell their stuff here.'

Khoda shook his head at a bunch of grinning kids indicating that no, he didn't want to buy a toy cellphone, red heart-shaped balloons, a plastic badminton racket or a pair of pink sunglasses. 'Yes-madam-bellies?' called out a rakish looking dude in a *Titanic* tee shirt, Kate Winslet and Leo di Caprio locked in a passionate embrace across his skinny brown chest. 'Yes-madam-tee shirts? Yes-madam-baggies?'

I shook my head at him, and he focused his attention on Khoda instead.

'You sure you don't want a bellies?' Khoda asked me grinning. 'Or a baggies? What *is* a "baggies" anyway?'

'No, I don't want either,' I told him. 'A "bellies" is a flat shoe that will make me look short and a "baggies" is a very outdated trouser. Come on, aren't we doing this for exercise?'

He followed reluctantly, trailing behind me a little, looking at all the crazy stuff on sale on the road, wooden spoon sets, suitcases of every size and colour, piles of spongy, squeaky children's shoes and frilly nylon frocks that looked like iced wedding cakes.

We passed carts piled high with rosy red apples, knobby grey-green water-chestnuts and bright yellow nimbus. We passed carts selling fake Dresden China shepherdesses and porcelain doggies, mosquito nets, fake flowers and digital watches. Then, at a cart piled high with plastic knick-knacks, Nikhil pounced on a red plastic fly-swatter-cum-back-scratcher. 'This is great!' he said enthusiastically, 'It's a two-in-one. I can kill flies and scratch my back as well.'

'That's kind of the idea,' I said, grinning as he waved the idiotic thing around, his eyes all shiny under his stupid sweatshirt hood and tried to swat me with it. I ducked and said hastily, my self-preservation instincts coming into play, 'You know what? I think I want one too!'

He fished out his wallet and bought two fly-swatter-cum-back-scratchers for the princely sum of ten rupees.

'There's so much energy in this place,' he said, leaping ahead and walking backwards in front of me. 'It's unbelievable!'

He couldn't have said anything to make me like him more. The KB Monday night market is my most favourite thing on the planet. I beamed up at him happily in the light of the bright naked bulbs strung above us, 'Isn't it?' I said, then added, 'Uh...watch out, bull ahead!'

We stepped around the placidly majestic bull and his steaming aromatic droppings and I led him towards a street corner where an old sardarji presided over a massive flat copper skillet, frying mashed potato cutlets to a rich golden brown, sending huge quantities of steaming potato vapours up into the air. The steam, coupled with the magical *tunnnggg! tunnnggg!* of his metal skewer hitting the skillet was attracting people to him in droves. We queued up for our turn, inhaling appreciatively, tucking our hands into our pockets. It was getting a little chilly.

'It's going to take a while, I think,' Khoda said.

The guy in front of us turned around and nodded, grinning. 'Ten minutes at least...Sardarji's very famous.'

Just then a runny-nosed little surdling came and handed us two cups of tea. 'Complimentary *hai ji,*' he said smilingly, exposing a gap in his front teeth. 'Waiting *de vaaste.*'

We thanked him and sipped our tea in silence.

Then Khoda said abruptly, 'Look, I'm sorry about that whole episode with the lawyers. Please tell your father that we'll fix it up any way you want, no conditions, no obligations. The important thing is for you to come to the World Cup with us.'

I didn't say anything, just cradled my glass of hot chai and blew on the icky brown-orange skin floating on the top. A million thoughts went through my head, number one being Anita Chachi's cheap Draupadi crack.

'Why?' I asked him straight up.

He looked surprised. 'You know why.'

I laughed, not very happily. 'Because I'm lucky. You don't really believe that, do you?'

'No,' he said doggedly, 'but my boys do. Even the ones who didn't come with us to Dhaka. They've seen that Australia match footage a million times and are convinced you're a miracle, a Goddess.'

'And *you,* Nikhil-sir?' I asked. 'What do *you* think?'

He said, with mild irritation, 'Will you please not call me Nikhil-*sir?* If you were born in June '83 you can't be more than two years younger than me. And it makes me feel really *old.* Like those dudes in the serials whom all the pretty girls are always calling *Mr* Bajaj or *Mr* Walia.'

'You watch those serials?' I asked, momentarily diverted.

He shrugged. 'Sure. They're pretty hilarious.'

'They're supposed to be *tragic*,' I told him. 'But look…uh…Nikhil, did you read that piece of paper they wanted me to sign?'

'I did today,' he nodded. 'Then I tore it up and threw it away. Forget about it. Just come as a guest, an honoured guest.'

I shook my head, swinging my fly-swatter-cum-back-scratcher around uneasily. 'I felt so cheap. You have no idea. There was this hairy troll in orange robes who went on about my "propitiousness" being directly proportional to my "purity".'

'Sounds like Jogpal Lohia's Lingnath Baba,' Khoda said dismissively. 'He's a joke.'

'Well, the joke was on me,' I said, rolling my eyes. 'And my dad…he was very quiet about it, but I think he was upset at the tone of the whole contract. He was already hassled because the family's been making snide remarks about Zahid and me.'

Nikhil placed his hand on the small of my back and nudged me closer to the sardarji's sizzling tikkis. 'I figured it was something like that,' he said. 'Do you think it'll help if I speak to him?'

I nodded, feeling that this could not actually be happening. 'Yeah, I guess. It should help.'

We'd reached the front of the line then and the old sardarji, a vision in spotless white, glowed at us benevolently from behind his skillet. He dished out four spluttering golden-brown tikkis into two leaf plates, sprinkled them with juicy, freshly grated carrots and sweet white radish, ladled on two kinds of chutneys – a sticky-sweet tamarind one and a lethal green chilli one – and sent us on our way.

Nikhil looked at his tikki gingerly, cocking one eyebrow. 'Isn't this seriously unhealthy?'

I grinned up at him. 'Worried you'll put on weight or worried that you'll get the runs?'

He laughed. 'Both actually.'

'Sports quota variety,' I said disparagingly.

'Karol Bagh type,' he smiled.

We walked home through the park, chatting easily, Khoda swinging the fly-swatter-cum-back-scratchers with one hand as we passed below the huge neem trees. A big gust of wind sent the neem leaves and tiny, star-shaped bittersweet neem flowers fluttering down upon us like confetti. He bought a paper bag of unshelled peanuts from an old lady and we ate them sitting on the swings in the deserted kiddie park.

He did this really nice non-starry thing with the peanuts. He kept shelling them and handing them to me to eat. I didn't have to shell a single one myself. Well, Lokey did the same thing, and with pistas, which are way more expensive than peanuts, but somehow I'd never gone weak at the knees thinking about how considerate he was.

'You know...' he suddenly said.

'What?' I asked, holding out my hand for more peanuts.

He dropped a shelled handful into my palm. 'We could've gone out somewhere fancy for dinner. Some place expensive. Gotten our picture in the papers...'

I looked up at him, puzzled. His tone was odd. I couldn't figure it out. 'But I'd eaten already,' I pointed out. 'And you said you wanted to walk. Sorry...did you want to go somewhere fancy?'

He shook his head. 'No, baba,' he said, looking at me, eyes alight with amusement. 'I didn't. But you're really a cheap date, Zoya.'

'It's all part of my simple unspoilt charm,' I assured him, shovelling peanuts into my face.

'Yeah, right,' he said laughing.

Then he leapt up and started running nimbly back down the lane to my house, while I trailed him slowly, surreptitiously fluffing up my hair and sneaking peeks at his butt. I wondered what Nikhil Khoda was doing here anyway, at a little past midnight, in my brother's grubby sweatshirt, the strings hanging idiotically around his chin, asking me questions about my life. Why wasn't he with the other rich beautiful people doing rich beautiful things? Or with his underwear-model girlfriend? What did he want with me?

Well, he wanted me to come to Australia with the team, that much was clear. But that was just a fifteen-minute conversation. And it was over. So why was he lingering? Was this usual? Did he do this with every mid-level advertising executive he met?

Of course, I didn't ask him any of these questions. I just chattered away as he ran circles around me, ignoring his complaints that I was walking too slowly, and acted like there was nothing extraordinary going on here at all.

And so, by the time we walked up to my gate, I realized I'd told him all there was to know about Tera Numbar and AWB, the twin pillars on which my life was built. He, on the other hand, hadn't talked that much, just nodded and listened, his eyes gleaming appreciatively every now and then.

A slight drizzle had started to fall, so we sheltered under the overhang of the madhumalati and he made me business card my dad's number to him, and then said formally, not at all out of breath, 'Thank you for a lovely evening.'

'Thank you too,' I answered politely. 'Goodnight.'

An awkward silence followed.

I reached out to take my stupid fly-swatter-cum-back-scratcher from him and in the process both of them fell onto the pavement. Khoda bent down to help me pick them from among the thickly strewn madhumalati blossoms and we knocked our heads together hard.

I saw stars and from the dazed look on his face, so did he.

He pulled back and looked at me, rubbing his forehead.

'What is *wrong* with you?' he asked exasperatedly.

'Sorry,' I winced and giggled at the same time.

'No, *I'm* sorry,' he said, rolling his eyes. 'My head hurts.'

'We should bang our heads together again,' I suggested. '*Nahi toh* a black dog will bite you.'

He raised his eyebrows at that. 'And who's being superstitious now?' he asked.

He had a point there. I shrugged. 'Me, I guess. It's just something Eppa says.'

'Maybe she just likes to bang Zoravar and your heads together,' he said, still rubbing his own ruefully. 'Maybe that's how she gets her kicks. Ever thought of that?'

'No, actually,' I laughed, warming up to him for talking about my family like he knew them.

'Anyway, who am I to argue about superstition?' he asked resignedly and came closer to me. 'So, where's your head again?'

I closed my eyes, still giggling, and braced myself for the collision. But nothing happened. There was just the feel of his lean, strong fingers cradling the back of my neck. Suddenly I was almost scared to open my eyes. But after a while, I did. I blinked and looked up. He was looking down at me. His face was very still, his eyes unreadable.

'Your hair's so soft,' he said.

I didn't know what to say. I mean, 'thank you' would've sounded idiotic in the circumstances. So I just looked up at him, though it wasn't easy. His Boost-brown eyes were mesmerizing. Then his gaze slid and I relaxed a little, only to realize that he was now looking at my mouth.

'I really want to kiss you, you know,' he said softly. 'I've been wanting to, all evening.' He touched the centre of my lower lip gently with one calloused thumb. 'Right here.' But then he said, even though his thumb lingered, 'But I'm not going to, okay?'

'Okay,' I whispered back idiotically, really for the lack of anything to say.

He shook his head and laughed, sounding half amused, half amazed. 'Aren't you going to ask me why, Zoya?'

'Not if you don't want to tell me,' I said, striving for a mature tone even though my heart was slamming against my ribs. 'And listen, if you're *not* going to kiss me, do you think you could get into your car and reverse it out of here, quickly? This is my Gajju Chacha's parking slot and he gets really antsy if anybody else uses it...'

'Well, of course. We can't go upsetting Gajju Chacha...' Khoda said, sounding faintly irritated and pulling away from me entirely. 'So why don't you run into the house now, isn't that your mongrel stirring again?'

Sure enough, Meeku's quick little feet had pattered to the gate and now he had his paws up against it and was beginning to bark up a storm. I picked him up in an effort to silence him and he started licking my face thoroughly.

Khoda watched wryly for a bit, then handed me my fly-swatter-cum-back-scratcher. 'So, goodnight then,' he said. 'And make sure your dad picks up my call, okay?'

'Okay.'

He waited for me to get to the gate, open it and latch it behind me. Then he got into the car and drove off.

11

Dad drove up to the gate a few days later, the car loaded with goodies from the farm. Warm, tangy buttermilk, round pats of fresh, white butter, bearing the imprint of my Dadi's palms, coarsely ground bajra flour and best of all, a massive lump of sweet, sticky, browny-orange gud.

Eppa had just finished watering the lawn, so it was cool and fragrant outside. I carried our evening tea out onto the veranda and we sat down to a cup of gud-sweetened tea with Meeku sniffing about hopefully at our feet. I sipped my tea, and listened to my dad as he gave me all Dadaji's news and wondered how best to broach the whole should-I-go-to-Australia subject.

Apparently, my grandfather had managed to set up an Internet connection in the village and was addicted to a Friends Reunited website. He'd propped an ancient photograph of his passing-out parade from the NDA next to the comp and was contacting all his old pals on it, one by one. I thought that was rather sweet till Dad snorted and said that Dadaji had got into the rather ghoulish habit of inking a marigold garland around the necks of all his batch-mates who had died, and crowing about the fact that he was still going strong. 'There are just seven ungarlanded faces left on that photograph, of a class strength of fifty-three.'

My dad shook his head. 'Pitaji says three out of those seven have some kind of cancer so they don't really count. He's convinced he's going to outlive the bunch of them. He keeps telling Amma she got a really good bargain. He also seems to be deriving a special pleasure from the fact that all the Generals from his batch have kicked the bucket...'

My grandfather retired from the army as a lieutenant colonel, the same rank my dad held when he took premature retirement a few years ago. According to Yogu Chacha that is as high as the people in my family rise in the forces, because, 'They just aren't socially savvy enough to rise any higher, kiddo.' Deciding to attempt some savviness myself, I put my cup down, and in a carefully casual voice asked, 'Dad, did Nikhil Khoda call you by any chance?'

'Yes, actually, he did.'

'Oh?' I said, a little taken aback. 'And what did he say?'

My dad grunted, '*Wahi, ki* Zoya *ko* Australia *bhejo*. We will pay for everything and take good care of her.'

'What did you say to him?' I asked, feeling seriously weirded out. Things like this just didn't happen. An Indian skipper, no matter how many matches he'd lost, didn't just call up your dad and have long chats with him. I mean, he lived in a different world. The fact that Nikhil Khoda and my dad had a talk over the phone seemed way more bizarre to me, somehow, than the fact that Nikhil Khoda had said he wanted to kiss me.

'I told him *ki* listen, young man, Zoya will not sign any contract. It will have to be a no-conditions arrangement. And I also told him,' he went on, breathing a little heavily, 'that I was *surprised,* or rather amazed, yes *amazed,* that a new-generation fellow like him should believe in all this luck-shuck.'

I winced. Poor Nikhil. That must've hurt. 'What did he say to that?'

'He said he was really calling on behalf of the IBCC chief

Jogpal Lohia. That taking you along was Lohia's idea and that he was just a go-between because you and he are' – Dad paused and looked up at me through beetling brows – 'friends.'

I went pink. Couldn't help it. 'Yes, that's true, actually,' I said, trying to appear cool. 'Not that we're friends,' I added hastily. 'That's an overstatement. He was just being polite. But it's true that Nikhil is not at all superstitious. It's Zahid and the younger boys really.'

Dad snorted. 'One trip to Dhaka and it's *Nikhil* and *Zahid*. And you want me to let you go to Australia?'

'I don't really need your *permission* to go,' I pointed out to him, flaring up instantly. 'I just...'

'Oh, I know, I know,' Dad said. 'You're twenty-seven years old, you'll do exactly what you please. But don't get too carried away. One match lost and these fellows will drop you faster than they drop catches.'

'I *know*, Dad,' I said. 'And I have no illusions on that score. But if there are no conditions, and if I can help India win, why not?'

He snorted again. 'It's all a bunch of rubbish. What is this country coming to? Anyway, it's your decision and let me tell you that your friend Nikhil also said that if there's no contract, the Board can't pay you anything.'

Hello! This was news! How come Nikhil hadn't mentioned that when we were talking tenderly under the madhumalati?

'What they *will* do though,' my Dad continued, 'is put you and two of your friends or family members up in style in five-star hotels everywhere. And pay for your tickets and all your expenses, of course.'

'But the IBCC's loaded!' I gasped. 'How cheap! Why can't they pay me? Especially because Sanks will never give me twenty-eight days' paid leave!'

'Just because somebody's rich doesn't mean they can't be cheap,' Dad pointed out. 'In fact, the two very often go together. But your *friend*, the captain, did imply that he would see that you were remunerated somehow. He said, this way you could still be a free agent, come and go as you please. He said that he got the feeling that it was important to you.'

'You seemed to have really bonded with him,' I said, feeling vaguely resentful.

Dad picked up Meeku and tickled him behind the ears. 'He seems to be a sensible enough fellow. Let's hope his team does well.' He looked at me worriedly. 'Now you be a sensible girl too, Zoya, and don't go giving yourself too much importance or start believing that it's all your fault if they lose.'

The next two months went by in a total whirl. The Shah Rukh film had finally broken and was doing amazingly well. The jingle especially was a super-hit and you couldn't go out anywhere without hearing it playing on somebody's cellphone. Luckily, Coke didn't come up with an outstanding campaign in that period, so that helped too. The openers' promo with Harry and Shivnath did all right. The HotCrust promo was a real cracker and I spent a lot of time with Zahid, travelling with him in a car from place to place delivering pizzas to deliriously excited aunties. He told me, rather naively, that he hadn't realized how popular pizza was amongst housewives between the ages of thirty-five to forty-five. I had to tell him that it wasn't the pizza they were after, but the hunk who was delivering it. He'd looked a little embarrassed, of course, but he hadn't blushed like he used to earlier.

I didn't see Nikhil after that night back in October. He hadn't been to Delhi since, to my knowledge, and then they'd been in camp. Neelo shot with him December-end for our cautiously optimistic spirit-of-cricket music video and had even been invited to the same New Year party as him. I'd questioned him in a very Subtle Bihari Vajpayee way about it and gleaned that Khoda had been with a bunch of hot-looking people including a Yash Chopra camp heroine he was apparently dating, with whom he had vanished post-midnight.

This big rumour about his engagement came out in the papers in January but then both he and his date denied it and it died down quickly. I agonized over sending him a text message to congratulate him but then decided it would be too desperate.

He had messaged me a couple of times. Once, to ask me to send his pictures from the still shoot to his mom who wanted them for his grandmom, who wasn't keeping too well. And one Happy New Year message that I think he sent to the whole list of contacts on his phone. That was all. No more I've-been-wanting-to-kiss-you-all-evening kind of stuff.

It was depressing, of course, and sometimes I wondered if I had misheard him or something (*kick* you all evening? *kid* you all evening?). That one measly remark had fully put me off all the nice, normal, well-to-do boys my dad had made me meet on various weekends, which was, of course, completely pathetic. I kept dreaming these cheesy dreams where Nikhil Khoda, resplendent in his India Blues, showed up with a bouquet of pink tiger lilies at the Mother Dairy booth where I stood in the queue with a stainless-steel doodh ka dolu on my arm. Really corny stuff. If anyone ever were to find out, the shame would kill me...

The sixth of January dawned bright and clear. Eppa woke me up at four-thirty in the morning, with a cup of adrak ki chai. 'Get up, Zoya,' she said, 'Rinku Chachi reddy alreddy!'

I sat up, reached for the cup blindly and took a large gulp. The flight was at nine and we had to be there by six, so I had to hurry.

'Your daddy says yu haft leave five o'clock sharp,' Eppa warned. 'Too much trucks on thee hai-vay.'

She went out of the room and I pulled on the clothes I'd left by my bed the night before. Comfy jeans, a short-sleeved turquoise tee shirt and a purple corduroy jacket I'd splurged on the previous week. (Whenever I've gone to pick up people from the airport, I've noticed that all the cool, well-travelled-looking types always carry or wear jackets. So, of course, I'd gone and bought one even though it was peak summer in Australia.)

I fluffed out my hair as I looked in the mirror. It was one of my good-looking days – hair very black and springy, cheeks not too big. No zits coming up either. Yesss.

My dad was walking up and down in the garden with Rinku Chachi and Gajju. She was to accompany me on the trip, much to Zoravar's chagrin. He'd been down on casual leave and had campaigned for the job enthusiastically. But Dad had said no, and, besides, I think Zoravar knew that he'd never be able to swing that much leave or get a visa anyway. Still, that hadn't kept him from groaning and grumbling about how he was so shareef, such a respectable boy, and would make a perfect chaperone, unlike Rinku Chachi, whom he claimed was carrying on with the DVD guy and the hot college kid next door. But Rinku Chachi had just smacked him on the cheek and told him to go play with his guns, which he'd done yesterday. He would be reaching his unit in Poonch anytime now. 'I'll be watching every match, Gaalu!' he said. 'We've got it all rigged up. Wave if the camera's on you, okay?'

I promised him I would, but I wasn't really anticipating any big media moments myself. Even the dudes from Jogpal Lohia's office had advised me to keep a low profile when I went to get my tickets and visas for the trip. 'For your own sake, bete,' they'd said, 'people there may resent you if we play well, you know.'

My dad said all that was hogwash and that Jogpal didn't want people to know what a ruddy fool he was, believing in luck and all that. 'Still, it's not a bad idea to lie low, Zoya,' he said. 'Eat breakfast with them, but otherwise give them a wide berth. Do your own thing. Go sightseeing, learn about a new country; and stick close to your Chachi and Monita, okay?'

Mon was to be my other companion in Australia. My dad's always been very impressed with her. 'Such a capable, handsome girl,' he always says. 'See how she balances her family life and her work! And her husband is so senior in American Express!'

Of course, Mon never swears or smokes in front of my dad. No foul Hindi abuses or blowing smoke rings or grumbling about her monsters. In fact, she'd gone all goody goody and taken it into her head that she was *chaperoning* me!

'Don't worry, Uncle,' she told my dad like a million times, 'Zoya is just like Armaan and Aman to me.'

Hello, at least I'm not a sex maniac like Monita's little monster! He was tagging along too, by the way. Monita thought it was a good idea for him to travel. 'It'll broaden his horizons you know,' she said eagerly. 'And I've neglected him so much lately. We'll show him Ayers Rock and the Southern Lights. Get his mind out of the gutter...'

To which all I could say was good luck.

I walked out onto the veranda and was greeted chirpily by the family. Even Yogu looked down from his window on the first floor and waved benignly. The only part of the house that stayed quiet was Mohindar and Anita Chachi's. She was very upset about the fact that Dad didn't choose her to accompany me abroad.

A big hug from Eppa, a furry wet embrace from Meeku, and I was ready to go. But Gajju was clinging to Rinku Chachi in a surprisingly raunchy manner. My dad raised one eyebrow and I heard Eppa *tch, tch* disapprovingly. Anyway, Gajju finally released his wife and she emerged, slightly dishevelled and moist-eyed, and said, 'Look after yourself, G. Singh!' in a suspiciously husky voice. He nodded silently and then we both piled into my dad's car and zipped to the airport.

Monita and Armaan were waiting for us outside the international departure terminal. He was perched on her trolley, swathed in her quilted jacket and looking very sleepy. Mon looked all wired and waved enthusiastically. We piled our bags onto the wobbly IGI trolleys while Mon assured my dad earnestly, for the *thousandth* time, that she would take good care of me.

And then it was time to say goodbye.

Dad pulled something out of his pocket and pressed it into my hand. It was a brand new cellphone – a much fancier model than the one I had, with Internet and a camera and everything. 'Here,' he said, closing my hand over it. 'I've got international roaming installed. You can call me any time you want to talk. And don't worry about the bill, okay?'

I nodded. 'Thanks, Dad.'

We'd reached the main gate and a surly 'sikorty' guy started grumbling about how we were holding up the traffic. '*Haan haan, bhaisaab,*' Dad snapped at him and stepped back, suspiciously red-nosed. 'Bye, beta, God bless.'

And, with one last wave to him, I wheeled my trolley through.

My spirits lifted quite quickly once we boarded the aircraft. The air in there was a heady blend of expensive aftershave, crisp air conditioning, Juicy-Fruit chewing gum and aromatic coffee – a bouquet Zoravar and I used to call 'abroad smell' when we were kids. (We used to crouch down and inhale it dreamily from the suitcases of visiting NRI aunties.) I took a deep intoxicating gulp and settled happily into my seat.

I was going through the list of movies on the first leg of the flight, when someone passing through to the rear went, 'Zoya?'

It was Vishaal, looking very sporty in white Dockers and a white-and-blue cricket sweater.

'Hey!' I beamed up at him. 'You're going for the World Cup too?'

He nodded, grinning.

'Because of Nike?'

'No, yaar,' he said, looking at the row behind me and waving to Monita. 'Hey Mon,' he said. 'Hey monster! (This to Armaan who frowned at him sleepily.) Because of biscuits. Didn't you notice that large uncouth contingent in Niceday tee shirts who just pushed their way past you?'

'No, actually,' I said, 'but why are you going with them?'

I learnt that Vishaal had worked his ass off on the Niceday Khao, World Cup Jao promotion. It had been insane. Apparently, they'd shot thirty-three short films over three days.

'Balaji, Thind and Harry,' he said, shuddering. 'It was like getting pieces of wood to emote.' Anyway, the films had turned out really well and the contest was a big success, so the client decided that Vishaal deserved a World Cup trip too. 'So, here I am,' he said, 'with the fifty fastest biscuit-eaters in the country for company. But, of course, I don't get to travel in style like you, you lucky little shit!'

He had to go to the back then and join his Niceday gang, who were fully in the mood to cheer. They were chanting,

'*Gandhigiri, Mohabbat, Love to alls – our cricket team will break your balls,*' as the plane took off.

Rinku Chachi curled up and went to sleep after the breakfast service and Mon was busy watching cartoons with Armaan. I shifted about in my seat, tucked my blanket in tight and thought of the days ahead, lying back in the semi-darkness and just letting my mind wander.

I'd watched the opening ceremony of the World Cup and a bit of the first match on TV – defending champions Australia against the other home team, New Zealand. The crowd had been massively excited and I had got very nervous looking at the scale of the event. And even though Dad assured me no team had lost in my presence, I was still a bundle of nerves. God, how could Khoda and Zahid and the rest of them handle this level of stress?

I gloomily reflected that Khoda probably handled it by working his way through proudly slavish *toinnngg* babes, Washington Redskins Cheerleaders, Bollywood heroines and chubby lucky charms, the way Armaan was working his way through the packet of airline peanuts behind me... *Crunch crunch crunch* and then an urgent ringing of the bell, 'Can I get another packet, please, Auntie?'

I had talked to Zahid about my anxiety while we'd been delivering pizza and he had just said, 'Some people say you should try and block out the crowd. Pretend *ki* they are not there. But I don't. *Kyunki* tension can work for you. You can use it to make you play better. If whole-of-the stadium is booing me also, I just think *ki, theek hai*, I will prove all these *behen-ke-*excuse-me-please fools wrong.'

Which was all very well for him to say, but *I'm* not going to be playing, *na*! Just sitting there and praying to God that my

luck holds. There was zilch I could do really, except maybe eat
a lot more than usual at the breakfast table. And though
everybody'd advised me to just relax and have a great holiday
and not take this thing too seriously, I was completely stressed
about it. I tell you, it's really weird to put on the TV and hear
Charu Sharma and Imran Khan discussing the Zoya Factor,
like it was something real. Of course, they were kidding around
and saying that kidnapping me and asking the IBCC for a fat
ransom was a good idea, *ha ha ha*, but it was pretty unnerving.

Anyway, the first India match was a fairly low-profile one,
against Zimbabwe, at the Gabba in Brisbane. Our flight was
headed there after a stopover in Singapore. The Gold Coast is
just a two-hour drive away from Brisbane apparently and is
supposed to be this cool place packed with casinos and adventure
theme parks. Mon was keen to take Armaan there to ride the
roller coasters and stuff, but I was not as keen. My *life* was a
roller coaster.

We landed late in the evening. I think it was seven-thirty p.m.,
Aussie time. It was a super-smooth landing and the lights over
the city looked really pretty. I grabbed my bag and complimentary
Bvlgari toilette set, bade farewell to the flight crew at the door,
and stepped off the plane jauntily enough. But then the fact
that I was in another country, a First World country chock-full
of unilingual white people, suddenly hit me. There would be
white people manning the Immigrations desk, I thought wildly.
White people driving about on the roads like everybody else.
White waiters in the cafés. I would have to *tip* white people!
People who knew only one language…which was *weird*.
Because, hello, what would they switch to if they started getting
pally, or angry, or fell in love? Suddenly, I just wanted to jump
back into the plane and head home.

But of course, I couldn't. I took a firm hold of Rinku Chachi's hand – catching our reflection in a mirror just then and realizing that we both looked really short and brown in this sea of white people – and followed the stream of mostly white people through the bewildering corridors to Customs.

There were huge signs with the word 'quarantine' everywhere, warning us to declare any plant or animal extract items or be fined fifty thousand Aussie dollars. There were also big white translites welcoming all the cricket-playing nations to the ICC World Cup 2011. Just like the ones in Dhaka, actually. That made me feel a bit at home, and Rinku Chachi ended up having a long conversation with the Immigrations guys, who were all very cocky as Australia had won the last three World Cups. No other team could boast of such an achievement. The West Indies, however, had come close once, winning the World Cup twice in a row and making it to their third consecutive final at Lords only to lose to India (on my Happy Birthday), to Kapil Dev's Eleven, in the lowest-scoring final ever.

Even the quarantine guys insisted India didn't have a chance. It seemed as if our team was the underdog of the tournament. Most of the junta didn't even know the names of our players.

Rinku Chachi got really hassled when she realized this and started giving them all a full who's-who lecture on the Indian cricket team but then had to pipe down when the burly quarantine guards and their sniffer dogs discovered a Lakshmi statue in her bags. The burly guards almost fell down and *died* when she told them airily that it was made of mud. We had to hang around for half an hour while they poked it and pried at it and put it through some complicated machines to check for mad cow disease and heaven knows what else. They checked all our bags after that. Armaan got all giggly and incoherent when Rinku Chachi's bags were rummaged through and her frilly undies were pulled out and shaken about. It was all a bit of nightmare. At last they finally repacked our bags and waved us through.

It was a long drive from the airport and the sun was setting over the hilly city of Brisbane. The roads were all uphill and down-dale, almost scarily so, and there was a river with lots of bridges over it. It all looked really idyllic, till the chauffeur told us that the quaint houses on stilts, called Queenslanders, which we were admiring, had massive carpet pythons living inside their roofs.

He also pointed out the Gabba to us as we entered the city area and drove down Stanley Street, one of the largest streets of the city which led on to Vulture Street.

Rinku Chachi got very excited. 'Stanley Street! See, Zoya, on TV they always say *ki* he is bowling from the Stanley Street end or the Vulture Street end!'

I nodded, and I had to admit that the stadium looked like a carnival, all lit up and gleaming like a massive doughnut, festooned with buntings for the match the next day.

At the hotel, the guy at Reception handed me a note from some IBCC sidekick saying they'd be picking me up for breakfast at seven o'clock sharp, so that put an end to any ideas I had of venturing out and discovering the city. I got an instant headache instead, wondering what I'd do if our team lost tomorrow itself... I couldn't possibly stay on and abuse the Board's hospitality, could I?

Breakfast was strange. The car swung me in to the boys' hotel by seven-fifteen and they were all sitting down and eating when

Wes's sidekick ushered me in and I entered feeling suddenly over-bright in my patriotic orange tee shirt.

I hunched down into my hair and tried to shuffle in unnoticed but Hairy leapt up, screaming, 'Zoya!' and rushed forward to pump my hand, thus causing everybody to turn and look at me.

I smiled at him and tried to shake hands, but he just leaned down and lifted me off my feet. An extremely undignified little struggle followed where I tried to walk to the table and he tried to carry me, and basically it ended with me sort of stumbling up, breathless, hair everywhere, feeling like a complete clown.

There were several unfamiliar faces around the table, boys who'd joined this squad after tons of shuffling and selecting and politicking. I'd seen it all vaguely in the papers without paying too much attention. Now they all looked at me in polite, but barely masked, astonishment.

I smiled back at them brightly, recognizing Laakhi's friendly face amid the sea of sky-blue with great relief. Next to him was horrible Rawal, the shoe stealer. I think horrible Rawal rolled his eyes as I took a chair, as if he couldn't believe I was there for real, and I instantly started feeling like a total interloper, instead of an 'honoured' guest.

The mood around the table was…intense. The Men in Blue weren't exactly grim but they seemed withdrawn somehow, even Hairy and Zahid. They weren't laughing half as much as they used to in Dhaka, or even at the IPL benefit match.

Well, this was the World Cup.

Wes was really sweet though. He walked up and waved a yucky Iodex-y looking bottle in my face, and went enthusiastically, 'Here, have some Vegemite, Zoya! It'll put hair on your chest!'

'Thank you,' I said politely, eager to blend in, and started spreading the yucky dark-brown goo onto my toast. Then, trying for a casual tone, I asked him offhandedly, 'Where's Nikhil?'

'Here,' a deep voice said behind me and I spun around in my chair to see his lean, dark face smiling lazily down at me.

'Oh, hi,' I said inadequately, face fully hot, mortified that he'd overheard me asking about him.

'Hey,' he said, his brown eyes warm as they lingered on mine. Then, very casually, he leaned over me to grab a toast from the rack. The collar of his two-buttons-opened, freshly printed India tee shirt brushed the top of my hair. He smelt like new newspaper mixed with a nice smell of soap.

It was the tiniest of physical contacts, but it made my heart zoom. I realized for the first time how totally fixated I had been on this one moment for the last two months.

Still, I covered it up well. I smiled demurely, capped the Vegemite bottle and tucked a lock of hair unnecessarily behind my ear. Khoda, chewing on dry toast, walked around and dropped down between Wes and Laakhi, and then they all left me pretty much to my own devices.

I took a bite of my toast, my heartbeat slowing down to something vaguely approaching normal.

Oh my God, this Vegemite stuff was absolutely foul!

'It's an acquired taste,' Wes said, laughing at my appalled expression. But I just sat there with my mouth full of the awful goo, too scared to chew.

The others started laughing too, even Nikhil, and suddenly, I was sure it had been their little scheme to shut me up, which was mean of them because I hadn't planned on talking much, anyway.

I swallowed it down somehow, chucked the rest of the toast,

and then quietly ate some fruit, feeling totally unwelcome while they talked around me.

A nice, pony-tailed waiter had just asked me if I'd care for coffee or passion fruit juice when Khoda stood up and went, 'Come on, boys, let's get on that bus.'

They got up with a general scraping of chairs and chucking down of napkins. There was a little commotion as Navneet Singh hurtled in very late and had to leave without eating anything. Everyone said goodbye to me a little awkwardly except for Zahid who smiled gorgeously as always and Hairy who doubled back after everyone had left to make a mock-reverential dive for my feet. I hastily tucked my feet under me and waved him away, saying, 'All the best, play well.'

Then I sat back, wondering why I'd done this to myself, and sipped my passion fruit juice.

Yuck.

The passion fruit juice was worse than the Vegemite.

I wished I was home.

12

The match began at nine so I had time to get back to the hotel and recover from the inexplicable depression that had descended on me so suddenly at breakfast.

Maybe it was just an anticlimax.

After all, I'd been gearing up for the big team breakfast for the last sixty days, and it had turned out to be so mundane. Vegemite and juice and monologues from Hairy about his strained groin. Really, I was starting to think he had a groin *obsession*. And Nikhil…well, after that first 'hey', he had said nothing to me at all. Life suddenly seemed very flat.

I opened my room door gloomily – and there were my three suite mates, sitting on the bed, spearing sausages. They looked up and smiled happily when they saw me and suddenly I felt this huge rush of affection for all three of them. *These are your family and friends,* I told myself. *They should matter much more to you than a bunch of stupid sports-quota-type cricketers and their I-want-to-kiss-you-but-won't captain!*

'I'm so glad you guys are here with me,' I cried, swooping down and squeezing them together into a big group hug.

Rinku Chachi looked pleased but Mon followed me into the loo and frowned down at me as I splashed cold water on my face. 'Is everything okay?' she asked mildly.

'Everything's fine,' I assured her, smiling brightly into the mirror.

'Balls.' She plonked herself on the pot, lit a cigarette and looked at me expectantly.

I patted my face dry with the hand towel while she exhaled a thin stream of smoke and waited for me to speak.

I sighed. 'I just feel like such a freeloader, Mon.'

Really. The whole team was so intense and focused that it made me feel really inadequate and full of fluff.

I mean, they are all hugely talented boys who've worked immensely hard to be able to earn a seat around that particular breakfast table. And then suddenly there is this chubby-cheeked person sitting right next to them going, 'Pass the butter, chootiye.' No wonder they look so pissed off.

Mon didn't look too affected. 'Don't be silly,' she told me firmly. 'You're *not* a freeloader. They've asked you to come, remember? They're paying through their nose for you, for all of us! If some of them are acting like jerks, it's because they don't want to own up to how superstitious they are!'

'It wasn't them who wanted me,' I pointed out. 'It was just Jogpal Lohia. They didn't have much of a choice in the matter.'

'Well, none of this is news to you,' Mon said reasonably. 'Why get worked up about it?'

'They don't like me,' I muttered. 'I could feel the vibes. I think they were *laughing* at me, I think they *hate* me, I think –'

'Oh shut up, Zo! I'm tired of your stupid insecurities. You're here in Australia on a fully paid trip for the *entire* Cricket World Cup! People would die to be in your place. Quit carping, will you? Now c'mon let's go, or we'll miss the start of the match!'

'Huh? We've got to go *see* the match? Why can't we go to the malls instead?'

In answer, Mon just perched my cool new Diesel sunglasses onto the top of my head – a present from Zoravar (Looks great, can hardly see your face, Gaalu) – and propelled me downstairs and into the car.

As we drove along the winding Brisbane River to the Gabba, we heard the radio commentator say that the Indian openers were coming in to play as Nick Khoda had won the toss and chosen to bat.

'See, Zoya, your luck is working already,' said Rinku Chachi triumphantly. She was looking very young and flushed in her blue *Zing!* India tee shirt, with 'RINKU 10' emblazoned across it. Neelo had got one printed specially for her. I nodded at her blankly, still wanting to argue the whole going-to-see-the-match programme.

Just then my phone beeped and I looked down and saw a message flash. *Relax. We'll cream them. Meet me after? Love N.*

Instantly the world became a better place.

I quickly messaged back. *Okay.* And beamed sunnily up at Rinku Chachi. 'I know, Chachi!' I said enthusiastically. 'Isn't it great?'

It was a medium-sized stadium, with seating for about 42,000 people, but it was only half full, January being full-on summer in Australia. The junta was pretty much stripped down to their undies. Everywhere we looked, hot-looking babes with every-coloured hair sipped beer in bikini tops, their tanned limbs and smooth midriffs gleaming in the sun. The place looked like an ad for Foster's.

All four of us had these fancy-looking IBCC badges slung around our necks. These entitled us to some really swanky seats in the president's box, which smelled deliciously of beer, popcorn and candy floss. There was a large TV screen, so we could see the match there as well as in front of us on the field. We took our seats with the cream of Brisbane's NRI community and presidents of the local cricket clubs, all in various states of undress, scattered around us. A smiling buxom type in jeans and a tiny camisole – Armaan's eyes totally popped – passed us stubby bottles of beer. Once we'd taken a big swig each and organized some *Zing!* for Armaan, we pulled our shades over our eyes and settled down to watch the game.

It was a lovely day, sunny, with just a bit of a breeze. Shivnath and Hairy were out in the field looking pretty relaxed, leaning on their bats like they had all the time in the world. The crowd seemed at peace, out more to have a good time than anything else. I spotted the Niceday gang a little further away, cheering lustily, with their very own dhols, trumpets and tambourines, some of them in very short, sleeveless, white tank tops with '*C'Mon India, Show Your Biscuits*' emblazoned across the chest. The match was rolling along smoothly, the run rate a decent 4.5, and no wickets down yet.

'So, Zoya, how was breakfast?' I turned around and saw Shanta Kalra, her salt-and-pepper hair glinting silver in the sunshine around her young-looking face.

'Great,' I replied, a little startled.

She looked at me searchingly. 'Really?'

I pushed my glasses higher up my nose and hoped I looked enigmatic. 'I can't give you any quotes, you know,' I said.

'I know, I know,' she smiled.

'No hard feelings?' I asked her warily.

'None,' she said warmly. 'But only if you let me sit with you.'

So, of course I did. I introduced her to our gang of four, who moved up and made room for her.

It was a slow match. Slow and steady, which was good, according to Shanta. 'Anyway, by the logic of things, this should be an easy win for India, our team's way ahead of theirs.'

She explained that for the World Cup, the system was a little different from say, the mini World Cup or any other event. This was the group stage, where there were four pools, of two strong and two weak teams respectively out of which only half would move on to the next stage.

Rinku Chachi stated, 'G. Singh says we should make it to the Super 8 very easily this time…'

'I think so too,' Shanta nodded, 'but the question is whether we'll survive till the semis.'

Rinku Chachi shook her head cheerfully, 'Kyon nahi, we've got Zoya, na,' she said, much to my embarrassment.

This caused a weird pause in the conversation. Shanta looked sceptical but said nothing, and we looked out at the match on the field. Armaan was fidgeting a lot so Shanta told him to pay attention because if the batsmen hit a six and somebody in the audience caught it, the stadium authorities would give that person four hundred Aussie dollars!

Armaan perked up at once. 'Really?' he said. 'Mummy, how much is that in rupees?'

Mon rumpled his hair, wrinkling her forehead. Multiplying by thirty-seven has never been one of her talents. 'Lots of money, baby,' she said finally.

Armaan jumped to his feet then and insisted on being taken out of the air-conditioned enclosure so he could catch a six and make fabulous sums of money. Mon gave Shanta a thanks-a-lot look over her chilled beer bottle, took a swig and said breezily, 'Later, baby, they won't really be hitting sixes till the last few overs.'

This made him glower and look so thunderously weepy that Rinku Chachi quickly said, 'Why don't you sing a song, Armaan? I will give you five dollars for singing a song.'

He scowled up at her, his brow all beetled and said, driving a tough bargain, 'Four.'

'Five is more than four,' I started to say, but Rinku Chachi said quickly. 'Okay, four, whatever. But sing, *na!*'

Armaan smiled shyly, sucking on one sticky finger. 'I know a new Christmas song,' he said hesitantly. 'Some boys in the hotel taught me.'

Mon smiled, looking pleased. 'See, he's been making friends, already,' she whispered to me triumphantly. 'He's learning about other cultures and religions too.' And then, in a loud, proud voice, she said to her son, 'Sing us the nice carol, baby!'

Armaan smiled angelically and warbled:

> *'Joy to the world! The teacher's dead*
> *We scissored off her head!*
> *What happened to her bo-dy?*
> *We flushed it down the po-tty*
> *And round and round it goes...and round it goes...*
> *And round and round and round it goes...'*

He finished with a grand flourish and then looked at his mother expectantly. She didn't disappoint him. 'What did you *say?*' she exploded.

Armaan's dark eyes widened. 'It's a real song,' he said, innocently. Then he gave a little giggle.

Instantly, Monita's eyes went all flinty. 'That's quite enough, young man,' she snapped. 'You and I are going to take a little walk.' She lifted him off his feet and marched him out while Rinku Chachi scurried behind them, holding out four golden dollar coins, crying, 'Hush, hush, good boy, good beta...'

Shanta and I had choked on our beers the moment Armaan had hit the second line but now we took a big gulp of air, and wiped our eyes. 'Kids...' Shanta said, shaking her head. '*The teacher's dea*...oh, look, he's out!'

I looked wildly towards the field, but unable to see what was happening, I looked at the TV screen instead. Shivnath was looking at the stumps behind him disbelievingly while the Zimbabwe wicketkeeper was doing a wild whooping war dance down the pitch and the dude in the Fly Emirates coat was pointing an index finger into the sky.

Yup, there was no doubt about it. Shivnath Singh was out. Laakhi came in to bat then and steadied things up a bit. He played a low-key game, just supporting Hairy who was hitting out happily in every direction. And then, when Laakhi got caught behind at 33, Khoda strolled out to play.

My heartbeat accelerated immediately, but, hello, judging from the way the cheering increased, so did the entire stadium's.

'These two are an excellent partnership,' Shanta said as Hairy and Khoda chatted briefly between overs. 'Don't you think so?'

I shrugged. 'I wouldn't know,' I said apologetically. 'I'm not really into cricket that much.'

She glanced over at me, one hand shading her face from the sun. 'Then what *are* you into?' she asked. 'Cricketers?'

'Wow, I thought you were Shanta Kalra of *Pitch-side*,' I told her coolly. 'Not Sonali of *Sonali's Gupshup*!'

She threw back her head and laughed, totally unoffended. 'Sorry, I didn't mean to pry, Zoya. It's just that you're in such a strange situation. I'm curious about what you're thinking...what's going on in your head. And not just from a story point of view. Though, of course, it would make a great one! I'd just like to know, for myself.'

'I'm pretty blank, really,' I told her. 'Comfortably numb.'

'Floyd!' she said, approvingly, but surprised. 'Didn't think many kids of your generation listened to them.'

'Oh, is it a song?' I said, surprised, and she just sighed and shook her head.

'It's an all-time great,' she answered and then added in an altered voice, her hand coming out to grip my arm: 'Speaking of which, look out for Nikhil now… You know I have a good feeling about this particular delivery…*yess!*'

We watched as Khoda hooked the ball away and headed smoothly down the pitch.

Shanta made a small, satisfied noise and sat back. 'He needn't bother,' she said, 'that's four runs for sure.'

I looked at her curiously. 'Is he really such a good player?' I asked, as neutrally as I could.

She looked away from the screen and back at me. The Niceday guys were screaming '*Chauka!*' in the background so she had to raise her voice to be heard. 'The best,' she said. 'He's finally about to come into his own. This World Cup is crucial for him. *And* he's a nice guy.'

Meanwhile, Hharviinder Singh was blissfully slamming the ball right around the stadium. Khoda was giving him 'solid support' according to the commentators.

I finally allowed myself to relax and when Shanta went off to join her press buddies, I pulled out my own phone and scrolled down to the message Khoda had sent me this morning. Yes! There it was – I hadn't imagined it. Just looking at it made me feel a little dizzy. *Relax, we'll cream them.* Well, that part of it was coming true right in front of my eyes, but what about the really interesting next bit? *Meet me later?* What did that mean? Did I have a date with him? A Friday night out with Captain Coldheart? And what about the best bit right at the end? *Love N.*

Not just plain *N*. Or, *See ya N*. Or, *Cheers N*.
Love N.

Okay, Mon's told me that in Bollywood *everybody* ends all their text messages with 'love' followed by their initials, even the GET messages they send to their phone company when they want to check their missed calls, but Nikhil wasn't from Bollywood! So *Love N* must have meant something, don't you think?

Mon and Armaan came back and sat down next to me so I put my phone away hastily. I felt weird around Mon, since she'd got it into her head that she was my 'chaperone'. Strangely, she spooked me out more than Rinku Chachi did. I decided to venture out of the plush VIP box and see what life was like in the rest of the stadium.

I was halfway out when a hot little hand grasped mine and I looked down to see Armaan trotting beside me. 'I have to go to bathroom,' he said. 'Take me.'

So I took him to the girl's loo, hauled off his shorts and Spiderman chaddis and plonked him on the pot. He looked very confused and asked me, 'Should I make?'

'Sure,' I told him. 'Go ahead, make.'

And that's how I ended up getting thoroughly splashed with susu at the Gabba, in Brisbane, Australia.

Armaan was more mortified than me. 'You only told me to make, Zoya,' he said tearfully as I rinsed my ganji and dried it under the hand-dryer.

'I know, baba,' I told him resignedly. 'I'm sorry, I forgot boys don't sit down and make. Don't worry, and don't look at me till I put on my shirt!'

The score had moved considerably by the time we emerged. I bought Armaan a drink with 'Woolloongabba' inscribed around it and we took a little walk.

'Hey, Zoya!' someone yelled. It was Vishaal, sitting amongst his contingent of biscuit-munchers. 'Come sit with us!' he yelled, putting out one arm for us to grasp.

So we jumped up and sat with them. A happy-looking pot-bellied sanitation engineer from Gajraula, UP, smeared tiranga face paint on Armaan's cheeks and offered me some genuine Bikaner bhujia and Old Monk Rum and *Zing!* pre-mix. I handed Armaan the bhujia and took a large swig of the rum. The alcohol burnt my innards and made my eyes water. As I brought the bottle down, spluttering slightly, the stadium exploded. Nikhil had hit a six close to where we were seated and Armaan leapt to catch it and missed and we all rose up in a huge Mexican wave and chanted, '*Nikhil Khoda dat gaya, Zimbabwe ka phat gaya!*'

It was awesome.

Things got a bit tense when Hairy finally got out at 85, and Navneet Singh got out for duck right after. But it steadied after that.

Armaan crunched steadily through two packets of bhujia and two of Niceday Jimjams as Nikhil, Saif and some new dude I'd never heard of called M. Mussaffar piled up a total of 310 for India with one last over still to play.

'It's unbelievable!' Vishaal yelled, and all of us leapt up and down cheering: 'India! India!' as some poor hapless Zimbabwe bowler ran up to feed a rampant Khoda another delivery. '310 for 4! Zoya, you've got to come eat with me before I do anything important in my life! Fuck. Where were you when AWB played Grey Worldwide for the Agency Cup, anyway?'

They finally finished off with 321 and then came off the pitch, looking sweaty but happy. Khoda spoke briefly to the anchors, but of course I couldn't hear what was being said, there being no TV in the Niceday enclosure. Then Armaan and I wandered back to our VIP box to find Chachi and Mon totally hysterical with joy at how well India was playing.

There was a really fancy champagne lunch laid out for us VIP types but I was too far gone on the Old Monk to appreciate it. Rinku Chachi loaded her plate with food, and then, finding it all too boiled and bland, kept trying to force it on poor Armaan.

The second half started while we were still eating and we had to scurry back to our seats to watch the Indians fanning out across the stadium into their fielding positions.

They showed Nikhil in close-up on the TV screen, he had the ball in his hand and was chucking it from hand to hand, his eyes narrowed to slits. Then he tossed the ball to Zahid who caught it deftly.

And then Zahid Pathan began that lithe, powerful run-up the girls all loved so much, his copper curls bouncing, and hurled the ball like a bomb at the poor red and green bakra at the other end of the pitch.

It was a massacre.

They were all out for 233, thus losing the psychological edge even for the matches to come, according to the commentator.

The Indians strutted back happily as the sun came down on the Gabba and the crowd cheered lustily. The choice for Man of the Match was obviously going to be Hairy – he'd made 85 runs in the morning, and had taken a couple of vital wickets too, when Khoda had tried something unconventional and given him the ball in the slog overs.

'He's a good captain, this Khoda,' Rinku Chachi said approvingly as we saw him vanish into the doorway directly below us, deep in conversation with the Zimbabwe bowler who'd batted so gamely in the last two overs. '*India toh aaj dat gaya.*'

Armaan chimed in happily: '*Zimbabwe ka phat gaya!*'

Mon looked at him, totally appalled.

We got back to the hotel in just under half an hour. The organizers had warned us about traffic, but Rinku Chachi said, 'What traffic? This whole country and all its cars will fit in our UP state only.'

As soon as we got back, I had a bath, brushed my teeth, dried my hair and started rummaging in my bags for the jeans and saucy little firoza-blue top I'd decided to wear after a painstaking mental review of my entire wardrobe while pretending to be absorbed in the second innings of the match.

Mon bounced into our room all ready to party at eight o'clock. 'C'mon. Let's go,' she burbled excitedly. 'There's a casino aboard the Kookaburra Queen at eight-thirty. Let's not miss it.'

She was looking really hot in a Goddess-like way, in a black sleeveless dress, her helmet hair clinging to her exquisite cheekbones. She smacked her lips to settle her lipstick, looked me over and nodded approvingly. 'Nice top, Zoya,' she said. 'I've never seen you wear it before.'

I tugged at the plunging halter top, trying to pull it closer to the waistband of my embroidered jeans. 'It's not too nanga-panga, *na*?' I asked uneasily.

'No way!' she said, 'it rocks. Besides, you can cover up with your hair if you feel conscious. But you may want to take a wrap along, it could get a bit chilly on the boat.'

'Uh, *actually,*' I told her, a little self-consciously, 'I'm not coming with you guys on the boat.'

Monita had been busy fishing out her phone and cigarettes from her capacious 'mommy' handbag and stuffing them into her skinny 'party' clutch but at this she looked up at me, an arrested gleam in her dark eyes. 'Really?' she enquired. 'So where are you headed? And with whom? Or' – her eyes narrowed – 'is somebody coming here?'

In answer, I smugly held up my phone and showed her the message on it.

She peered down at it short-sightedly and then slowly this huge grin broke across her face. But all she said was, 'Uh huh? And who might "N" be?'

'Naveen Nischol,' I told her sweetly. 'I'm his greatest fan. I'm in love with his pudgy face and flared pants and negligently knotted neckerchief.'

'Okay,' Mon grinned. 'Just make sure *Naveen* pads up before he bats, okay?'

So I sat down on the sofa, with my phone in my hand and waited for Nikhil to call. And waited. And waited.

Of course it would've been perfectly acceptable behaviour for me to call and congratulate him and gently remind him about our date but there was no way I could bring myself to do it. Not on top of that overeager *Where's Nikhil?* I'd come up with this morning.

So I made a deal with myself. If he didn't call by ten I was going to change into my pajamas and order Room Service. Decision made (more or less), I flicked on the TV and started watching the highlights of the day's match.

The two commentators, who'd been on all day, were still going strong, talking to a bunch of people in a live studio. I glowered at the two of them blankly, even as, at the back of my mind, I brooded over the Khoda no-show.

The programme was called *'Jay and Beeru ki Show le!'* – a name that made sense to everybody who hailed from the Indian subcontinent and to nobody else. Jay (Jason Plunkett) was a laconic English ex-captain, very dry and precise, and Beeru (Birendra Singh) was a motor-mouthed Indian ex-opening batsman, with a not very strong grasp of the English language.

Anyway, the Jay and Beeru show was on in full swing. Beeru was going on about how Nivi had not only got out for a duck but had also dropped two catches. 'Vul, all I can say is that Navneet Singh is a bit of a slacker,' he said, shaking his head from side to side gravely. 'His captain should pull his socks.'

Jay nodded. 'I agree. I was surprised to see Nick Khoda giving the ball to Hharviinder Singh. Bit of a gamble, that was, wasn't it, Beeru?'

Beeru placed his fingers together, frowned broodingly and said, 'Vul, gumballs are like girlfriends, my friend.'

Jay looked at him blankly. 'Sexy?'

Beeru shook his head sombrely. 'Very, very expensive. But Nikhil's paid off today. Of course, Harry can bowl a little bit. He's done it in school and at A-level matches. It's a good strategy because it let them get an extra batsman in. And it did not affect his batting also! Hats off to him, that was a great knock he played today.'

'Well, one batsman who's on his way out of the eleven is Navneet Singh,' Jay said. 'He'll be lucky if Khoda plays him again in Sydney. That was an altogether pathetic performance today.'

Of course I couldn't help thinking at this point that Navneet Singh had missed having breakfast with me this morning. Maybe *that* had something to do with his abysmal show today. Okay, I know what Neelo would say. *You're becoming a victim of your own hype*, Zoya. But really, I was feeling so low and unwanted thanks to Khoda not showing up that I was ready to cling to any straw. If you thought about it, Hairy – my truest acolyte – had been Man of the Match today! So maybe I really was a kind of god-woman after all! I'd worn orange to breakfast today, had big curly hair and was doling out victory to my devotees and ignominious dismissal from the side to disbelievers!

Hah!

It was an intoxicating thought. But I couldn't hold on to it.

The fact that there were eleven matches to go for India in this tournament – that's if we *made* the Super 8 of course – dampened my spirits considerably. What were the odds of our loser team winning them all?

I sighed, ripped open a packet of minibar goodies and wondered if there was anything I could do to make my Luckiness last. I could pray, I suppose, but all of India was praying every day, anyway. And what about the use-up-all-your-good-luck-on-cricket-and-be-doomed-to-bad-luck-in-your-own-life theory? Nothing was going good in my personal life, was it?

I mean, everybody else was at a floating casino having a blast, and I was overeating in a hotel room, after being urinated on by a five-year-old, waiting for a world-famous person to call me. God, I was such a loser. How much worse was it going to get, anyway? Maybe I was destined to help India win the World Cup and then *die* or something!

Oh my God! That was it!

I had a sudden, perfect flash into the future. Khoda was going to clinch the final with a huge six. The ball would fly into the stands, knock me on the head, cause a horrible spurting wound and decapitate me in front of a million viewers. An ugly bat-shaped monument would be erected in Shivaji Park in my honour. Khoda would stand brooding before it, blue cap in hand, crying in the rain, as the credits rolled down on the movie of my life.

I zapped off the TV, collapsed onto the bed and covered my head with my pillow.

13

The first thing I saw the next morning was Khoda's face in the *Herald Sun*. He was laughing, brown eyes warm as they gazed into the dulcet dark ones of some hot-looking babe showing too much cleavage. Underneath, it read: *Indian skipper Nikhil Khoda with local restaurateur Reita Sing, at the latter's restaurant Sultry South at South Bank, late last night.*

Tears sprang to my eyes. I chucked the paper onto the floor and headed for the loo.

When I emerged, a good forty minutes later, Monita and Rinku Chachi told me kindly but firmly that we were all going to the Gold Coast for a day of sun and fun. So I ended up trailing along behind them in the Movieworld theme park while Armaan skipped about ahead of us, sticking his tongue out at everybody who passed us by.

'Armaan, stop showing your tongue to all of Australia,' begged his overwrought mother.

'No, no, Mummy,' he replied earnestly, 'I am not showing my tongue to Australia, I am showing *Australia* to my tongue! Because it lives inside my small, dark mouth hole and doesn't get to see *anything*. See Tongue – see the pretty girl in the shorts, see Tongue, see the fat man in the shorts, see Tongue, see Zahid Pathan...'

I looked up, surprised, and sure enough, there was Zahid,

all Mickey Mouse tee shirt and tousled curls. He was waving out to us, flushed and grinning and seemingly oblivious to the fact that he was being tailed by a gaggle of giggly Pakistani girls. 'Hi Zoya!' he said as he bounded up. 'I just did all the wet water rides, it is superb, awesome, too good, *matlab ki* you will love it!'

He then started telling me that I simply had to do a bungee jump. I told him to go do it himself but he said Dieter-sir would kill him if he tried it. Then Monita chimed in too, whispering all kinds of corny agony aunt stuff like, *C'mon, snap out of it, stop brooding, do the bungee. Don't let other people take control over your happiness…*

The two of them hauled me over to a huge crane, fully covered in graffiti, where a bloodthirsty crowd had gathered to watch all the deranged loons who were paying large sums of money to risk killing themselves in the flower of their youth.

A guy with tattooed tits, dark glasses and big black jack boots yelled down to us, 'You folks wanna swing?'

'She does!' Zahid yelled back, giving the guy a big thumbs up sign. The crowd cheered happily. 'Well. Get on up then!' The guy made us shell out two hundred and fifty Aussie dollars. (I started multiplying by thirty-seven, but then Zahid said it was his treat. He actually used that word – *treat*, hello, this was a *treat*?) Then this guy with a video camera started briefing me about where to look and wave while he shot the video of my jump. Which made me get all worked up about the fact that my little cropped top would flip over my head when I fell and my new, specially-bought-for-Australia-bra-encased boobs would be captured on camera for all to see.

I tried to explain this to Zahid. It took a while for him to get it, but then he nodded, whipped off his shirt, and told me to put it on. (A few of the Pakistani girls swooned and Monita instantly started humming *dard-e-disco* under her breath.) Somehow managing to ignore the seriously lethal torso on display I put it on, and then he tucked the bottom snugly all the way around into my shorts.

The next thing I knew, I was walking up the first series of stairs, a weird plummeting feeling in the pit of my stomach, which up till now I'd only associated with encounters with Nikhil Khoda.

Below me, the crowd cheered lustily. *What a bloodthirsty bunch of people*, I thought, surveying them from a lofty height. Really, it would serve them all right if I threw up large amounts of semi-digested candy floss and coke on them as I fell...

I took a deep calming breath.

Oh well, I reasoned, as I walked off the edge, *I'm feeling so suicidal, maybe simulating it will actually be kind of cathartic...*

I strutted happily into the lobby of my hotel that evening, feeling totally at home in Australia, the adrenalin rush from the bungee jump still very much with me. The guy at Reception got all excited when he saw me. 'Miss So Lanky?' he went (hah, I only wish I was!). 'There's a gentleman waiting to see you. He's been waiting for a long time, two hours or more. He's right over there, behind that screen.'

Khoda. It had to be Khoda, I thought instantly, my heartbeat zooming. So much for not letting other people take control of your happiness.

I spun around and hurtled towards the Aboriginal screen he'd pointed at, fluffing up my hair as I went past, to see a familiar face all right, but not the lean dark one I'd been hoping for. Plump and fair and shinily bald-pated under the fancy hotel lights, Lokendar Chugh beamed up at me benignly. 'Hello,

Joyaji,' he said, all avuncular charm. 'Why you are not picking up thee phone?'

We had a beer at the poolside coffee shop. Lokey chatted about this and that and inquired after my family in such a familiar way that I started to wonder if he had a *file* on me or something. He asked about Gajendraji and Zoravarji. I was almost surprised he'd missed out Eppaji and Meekuji.

Basically he had an offer for me. That was why he was skulking around here. 'It's all very hush hush,' he said, pulling his chair closer to the table and looking at me with round-round eyes. 'You used to be an agency girl, you will understand.'

Hello, used to be? I was still an agency girl unless Sanks had found some other sucker who'd work for less to do my job.

Lokey sweated profusely, looking here and there, like a man in a bad spy movie who's always clutching a briefcase and ends up getting stabbed in the parking lot before one-fourth of the film is over. 'I have an offer for you,' he whispered hoarsely, wiping his sweaty brow with a large white handkerchief, 'to endorse a product.'

Wow, was he serious? 'Wow, are you serious?' I asked him.

He nodded solemnly. 'It is a very big brand. It will be coming on TV for thee very first time.'

Bit of a contradiction there, I thought. If it was such a big product, why wasn't it on TV yet? 'What's this product, Lokey?' I asked him.

He gave this long, impressive pause, shelled a particularly recalcitrant pista, popped it into his red mouth and said, 'Sher bidi.'

'Sher bidi?' I repeated, hugely let down. 'A *bidi*?'

Lokey beamed. 'Not just any bidi, Joyaji, Number One bidi in Indian subcontinent and Middle East!'

'But tobacco products can't be advertised on TV!' I said, scandalized. 'And anyway, I won't endorse smoking.'

'You won't have to, Joyaji!' Lokey said earnestly. 'Because Tauji is diversifying specially into agarbattis for being able to do TV commercials.'

'Proxy ads, you mean, Lokey,' I said. 'Apple juice instead of whisky, playing cards instead of beers, and music CDs instead of white rum.'

'But this is genuine product, Joyaji!' he assured me. 'Otherwise would I ask you to endorse? I also have my integrity.'

I let that pass for now. 'What's it called?' I asked him instead, genuinely intrigued about how a bidi king could diversify into joss sticks and not lose face.

Lokey beamed. 'Ekchully, Mr Jogpal Lohia has suggested very good name. He is a friend of Tauji, you know. The idea to cast you is also his. You must thank him, Joyaji.'

'What's the name, Lokey?' I asked patiently.

'Sheraan-wali,' he said. 'Good name, no?'

It was genius, the name. Genius in a twisted, sick, totally commercial kind of way, but genius all the same – the kind of thing Sanks would have thought of. Because Sheraan-wali Agarbatti literally means the tiger's agarbatti, but more importantly it means the agarbatti of the goddess who bestrides a tiger, who of course is Durga Mata, the main goddess of the Hindu pantheon.

'Yes, good name,' I told him slowly as he nodded, looking at me intently, like a fat cat outside a rat hole.

'Tauji is very excited about thee Joya Factor. He thinks you and Sheraan-wali Agarbatti are a match made in heaven. He wants to sell six million packs of agarbatti this year. This is slump time to launch thee agarbattis because all thee festivals are over but the ad will do double-shift and advertise thee bidi also.'

I didn't say anything, mainly because I didn't know what to say. An agarbatti ad. It was seriously SEC D minus. Like doing an ad for Navratan Tel or something. But hello, Govinda, Amitabh Bachchan and Shah Rukh Khan have all done that...why not me?

'They want to shoot an ad with you now, asap, which they will run *only* if India wins the World Cup. It will be thee first thing you see after Khoda lifts the Cup and we cut to thee ad break.'

'D'you have the script?' I asked Lokey.

'*Ufff!* What script-vript?' he shook his head. 'Joyaji, start thinking like a celebrity, why you are asking for the script? Ask for the money first.'

Yeah, right, stupid me. 'So show me the money, Lokey,' I said, just to humour him. It all seemed so totally unreal.

He grinned happily, held up four stubby beringed fingers in my face and waggled them obscenely, shaking with silent, triumphant laughter.

'Four?' I said, slightly insulted. 'Four lakhs?'

Lokey shook his head gleefully. 'Forty,' he chortled. 'That's what I have negotiated. Forty lakhs either way.'

'*Matlab?*' I asked, my head spinning at the thought of so much riches.

'*Matlab*, forty lakhs whether they run the ad or no. Whether India win or no. But they'll only sign the contract if India gets to thee semis.'

Well, that was reasonable enough. Why shell out money to a lucky charm till it's proven itself? Tauji *ka* logic was sound.

'But they'll be booking space on Sony, won't they?' I pointed out. 'Won't they lose a lot of money if we lose and they don't have an ad to run?'

'That is risk they are taking, Joyaji,' Lokey replied. 'Tauji's pockets are very deep. They will make out thee payment thee day you shoot,' he added. 'There's a five-day gap between thee semi and thee final. They will fly you to India for shoot and back.'

'Okay,' I said cautiously, my head in a total whirl. 'I need to think about it, okay? Let me call you and tell you soon.'

'Of course, of course,' said Lokendar magnanimously, reaching for his beer mug like a man whose job was done. 'Definitely. Take your time. What's there.'

Lokey had certainly given me something to think about. I went up to my room, mulling over what he'd said. Of course it was all notional at the moment. I'd only get the money if we made it till the semis, which were still a good ten matches away. Still, it was all very exciting. And to think I had been moping around last night feeling unwanted.

In this gung-ho spirit I strutted up to my room, fluffing my hair out and looking at myself in every mirror I passed. I was looking really good. All that blood rushing to my head during the bungee jump must've been like a facial or something, 'cos I was positively glowing, mate.

Rinku Chachi was all over me the moment I entered the room. 'Zoya, *tabse* number *mila rahi hoon*, that fat man has been waiting downstairs for you for hours!'

I looked at her blankly for a moment. Come to think of it, the first thing Lokey had said to me was, 'Why you are not picking up your phone?' Hey, maybe there was something wrong with my phone…and Khoda, after trying my number a million times had gone out with that sultry south Indian babe instead and made mad passionate love to her all night just to get over the trauma of my not returning his calls and was, at this very moment, having to make an honest woman out of her!

I dug my phone out of my red rucksack frantically and looked at it.

Rinku Chachi heaved this really long-suffering sigh and took it from me. She pressed some keys and then looked up disgustedly. 'Zoya, it's working. It was on silent, that's all.'

I grabbed the phone and checked all the missed calls. There was one from Hairy, one from my dad, two from Lokey and Zoravar and tonnes from Rinku Chachi. But none from N. Khoda. So much for that theory.

But somehow the whole thing gave me some momentum. Or maybe I was just tired of waiting for him to call. Whatever it was, I put down my bag, scrolled down to Nikhil's number, pressed call and, phone in hand, walked right into the loo and shut the door in Rinku Chachi's confused face.

It rang. Once. Twice. Thrice.

Before it could ring the fourth time – I was going to disconnect on the fifth ring, I'd promised myself – he picked it up.

'Hello?'

'Hi!' I said, all bubbly.

'Zoya?' he said suavely. 'What's up?'

But I wasn't falling for that. I knew he had my number saved, it must have flashed when I rang, who did he think he was kidding with that surprised *Zoya*?

I shrugged, looked in the loo mirror. I was still looking really good. My hair was positively angel-like under the lights. I said airily, 'Lots actually. Sightseeing. Negotiating contracts. How are *you*?'

'I'm well,' he said, sounding more amused than anything else. 'Very well, actually. Aren't you going to congratulate me?'

'Huh? Oh yes! Congrats, great match,' I said, automatically. Then, telling myself I was a girl who'd gone bungee jumping today, I took my courage in my hands and said casually, 'I thought we were meeting up yesterday, why didn't you call me?'

I thought I had him pinned then, but imagine my surprise when he turned around and said, 'Why didn't *you* call me, Zoya?'

Damn, I didn't know how to answer that. I gaped at myself in the mirror and finally came out with a lame, 'Uh, I forgot?'

'Please,' he said, 'you know, I really don't think I'm *that* forgettable.'

'No, you're not,' I said, dropping all pretence, 'and as you're so *famous* and *unforgettable*, don't you think *you* should've called me, because if I called you I'd have felt like some overeager pile on?' I couldn't believe I had said that. It had to be the most pathetic, needy speech of all time!

But all Khoda said disbelievingly was, '*Pile on*? Zoya, all you sent me was an sms saying "okay". It didn't sound like you were very keen to meet me. And you barely spoke at breakfast. What was I to think? I figured if you wanted to meet me, you could call. God knows a million people called me last night!'

'Oh, I'm sure you had a great time last night!' I replied, stung to the quick. 'There's a picture of you in the morning paper, with Miss Sultry Mouth!'

'South,' he corrected, 'Sultry South. It's the name of the restaurant, not the owner's daughter. I always go there for dinner in this city, I co-own it. And if we're trading damning press clips then there's a photo of *you* in the afternoon paper with a shirtless Zahid. Beat that.'

That gave me pause. 'There is?' I asked.

'Stop sounding so excited,' he said sardonically. 'Sound a little bored with the whole thing or I'll think you're...what's that word you use so often? Yeah, *uncool.*'

That made me laugh. I couldn't help it. 'Please can we meet today?' I heard myself asking, too eagerly.

'Pick you up in fifteen minutes,' he said instantly and hung up.

It was seven-thirty in the evening, so I figured we'd be going out for dinner. Rinku Chachi was packing and stuff. We had to fly to Sydney for the next match tomorrow. So she looked rather bemused when I bounded out of the loo and announced that I was going out for dinner with Nikhil Khoda.

She cleared her throat self-consciously and said, 'Vijay Bhaisaab has sent me here as your shaapper-own, Zoya. Tell me the truth. Where are you going in the night with this Khoda?'

'*Uff*, we're only going to a restaurant, Chachi,' I said, rootling in the suitcase for my nicest clothes. 'Fully public place. We're only friends. Don't you worry.'

But she looked worried as I slipped into a long slinky black halter dress and brushed out my hair vigorously. She pursed her lips as I plumped out mine, narrowed her eyes as I widened mine with kaajal.

'Tell him to come upstairs,' she said in a steely voice when Nikhil rang saying he was in the lobby.

'Chachi!' I whispered, cupping the phone with one hand, 'Please, *nahi*, it'll look so uncool!'

She shook her head, a formidable little figure in her pastel pink salwar kameez. 'No, Zoya, my mind is made up.'

So I sighed and said, 'Uh, Nikhil-sir? Can you come upstairs? My aunt wants to meet you.'

He agreed, not sounding too surprised.

I glared at Rinku Chachi. 'If he turns around and leaves now it will be all your fault,' I hissed.

The doorbell rang and I opened it.

Khoda was leaning against the door-jamb, looking dishy in a white tee shirt under a dark blazer. He did a bit of a double take when he saw me – because I was looking good, I hoped, not because I was, you know, an over-the-top fashion disaster.

'Come in,' I said, rolling my eyes. 'My Chachi awaits.'

He gave my hand an admonitory squeeze as he moved past me into the room. 'Behave,' he whispered.

I followed him into the room and was totally gobsmacked when he approached the resolute pink figure on the sofa.

'Rinku Chachi? I'm Nikhil. Zoya's told me so much about you.'

She was totally floored, of course. Who wouldn't be? By the time he'd finished telling her that she was my favourite aunt (hello, the only competition she had was Anita Chachi, the hag) and that he'd heard so much about her rajma pasta, she would have let him take me to dinner absolutely anywhere in the world.

He got us a deadline of eleven o'clock. She'd have made it later but he said he had to be up early for net practice the next day. He even said we'd be back sooner than eleven! Then he earned her total approval by insisting I carry a warm wrap with me, if you please. So I had to put on this totally not-happening hot pink pashmina over my black halter dress.

We didn't talk much on the way downstairs. I was worried we might run into Shanta Kalra or some of the other journos in the hotel, but we made it to the back of a big black hotel car without being spotted by anyone.

The car took off smoothly, obviously the driver knew where to go. Then, once we'd got our seat belts fastened, Khoda smiled down at me.

'I got you a present,' he said.

I sat up, excited. 'Really?'

He laughed, almost as if he couldn't believe it himself. 'Really!' he said, and pulled something out of the inside pocket of his blazer and handed it to me. 'Look!'

It was a little dark in the car but once I'd got the wrapping off I could tell it was a very dainty gold charm bracelet.

'A charm bracelet?' I asked, surprised.

He nodded, smiling, his eyes warm. 'Yes.'

I didn't quite know what to say. I just sat there looking at him, at a loss for words.

'It made me think of you.' He shrugged casually.

I thought of him going into some fancy jewellery store and looking at stuff, asking them questions, fingering the bracelets with his lean strong hands. Picking out something so carefully for me. Just for me!

'Thank you,' I said, somewhat inadequately.

'I got it from New Zealand.'

I held it up to the passing light and looked at it carefully. 'I can tell,' I said. 'See, this one really cute sheep has New Zealand tattooed on its bum.'

'It what?' he asked, startled.

'NZ,' I said a little more loudly, holding up the sheep for him to see. But even as I did so, a new and thrilling possibility popped into my mind. 'Oh,' I said faintly, and then shut up.

He was looking at me in total exasperation. 'Do you really

think NZ stands for New Zealand, Zoya?' he said very casually, plucking the bracelet from my suddenly nerveless grasp and putting one arm around me so he could clasp it around my wrist.

'Of course,' I said, my cheeks flaming, fully giving the *duh* ones. 'It must. New Zealand is famous for sheep, isn't it?'

'What *incredible* general knowledge you have,' he said sarcastically.

'Thanks,' I said, like an idiot.

He leaned in to murmur into my hair, his voice all deep and growly, 'Does no other possibility present itself to your tiny mind?'

I shook my head.

He gave my ear a little nibble. 'Like, um, people's *names* for instance?'

'People's names...' I repeated faintly. His breath against my ear was destroying my ability to string two coherent words together. 'Um...no.'

He let me go, moving away to his half of the car seat. 'Okay, then it must be New Zealand, mustn't it?'

Taken aback at this total volte-face, I opened my mouth to argue, and his gaze met mine, challenging me laughingly. He raised an eyebrow quizzically. 'Well?'

I raised my chin. 'I guess so,' I said.

Nikhil took me to this lovely Italian pub along the riverside market, all warm wood and checked tablecloths and candles stuck into empty bottles of wine. There was a trio of geriatric Italian men, playing string instruments and singing what sounded like romantic songs in cracked voices.

An extremely large waitress got us a table with a view of the river and the winding market street. She took my wrap and his jacket, plonked a jug of iced water at our table and teetered away on her red high heels, leaving us quite alone.

Suddenly feeling idiotically awkward, I poured the water into our glasses, admiring my new bracelet as it glinted in the soft candlelight.

He watched me pour, then said, as he reached forward for his glass, 'Your Chachi's really nice.'

I looked up at him, 'No, *you're* really nice,' I said sincerely. 'How sweetly you spoke to her, you remembered all that stuff I'd told you about her.'

He said, looking steadily into my eyes, 'I remember everything you've ever said to me. Even the nasty things.'

Okay, that was embarrassing. Some of the things I'd said to him would have to classify as pretty mean. 'Hey, I was totally prepared to like you the first time we met,' I protested, 'but you were so horrid to me.'

He raised his eyebrows. 'When? When you borrowed my ball pen to fake a Nike swoosh on Rawal's shoes?'

I shook my head impatiently. 'Not then. Later. When you said I was *stupid* for lighting rockets.'

'You *were* stupid,' he said, putting his glass down and glaring at me. 'I thought I was hallucinating when I looked out of my window! There was this under-sized capering creature lighting industrial-sized bombs with tiny little matchsticks. You were tossing your head crazily and singing too. Weren't you singing, Zoya?'

I shook my head indignantly. Of course I'd been singing. *Bach Ke Tu Rehna...Khallaas*, actually, but there's no way I was going to admit to it. 'No, I wasn't,' I said, lying through my teeth.

He looked at me, one eyebrow cocked. 'Are you sure?'

'Yes,' I said fiercely and quickly added, 'and then, just when I started to *like* you, you swept the boys away before Neelo and I could get our shots!'

'You were so Corporate that day,' he said reminiscently. 'Giving the over-all-incharge-of-everything ones, still smelling of crackers and gun smoke, looking about four years old...'

I flushed. 'And you were giving the I-am-the-Indian-captain ones,' I said defensively. 'Look at me, Ye Mighty, and be afraid.'

He choked into his glass. 'What rubbish!' he said. 'I did no such thing!'

But I was in full swing now. 'Of course you did! And the next day you totally *mangled* me under the big Bong tree! "Do me a *service* and lay off my boys!" And then, of course, in my hotel room you were so...'

'Zoya,' he said, in a shut-up-and-let-me-talk voice. I piped down and took a sip from my glass.

His hand reached for mine across the table. 'I'm really sorry for saying what I did that day in the room, okay?'

I nodded, feeling miserable. 'And I'm really sorry for what I said to you too.'

His face got this odd shuttered look and he said, shrugging a little, 'Well, what you said was true...'

My snide little comment hung in the air, almost like I'd said it again and I wished I hadn't reminded him of it.

I said earnestly, 'I'm sure you're the best captain ever, Nikhil. This is *your* World Cup.'

But he just shrugged again, smiled and said, 'Shall we order?'

It was a magical evening, in a tantalizing, indescribable sort of way. We talked but nothing really got said, you know? I never asked him why he'd got me a bracelet when he seemed to have such a bevy of admiring girlfriends. I never asked him why he hadn't kept in touch over the last two months. I never asked him what his scene was with the restaurateur babe.

And he, well, he told me a lot about his school days and his first cricket camp but we didn't discuss the World Cup, or my Lucky Charm status or the obscene amount of pressure on him.

I did tell him all about my bungee jump though. He refused to believe I'd done it, so I told him I'd show him the video and he said that I was a tech-savvy advertising girl and that I would doctor the footage. But he was just kidding. I could tell he was impressed.

'Is this a very expensive restaurant?' I asked him after the old lady had taken our order.

'Depends on what you consider expensive,' he said with a grin. 'It costs more than two plates of aalu tikki, definitely.'

I must have looked uncomfortable, because he leaned in and said, very kindly, 'Probably doesn't taste half as good though.'

Which made me laugh. Which made him say, as he got up and pulled me to my feet, 'You really are a cheap date, Zoya.'

He put one large warm hand in the small of my back and propelled me onto the dance floor. The music was slow, incomprehensible, of course, but nice. Almost without realizing it, I slid my hands into the pockets of his jacket, snuggled up against his soft white tee shirt, and, remembering how I'd rated his torso 'gorgeously biteable' at the Men in Blue shoot, giggled to myself.

'What's so funny?' he asked lazily.

I kept my head down, certain he'd be able to read my mind if I looked up, and just shook my head.

He pulled me a little closer and buried his nose into my

hair. 'Gun smoke,' he said, taking a deep breath in this very corny way. 'Definitely.'

We drove back to my hotel, well within time and parked in the portico. The valet service guys kept shooting us dirty looks so we had to keep the conversation short.

He held my hand and said, 'I'm not sure when we'll be able to do this again.'

Huh? What was that?

He pushed his hair back from his forehead and said, looking out through the window as he spoke: 'I can't – none of us can – afford any distractions just now. There's too much at stake. After all, I've spent my entire life preparing for this...'

He turned to look at me searchingly then, his brown eyes intense.

I somehow managed to suppress the urge to say *it's just cricket, you know* and nodded understandingly.

'I get it,' I said. 'I understand.'

'I knew you would.' He smiled, looking relieved. 'See you then.'

I nodded, as cheerfully as I could. 'See you.'

Shaapper-own No. 1 was snoring lightly when I tiptoed back into the hotel room. In the next room, shaapper-own No.3 was in Spiderman pajamas, almost asleep, with a video game in his hands. And shaapper-own No.2 was sitting bolt upright on the sofa, waiting for me like her life depended upon it.

'Zoya,' she squealed, the moment I walked in. 'Give... gimmeee! Spill!'

I collapsed on the sofa next to her, closed my eyes, sighed and said, 'Mon, please, let me just juice it all on my own a little?'

'No way!' she said, scrambling closer. 'Don't be selfish!' She touched my shawl, 'Love what you're wearing, by the way. You look so good! That pink pashmina is a touch of genius!'

I opened my eyes. 'Really?'

'Sure,' she said. 'Khoda finally called, did he? I thought you were going to do yourself an injury or something last night.'

'I called him actually,' I said, propping my elbows on a bolster and looking dreamily at my bracelet.

Mon shook a hand dismissively. 'Details!' she said. 'Who cares who called whom, the point is you guys spoke! You could've knocked me over with a feather when Armaan and I got back from the Red Rooster and Rinku calmly said you'd gone out with him. I acted really casual, don't you worry,' she added hastily, seeing the start I gave. She tweaked a curl on my head and said, 'Now spill.'

I just held up my wrist.

Mon gasped. 'He gave you that!' She zoomed in to the intialled golden sheep unerringly, and then said, 'Oh my God! Nikhil–Zoya!' she shrieked, happily articulating for the whole hotel to hear what I'd been unable to the entire evening.

I gagged her with both hands, and we collapsed giggling on the sofa. 'Nikhil–Zoya,' Mon said happily to herself. 'Nikhil–Zoya.'

Rinku Chachi snored on, but Armaan did stir sleepily and mutter, 'Nikhil–Zoya dat gaya, Zimbabwe ka phat gaya.'

14

I slept in late the next morning, and woke up only when my phone beeped. I reached for it sleepily, held it up and read, much to my horror, *Not good, Gaalu, you're in the TOI hugging a nanga Pathan. Baap livid. Think up something good.*

My instant reaction was to switch my phone off.

I didn't want to talk to my dad till I'd seen the damn picture, and maybe not even then.

Then I leapt out of bed, and cupping the receiver tight so Rinku Chachi wouldn't hear, asked the hotel staff to bring me all of yesterday's papers.

Lots of mad shuffling later, I found it. It was about the size of a 100 cc ad, not too big, not too small. It had been taken in the theme park. I was clutching on to Zahid, laughing, my hair totally wild. He had his arms around my waist and was looking down at me, smiling very fondly. We looked totally connected. And, of course, he was shirtless and looking really hot, in a rather washboard ab-ed, boy-band way.

I started frantically wondering how was I going to explain this to my dad. If I was lucky, he would take the broad view and it would all blow over by the time I got home. And if I wasn't lucky, he'd be calling on Rinku Chachi's phone any time now, ordering me to come home immediately. I scrunched the paper into a ball, chucked it into the bin and ducked into the loo.

It was a two-hour flight to Sydney. The fifteen-member World Cup squad and all their coaches and managers had left on the early morning flight. So when we boarded the plane there were no familiar Indian faces on board. There were, however, some South African ones.

'Look,' Mon nudged me, as she buckled on her seat belt, 'that's their captain.'

I turned to look at him curiously. So *this* was the guy everyone was sure would take the World Cup home. He seemed okay, a little rumpled and sleepy actually, and was asking the stewardess for a blanket. He had a long, lumpy kind of face, short, sticky straw-coloured hair and slightly boiled-looking big blue eyes. The guy sitting next to him was pretty cute though. I asked Mon if he was in the team too.

'*Sacchi*, Zoya,' she whispered, totally exasperated, 'don't you know anything? He's their star batsman, and the wicketkeeper too.'

Of course, we were talking in Hindi, but they must have caught the essence of what we were saying because the good-looking dude flashed us a quick grin before he went back to talking to the captain.

Feeling mortified about being such an ignoramus, I asked for a sports magazine when the stewardess came around, and settled down to increase my cricket GK.

I found this big article with a picture of the cricket World Cup trophy splashed across it, a big round silver ball held up by three silver stumps, at least that's what I thought they were.

The headline read, 'The Spoils of War':

The Cricket World Cup trophy, a solid silver sculpture, is currently displayed in a glass showcase in the Melbourne Cricket Club. It's been resting serenely there for the last four years, gathering a little dust, waiting in the silent darkness for the sixteen strong contingents that it knows will arrive one day from over the seas, storm its citadel with pennants flying high, engage in pitched battle for forty-odd days till a victor emerges, bloody but unbowed and bears the spoils of war away triumphantly to the land he calls home...

Wow, the prose was pretty purple, huh? This guy was obviously into military metaphors with a vengeance. He'd actually compared all the different captains to different generals or conquerors through history. The art director had done this really bad Photoshop job, superimposing the costumes and helmets of Alexander, Nelson, Chengez Khan, Julius Caesar et al., on the mugs of the Aussie, English, Pakistani and South African captains respectively. Khoda, I was hugely amused to see, was Che Guevara. They'd put this really dumb cut-pasted beret on his head and given him a goatee, long romantic black hair, and a cigar in one hand. According to the writer, Khoda was destined to crash and burn and not even make the Super 8. His money was on the South African captain – the dude with the boiled-looking eyes – whom they had rigged out in sandals and a long, white, revealing toga with a laurel wreath on his head. No wonder he was sleeping through a day flight and not looking anyone in the eye. But the writer didn't rule out the Aussie captain (portrayed as Alexander) or the West Indian (portrayed as Saladdin) either.

Nikhil Khoda leads a young, more-or-less untested side of fiery revolutionaries. Gone are the days of the diffident

Indian, this side's body language is cocky, their eyes full of
an uncalm confidence. But while the team's youth is its
strong point, it is also its Achilles heel. Quick tempers and
rivalries abound, some of which are reportedly fuelled by
Robin Rawal, the southpaw who was elbowed out of the
captaincy some months ago, but who has still arrived in
Australia as a bonafide member of the sixteen-men World
Cup squad. This squad looked good at the ICC Champion's
trophy, two months ago in Dhaka, scoring two big wins
over England and Australia, before collapsing utterly against
a confused but grateful Bermudan side…

Thankfully, the article didn't mention me, I was a more recent
phenomenon, and anyway, he didn't sound like the kind of guy
who did too much research. I flipped the pages to another
cricket article, written by Shanta Kalra, where she said that
people could say whatever they liked about South Africa finally
coming into its own, but her money was on the Indian
subcontinent. 'It's going to be one of these three sides definitely.
The cup is coming home to the subcontinent and about time
too!' She went on to say that Pakistan had just done a forty-day
Test tour of Australia and that the pitches there held no surprises
for them, that India were an extremely talented and young team
united under a strong and savvy captain, and that the suspect
bowling action of both the star Sri Lankan speedsters had finally
been okayed and their batsmen were amongst the world's best.

Mon was asleep and Rinku Chachi and Armaan were
engrossed in cartoons behind me, so I just sipped my drink and
mulled over this information. I hadn't known that Robin Rawal,
the shoe-stealer, had been hoping to be made skipper. But then,
I didn't know anything anyway. But why had Khoda – who was
both 'strong and savvy', according to Shanta – picked out such a
troublemaker to be part of his World Cup squad?

I put this to Mon when she woke up and she said, 'Your boyfriend isn't all powerful, you know,' impatiently finger-combing her hair and rummaging through her bag in search of a lipstick. 'There's something called a Board of Selectors. They have a say too, and sometimes, if the captain or the coach doesn't like it, he just has to lump it. Nikhil was selected as captain after a major slugfest last year, and Rawal's been around a while, he's cosy with a lot of the selectors. In fact, if Jogpal Lohia had been IBCC chief then, he'd probably have picked Rawal, not Khoda.'

Oh great, it was nice to know dumb-ass Rawal and I were a cosy little club of Lohia protégés.

As the plane circled over Sydney and Rinku Chachi and Monita oohed and aahed at their first sight of the Opera House, I brooded over whether I'd been foisted on Khoda, and if he resented this at some level.

Rinku Chachi's phone rang the moment she switched it on after we landed. I winced and waited for her to hand it to me. It had to be Baap, snorting fire about my photo with the nanga Pathan. But then she said a hurried *wrong number* and hung up, so I relaxed a little, but not enough to put my phone on, no way.

I got a surprise when we reached the hotel. The guy at the desk went, 'Oh, Miss So-Lanky, we're holding a message for you,' and handed me this letter in a fancy envelope.

I opened it, and found it was a really polite note from Jogpal Lohia, asking me – and my family – to have dinner with him that evening.

I showed it to Mon, who grunted and said, 'About time, he's been neglecting you a little, don't you think?'

Rinku Chachi got all overawed and said she couldn't possibly meet him, wouldn't know what to say to him and that she would stay in the hotel with Armaan.

'But you were so cool with Nikhil yesterday,' I said.

'He's a young boy,' Chachi said, 'and that was my duty, you know, Zoya. I promised Vijay Bhaisaab I would look after you properly. But this dinner, all those forks and spoons, *baap re*, I can't come. You and Monita go.'

I was a little puzzled. It wasn't like Rinku Chachi to miss out on any fun stuff – and this was a guy Gajju Chacha had such a high opinion of. Still, I didn't press her. She *was* looking a little tired, but Mon insisted she wouldn't foist Armaan on Chachi if she wasn't well. 'I'll take him along,' she said, 'after all, he's invited *all* of us.'

And so it was settled that Mon, the Monster and me had a date with the Big L that evening.

The three of us reached Jogpal Lohia's hotel a little late. This was partly because we'd overslept and partly because Armaan had thrown up huge amounts of vile-smelling *Zing!* and peanut puke just when we were leaving and had to be put under the shower again. Mon had towelled him off, crumpling her crisp chikankari sari in the process, cursing the stewardesses for slipping him so much junk food. 'And of course he could never have said no to them,' she said, as she grabbed his chin and sliced a parting viciously through his damp curls. 'Their skirts were so short!'

Anyway, the moment we got out of the car, this minion in a dark blazer came up and said, 'Zoyaji? Please come,' and ushered us smoothly to this fancy suite on the first floor. He rang the doorbell, all the while bowing repeatedly to us, almost wilting with relief when it opened and he could hand us over to another minion inside. This second minion smiled and led us into a room smelling vaguely of incense. The suite was full of ornate Indonesian furniture, with a photo of Lingnath Baba on one wall, which clashed horribly with the sweeping view of the glass and chrome city from the window.

'Please be seated,' the second minion said in a hushed voice. 'Sir will be with you shortly.'

He retreated, without turning his back to us, as sure-footed and silent as a cat. When he vanished Mon giggled, really loudly – one of those snorty, through-the-nose giggles.

'Shut up!' I whispered.

'Shut up, Mummy,' Armaan whispered too, delighted that somebody else was being yelled at for a change.

Red-faced and contrite she nodded, and then looked up, eyes fully round. Armaan and I both turned to look at what had just walked through the door.

I'd read articles that had described Jogpal Lohia as 'vulpine', so I'd imagined him to be like Amitabh Bachchan in *Sarkar*. Brooding and droopy-eyed and exuding power from every pore, you know?

The man in the doorway looked more like a warthog. He had massive, gently undulating nostrils peering coyly out from above a huge walrus moustache, large, startled-looking eyes and a trapezoid grey beard that came halfway down his chest. He was chewing gum too, his beard moving busily, but somehow he managed to make it look like he was chomping paan. 'Zoya!' he chuckled, folding both hands into an extravagant namaste. 'How are you?'

I shook my head, clearing it. 'I'm fine, Uncle,' I said dazedly.

He nodded, breathing heavily, his nostrils going big-big-big and then small-small-small. Then he turned to Mon and Armaan and greeted them politely. Armaan nodded vaguely, he probably thought he was meeting Pumba from *The Lion King*. Then, noticing that a tray of chilled *Zing!* had just been borne into the room, he brightened up and reached for it with both hands, reverentially, the way people reached for blessed prasad in temples.

Mon glared at him, her face above her (still slightly crumpled) sari quivering in reproach, but before she could say anything Jogpal boomed in his strange Bikaneri-Yankee accent: 'So! Ladies! How are you? How are you finding Australia? Are you enjoying?'

Yes, we assured him enthusiastically. 'We love cricket! Thanks for sponsoring our trip.'

Then Jogpal sprawled onto the sofa and, without any preamble, started telling us the story of his life.

It was pretty interesting, actually. He was a self-made man, he told us. He had spent his childhood playing cricket and looking after his uncle's grocery shop. A cricket scholarship got him into college where he did a B.Com and then joined a detergent company and started selling kitchen cleaners door to door. It was while pushing detergent that he met his wife-to-be. She opened the door when her mum was out and the young Jogpal came in and cleaned the gunk off the kitchen sink and wormed his way into her heart for ever. A runaway marriage followed as her folks were very rich, and from a different caste. But after the first bouncing baby was born, the father-in-law set Jogpal up with a grocery business and adopted him as his son.

'My wife is my good luck, ladies,' Jogpal said. 'Everything has turned to gold since I met her. Business went up and up, my sons look after it now and I am free to pursue my first love, cricket.'

'So were you a batsman, Uncle?' Mon asked, smiling at him.

Lohia slapped the table so hard, she jumped. 'What batsman-shatsman!' he demanded. 'I was all-rounder. Batting, balling, fielding – I was good in all.'

Armaan, of course, zoomed unerringly onto the one juicy word in that sentence. 'Balling,' he repeated happily. 'Balling. Uncle is good at balling.'

Lohia nodded benignly at Armaan, humming to himself a little and then suddenly said, 'Tell me, Zoya, I found you a good business opportunity through my friend Tauji. You are pursuing it?'

I nodded. 'Yes, thank you,' I said.

'Don't mention,' he said graciously. 'I myself was feeling very bad that Board is not giving you any fee without a contract, so I organized this instead. It will be good for everybody concerned.'

Wow, he's a nice guy, I thought, surprised. I told him as much and he waved his hands about. 'No, no,' he said, 'it is my duty to look after all the children, that's all.' Then, turning his nostrils on Mon, he asked suddenly, 'Monita, you like music?'

It was rather unexpected. We'd been brushing up on our cricket GK in anticipation of meeting him. We both nodded, very relieved, blithely unaware of the horrible trap he was setting for us.

'Sure,' we chorused. 'We love music.'

'Nothing like music,' Jogpal said. 'Music is our culture, our soul, our heritage. Who needs alcohol or doctors when they can have music, I say? Music is life.'

He then glanced at one of his hovering minions, who bowed respectfully and went out of the room, to return in a little while bearing a strange looking string instrument and a bow. While we gaped open-mouthed, Jogpal took the instrument, placed it solemnly on his lap and set bow to string. He nodded at us over the stem a couple of times, cleared his throat and announced in a hushed, intense voice, 'Raag bhairavi. On the sarangi.'

And then he started to play.

Very badly. Very, very badly. And if that wasn't enough, he started singing too. It was a poignant little song about the cowherdess pining for Krishna and Jogpal attacked it with full gusto.

> 'The sun is setting,
> The cows are fed
> Only I am hungry,
> Krishna Krishna, you are my bread
> I am a timid tremulous deer
> Wandering hither and thither
> Slay me with your lotus-smile
> Oh my navy-blue hunter...'

It was like a bad dream. The little song had just eight lines, but Jogpal warbled on, repeating the words again and again, scraping his bow across the sarangi strings enthusiastically. Mon and I somehow managed to keep our faces straight, but Armaan started to giggle and fidget. A quick-thinking minion smoothly slid a huge bowl of potato chips in his direction and he grew still and just crunched steadily through the whole recital.

Jogpal cunningly kept varying the tempo, so we'd keep thinking the end was near but whenever we got our hopes up, he'd slow down again, toss one little curl off his forehead with an almost feminine gesture, and keep on going. A good twenty-five minutes had passed before he hit the high notes with an awful flourish, his nostrils working overtime: 'Oh slay me with your lotus eyes, my navy-blue hunter!'

And then he dried up, teary-eyed, flushed and obviously expecting applause.

We clapped enthusiastically.

Jogpal smiled modestly and took a delicate sip of water. 'So did you like my song, beta?' he demanded of Armaan, his Yankee twang coming and going in waves. With a gracious wave of the hand, he indicated that the sarangi was to be taken away. Monita and I perked up instantly.

Armaan surveyed Jogpal solemnly over the rim of his third *Zing!* glass for a bit and then asked, 'Now can *I* sing a song?'

Jogpal looked a little taken aback, he obviously hadn't thought of himself as a mere opening act. 'By all means. Of course of course...' he said with fake heartiness and Armaan nodded quietly, hopped onto his feet, wiped the golden-brown *Zing!* moustache off his upper lip, clasped his hands together and chirruped:

> *There's a bear in there*
> *And an elec-tric chair*
> *There are hand grenades*
> *And people with AIDS*
> *Come on inside*
> *Commit soo-cide*
> *Welcome to Gay School...*
> *Welcome to Gay School...*

Monita muttered something incoherent in Bengali, moved as far away from her son as she could, and started fanning herself with her pallu. Her whole attitude was one of I-disown-this-demon-child-he-has-so-not-emerged-from-my-womb.

I gave a stupid, nervous laugh. 'It's a social service song,' I told a stunned Jogpal. 'Armaan bete, very nice, *ab Zing! piyo*, drink your *Zing!*'

Armaan nodded, and after giving Jogpal a triumphant 'beat-that-if you-can-you-amateur' look, promptly disappeared behind his *Zing!* glass.

'*Arrey*, by the way,' Lohia said, swivelling his nostrils towards me with a whistling sound, 'your papa phoned me today, Zoya.'

I almost spilt my drink. I'd been nodding politely, wondering how quickly we could leave, and this remark caught me off-guard. 'How come?' I asked, with a sinking heart, but I knew already.

My dad had basically bypassed Rinku Chachi and rolled out the big guns. Or maybe she knew. Hey, no wonder she'd passed up dinner with Jogpal Lohia this evening!

With a numb feeling of inevitability, I watched him pull out the photo of the nanga Pathan and me from a file and put it down on the table. Then he looked at me, his nostrils suddenly resembling the bores of a double-barrelled gun and inquired mildly, 'What is this?'

Armaan instantly leaned forward to have a look. Monita looked from the chubby old warthog to me and stood up smoothly. 'Armaan,' she said, 'let's go look at the view from the balcony. You can see the bridge and everything.' She made him put the picture down, taking a quick look at it herself, and then they moved away.

I looked Jogpal in the eye and said, 'It's Zahid and me. So?'

Lohia frowned. 'So? So? That's what your papa wants to know,' he said. 'I told him, "Colonel Saab, Zoya is like my daughter too." I told Zahid also *ki…*'

'You spoke to Zahid about this?' I squealed, horrified.

He nodded. 'Then what?'

Oh my God, how horribly embarrassing!

'But, *bacche*,' said the Lohia, breathing heavily, 'have I not been a good host? Are you not staying in the best hotels? Three members of your family are travelling with you! Why you're doing all this?'

'All what?' I demanded hotly. 'I haven't done anything! And as you rightly said, three people are travelling with me. It's their job to look after me – not yours!'

'But it is also your papa's job, no?' he said simply. 'And he requested I find you and connect you on the phone to him so that you both can talk.'

Oh my God. I can't believe that my dad would gang up with this, this...*Lohia* on me. Rinku Chachi...she knew too. Only Zoravar was on my side. I knew it had been a bad idea to put my phone off!

I stood there, smoking gently, as Lohia punched the familiar number of the house in Karol Bagh on his fancy cellphone.

Really, how old did Dad think I was?

'*Haan*, Colonel Saab?' Lohia said, lumbering to his feet. 'Zoya wants to talk to you.' He handed me the phone, and actually had the gall to smile at me.

'Hi, Dad,' I said, as calmly as I could.

'Zoya.' He sounded angry, anxious, affectionate, all at the same time. He even sounded, I thought, embarrassed, like maybe he was feeling he'd overreacted a little by getting Lohia involved. But the embarrassment was evenly balanced out by a defiant tinge of why-the-bloody-hell-shouldn't-I-overreact. The moment I heard his voice, I felt terribly homesick. I knew exactly where he was standing, in the pillared veranda, speaking on the cordless phone. It would be late afternoon in Delhi, the prettiest time of day to hang out in the lawn. Eppa and Meeku would be running around in circles on the grass, and Dad would be trying to keep his voice down so that Anita Chachi didn't overhear and go all I-told-you-so.

'Why aren't you using that new phone I gave you?' he demanded.

I felt instantly guilty, remembering how sweetly he'd given it to me at the airport, and how good I'd promised to be. I mumbled something about switching it off for the flight to Sydney and forgetting to put it on afterwards.

'I called Rinku a million times when I couldn't get through to you, but she's such a coward...she just kept saying *wrong number, wrong number!*' my dad fumed. 'Must've seen that photo, I suppose.'

I felt a sudden surge of affection for my Rinku Chachi. 'Uh, Dad, the photo... It's nothing, *kuchh nahi*, okay?'

'If it was all so innocent, why have you been avoiding my calls?'

'I haven't,' I said, untruthfully. 'It's just that I haven't figured out how to use that new phone properly yet...' Then as calmly as I could, I told him how I had gone bungee jumping just before the picture was taken. 'That's why I was looking so excited and hanging on to Zahid so animatedly.'

Bad mistake. 'Bungee jumping?' Dad exploded. Across the room, Lohia, who was humming horribly to himself and trying to look invisible, jumped a little. 'You could've been paralysed for life! Those things are dangerous. *What is that bloody Rinku doing?*'

'Dad, I'm sorry, I'm sorry. Relax, I'm fine, nothing happened...They even took a video, I'll mail it to you, okay? I'm not seeing Zahid or anyone else. You can ask Lohia Uncle. I just see them all for fifteen minutes every five days or so. Honest!'

I was fibbing, of course, there was no way I was going to tell him about my 'NZ' bracelet and all the close dancing I'd been up to, or how good Zahid's gorgeous washboard abs had felt under my fingers. But I did make a promise to myself, right there and then, to keep my distance from the cricketers for the rest of my stay. After all, my propitiousness was directly proportional to my purity, according to old Lingnath whose picture was grinning at me from the wall across the room. And from the way Dad was yelling, my being disowned by my only living parent was directly proportional to my purity too...

To calm him down, I started telling him about Sydney and the match and our fancy hotel.

'Okay, okay, don't you try and manage me,' he said at last, with bad grace. 'And keep your phone on, I want to be able to get through to you at a moment's notice, *suna tumne?*'

'*Haan, haan*, Dad,' I promised. 'Love to Eppa and Meeku.'

He muttered something in reply and hung up.

Feeling extremely stupid, I walked across the room and handed the phone back to Lohia.

The evening ended pretty soon after that. Lohia had to go out for some high-profile dinner, so we cleared out of his ornate suite fairly early.

Mon was fully mortified about not having kept a closer watch on me. The first thing she did after getting into the car on our return was to message her number to my dad and assure him that she'd pick up his calls 24/7.

They all slept late the next morning but, of course, I had to be up bright and early for breakfast. I'd set the alarm for six a.m., but I needn't have bothered. Zoravar woke me up at five-thirty in the morning, calling from Poonch. 'You alive, soldier?' he yelled down the line.

'Yes,' I said grumpily. 'Thanks for the warning.'

'Anytime,' he shouted.

'And listen, just for the record, there's really nothing going on between Zahid and me.'

'Never thought there was!' he yelled. 'Now what about the *other* guy? *You* know, Kuptaan Saab? Don't bullshit me, now, I know you like him, Gaalu.'

'Well...' I giggled happily, looking at the pretty gold bracelet on my wrist, 'it seems he likes me too!'

There was absolute silence at the other end; just the wind whistling through the mountains of Poonch. I'd just started worrying that a Pakistani sniper had put a bullet through my brother when he finally said, very quietly, 'Really? How d'you know?'

I told him all about my dinner date in Brisbane. Well, not all, but most of it.

He heard me out and then said urgently, 'Gaalu, look I've gotta go, but listen, ask yourself why this guy's being so nice all of a sudden? He's surrounded with hot babes constantly, why's he training his sights on you?'

I started to protest but he cut me off. 'He's a good captain, I'll grant him that. Maybe sucking up to you is part of his winning strategy. Fair enough. But keep your defences up. Guys keep using you all the time – and I don't want you to become collateral damage, okay?'

'Zoravar, listen,' I started to say, but he'd hung up, leaving me absolutely shattered.

I sat down on the loo floor, thinking, *Oh thanks, Zoravar.* Obviously, I am so damn ordinary, so damn boring, so damn *ugly* that no one could possibly like me just for myself. There would have to be an ulterior motive, wouldn't there?

And thanks for reminding me I've been a dumpee twice before.

As if I've ever forgotten it...

The first time hadn't been so bad, actually, I'd come out with nothing more than a slightly bruised ego and a real appreciation for heavy metal music. (The dumper in question had played bass guitar in a Delhi University band called *Hymen Busters* and had dumped me for the husky-throated lead singer. In his breaking-up speech he'd confessed he was only going out with me because Dad had let the band practise on our terrace.)

But the second time – that had been bad.

My second dumper, with his sexy Bangalore drawl, his Hubba Bubba grapefruit-flavoured deep kisses and his brooding intellectual brow, had destroyed me utterly when he wrote to me from Columbia University (where he'd got a scholarship basically because G. Singh had pulled a lot of strings) that he felt the two of us should give each other 'space'.

We'd been going out for four years. I'd met him at a college social, he'd just walked up and said hello, we'd slow-danced to Enrique Iglesias's *Hero* and then sat on the college steps and chatted for hours. He was super-bright, had maxed the CATS and gone to Ahmedabad for his MBA. (Unlike me. I'd got mine from some shady place in Ghaziabad.)

I should have seen it coming, really. After all, anybody with an IQ that high was sure to work out that once the scholarship came through, he had no further need for a loser like me.

And now Zoravar was implying that Nikhil Khoda was dumper number three – my *third* tryst with a destiny that just couldn't seem to get enough of rubbing my chubby face into the mud.

I brooded as I showered and brushed my teeth, thinking resentfully that Zoravar didn't know what he was talking about. He had no notion how much integrity Nikhil had, what a straight guy he was. Why, he'd tried so hard to keep me away from the team table before finally capitulating after the IPL benefit match! I was going to pay no attention to my big brother's stupid ravings, I decided, as I brushed my hair so viciously that it crackled. And headed towards the car in time for breakfast.

Breakfast this time was at the Sydney Cricket Ground itself. We drove into Moore Park by seven-fifteen and the place was still pretty quiet. Actually, I was starting to miss India, where the World Cup fever was way higher than here. In India, Durga pooja pandals had the goddess decked out in the Indian uniform – bats, balls and stumps in every arm – a good three months before the event started. By now, self-styled cricketing gurus would be explaining India's position, or rather *'poishun'* at every street corner, and calculating if we would make the Super 8. Neelo and gang would be writing banner lines feverishly and firework stalls would be coming up everywhere. There would be the inevitable match-fixing allegations, cursing of sponsors and *tsk tsking* over the crass commercialization of the sport. All the cool people would be pretending to be unaffected by the fever, talking about how painfully slow ODIs were compared to Twenty20s and then running to the TV frantically when a big wicket fell. And, of course, Sony Entertainment Television would be charging obscene rates and raking in the moolah by the truckload.

The boys looked almost ready to leave when I showed up. They grinned at me and shifted to make room. The sofas had been moved out of the way and the tables pushed together to form a long one.

Rawal, of all people, called out from the other end of the table: 'Not fair, huh? Zoya won't really be at *our* table.'

Wow, he was being friendly. I gave him a rather-too-bright smile out of sheer surprise and he responded with a constipated one of his own. I wriggled in between Shivnath and Hairy, even though there was a little space next to Zahid. He didn't seem to notice though. He was looking really intense as he chewed furiously. Khoda, of course, was at the top of the table with Wes, Dieter Rund and Laakhi. He looked up, flashed a grin, and I smiled back, thinking what a suspicious piece of shit my brother was...

Shiv and Hairy, usually so animated, were very quiet. Maybe because it was a very big match? But this time, I didn't feel so resentful, or like an intruder. I grabbed some toast, reached for the butter, ignored the Vegemite, and poured myself some coffee.

I think they had been waiting for me to show up, because the moment I'd downed one cup, they were ready to go.

'Umm, best of luck, guys,' I said through a mouthful of toast as they all wriggled out from behind the sofas and started grabbing their stuff to leave.

Everybody smiled at me, some of them said thanks, some just slouched away, like they were embarrassed to say anything at all. But my trio of diehard fans – Hairy, Shivee and Zahid – grabbed me one at a time in a bear hug. I hugged all three back, fervently wishing them victory.

Khoda caught my eye as he left the hall. He had a strange expression on his face. He didn't look upset but definitely wasn't happy either. I smiled at him, but he didn't return the smile, just nodded and pushed his way through the swinging batwing doors.

Julius Caesar lost the toss. Khoda decided to bat, and I relaxed, thinking that the charm was working. Thank you, God. Mon and Armaan were bunking today's match but Rinku Chachi joined me at the stadium by nine. We'd had a little chat, she'd fessed up to avoiding my dad's calls and I'd told her not to feel too guilty. We settled down happily in the Members' stand, flanked by the dressing rooms on either side, so we could watch the players come and go and hoot rudely if we so wished.

The SCG is supposed to be a pretty old stadium, established in 1848, but it sure wasn't showing its age today. Its green roofs shone, its green grass gleamed and, through my new binoculars, I surveyed the bright blue *Zing!* ground signage with satisfaction. The Brewongle Stand was right opposite us, where Vishaal and the huge Niceday contingent were already chanting *Indiya! Indiya!* The other stands were full of people who looked all set to start stripping the moment the temperature went up a notch.

When Harry and Shivee walked onto the field the Niceday guys started this huge Mexican wave and the commentators said, 'And here comes the first delivery from the Paddinton end...'

The first few overs were pretty slow so Jay and Beeru rabbited on about how this stadium, which once had pitches that favoured the batsmen and where Don Bradman had made his personal best of 452 for New South Wales against Queensland, had somehow mutated over the years into a spinner's paradise, and that even Allan Border, with his left-arm orthodox spin had managed to claim an unlikely eleven scalps here in '89. They wound this up by saying that Khoda's decision to bat first was a good one, which was a little scary because usually they said he took a *bad* decision and then we'd end up winning.

Rinku Chachi and I tuned out after a bit, because it was so slow, though half the people in the box were *oohing* and *aahing* about how stylish the boys were. The only type of cricket I can understand or enjoy is when people hit lots of boundaries or get lots of wickets. And anyway, today's match wasn't too vital, we'd creamed Zimbabwe, South Africa had creamed Bermuda and both winners expected to cream the teams that the other had already creamed. We were in a good *poishun*.

I had just settled down with a crime novel when a shriek sounded from behind me, piercing my eardrums and making my tooth cavities rattle: '*Zoyaaa!*'

I turned. It was Vishaal, looking very grumpy, and the person who'd let out that bone-rattling shriek: Ritu Raina, my pal from Dhaka, looking drop-dead gorgeous as usual. Her hair was super straight, her clingy clothes were in yummy ice cream colours and, as she enveloped me in a massive hug, I discovered that she smelled divine.

I introduced her to Rinku Chachi who was thrilled to bits, of course, and the two of them settled down next to us. The guy whose seat it was did try to protest, but Ritu smiled at him and said 'please' so prettily that he muttered 'no worries' and wandered off, dazed.

'So?' demanded Ritu. 'How are you?'

'I'm fine,' I told her. 'And how have *you* been?'

She shrugged. 'Oh, I'm great,' she said airily. 'Life is fab! But what about you, Zoya? So much has happened since I saw you last, you're a real star! And I *love* what you're wearing!'

I found this extremely flattering of course, because, hello, in Dhaka, all she'd done was fuss with my clothes and my skin and tell me to get my hair straightened. 'Thanks,' I beamed, smoothening down my boring jeans and white cheesecloth shirt. 'Coming from you, that's a huge compliment!'

Vishaal rolled his eyes rudely and said, 'Zoya, c'mon let's grab a couple of beers.'

I opened my mouth to tell him that they'd serve us right here, but something about the look he gave me made me change my mind. 'Okay, come on.'

The moment I got up, Rinku Chachi and Ritu moved closer together and started chatting animatedly.

Vishaal and I grabbed a couple of beers and found a cosy place to sit, higher up in the stall.

'What was that?' asked Vishaal after he had taken a large swig.

'What?' I asked him blankly.

'*That!*' He rolled his eyes and gesticulated towards the back of Ritu's gloriously re-bonded head.

'Ritu?' I asked, surprised. 'But you looked so pally, aren't you guys friends?'

'No way, yaar,' Vishaal shook his head. 'She did one still shoot with me three years ago and ignored me completely in Dhaka. But today she renewed our acquaintance with gusto. I was flattered till I figured out all she wanted was to hook up with you.'

'With *me*?' I said, quite pleased with the idea. 'Yeah, maybe, we had fun in Dhaka…'

'Or maybe with the Boys in Blue…*through* you,' Vishaal said.

'But she knows all of them,' I pointed out. 'She doesn't need me.'

Vishaal frowned, obviously irritated with my naiveté. 'Use your head, kiddo,' he said, sipping his beer in a marked manner. 'She broke up with that Nivi guy recently, she's obviously here to attempt a reconciliation. Anyway, why do I care? I'm screwed anyway, Zoya.'

'What's wrong?' I asked, stealing a look at the closest screen, where Shivee and Hairy were plodding on, pausing now and then to make that disgusting little 'adjustment' to their crotches while Jay and Beeru rhapsodized over their sublime strokes and silken grace.

This match was way too slow, it was starting to scare me. I started muttering *Please God, Please God* under my breath, only half-listening to Vishaal.

His Nike film had no takers.

'I'd made it on spec, Zoya,' he said. 'Clubbed it with another shoot they were doing with Nikhil. He'd made time especially for it because he liked the script so much. Now, after all the expensive post-work I got done, the marketing guys have just washed their hands off it. They're saying the wind's blowing the other way now. Luck is in. And they've done some research, apparently you're more popular than Sania Mirza at the moment! I've spent all the advance they gave me and ten lakhs besides.'

Of course I was thrilled to be more popular than Sania. But I didn't let it show on my face as I made sympathetic noises, genuinely feeling bad for Vishaal who was a good bloke and passionate about his work. 'So what are you going to do with the ad?' I asked him.

'Put it in my showreel, I guess,' he said with a wry grimace. 'And keep shooting stills. What else to do?'

There was a commotion, and everybody leapt to their feet. Vishaal and I looked up to see that one of Shivnath's 'stylish' shots had ended in a run-out. Hairy was out and Laakhi was the new man in.

We won, in the end. By the skin of our teeth. The only reason we made it was because the South Africans had bowled too slowly and that had got us a couple of extra overs towards the end. Even then, it was a close thing. Julius Caesar's much-fancied side fought right till the end and finally lost by only eleven runs. He looked like he couldn't believe it and shook hands with Khoda like a zombie after the match. Khoda, on the other hand, looked relaxed throughout, scowling as he chewed gum and back-slapped his boys. I think I was the only person anxious about the result of this match. The team knew they could afford to lose it as long as they won against Bermuda, which was practically a walkover. I, on the other hand, would not have been able to show my face if they lost. My days of being considered the lucky charm would be *so* over.

Anyway, as I'd received no more *Love N* messages I was at a loose end that evening, we all had dinner down at the nice poolside restaurant at our hotel and got into bed early.

I was rummaging through my rucksack in search of a nail-cutter when I came upon my passport and flicked through it, feeling very well travelled now that I had an Australia stamp besides my Bangladesh and Bali ones. But something seemed to be missing. I flipped through the pages again, more frantically this time.

'Where's that match day after tomorrow, Chachi?'

She looked up startled. She was in bed, the sheet over her head. '*Hain? Beta*, Auckland *keh rahe the na*?'

That's right, the India–Bermuda match was in Auckland, which was in New Zealand, which was the other country hosting this shindig Down Under. But where was my visa to travel there? I told Rinku Chachi that I seemed to have lost my New Zealand visa and she started beating her breast immediately. '*Hain? Ab kya karen?* I've got my visa…Zoya, check *properly!*' She scrambled out of bed, her kaftan riding way up her chubby legs and fished out her own passport from her shiny purse. She opened it and showed me. 'Look!'

I looked. I remembered it well. A seal with a babe and a
Maori dude on it. I flipped through my own passport frantically
for the third time. I could've sworn I had seen it three days ago
but now I didn't have it. 'Oh shit, oh shit, now what do I do?'

'Call Mr Lohia, no...' Rinku Chachi cried.

I grabbed the phone to call him, but then thought it was too
late in the night to call. Besides, I didn't want him to think
father and daughter were getting trigger-happy with his phone
number. He was probably doing late night riyaaz or something.

'*Kya* Zoya?' Chachi looked at me. 'Phone *karo na.*'

Instead, I checked the passport three more times, extremely
slowly, rubbing each page between forefinger and thumb to
make sure they weren't stuck together.

No New Zealand visa.

So then I decided I could phone Nikhil, without being
labelled either desperate or distracting.

I scrolled down to N and called him, my heart beating hard,
partly with worry about the visa and partly with excitement
about speaking to him.

The phone rang for a long time. If it hadn't been a bonafide
emergency, I'd have hung up. But I waited, pacing the floor in
my baggy pajamas and finally, he picked up.

'Uh...hello?' He sounded super sexy and super sleepy. My
toes curled up in my bathroom slippers immediately.

'Hi,' I said awkwardly. 'Listen, I know it's late and you said
you don't have time for me but I have a real problem. There's
no New Zealand visa in my passport.'

He took a while to grasp that. There was a long pause and
then he said, 'Are you sure?'

I nodded vigorously. 'Absolutely. I checked every single
page. Rinku Chachi has one though.'

'Like that helps,' he groaned, sounding like he was throwing off the sheets and swinging himself out of bed. I found myself wondering what he was wearing...linen pajama bottoms with nothing on top, I decided. Creamy white. And the bed would have creamy white sheets too. My heart did a lazy belly flop at the thought. Then I realized he was saying something.

'Send it down to Reception.'

'What?' I asked blankly.

'The *passport*, Zoya! Are you sure you're awake and not dreaming up this whole thing?'

'I'm awake,' I said indignantly.

'Good, I'll get Jogpal's guys to pick it up right away. Maybe they can swing your visa by tomorrow afternoon, okay?'

So I trundled down to Reception, handed over my passport, then came back and reported to Nikhil again – happy to have an excuse to speak to him. 'I dropped it off,' I announced when he answered, sounding wide awake.

'Good girl,' he said.

An awkward pause followed. I desperately wanted to keep him on the phone but couldn't think of anything to say.

Finally, he said, and I could tell that he was smiling, 'So, how was your musical soirée the other night?'

Thrilled that he wanted to talk, I replied, giggling a little, 'You knew? You could've warned me. I would've said I *hated* music! The guy's a lunatic!'

'Not really,' Nikhil said. 'He's actually sharp as a whip. Do you know why he sports that huge bushy beard?'

'Why?' I asked, not at all interested in the answer, but hey, that was hardly the point. Nikhil Khoda wanted to talk to me, who cared what the conversation was about?

'Guess,' he said, his tone intimate.

'Because he's hideously disfigured?' I hazarded, rather huskily in a daring attempt to sound sexy.

'What?' said Nikhil. 'I didn't catch that.'

I sighed and repeated the question in my normal voice. 'Because he's hideously disfigured?'

'No,' Nikhil replied. 'He used to be clean-shaven till '84, but when all those riots happened after Mrs Gandhi died and Sikhs everywhere were shaving their beards to avoid being persecuted, he grew one, to show solidarity with their cause.'

'He sounds nuts,' I said a little resentfully, thinking about how he'd ganged up against me with my dad.

Nikhil carried on like he hadn't heard me, 'Then he shaved it off and was clean-shaven for a long time. But the day after 9/11, he was living in the States then, he started growing it again.'

'To show solidarity with the Taliban?' I asked.

'No,' Nikhil chuckled, 'not really. To show he's not intimidated by the Americans, I think. He's always getting stopped at international airports by Security. Sometimes he carries little books in Arabic script just to give them a scare. He's quite a character, Jogpal.'

I snorted. 'Jo Lo you mean,' I said, irritated because he sounded so fond of him. 'Because he's a singer and all. Kind of like J. Lo, only with a bigger butt.'

Nikhil laughed. 'He's a good guy. Just eccentric as hell.'

There was another long pause. I racked my brain for something intelligent to say, but all I could think was: *Please don't say goodnight! Not yet!*

He said, 'By the way, the Indian officials are very sure they'd got you a visa for New Zealand in Delhi. They suspect somebody tore a page out of your passport.'

I almost dropped my phone. 'What! But why? But who…?'

'I don't know. Maybe they are just trying to cover up their

own negligence, but I don't think so. Where d'you generally keep your passport?'

'In my red rucksack,' I said, glancing across the room to where it lay on the sofa.

'In that thing?' Khoda asked, clearly not very impressed. 'Then it could've been anybody. You're always leaving that sack around.'

'It's not a sack,' I protested. Though I was secretly rather pleased that he knew what my bag looked like. *Nikhil Khoda knows what my bag looks like*, I thought dreamily. He knew I was careless with it. He was bossing me around at four in the morning, topless and tousled.

'You're a very careless girl, Zoya,' he was saying reprovingly.

'No, I'm not,' I replied with soft idiocy, every bit of me rolling over and purring at the commanding tone in his voice.

'Yes, you are,' he said, authoritatively.

I loved the way he sounded, but my hackles rose a little. I managed to pull my wits together enough to say, fairly composedly, 'Look, I'm really sorry that I won't be able to come with you guys to Auckland.'

Sounding just a little taken aback at my change in tone, he said, 'Hey, it's cool, stay here and do some sightseeing.'

I said, rolling over onto my tummy, 'You'll be okay, *na*?'

He sounded just a little dry as he replied, 'I think we can manage this one without you, Zoya.'

I thought, but didn't say, *Hello, you said the same thing to me in Dhaka too, and you lost. To Bermuda only. Remember?*

But I think he heard me anyway.

His voice got just a little distant as he said, 'Gotta get some sleep now. Goodnight.'

And I didn't have any option but to say lightly, albeit with a sinking heart, 'Okay. Goodnight, Nikhil.'

15

Zahid woke me up the next morning sounding slightly panicky and wanting to be 'blessed' before he caught the flight. He was full of conspiracy theories about the alleged 'passport tampering', blaming the Bermuda team, the Aussie press, and for some strange reason, the ISKCON temple priests in turn. He said, 'Anyways, we are through to the Super 8, *par* you know, we will get two more points if we win this match.'

'Of course you'll win, Zahid!' I said, irritated. I was a little weirded-out by the way the conversation with Nikhil had ended last night. 'Bless you. Kick some butt, okay?' I hung up, frowning a little, hating to admit it to myself even, the way the ugly, world-famous Indian Crab Mentality had suddenly risen up and tightened its slimy pincers around my erstwhile patriotic heart.

I had wished Zahid very half-heartedly.

Because a certain part of me wanted him to lose.

Let me be absolutely clear. Not lose his *virginity*.

Not lose some *weight*.

Lose the match.

I wanted *India* to lose the match.

Why? Because – and this is pretty gruesome stuff to know about oneself – if they won they would start thinking they didn't need me any more.

No more special status.

No more Agarbatti contract. No more Nikhil Khoda.

So much for being a patriotic girl whose whole family had served in the army and whose uncle had got a Mahavir Chakra in the '71 war.

It was in this sorry, schizophrenic state of mind, that I sat down in front of the TV to watch the match with Mon, Rinku Chachi and Armaan.

The match started badly for India because Khoda lost the toss and Bermuda said they wanted to bat. In a little while their openers strolled out and the match began. It was all okay for a bit. Jay and Beeru were saying the Bermudans were clearly intimidated by India but had apparently given Zimbabwe a couple of bad scares, before finally losing by thirty-two runs in the match before this one. They had three really good batsmen, Jay said, but the middle order wasn't too hot and the bowlers couldn't bat for toffee. Then Beeru said that opting to field first was not a very good thing to do because this team's strength was their bowlers (some of whom played county cricket in England all the time and were very savvy).

Anyway, there was this exciting moment in the eleventh over when their star opener lobbed a ball way too high and short and Robin Rawal leapt on it with a cry of joy. But he fumbled it somehow, and of course they cut to Pathan, all blazing eyes and rumpled curls, coming down from his triumphant whoop of victory and shooting filthy looks at Rawal in slo-mo for the next five minutes.

He looked all leonine and heroic, but my heart didn't go out to him.

Because, you see, my heart had a big black Indian crab

wrapped snugly around it. *Good scene,* the hairy black crab muttered exultantly. *Good boy, Rawal.*

(Of course I cunningly pretended to be disappointed so that Mon and Chachi and Armaan would think I was a good, patriotic Indian girl.)

Jay and Beeru just couldn't get over the catch-that-could-have-been. Beeru said sombrely that Rawal had just dropped the ICC World Cup 2011, which was a stupid thing to say, because, hello, we were through anyway. But I'd realized by now that Beeru wasn't really a very clever guy...

Then Jay went into this long monologue about Rawal, and how stylish and wristy he was; how being left-handed he was vital to the side, and how he'd been such a great opener till Harry came along and he had to be shifted down the batting order. He mentioned some old injury of Rawal's which could've maybe caused the fumble...

'But the intelligent insect can suck nectar from the bitterest of flowers,' Beeru pronounced. 'Robin Rawal needs to be more of an intelligent insect.'

There was a long pause as Jay digested this. Then he said, 'Well, I'm seeing that Nick Khoda's giving the ball to Balaji, that's unusual so early on in the game.'

'Yes, vul! It looks like another day of experiments at the Khoda and Hardin laboratory. I'm telling you, Jay, this duo will end up making rhesus monkeys of us all!'

I tuned them out at this point as the camera cut to Nikhil, looking positively murderous, Boost-brown eyes burning as he glared at Rawal. He didn't look like he was experimenting. He looked like winning this match mattered.

Hah, he probably just wants to prove he doesn't need you, the hairy Indian crab whispered megalomaniacally into my ear. *You. That's all this whole match is about.*

The Bermuda opener played it very cautiously after that.

It went on and on and Zahid finally got him out and then they all kind of fell apart but managed to finish it off with a respectable 232 all out in the forty-sixth over.

When they went in for lunch, I saw Khoda with his arm around Rawal, saying something to him pretty earnestly. Then the Bermuda captain came up to them and started chatting, a fully hero-worshipping look on his silly face.

What a sap.

Didn't he get it? These guys were the enemy. Show me some Indian blood, Bermuda boy!

They lost. (The Indians, I mean.)

They had got off to a good start but then Harry and Shivee got out pretty quickly. Then, for some strange reason, Rawal came in third instead of Laakhi. (The commentators said Khoda was experimenting because this match wasn't vital or anything, but I think he just let Rawal come in one down because he was in a sulk.) Then, when Laakhi and Rawal were doing pretty good, there was some confusion with the calling and Laakhi got run out. At this point, Nikhil came in and settled things a bit but Rawal got out LBW and then Nivi totally collapsed and got out for like five or something. Khoda soldiered on but Bala and Thind never looked comfortable, Ali got out ludicrously (the Bermuda guys actually *laughed*, so did Jay and Beeru) and finally Zahid was on strike for the last ball and had to make a six, and couldn't.

He looked completely bereft. He'd hit a four but that was no consolation and he was positively drooping when Khoda put an arm around him and they both shook hands with the chubby Bermuda captain. The Bermudans of course were thrilled to bits; as the commentators said, they weren't through to the Super 8 but this was a huge, huge victory for them, they could go home very proud indeed. They'd defeated India, after all.

'That's twice in a row, Beeru!' Jay said. 'What *is* going on with India and Bermuda, anyway?'

Those seemed to be Khoda's sentiments exactly, when he came up to receive the Man of the Match award for his unbeaten 103, frustration writ large on his handsome face.

The commentators asked him lots of questions, which he answered frowningly, pushing his dark hair back from his forehead. He got pretty nasty when they asked him about his team's performance today and said his boys needed to pull up their socks big-time. He said the fielding had been pathetic, the collapse of the batting order even more so and dismissed his own fifteenth One-day century as *not good enough.*

He looked incredibly hot as he said all this stuff. And I loved him with almost all my heart.

But I didn't cry for him, Argentina.

I gloated with a secret joy.

Even at that key moment, a moment designed to bring out the patriotic deshpremi in even the most hardened of hearts, the moment when Zahid Pathan *thwacked* that last ball away and it soared up into the air and started dropping too early, my heart hadn't dropped with it.

Oh no.

My heart had soared on through, all the way over the boundary for a six, singing a vile victory song.

It was only after we switched off the TV and I turned around with a smug satisfied smile to see the tears standing large in Armaan's huge black eyes that the hairy Indian crab loosened its hold on my heart a little.

'We lost!' Armaan said tearfully. 'India lost! They *beat* us, Mummy! You said we were going to win but we didn't! We're *losers*. We're *losers*.'

And that's when the hairy crab finally dropped away from me with a hollow *clunkkk*, leaving me shame-faced and guilty and wondering what exactly I was turning into…

The next few days were pretty quiet (except for a rash of mean sms-es doing the rounds from India saying things like – *What did Nikhil Khoda's mother say to him when he wouldn't drink his milk? Doodh peele'beta, nahin toh Bermuda aa jaayega…*). The first round was drawing to a close all over Australia and New Zealand, but India had been one of the first to finish all their round robin games in the group stage. So our boys now had almost a week off, in which time they could hang loose, practise at the nets and nurse any lingering injuries. They'd holed up in a fancy hotel in Melbourne and gone all quiet. They were probably licking their wounds. I, of course, didn't dare call them. I was too scared that they would think I was gloating.

Meanwhile, the four of us did a lot of sightseeing around Melbourne. We rode on romantic trams everywhere, hired bikes and went cycling and took the Met to look at the World Cup trophy in the legendary MCG gallery.

It was on the train back from the MCG that Rinku Chachi suddenly got a call from Gajju. '*Haan, G. Singh?*' she went, her face lighting up happily. '*Hain? Kya?* Oh, Zoya *se baat karni hai…*' Looking a little miffed, she handed me the phone. 'He wants to talk to you,' she said, disgruntled.

'Hi, Chacha,' I said cautiously.

'Zoya!' Gajju sounded excited. 'What is the true story? Everybody is asking me! They are saying you will know for sure!'

'Sorry, Chacha, what true story?'

'*Uff*, you don't know?'

'No,' I said puzzled.

He *tched* in an irritated sort of way. 'Hardin's e-mail. Get a newspaper, child. What is the use? You must know all these things. Information is power, you know!' And with that ambiguous remark, he cut the line.

Rinku Chachi snorted. 'Stingy as always,' she said. 'Worried about the phone bill. What did he want, Zoya?'

'He wants me to read the paper, Chachi,' I said, as puzzled as she was. 'Something about an e-mail...'

We grabbed one as soon as we could.

The Age Sports Section

WesHard@gmail.com to JoLo@yahoo.com
cc NikKhoda@gmail.com.

Dear Sir,

Twelve months ago, your predecessor met me in Sharjah and very kindly asked me to coach the Indian team in preparation for the 2011 World Cup. You accompanied him, and may remember that I had another, very flattering offer in hand at the time, but the youth, malleability and potential of the side and the promise of a free hand, won me over.

At that very time I had voiced a few misgivings about the process of player selection in India which is infamous across the ten Test-playing nations, to say the least. At that time your predecessor gave me the verbal assurance that your captain and myself would be allowed to pick the side we wanted without any outside interference. Advice of the senior players on the side, senior ex-players and the more savvy selectors was, of course, most welcome, if it was without zonal bias of any sort.

A year has passed, and I am still to receive that assurance in writing.

I had also been apprehensive about the continued presence in our proposed World Cup squad, of a player who seemed to be lacking both passion and performance in alarming quantities. On top of that, he was plagued by constant injuries, wore a crepe bandage sometimes on his left arm and sometimes on his right and was an unsettling presence in the nets and dressing room alike.

His cynical attitude towards discipline, training and the noble concept of patriotism itself was having a bad influence on the youngsters on the side.

I expressed my doubts about his inclusion in the World Cup repeatedly, but was informed, by you personally, at the time of your installation as IBCC president, and by the chairman of the selectors committee on many occasions, that Robin Rawal's inclusion was non-negotiable.

Ever since our arrival in Australia his attitude has been arrogant and negative to the extreme. Tardiness and no-shows at the nets have been frequent. He has given interviews and made public statements that deviate diametrically from the point of view of the captain and coach. His sour demeanour and mysterious straight-from-the-mouth-of-Jogpal-Lohia utterances have been playing havoc with the morale of our young side.

This kind of behaviour is totally unacceptable from a player who has worn the country's colours for over nine years. And now he has upped his game from the merely irresponsible to the downright criminal.

I am not making the following allegation loosely.

I have just finished watching three hours of slow-motion television footage, capturing the dropped catch against Bermuda from every conceivable angle.

And I can confidently say that the blame for Tuesday's ignominious loss can be laid squarely at Robin Rawal's door. Desultory fielding topped with a dropped catch that a child of five could have taken would be enough reason to have shown him the door from the playing eleven. Add to that his eleven runs in thirty-nine balls (two of them extras) and the fact that he got a set player run out when he was looking good for a big total at a vital point in the game and a clear case for criminal prosecution begins to emerge. I am aware of what everybody must be saying on the streets in India, and just this once, I tend to agree. Robin Rawal, Navneet Singh and Anzaar Ali should be recalled to India and investigated thoroughly for throwing matches.

Which is why I must state, in the strongest language possible, that it is no longer possible for me to function with this player on the side.

It is not fair to the rest of the side, which has worked long and hard to make India's World Cup dream a reality. It is not fair to the lads who lost their place on the World Cup squad so that there would be room for Rawal and his ilk.

One more thing.

While I respect your religious beliefs, and those of the beautiful country of India, very much, the fact that you have foisted a so-called good-luck charm onto my squad at the behest of your guru, Swami Lingnath Baba, is causing me no end of discomfort. It's a flagrant departure from every cricketing norm to have a strange young lady present at our breakfast table.

The fact that she could not be present at the match in New Zealand is being touted as proof that 'her medicine is good'. This is sure to either make the side complacent,

if she does make an appearance before a match, or eat
into their self-belief, if she does not. I am not asking for
her to return to India. I am just pointing out that I am
putting up with a lot of unorthodox practices already.

Please do not expect me to put up with Robin Rawal
too.

Yours sincerely,
Weston Hardin

Mon read it aloud as we zoomed back to our hotel on the Met.
It was potent stuff. We discussed it heatedly, all of us talking at
once. Who'd have thought the strong and silent Wes Hardin
had such depths to him? Had Rawal really thrown the match?
Him and Ritu-dumper-Nivi and that quiet guy, Ali?

Judging by tolerant Indian standards – not Hardin's self-
righteous Aussie ones – was it really such a horrible thing to do
(throwing that match and getting rich, I mean)? Because we
were in the Super 8 anyway! I'd been hoping for more or less
the same thing myself!

Would Jogpal Lohia back down and send Rawal home?

No way, we all said immediately. So would Wes quit? Or
deny the e-mail was actually written by him? And what was
Khoda's take on the whole thing?

We pored over all the other related articles in the newspaper
and speculated madly about *how* it had leaked, *who* had leaked
it and so on.

Investigative journalists scrutinized the Rawal–Lohia
friendship from the day it began, saying they'd been as thick as
thieves for years and that he'd tried really hard to get him made
captain, and that Rawal had named his first child (from his ex-
wife) after the old man. They were both from Rajasthan and
Rawal was Jogpal's first big discovery.

They'd met when thirteen-year-old Rawal smashed a six through Jogpal's fourth floor drawing room window during a game of galli cricket. The big man had come out, given the little street urchin a blistering tongue-lashing, then tossed the ball back to the kids and asked Rawal to play a few strokes...

It was a sweet story. I had a vision of a husky young Rawal and a slimmer, beardless Jogpal walking arm in arm, bats resting jauntily on their shoulders as the sun went down behind them over the spectacular Jaipur Fort...

Cho chweet.

Rinku Chachi said, 'D'you think they're *gay*, beta?'

I groaned. 'No, I don't think they could be gay, Chachi, okay?' I said. 'Maybe...maybe he's on the take too, huh? How about that? Maybe they all divvy up the money the bookies shell out?'

And then Monita's eyes widened. 'Hey, maybe *he* tore out the visa from your passport!'

Of course I phoned Nikhil the moment we got back.

He didn't sound at all surprised. 'Hi,' he said, lightly. 'Been reading the papers?'

'Yes, of course,' I said. 'How are you?'

He laughed. 'Great, actually. I've no idea how that e-mail leaked. But I'm happy. It's quite a relief actually.'

'How's Wes?' I asked.

'He's right here,' Nikhil said. 'He's been singing philosophical country songs all morning. *Freedom's just another word for nothing left to lose*, did you know that one, Zoya?'

'Are you *drunk*?' I asked, horrified.

He chuckled. 'No, of course not. I wouldn't hit the juice over Robin Rawal!'

'Where's he?' I asked.

'I don't know. Shut up with his godfather in his fancy suite, I guess. Would you believe he hasn't spoken to either of us since this news broke?'

'Maybe he'll give a press conference,' I said.

Khoda said, 'You know what? You could be absolutely right.'

'What about Wes?' I asked. 'Is he talking to the media?'

'He's switched off his phone,' Nikhil said. 'He still hasn't recovered from the fact that somebody leaked his confidential e-mail…'

'Tell him, I'm flattered he doesn't want me sent home too,' I said, 'and listen, Monita's got this weird theory. She thinks maybe Rawal tore out my New Zealand visa.'

'Really?' Nikhil said. 'D'you know one paper in Lucknow is saying you're on the take too and that you tore out the visa *yourself*?'

Oh my God, I'd never thought of that!

Then Nikhil went, 'Another call coming. I have to take it. Don't give any quotes, stay put in your hotel and – I'll try to come see you in the evening, okay?'

'Okay,' I said, but he'd cut the phone already.

We stayed in our rooms and watched TV. The leaked e-mail scandal was on all the sports channels. In India it was the only thing the junta was talking about. Zoravar called me, on a crackly, buzzing connection from Poonch and yelled down the line, 'Shame on you, Gaalu! Taking ghoons from the chaddiwallahs! All my buddies are shunning me here.'

I told him to shut up and get lost, but he went on and on for a while, hiding his concern for me under all kinds of inane utterances. 'How are *you*, anyway?' I asked him finally. 'All quiet on the western front?'

'Eastern, actually,' he said. 'Yeah, everything's quiet. Major snowstorms, of course, but I still have all my fingers and toes and am making good bowel movements every five days.'

'Gross!' I said. 'Your tent must stink.'

'No, no, Gaalu,' he assured me. 'Our sleeping bags are totally airtight, you know. They just balloon up slowly in the night, and sometimes I wake up floating in the air on all that hot gas. The guys have to shoot me down.' I groaned, he chuckled and said, 'Be good, okay. And tell Rinku Chachi to remember she's a married woman. Tell her to leave all those hunky West Indian players alone. If her foot slips, we will not be able to show our face to the clan in Karol Bagh...'

He kept chattering away about inconsequential things for a while, but he wasn't fooling me. Sure enough, as he was winding up, he asked casually, 'So, did you think about what I told you last time?'

I said sweetly, 'No, Zoravar, I didn't,' and hung up on him.

I got a lot of calls after that from numbers I didn't recognize (journos, I assumed) and ignored them all. The list of all the Super 8 teams was almost complete, there were just a couple of matches left to go. The next India match was still three days away, and on TV, the sportscasters were speculating madly about who the playing eleven would be.

By seven-thirty in the evening I figured Nikhil was too busy to come over and got into my baggy pajamas and sat on the floor to put coconut oil in my hair. Rinku Chachi got behind me on the sofa and started giving me a teeth-rattling champi, talking about her daughter Monya, so far away in boarding school.

That's when this breaking news came on and a thin Aussie sportscaster said: 'Indian southpaw Robin Rawal finally broke his silence with a press conference this afternoon, saying that' –

they cut to Rawal-the-creep's ugly mug talking into like a *million* channel mikes – 'he was sure that the leaked e-mail was the work of mischievous elements and had not been written by Weston Hardin at all and was confident that Hardin had the utmost faith in him. He said there was no question of him returning to India, and that he was looking forward to putting the bad memories of New Zealand behind him and giving a cracking performance in the Super 8s for the benefit of fans of the game everywhere.'

So Rawal wasn't going home quietly. He'd cleverly given Wes a way out, by which he could save face and stick with the team till the end of the World Cup. My respect for Jogpal Lohia rose; he'd turned out to be quite a Subtle Bihari behind that beard, after all.

I didn't think it would work though. Wes didn't sound like he was in the mood to deny the e-mail. Not from what Nikhil had described to me of his state of mind in the morning.

But Mon and Chachi thought otherwise. 'Wait and see, they'll patch up and come to a compromise, Zoya,' Chachi told me, banging the top of my oily head vigorously. 'This Weston will be on TV soon, saying *ki* I never wrote any e-mail, Rawal is like my younger brother, it happens all the time. That fellow' – she yanked my hair into a plait so tight my eyes watered – 'tore up your passport, threw the match, betrayed his country. And nothing will happen to him, nothing! Because he is president *ka* aadmi. Jogpal's man.'

'I think so too,' Mon said. 'After all, he wriggled his way into the side, didn't he? None of us thought he'd make it. *Zing!* didn't even want to renew his contract!'

I wanted to say that I didn't think Nikhil Khoda was the sort of man who made compromises. But he'd let me pile on to his team table, hadn't he? And he'd accepted Rawal into his squad too. So maybe they had a point...

Then when we were eating dinner, the same sportscaster, wearing a smug, cat-that-got-the-cream expression came on and said, 'And with us in the studio is the vice captain of the Indian Cricket team, Luckshmun Singh Teja.' He grinned toothily. This was obviously some kind of coup he'd scored over the other channels.

They cut to Laakhi, looking like a benign man-mountain, closely shaved and middle-partinged, his eyes twinkling naughtily, like the whole thing was a huge joke.

'Laakhi, how are ya?' asked the sportscaster.

'Good, thenkyou,' Laakhi said, right on cue.

The sportscaster, a thin guy with protuberant teeth, leaned forward and, pinning Laakhi with his hugely-magnified-behind-horn-rimmed-glasses eyes, asked with what he obviously believed was disarming frankness, 'Laakhi, what the hell is going on?'

Laakhi laughed expansively, his mighty shoulders shaking. 'Nothing, nothing is going on,' he said cosily. 'We are all one happy family, there are arguments between youngsters and seniors in every family you know, nothing is wrong, all is in the well.' He slapped the sportscaster on the back, making his glasses slip off his nose a little, and winked reassuringly.

The sportscaster was one of those people whose lips and spectacles, if they don't stay vigilant, tend to *slip*, the lips *backward* over the sticky-outy teeth and the spectacles *downward* over the nose. Such people, I've noticed, deal with this unique two-in-one problem by making a peculiar snarling movement that hitches up their cheeks higher and then drops them down again. The first part of this movement makes their specs ride up higher and the second part makes their lips drop lower, covering the teeth.

The sportscaster made his little snarling, cheek-hitching-up movement, startling Laakhi, who drew back slightly.

'So who is the head of the family then?' the sportscaster asked, his glasses glinting.

Laakhi eyed him warily and adjusted his collar (he looked like he'd have liked to adjust other parts but was heroically resisting). He said, 'Wes is head-of-the-family, of course. I know him for many years. He is great player, great man, great coach. He only has team's best interests at heart.' He nodded firmly and sat back.

The sportscaster nodded, snarled and hitched up his cheeks, moving in for the kill. 'But what about your president, isn't he head-of-the-family too?'

'But definitely,' Laakhi nodded vehemently. 'He is head-of-the-family also.'

The sportscaster inched even closer to Laakhi (a bad move as we shall see in a moment). 'So is the family headed for a divorce?'

Laakhi laughed his deep, barrel-chested laugh, slapped the sportscaster on the back so hard his spectacles slipped again and said, 'In India we don't believe in divorce, man!'

The sportscaster snarled and hitched again, as Laakhi watched in horrid fascination. 'So am I to understand a compromise is being worked out?'

Laakhi, looking a little intimidated with this hound-like persistence, not to mention the constant snarling and hitching, said, 'Look, this is husband–wife internal matter. Nobody can say anything!'

The sportscaster smiled a constipated little smile. 'One last question before we move on, who is the husband and who is the wife?'

'It depends. Sometimes one, sometimes the other. They take turns.' As the sportscaster looked totally flummoxed, Laakhi laughed uproariously, slapped him on the back again with violent desperation, obviously hoping to bludgeon him into unconsciousness, so the snarling and hitching would stop and so would the questions.

I'd been fast asleep for over an hour, I think, when the phone rang.

'Hello?' Nikhil's deep voice came crisply on to the line.

'Hi,' I said, sleepily.

'Are you up?'

'Just about,' I said, sitting up in bed and cuddling the phone to my ear happily.

'Can you come down to the poolside?'

Could I ever! I jumped out of bed, caught sight of my reflection in the mirror and froze in my tracks. My hair was all tied up in a fat oily plait. I looked like a greasy laddoo.

'Uh, can't we just talk on the phone?' I said.

There was a little pause, and then he said, a little formally, 'Is there a problem?'

'No, yes...not really.'

'Then come, no,' he said. 'Please. I don't have much time and I really want to meet you.'

I looked at myself in the mirror and sighed. I looked truly awful. 'Okay...I'm coming,' I said, with bad grace. 'Just don't *laugh* when you see me, okay?'

I hitched up my baggy pajamas, slipped on my fluffy shoes and headed for the poolside. He was sitting in the shadows on one of the deck chairs, and I don't think he recognized me at first. The light from the lobby made me practically a silhouette and it wasn't till I was standing right in front of his face that he said, in an unsure voice, 'Zoya?'

'I look horrible, I know.'

He laughed. 'No, it's just that I didn't recognize you at first. Is that why you didn't want to come downstairs?'

I nodded crabbily.

'*Seriously?*'

I nodded again, feeling oddly exposed. I'm so used to lurking vampishly behind my curls. 'Yes, okay?' I said crossly. 'I don't like meeting people when I look like a gaalu aalu.'

'You don't look –' he began to say, then a slight hint of impatience crept into his voice. He shrugged and said, 'Never mind.'

Oh God, he's got all this stress on his head and he thinks I'm only bothered about how fat my face looks.

Quickly, I sat down next to him and asked, in this very sensitive way, 'So, what's the latest on the stand-off?'

He sighed. 'It's still just that. A stand-off. Wes refuses to deny the mail, Jogpal refuses to drop Rawal.'

'What are you going to do?' I asked.

He shook his head. 'I don't know. The whole thing has turned into a media circus. There's rioting in Rajasthan. There's even an sms going around asking all true Indians to burn their Bermuda shorts.'

I giggled. 'Really?'

'No,' he said, his voice smiling in the dark, 'not really.' He paused and then said, 'Well, the good bit is that it's all come out into the open before the Super 8s. It's a chance to sort things out before the matches start getting tougher.'

'That's good,' I said idiotically.

He said, 'In a way it's a second chance for me to fight for the squad I really wanted.'

I nodded, muttering something non-committal, feeling way out of my depth, but at the same time also feeling very *important*, because he was having this high-level-type conversation with *me*.

And then he said, 'What do *you* think, Zoya?'

Oh no, what would I know?

'I don't know,' I said hesitantly. 'What's the worst that can happen if you guys deny Wes wrote the mail, anyway?'

'We can't really. The boys know how Wes feels. He didn't exactly make a secret of it. Yelled the place down, actually. He totally bawled out Zahid too, for not getting that last six.'

I winced, remembering guiltily how happy I'd been when that happened. Good job Khoda couldn't read my mind, he'd have probably thrown me into the pool instead of stroking the back of my oily neck in the absent way he was doing now.

'Basically, they all know he's written it. If he denies it, he'll lose respect. If I back him up on it, *I'll* lose respect. Morale will plummet. And, of course, it'll mean fielding the same team we've got now. Ergo more dropped catches and run-outs.' He paused and then added, more bitterly than I've ever heard him speak before, 'All because of the glorious uncertainties of the game...'

'And supposing you both say that yes, Wes did write it?'

He shrugged. 'Well, the boys will rally around us, but if we lose the World Cup, we'll both lose our jobs practically as soon as we get home. Which will be okay for Wes, he can get another team to coach, but not so okay for me.'

'And if you win?' I asked.

'Then it should pan out all right, I guess,' he said. 'All will be forgiven. Happiness all round. But that's easier said than done, Zoya. There are *nine* matches to go still, and we're not exactly the best team in town.' He pushed his dark hair back from his face with a frustrated gesture and glowered down at the calm swimming pool waters, a queer smile twisting his (seriously sexy) mouth.

I watched him with eyes full of trepidation. I was crazy enough about him to tell him whatever he wanted to hear. Trouble was, I didn't know what he wanted to hear. And then he looked up at me, the queer little smile almost savagely challenging. He asked again, Boost-brown eyes boring right into mine, 'So, what do you think I should do, Zoya?'

'See only thee eye of thee cupboard,' I said, feeling a little foolish.

There was a little silence. 'What?' he asked, uncomprehendingly.

'Only' – I said in a dramatic whisper, giggling a little out of sheer nervousness – 'only...thee eye of thee cupboard.'

He gave an unamused laugh. 'Oh! That.' He pushed his hair back from his face again and said deliberately, 'Focus *only* on winning. Defy Lohia, you mean.' The words hung in the air for a bit. Then he said, 'And what if I stick my neck out and we lose anyway? What about *then?*'

I said, hesitantly, scared of him almost, with this odd mood upon him. 'Then you'll know you did the right thing?'

Khoda gave a short laugh, and got to his feet. 'Do you have *any* idea,' he said, his voice shaking a little, 'how difficult it was for me to get the captaincy a year ago? Any idea at all?'

I had to shake my head, no. Because I usually use the sports sections of newspapers to pick up Meeku's potty in.

'This is a very new, and very unstable team,' he said. 'There are no givens at all. Those guys can change us around, drop us, do whatever they like. All I have to do is make one mistake. Just one. And I'll be playing galli cricket for the rest of my life. So, what was that you said just now? Yes, *knowing I did the right thing* will be very cold comfort if I end up being that completely *uncool* thing – an ex-captain.'

I didn't say anything. There was really nothing to say.

'I have to go now,' he said.

I nodded, relieved almost. 'Sure.'

The queer glittering look left his eyes then. He let his hands rest on my shoulders, smiled and said, 'Thanks for the chat.'

'Anytime,' I said, relieved, smiling up at him like a lovelorn gaalu-aalu.

He stood looking down at me for a while, then said mildly, 'What a pugnacious little chin you've got. I've never noticed it till today.'

'Thank you,' I said crossly, giving him a little push. 'Goodnight.'

He pulled me in for a long tight hug. 'Goodnight, Zoya from AWB.'

I crawled back to my room and slept like the dead. When I woke up, there was no sun in our usually gorgeously-sunny-in-the-morning room and I realized it must be practically midday. My first thought was of Nikhil. What had he decided? I grabbed my phone and dialled his number but he'd switched it off.

So I put on the TV and flicked through the sports channels, but there was no breaking news or anything on it. Then, when I found a note for me next to my toothbrush, I realized that Rinku Chachi was missing.

She'd gone shopping with Mon, apparently, and they wouldn't be back before three. Oh great, so now I would have to fret and worry all alone.

In a bid to relax, I ran a hot bubble bath and soaked in it for a while. I got rid of all the oil in my head, then sat on my bed to comb it through with a wide-toothed comb. As I made neat sections and worked my way through the knots from tip to root, I wished there was a way I could untangle all the thoughts that were swirling around inside my head and giving me a killer headache. Basically, I was worried that my advice to Nikhil had been too filmi and unreal and that he might be hassled with me for being such a fake.

(I mean, I had been a total humbug, hadn't I, telling him to put Indian victory before all else, and *see only thee eye of thee cupboard* considering my dirty little secret, which was that I'd been thrilled to bits when India lost to Bermuda without eating breakfast with me-the-great.)

Supposing he woke up this morning and thought, *Hmm, who does that pompous, pontificating, chubby-cheeked chick with the oily plait think she is anyway? I'm so done with her. Where's my little black book full of the phone numbers of genuine, honest people like calendar models and Bollywood actresses?*

It panicked me so badly I started feeling hungry. Not just normal hungry, but *Indian* food hungry.

I scanned the Room Service menu but they had nothing desi on it. A quick rootle through the Mel-pages revealed no Indian restaurants close by. The closest thing to Indian food in the vicinity was a tandoori pizza from Benito's, so I ordered it and sat down to wait the mandatory half-an-hour, mindlessly flicking channels and worrying myself sick.

Maybe Nikhil values people who tell him some hard truths, I tried telling myself. He's so surrounded by sycophants and insecure people all the time.

'But you're insecure too,' my brain whispered. 'You want

him to like you, you just told him what you thought would make him respect you more as a person. Would *you* ever see only thee eye of thee cup birrd if it meant losing your job?'

Sure I would, I thought unhesitatingly.

Not your crummy twenty-grand-a-month job, my brain said snidely. '*His*, like, thirty-lakhs-a-week job or whatever. Would you stick your neck out if it meant losing *that?*'

The truth is, I wasn't sure.

I mean, I stand up for the national anthem, and I cried when that fat kid made all the goras sing *Saare jahan se achchha* in the school scene in *Kabhi Khushi Kabhi Ghum* but the truth is that my patriotism has never really been tested. So, basically I had no business advising Khoda the way I did. I had no idea about how much he'd struggled to get where he was today.

Damn.

Where was the tandoori pizza anyway? I was starving.

I waited and waited and was finally reduced to eating *everything* in the minibar before calling Benito's and abusing them. They said they were very sorry, but my delivery boy had met with an *accident* (they actually expected me to *believe* that?) and that they'd send me a free pizza in the evening.

So I was full of Planters' peanuts and Ferrero Rochers and very, very crabby when my three shaapper-owns trooped in at three-thirty.

Armaan instantly put on Disney channel in his room and Chachi went to sleep in ours so I couldn't watch the news there any more. I did try to bully Armaan into giving me the remote but Mon gave me such a filthy look that I desisted. 'Don't you dare,' she hissed. 'The child needs his daily dose of nice nourishing television and I need some adults-only conversation or I'll crack up.'

So we poured ourselves a couple of adults-only drinks and sat out on Mon's balcony, watching the sun go down.

And that's where Nikhil Khoda strode in at seven-fifteen, brandishing a copy of that evening's tabloid. He lifted me off my feet, swung me around in the air, kissed me resoundingly on the mouth, and declared laughingly, 'Zoya, I believe it now, you really *are* a lucky, lucky charm!'

The Evening Star **Sports section**

LUCKY CHARM BREAKS AN ARM
DOCTORS SAY NO WORRIES,
NO LONG-TERM HARM!

The stand-off between the Indian Board president and the Indian coach Wes Hardin had reached a total stalemate last night. Neither of them was budging an inch. The president wanted to retain his protégé, stylish southpaw Robin Rawal, while the coach wanted him sacked and investigated for match-fixing (the surprise loss to Bermuda in Auckland, last Tuesday). The captain, Nikhil Khoda, it was rumoured, had thrown in his lot with the coach, saying three extremely talented youngsters deserved a chance to wear the country colours more than Rawal did.

'Basically, we Indians are washing our dirty groin guards in public again,' commented a disgruntled Shanta Kalra, leading sports journalist and columnist. 'Why these things aren't decided and worked out in India well before the event starts is beyond me.'

Late last night the situation reached a state of total deadlock when Wes Hardin stormed out of IBCC president Jogpal Lohia's hotel suite refusing to deny that he'd written an e-mail that somehow got leaked to the press day before yesterday. The coach allegedly threatened to quit if Rawal was retained.

Lohia mulishly showed no sign of backing off, even though he is said to have received several long phone calls from India last night, even one from the Rashtrapati Bhavan (the official residence of the Indian president). He said Hardin had no proof whatsoever, that Rawal would be suing him for libel and that Hardin was just trying to cover up how badly his team had collapsed against the puny Bermuda attack. He said Weston Hardin had an attitude problem, that he was crashing around like a bull in a china shop and had no understanding of the Indian temperament.

When questioned on the rumours of him siding with the coach, skipper Nikhil Khoda said, 'There's no question of taking sides. I respect both Mr Lohia and coach Hardin. I am positive they will come to an understanding soon.' Such sunny optimism seemed slightly unreal – especially as riots broke out last night in Rawal, Lohia's native state of Rajasthan, further fuelling the president–coach divide. Rioting mobs took to the streets, smashed shops and set ablaze three *Zing!* Cola trucks in the mistaken belief that coach Hardin is American, not Australian.

And in this, India's darkest hour, salvation came through the diminutive form of the team's very own 'lucky charm' Zoya Solanki who woke up this morning feeling peckish (and no doubt a little homesick for the lovely land of India) and ordered a tandoori pizza from the Benito's outlet on Brunswick Street, Melbourne.

The delivery boy, rushing through traffic to make the half-an-hour delivery deadline, crashed into a pedestrian who was crossing the road to enter his hotel.

The pedestrian, who broke his left arm and requires a full arm plaster for one whole month, turned out to be (oh the beautiful ironies of cricket!) controversial man-of-the-moment batsman Robin Rawal himself. The name of the person the pizza was meant for, Ms Solanki, was discovered by our reporter on the crumpled Benito's bill at the scene of the accident.

'It's a clean break,' said Dr Matthew Patnaik of St John's Hospital Fitzroy, where Rawal was rushed moments after the collision. 'There's no reason why Rawal shouldn't play as well as ever once the plaster is removed,' said Indian physio Dieter Rund. 'Cricket lovers need not worry.'

Yes, cricket lovers need not worry indeed, because the bone of contention having being removed (or rather broken), the Board president and coach have made up again. Mr Lohia has not lost face, India has retained their tactically brilliant coach and Vikram Goyal, a capable young all-rounder (whom Aussies will remember from the Under-19 cup a year ago), will be making his World Cup debut in India's first Super 8 match against New Zealand on Friday.

Of course, Lucky Charm Zoya Solanki will be there to cheer the team on.

All, as the Indians say, delightfully misquoting the immortal Bard, is in the well!

I hadn't had time to recover from being whirled around the balcony when my phone rang, and I picked it up, fully breathless.

'Traitor,' said a very familiar, irascible voice fondly.

'Sanks!' I cried. 'How are you?'

'Don't you Sanks me, Zoya, you brat!' he said, between snorts of laughter so hard I thought he would choke. 'How dare you order baasi thakela, no-good, stale-dough, frozen-chicken, bottled-tandoori-paste, Benito's pizza? Do you have any idea how hassled the HotCrust people are?'

We all just stayed in Mon's room that night. Nikhil hung around, lying on his stomach on the bathroom floor, playing

Beyblades with Armaan (it was the only uncarpeted area in the suite). Armaan won every match and crowed about it, while Nikhil chewed gum and grinned indulgently. And when my complimentary Benito's pizza finally arrived, we all fell on it with cries of glee and absolutely no guilt pangs about betraying our client whatsoever.

Armaan went off for a bath, emerged looking angelic in his Spiderman pajamas, and sat down between the two of us, as we watched a recap of the news, wanting to know why I was so important. 'You are the Boss of India,' he said pointing at Nikhil. 'What is *she?*'

I think Nikhil muttered *good question* under his breath but all he said, feigning ignorance of the world-famous masked menace, was, 'What's this suit you've got on, dude?'

Then, of course, we all got a long lecture on Spidey and how he does *phhfchikkk phhhchikkk* and shoots out webs from his wrists. 'But, shall I tell you, he only webs the bad guys,' Armaan said, waggling one chubby finger at us solemnly. 'Not the good guys. Or the weak guys. He is very powerful but he doesn't…uh…*mis-yooooz* his powers or robs banks or steals cars or doos bad stuffs…if he did, he would just be a selfish bully.'

'That's cool,' Nikhil said approvingly.

'Spidey's uncle Ben told Spidey that with Grrreat Power comes Grrreat Res-*ton*sibilty,' Armaan informed Nikhil, rolling his rrrs impressively.

That made me giggle, because it was really such a Nikhil Khoda thing to say, totally the kind of Nike-ad philosophy he was always spouting at me.

Sure enough, he told Armaan, 'You, young man, are wise beyond your years,' lifted him up by the seat of his pants the way I would lift a kitten, and started flying him around the room.

Then Mon, after a couple of extremely theatrical yawns, grabbed Armaan and went off to crash in the next room with Rinku Chachi, leaving the two of us to chat on our own. (She left the door very pointedly half-open, though.)

Nikhil made the wryest of faces at the sight of Monita's hot pink bathroom slipper jammed in the door, keeping it from locking shut, shrugged, and turned to me. 'That was good advice you gave me last night. Thank you.'

But I shook my head guiltily. 'It was all fake, really,' I confessed. 'I wanted you to think I'm a *good* person. A *brave* person. I would probably never have done what I told you to do if I'd been in your place! I did the whole remember-what-the-children-said goody-goody act just to impress *you*.'

I had thought he would laugh at this vacuous-sounding speech but he didn't. 'Well, I was very impressed,' he said seriously. 'And very inspired. You may not believe it, Zoya, but if you hadn't intervened with your pizza this morning, I was planning to call a press conference and side openly with Wes today.'

Wow, thank God it hadn't come to that. Lohia would've probably strangled him to death with a sarangi string or something.

He said, very formally, his deep voice smiling, as he lounged back on the sofa and looked at me, 'So, what are you doing tomorrow night, Zoya from AWB?'

'I'm having dinner with the Indian skipper,' I told him airily.

He laughed. 'You'll be lucky if he's still awake after a long day at the nets.'

I looked up and smiled demurely. 'Oh, but I *am* lucky,' I told him cockily.

16

The Super 8s began six days later. There were no surprise upsets in the teams that had made it through – all the usual suspects were in. Australia, South Africa, India, Pakistan, Sri Lanka, England, West Indies, New Zealand. They would all play each other once (seven matches each) and the four teams that won the maximum number of encounters would make it to the knock-out semi-final stage.

'This is where the real fun begins,' Shanta Kalra told me, practically licking her chops as we chatted at the lunch table at our hotel in Melbourne. 'Now we'll see some world-class cricket!'

I smiled politely at Shanta and said, 'Can't wait.'

She put her hand upon my arm and said, 'Hey, Zoya, d'you girls want to go out pubbing with me and some journos tonight? We'll go up to St Kilda, you know, the boho district by the beach.'

It sounded like fun. Better than staying in the hotel and watching television. I looked at Mon and Chachi and they both nodded happily. So, at eleven in the evening, we left a sleeping Armaan in the room with the hotel babysitter and sneaked out, all duded up in our clubbing clothes.

'You know, girls,' Rinku Chachi said, tightening the clasps of her dangling earrings as we all piled into the hotel cab, 'this is the first time we're all three going out together for a night-out in Australia!'

'You're right, Rinku!' Mon said, adjusting the bosom of her clingy dress. 'Let's have a bloody blast!'

We followed Shanta's car all the way to St Kilda. It was a pretty hip quarter, full of people in purple and black clothes with piercings and spiky, odd-coloured hair. There was a winding main street full of cake shops, hat shops, painting galleries and lots and lots of pubs. Mon totally loved it. 'D'you know this is where the AWB office is, in Melbourne!' she told me. 'Think of us, stuck in Vanijya Nikunj, Phase 5!'

Shanta really seemed to know her way around. She swung us into this happening nightclub kind of place and snapped a finger very authoritatively at the burly-looking barmaid.

'*Yeh toh badi* cool *nikli!*' Rinku Chachi muttered into my ear as she hauled her bulk onto the zany-looking bar stools. 'Beta, she must be my age only, no?'

I looked at Shanta carefully, even as I inhaled great gulps of the wet woody aroma of draft beer. Yes, she'd be about Chachi's age all right. Maybe a few years younger. 'No way, Chachi,' I said comfortingly. 'She looks *at least* ten years older than you!'

Soon we had all ordered naughtily named cocktails and had been introduced to Shanta's little gang. Most of them were younger boys, all vaguely familiar because they were cricket reporters from various television news channels. A couple of sporty-looking babes were there too, and – a bit of a surprise this – Ritu Raina, ravishing as always in a tight pair of jeans and an extremely abbreviated version of the India team tee shirt.

'Zoya!' she squealed excitedly, on seeing me. 'How are you, *baba*? You look so cute!'

'Hi, Ritu,' I said smiling. 'You definitely don't look *cute!*'

She laughed, flicking her shiny long hair back over her

gleaming bare shoulders. 'I know,' she twinkled back at me. 'I don't *do* cute.'

She greeted Rinku Chachi like an old friend and got into a giggly little huddle with her and Mon. And then Mon wanted to rate all the men in the bar on what she called 'The Return Gift' scale. 'You know, how we give kids return gifts at the end of birthday parties so they go home happy?' she yelled across at me above the din. 'They play with them in the car on the way home and forget about them by the next day? That's what I'm talking about here!'

According to Ritu, the place was littered with dishy return gifts whom she wouldn't mind playing in the car with but Mon insisted that she was doing 'lenient marking'. This got the boys who'd come in with us all worked up and they all demanded to know what kind of return gift was a 'good' one.

'Big. Expensively wrapped. Should feel heavy in the hand and make a noise when you shake it!' Mon yelled, making graphic thrusting movements.

One of the boys nudged me and asked wonderingly, 'Isn't she supposed to be your *chaperone?*'

I nodded glumly.

And then Ritu drawled, 'How about *imported?*'

She'd spotted what she claimed were some of the Aussie players by the pool table, but it was too dark and smoky to be sure really. Ritu wanted to get closer and make sure, saying large-heartedly that she had quite a crush on *all* of them and was rather taken aback when Rinku Chachi went: '*Chhee*...they're so pink arsed! Don't be *paagal*, beta!'

'Chachi!' I protested mildly. 'You can't just go around calling people pink arses in their very own country!'

'But why?' Chachi said, honestly surprised. 'It's true, isn't it?'

'I don't know,' Ritu said musingly. Then she added with a deep gurgling laugh, 'but I wouldn't mind finding out!' She nudged Mon in the ribs and both of them started giggling idiotically and making plans about how to approach the pink-butted boys.

We played a rowdy game of pool (very badly, Mon was the only decent player and I, of course, disgraced myself totally by scratching the baize). Then when Mon was chalking her cue (unnecessarily languorously, I thought), Ritu brightened up and nudged her saying, 'Look, awesome non-pink Return Gift! There, by the window.'

We all swivelled to squint through the wooden beams and saw this dude flanked by a posse of hot-looking babes and hopeful-looking guys. He had on interestingly ripped denims and a tight dark blue tee and was leaning at the bar, with his back to us, reading the menu or something while his buddies chattered around him noisily. There was a promising width to his shoulders, and sun-streaked copper curls at the back of his neck.

'*That* is not a *Return Gift*,' Mon said, pointing at the jean-encased butt with drunken emphasis, '*that* is a fully loaded *Khoeee bag*!'

'What's *Khoeee bag*?' Ritu asked, hiccupping gently. She was not on the mommy circuit, obviously.

Mon turned to look at her reproachfully, her big dark eyes appalled at this ignorance. She made a large mystic gesture with her hands. 'Ahhh...the *Khoeee bag*!' she intoned reverentially. 'A *massive* bag, full of goodies, that *bursts* upon the thankful public at the end of the celebration. The *climax* of the birthday party, baby!'

They giggled again. Ritu let out a piercing wolf whistle, then chickened out and ducked quickly under the table. The perfect Return Gift turned around to look at us, and all our jaws dropped at once.

It was Zahid. Zahid Pathan.

Zahid Pathan, India's ace-in-the-hole, the man everybody was depending upon to quash the Kiwis tomorrow.

'It's Zahid,' Mon said rather unnecessarily.

'What's he doing out of bed?' Rinku Chachi wanted to know.

'He looks drunk,' Shanta said, squinting a little.

'Zoya, go talk to him,' Ritu said, emerging from under the table to give me a little push.

I started to protest, but they all chorused so loudly that everybody in the bar turned to look at us. So I got up from my stool, tripping a little, smiled stupidly, and walked over to Zahid's gang of friends, who didn't even notice me; they were so busy trying to talk him into something.

'It's a *great* proposition I'm putting to you, mate,' one of them, with flashing rimless glasses and a vaguely medical air, was saying. 'I mean, look at that babe, Evalene Adams, she really wanted to have a top-level sportsman's baby...and she got it free! Your captain's a fool, man. You guys have superior DNA – you should capitalize on it.'

Zahid, looking a little bewildered, said, '*Matlab ki*? I don't understand...' The bookish guy looked about furtively, then lowered his voice and said, 'A Sportstar Spermbank. If you want a piece of that best-quality, Alpha-male, baby-making stuff, lady, you have to pay for it!'

'*Kya*?' Zahid started to say, but the rimless dude kept talking, faster now.

'You'll be surprised to know how many sportstars have already signed on with me, dude! I have a freezer compartment right here, so take these sterilized vials and *Playboy* magazines and go to the men's room right there and think sweet thoughts...'

Zahid's blank look was slowly replaced by one of complete horror halfway through this speech, but before he could go on from there to anger and full-scale violence, ending with the rimless guy's face being embedded in the oakwood bar top, he spotted me and complete consternation spread across his face. 'Z...Zoya,' he said weakly.

'It's an *awesome* proposition,' I told him. 'Hey, you'll be making money hand over fist.'

A couple of the guys in the gang tittered nervously, but Zahid didn't look too amused. Or maybe he didn't get the joke – he's not really all that bright – or maybe, who knows, he has a different technique. Anyway, he turned his back on the lot of us and started watching the dance floor.

A little pause followed, broken by the rimless-glasses guy asking, 'Sorry? I didn't get your name? I'm Jag, are you a friend of Zahid's?' In this really proprietorial way, like I was a pile on or something.

'Never mind me,' I told him, shaking a slightly wavering finger into his face. 'The question is, are *you* a friend of Zahid's?'

Jag backed down a little then and had the decency to look embarrassed. 'Listen Jag*dish*,' I told him roundly, 'he should be in *bed*.'

The dude shrugged, backed off a bit and said, 'Yeah...*good point*. Listen, whyn't *you* tell him that, babe. Read him the Riot Act, go on!'

He was being sarcastic of course, but I squared my shoulders and rounded on the Pathan. 'Zahid!' I yelled above the music.

He said something then but I couldn't quite make it out. 'What?' I yelled.

His lips tightened and he suddenly grabbed my arm and pulled me out through the long windows and onto a little balcony outside. It was very cold and quiet there. I said, stupidly, 'Hello.'

He didn't say anything, just turned away from me and grabbed the railing and glowered down at the street below. His knuckles were almost white.

I said, 'It's eleven-thirty, Zahid. Why are you out of bed?'

He tossed his head violently, copper curls tumbling every which way. 'My wish,' he said.

This rather childish crack gave me hope. I took a step closer to him. '*Dekho*, Zahid,' I said persuasively, 'this place is full of Indian journalists. They'll report they saw you here, on the night before a big match. *Bahut* negative publicity *hogi.*'

He turned around to look at me suddenly. 'Negative publicity *toh* already *hai*!' he said. 'Last ball *pe* six needed *tha* and I couldn't do it!'

Oh, shit, this was about Wes bawling him out.

'Zahid, you're talking crap,' I said firmly. 'It wasn't an important match, we're through anyway. Who cares?'

The next moment, the entire street below that balcony knew that Zahid Pathan did. He yelled it out so loudly my eardrums vibrated and hummed. Really.

Then he turned and glared at me, panting lightly. I managed to look unimpressed though actually I was shaking in my shoes. 'Okay, so you care,' I told him placatingly. Then, feeling like a student helpline operator giving *dilaasa* to suicidal kids during the tenth class board exams, I added, 'So why don't you stop thinking about the *last* match and start focusing on the *next* one, hmmm?'

Zahid patted my hand and assured me, slurring slightly, that he would play *superbly* tomorrow, not to worry.

I nodded. 'Maybe a good sleep will help your performance?' I suggested cunningly.

That fully backfired. He got all combative and demanded: 'You think you know more cricket than me?' I shook my head hastily but he just raged on. 'Actually, why only you? *Everybody* thinks they know more cricket than me! Even that *machchar*, Vikram Goyal, thinks he knows more cricket than me! That's why Hardin sir is saying *ki* "Okay okay, well tried Zahid, well tried." But inside he is thinking, "this boy can't take pressure, *badal do*, change him for Goyal…"'

'You're mad,' I said bluntly. 'Nobody thinks they know more cricket than you! And even if they do, the only way to shut their mouths is to play well tomorrow.' His eyes smouldered at this and he started to say something, but I didn't give him a chance. 'And *that's* why you should be in bed!' I finished.

He glared at me defiantly, swaying a little. 'Nothing happens by sleeping-veeping,' he said finally, his tone dismissive. 'Nothing happens by *discipline* and *diet* and *technique*.'

Okay. Stupid me.

'Everything is *here!*' He banged one big fist into his chest. '*Here!* In the heart!' Then he dropped his hand to the washboard abs we'd all been admiring inside. 'Here! In the guts!' Then he dropped his hand even lower. 'Here! In the ba…' he stopped short, shook his head and raised his hand to pat mine reassuringly again. 'I will be *superb* tomorrow,' he said again, very gently. 'Not to worry, Zoyaji!'

I shook my head, stubbornly and repeated, 'You should be in bed, Zahid.'

'Go to the bloody hell,' he said with abrupt rudeness and turned around to glare down at the street again.

Faced with his back I had just started thinking, *okay, not my bloody problem*, when, with a lovely wafting whiff of perfume, Ritu Raina tick-tocked her way delicately onto the little balcony.

'Zoya?' she inquired softly.

Zahid turned around quickly, ready to snap, and then saw who it was and subsided.

Ritu walked in, prettily hesitant, and said, 'Oh, hi…' to him in a vague sort of way. Then she turned to me and said with a little laugh, 'I know it's silly, but I'm a little scared of driving back to the hotel alone, so late. Will you come with me?'

I opened my mouth stupidly to ask her what she was on about, but she didn't let me speak. 'I'm at the Hilton,' she said, enunciating her words very clearly for some reason. 'Nobody else seems to be putting up there…'

Huh? I thought Ritu was staying with friends, not at a hotel. That's what she'd told me earlier in the evening. I started to say so but just then I heard Zahid say, very slowly, *'I'm* staying at the Hilton.'

Ritu turned around to face him, her face eager. *'Really?'* Then she looked doubtful. 'But you're having so much fun…you mustn't leave…I'll go alone…there are some dodgy characters outside the pub but' – she swallowed bravely and squared her shoulders – '…what's there? I'm a big girl!'

'Arrey aise kaise?' Zahid said, with weaving chivalrousness. 'I will 'scort you back. I will 'scort you to your hotel. It is my duty…You are an Indian girl…'

Hello? And what was I? *Namibian?*

Ritu kept protesting, brushing her glossy hair off her shoulders, but he grabbed her arm and steered her gently off the balcony. A moment later, I saw the two of them emerge onto the car park down below, both looking tall and lithe and impossibly beautiful.

I saw her bundle him into his seat and click his seat-belt shut. He didn't protest once. She tick-tocked around to the driver's door, got in and slammed it shut. Then she cranked up the glass and drove off purposefully.

Feeling a peculiar mix of relief and regret, I made my way back to a much more sober-looking gang of lady revellers inside, settling the bill. I told them what had happened and they nodded, relieved.

'*Chalo*, Zo,' Mon said. 'Let's go. Armaan always wakes up for water around two o'clock.'

Chachi nodded. 'Yes. And team breakfast at seven-thirty.'

'Seven forty-five,' I said crabbily. 'You think you know more cricket than *me?*'

I woke up the next morning to find a message from Ritu on my phone. *Zed in bed by two-fifteen*, she'd written. *Virgo intacta. Regretting it ever since.* I laughed and swung out of bed. I had a very, very good feeling about today's match.

Breakfast was at the team's hotel and when I ducked out of my car and into the lobby a few cameras clicked. Feeling pleasantly paparazzied I scuttled in through the entrance and went down to the coffee shop.

It was a bit early and Wes was the only person at the table when I entered, pottering around near the industrial-sized toaster. I stopped and looked at him doubtfully, feeling awkward, but he smiled, his blue eyes twinkled, and he held his arms out wide. 'Zoya!' he went. 'Well done!'

Much relieved, I walked into his arms saying, 'I didn't do it on purpose, you know.'

'Of course you did!' he said comfortably, enveloping me in a huge hug and patting my back thoroughly. 'You can be honest with me! Ruthless little girl, you called up the Bombay underworld, dintchya, and took out a *soup-ar-rey* on him, you told them to take him down, tell the truth now...'

I shook my head, laughing, and then, thinking this was probably the only chance I'd ever get to chat with him alone I took a deep breath and said, 'Listen, I'm sorry I've been foisted on you like this, I –'

But he cut me off. 'Hush!' he said. 'I'm honoured to have you at our table. You're an official Girl in Blue!'

A stupid lump rose in my throat at the kind tone in his voice. I hadn't realized till that very moment how defensive I felt around him. A huge load seemed to lift and I smiled over-brightly, reaching blindly for the water jug and promptly knocking it over.

Nikhil entered just then and raised an eyebrow, 'New tradition?' he asked. 'What does that mean, that we'll *drown* the crowd in boundaries?' He shovelled large amounts of fruit onto his plate, sat down at his usual place and started to say something to me, but just then the doors swung open and the entire gang streamed in, chatting loudly, and the moment was lost.

I sneaked a quick concerned look at Zahid as he came in. He looked well rested, just *very* slightly red-eyed. He caught me looking at him and flushed, embarrassed. Then he grinned guiltily at the table, pushed his curls off his forehead and got into a serious-sounding conversation with Laakhi, the sportscaster-slapper. Nobody had snitched on him then, I thought, and relaxed. Thank God!

Hairy and Shivnath looked like they wanted to talk to me about the whole lucky-charm-breaks-an-arm incident, but I think Wes had warned them not to. So they just shook hands with me very meaningfully and kept offering me good stuff to eat right through the meal. Gargantuan watermelons, whole salmon with dead glaring eyes and a massive boiled ham, all offered to me with the most dramatically speaking looks possible. And if I passed *them* anything they went, *Thank you, Zoyaji, Oh thank you very much, ji* and *tussi great ho ji,* in these broken grateful voices till Wes looked around and glared and that shut them up.

They introduced me to Vikram Goyal too, whom Mon had seen on TV last night and called an infant with facial pubic hair. He smiled at me and said, in a slightly oily, just-broken voice, 'It's an honour.'

Of course, Navneet and Ali were still part of our fifteen-member squad. They didn't look sulky or guilty, quite the opposite. They were being pretty boisterous and nobody was *not* speaking to them or anything.

They all ate quickly and sparely and were soon ready to troop into the elevator and leave.

I jumped up and hugged everybody in turn, and it seemed quite natural and unforced. I didn't feel unwanted or Durga Khote-ish any more. A little chat with the coach had done wonders for my comfort levels at this particular table.

I think Nikhil manoeuvred cleverly to be the last one out. As I finally turned to him, he gave me this really business-like look, cleared his throat and went, 'Umm...Zoya, a word with you in private, if you please.'

So I put on this blasé, *whatever* expression and trailed behind him into the elevator. We stood side by side looking straight ahead at the door as it slid shut smoothly before us. Then he turned towards me, slid his large warm hands very deliberately into the back pockets of my jeans and drew me in towards him.

It was very, very intimate. 'Hey,' he said softly.

I looked up, shaking the hair off my face as nonchalantly as I could, my hands coming up to hook the collar of his blue tee shirt. 'What?' I asked his superbly muscled chest, as for some reason I couldn't quite meet his Boost-brown eyes.

'How about a lucky kiss?' he asked, his fingers warm as they raised my chin.

A *lucky kiss?* I thought dazedly. *Nikhil Khoda's asking me this?* I could instantly hear Zoravar's urgent voice going, *He's surrounded by hot women, why's he zeroing in on you?*

I said, 'I thought you didn't need luck to win a match?'

'Oh, I can manage without the *luck*, all right,' he said ruefully, pushing me up even closer against him, 'but I'm finding I can't manage without the kisses.'

They won. Easily.

Khoda demolished their attack by contemptuously slamming a hundred off 63 deliveries, and wound up being declared Man of the Match.

I should've been ecstatically happy I know, but I was really, really low. *See see*, my mind whispered. *Zoravar's right! He lured you into the elevator, kissed you thoroughly and went out there and scored.*

Then when he'd called me right after the match and wanted to come over and see me I'd said yes, and now I was waiting for him, very wound up, scared of what might come out of my mouth when we met.

I sat curled up by the poolside, fiddling with my hair, trying to stay calm. And when he walked in, very lithely confident, flashed me a cocky, quizzical grin and opened his arms wide, I just looked at him stonily.

'Congratulations, Nikhil,' he hinted mock-reproachfully,

dropping down on the deck chair beside me and nuzzling my neck. 'You played an awesome innings, you brute of a man, you!'

I shifted away from him, hugging my knees.

'Zoya?' he asked, his voice changing. 'Are you all right?'

I turned around to look up at him, tears brimming bright in my eyes and blurted out, 'Zoravar says you're pretending to like me because I'm lucky.'

There was a long silence.

The water lapped quietly against the pool walls, a gentle breeze blew, flies hummed busily around us, and the silence stretched out, like forever.

Nikhil sighed and leaned back against the deck chair. He crossed his arms and closed his eyes meditatively. 'How long,' he asked mildly, 'has this been on your mind?'

'How does that matter? It's true, isn't it?'

He shrugged. 'What do *you* think?' he asked, opening his eyes, not looking at me but at the cluster of frangipani trees in front of him. 'Do you really think I made a 103 out there today because you *kissed* me? *Really?*'

I couldn't talk. I was all wound up and shaking. The back of my throat hurt crazily with suppressed tears. I waited tensely for him to tell me it wasn't true, that my brother was nuts. I wanted reassurance like I'd never wanted it before in my life.

'You know, Zoya,' Nikhil said deliberately, still not looking at me, 'a lot of people might say you just like me because I'm the captain of the Indian cricket team.'

That struck me like a blow to the solar plexus. My mouth opened automatically to refute the allegation, even as my brain went reluctantly, *Well, he does have a point...*

He turned on me then, his brown eyes gleaming savagely.

'Would you like me so much if I *wasn't* the captain? Would you like me so much if I was a *reserve* player, the sixteenth man? Would you like me so much if I was a Ranji player, huh? Or what if I was a life insurance agent or a…I don't know, a *banker* or something?' He said it really fast and nasty. I couldn't get a word in.

He went on, talking without any intonation or feeling in his voice. 'I see you hug my boys before every match. Every single one of them. And if *I* want something a little more, from *my* girl, before I go in to play, my motives are suspect.'

I tried to reach for him, but he shook me off, shaking his head. 'You know, at *this* point in time' – he gave a bitter laugh – 'all I need is absolutely unconditional support.' Then he looked up at me, his eyes so cold they seemed almost opaque, 'But it was too much for you to give, wasn't it?'

'Nikhil, no – ' I started to say.

But he got up. 'It's cool, Zoya,' he said. 'You keep your distance. Stay away from me. Don't even come for breakfast if you'd rather not. I don't need your bloody blessings to win me a World Cup!'

And with that, he turned around and strode out of the hotel, and out of my life.

Things got pretty grim after that.

Oh, of course I kept going for breakfast with the team, but as far as Nikhil was concerned, I might as well not have been alive. He was the first to leave the team table every time, with not even a nod in my direction. So, obviously, I ignored him right back. I laughed and kidded around with the others, but inside I was pretty close to cracking up.

It didn't help that he was in superb form. Jay and Beeru

couldn't stop raving about him. Here's a captain that leads from the front, they rhapsodized constantly. Great cricketing mind, cool under pressure, deservedly arrogant, and so on and so forth.

'Vul, with a rampant lion at its head, even a herd of cattle can win a war, my friend,' Beeru had declared just the other day. 'And the Indians are not cows.'

I glowed with pride when they said all that stuff, swore to myself that I'd speak to him the next time we met (he didn't return my calls and after three times, I stopped trying) but then, whenever we'd meet he'd freeze me out with that distant, dismissive look in his eyes and my courage would shrivel up inside me, shrinking down to a size where all it could power me to do was toss my hair and smile a brilliant, radiant smile around the table.

Privately, I had to admit that everything he'd said to me was justified. I did fall for him because he was the captain, so glamorous, so gorgeous, so successful. Would I have felt the same if he worked on Maximilk, pushing layouts to a pharmaceutical company for a living?

I tried to imagine Nikhil Khoda with a small-time, plastic briefcase, his lunch in a steel tiffin carrier, rattling up to AWB in a Maruti 800 wearing a jacket and tie.

But I couldn't visualize it. Because, every time he opened the Maruti door and strode into the conference room, the scene would slide into slow motion and the back of his coat would fly up, all *Matrix*-like. His eyes would narrow into slits and he'd start chucking Junior Maximilk layouts up in the air and catching them again without looking at them, his eyes boring into the eyes of the cowering clients across the board room table, just like in the Boost ads. 'Buy these, you morons,' he'd say. 'Buy them, or die…'

Basically, I really had it bad.

Meanwhile, 'my bloody luckiness' seemed to be working wonders. The boys won the next three matches on the trot. (They'd have won four, but one got rained out.) Apart from my rift with Nikhil, it was a crazy, heady time to be Indian. We whooped and cheered and drank ourselves silly in the stands in different stadiums all over the country. Cries of *Chauka! Chhakkaa! Indiyaa!* rose constantly into the surprised Aussie skies.

The sequence of events was more or less the same everywhere. Khoda would saunter in, and win the toss. He'd tell the umpire what he wanted to do and then, he and the boys would just do it. No fuss, no fumbles. One of them would pick up a Man of the Match trophy at the end of day's play and the Indian 'poishun' would be a little more secure.

They were making it look incredibly easy.

The commentators had started calling the season an Indian Summer and were all busy claiming they'd been predicting an Indian victory or at least an Indian side in the finals for, like, forever.

The media had also, ever since that dumb episode with Rawal and the Benito's pizza guy, developed a huge fascination with me.

The Zoya Factor was being debated on every possible channel and forum. Panels full of balding men, of every colour, accent and nationality, held forth on Luck as a Factor in Cricket. An entire half-hour programme had appeared on Channel Seven about me, with lots of footage on me that God only knows how they'd managed to get hold of. They'd started with my baby pictures, interviews with Zoravar's old colony friends, that wretched retired colonel again. They'd included the old footage of Zahid and Khoda that had run in India too and there was even an interview with Jogpal Lohia's Lingnath Baba. I prayed he would say nothing about my propitiousness being directly proportional to my purity, and luckily he didn't. Instead, much to my horror, he pulled out my janam-patri!

They'd done full 3-D graphics on it, so all these planets revolved most majestically as he pointed them out one by one, saying how my Mangal and Shani and Braspati were super-shubh and that if I'd been born even a nano second here or there I would've been no use to the team. 'When an individual longs for something with his whole soul, the entire universe conspires to make sure he gets it,' Lingnath said, lisping slightly and making large mystic gestures with his hands. 'And we are talking not of an individual here, but of an entire nation. The very cosmos bowed to the prayers of a united Bharat and wrought mighty changes in the arrangement in the paths of the planets that day in June 1983. Owing to which an entirely propitious girl child, an avtar of Durga-ma herself, was born.'

It was unadulterated crap from start to finish, but the goras seemed to love it. Either that, or they were running out of things to discuss on all those panel discussions. They even had a debate on whether I should be allowed to sit at the table with the boys, because I was giving them an unfair advantage.

Of course it was all very heady and I did lap it up a bit. But it was just so very fragile, dependent totally on how the boys performed. Dependent totally on Nikhil actually.

The third point the commentators were kicked about, besides Khoda and me, was how well everybody on the team was playing. 'Indian cricket has always been about individual brilliance,' they said, 'now here's an entire team that's brilliant!'

It was true. Maybe buoyed by the dropping of Rawal or

whatever, the boys were playing superbly. In all three matches, different people had come through to take us to victory. It was truly a team effort.

The old Indian hands, however, still looked all dour and pessimistic about India taking the 'spoils of war' home with them next month. All the usual phrases – 'peaking too early', 'Indians are chokers', 'lack of killer instinct', 'psychological disadvantage' and 'snatching defeat out of the jaws of victory' were trotted out.

'It's just the superstitious fear *ki nazar lag jaayegi*,' Shanta explained to me. 'As in, "Let's not get too excited or our boys' splendid performances will attract the"' – she made a graphic, jabbing gesture with her index and little finger – '"Evil Eye"!'

But you could smell the hope in the air.

It dripped out of everybody's pores even when they were being all balanced and careful, scented the air with a heady mix of spring-fever and monsoon madness and hung above us everywhere we went, sparkling tantalizingly.

'It's the manic *dhak-dhak*-ing of a billion brown hearts, Zo,' Vishaal told me one morning by the poolside of some hotel in Perth. 'Hesitant *and* insistent! Isn't it driving you crazy?'

It was actually.

Because every time I sensed the pressure (which was constantly), I was eaten up with guilt over the last thing Nikhil had said to me. *At this point in time, all I need is absolutely unconditional support.*

And I'd been unable to give it to him.

The next match was in Brisbane again. We got there a full day before the match and stayed at the same hotel we'd stayed at before.

'C'mon,' Monita said to me in the evening when I was moping about in my room. 'Let's go out for a fancy dinner.'

'*Haan*, Zoya,' Rinku Chachi said, 'last time you didn't come with us to the casino! You have to come today!'

I'd been sitting hunched up by the windows looking out at the river and thinking about how I'd overheard Nikhil talking to somebody on the phone a couple of days ago. He'd been saying, *I miss us too*, in this very half-exasperated, half-caressing manner. For a single ecstatic moment I'd thought he was talking to *me*, till I'd seen the headphone clipped to his ear...

'I don't know, Chachi,' I said vaguely

'Zooooya? Are you coming? Come *na*, we can share a red pizza.' I looked down to see Armaan hugging my knees insistently. I sighed and shoved Nikhil Khoda back into my subconscious where he seemed to have taken up permanent residence. 'Okay, dude,' I said, smiling brightly, 'but only if you'll be my date for the night!'

He nodded. 'I want to wear my suit,' he said solemnly.

'Of course you must wear your suit,' I said, planting a smacking kiss on his cheek, 'and I'll wear a "suit" too!'

So Armaan wore the black, two-piece tuxedo Mon had got for him in Sydney along with wrap-around sunglasses and gelled hair, while I wore a sleeveless rose-pink salwar kameez with a floaty pink-and-white dupatta.

Armaan and I strutted down to the lobby, arm in arm, Mon and Rinku Chachi clattering behind us, wafting expensive perfume.

'There's a very nice Indian restaurant close by, ma'am,' the concierge said, taking in my outfit. 'Shall I book you a table?'

I looked questioningly at my three chaperones (not that I needed them any more, I thought sadly; Zahid was so cosy with

Ritu now and Khoda, of course, had given up on me forever) and they all nodded. 'Book it,' I said.

It was just a short drive away, in South Bank, and it wasn't till we reached the entrance and I looked up and saw the neon sign glowing The Sultry South above that warning bells went off inside my head. By then, of course, it was too late.

Maybe she won't be there, I told myself as a pretty dark girl in a *pavada* choli came up noiselessly to show us our table. *Maybe he won't be there!*

But no sooner had our tamarind-tomato savouries arrived that Armaan stood up and chirped, 'Look, look Nikhil Bhaiya!'

I promptly dropped my soup spoon and then dived under the table to retrieve it.

I heard Nikhil's deep voice going, 'Hi monster,' and winced.

'*Arrey*, Nikhil!' Rinku Chachi was saying, sounding very pleased with herself. 'How are you, beta?'

'Great performances!' That was Mon.

'Sit with us! Sit with us!' Armaan shrieked. I could see his feet jumping up and down.

'*Chup*, Armaan, he's with somebody,' Monita remonstrated and then, with a sinking heart I heard her say pleasantly, 'Hello, I'm Monita.'

And this really husky, exquisitely pitched voice answered, 'I'm Reita, hope you're having a good time.'

Everybody chorused in agreement and then I heard Khoda say casually, 'Is it just the three of you, tonight?'

Okay, I couldn't lurk under the table forever, could I, so I decided this was the time to make my entry. I shook back my hair, squared my shoulders and emerged, slightly red-faced, with my spoon held out before me like a talisman. 'I dropped this,' I said idiotically, and then, 'Oh *hi*,' to Nikhil and Reita Sing.

She was super hot, half Mallu half Singaporean, I think. With a sinking heart I took in her long, black, luxuriantly curling hair.

'Zoya!' Reita gushed warmly. 'What an honour to have *you* in my restaurant!'

I muttered something idiotic and spooned some soup into my face.

'Sit with us, sit with us,' Armaan prattled on at Khoda. I gave him a dirty look.

'Actually, why *don't* you, Nikhil?' Reita said, putting one hand on his arm appealingly. 'This is a working dinner for me, anyway!'

Nikhil hesitated, his hand on the back of Armaan's chair, and I – smarting from the fact that I must have called him at least *six* times only to hear his stupid voicemail message – said, 'Hey, Armaan, you said you're *my* date tonight!'

Nikhil's face hardened instantly. 'I'll be with the rest of the guys by the bar,' he said and stalked off.

Reita smiled unsurely at us, then said, 'Okay, enjoy!' with a nervous little laugh and hurried away too.

Leaving me to face three reproachful faces. 'What is your *problem*, Zoya?' Chachi said.

'Nothing,' I said defiantly. 'What's *yours?*'

The encounter with Nikhil made me completely lose my appetite. I pushed back my chair and headed towards the washroom where I banged into Lokey. He drew back and grinned at me. 'Joyaji! Where are you hiding? I am calling and calling you every day.'

'I'm here only, Lokey,' I said, smiling back at him, happy to see a cheerful face.

'Well, we have to have a serious chat soon, y'know!' he said, fishing out about half a kilo of shelled pista from his pocket and offering it to me. 'Please have.'

'No thanks,' I said.

He registered astonishment at this lack of good taste, then shrugged and tossed the entire consignment into his capacious mouth and chewed on it thoroughly. Then he beamed at me. 'I have some papers for you to sign.'

'Lokey, I've been meaning to tell you,' I said, 'I'm not very sure about doing Tauji's ad.'

'*Hain?*' His ears cocked instantly. 'Why why why?'

I shrugged. 'I think my doing an ad, claiming credit for India's World Cup victory, will do neither me nor the team any good.'

Lokey looked completely scandalized. 'Why are you kicking your foot into my stomach like this?' he protested. 'If people like you take this kind of approach then how will I earn my livelihood?'

I just looked at him, wondering if I was being too moralistic.

Sensing my ambiguity, he looked here and there, then put one burly arm around me. 'Think it over carefully, Joyaji,' he said hoarsely. 'Tauji may even be persuaded to up to fifty.' He waggled all five meaty digits of his left hand at me tantalizingly.

Fifty lakhs, I thought dreamily. Fifty *lakhs* before I was even twenty-eight years old? Fifty lakhs was a pretty good consolation prize for a broken heart.

'And we can arrange it so you have to pay *minimum* taxes,' Lokey said. 'We'll give the government just one tiny little bite, eh?'

'And what about you, eh?' I asked, getting into the mood of the thing. 'You'll take a big fat bite out of it, won't you?'

He rubbed his hands together, with happy glee. 'Now you're talking!' he said, chuckling fatly. 'Now you're talking business, Joyaji!'

'Thank you,' I said. 'Now can I go to the loo, Lokey?'

'By all means ji, why hold it back?' he said and oiled away.

I was walking back to my table, when suddenly, a large pink person waylaid me and shouted out my name. I blinked up at him, mystified, and by listening with great concentration, managed to decode that he was 'Butch' and that he knew me from the IPL match, where he'd played for Kings XI, Punjab. 'Butch' led me triumphantly to 'the guys in the bar' Nikhil had mentioned earlier, who turned out to be most of the Aussie team plus half the Miss Universe contestants crop of the year.

The Aussies set up a loud cheer when Butch announced who I was, while the babes in the group looked at me curiously, obviously wondering *what is this short fluffy person doing in our fabulous midst?* I couldn't speak much (having been hit by a sudden relapse of an oh-my-God-white-people attack) but I smiled benignly at all of them as they shook my hand like it was made of glass, and tried to talk to me in the broken Hindi they'd picked up from the crowds who routinely hurled abuses at them in Eden Garden. Then some song they all liked came on and they took to the tiny wooden dance floor, leaving me alone with Nikhil.

He was frowning down into his cellphone, looking like he didn't want to talk, so I hoisted my red rucksack onto my shoulder and muttered 'bye' and started slinking away.

He looked up suddenly, startling me, and I was so jumpy that I promptly dropped my rucksack and it crashed against the table and fell to the floor, taking his fancy phone down with it.

'What is *wrong* with you?' he said exasperatedly as we both knelt down to the floor scrambling for our stuff and suddenly I was back at the Tera Numbar gate, groping through the scattered madhumalati blossoms for a pair of red, plastic back-scratcher-cum-fly-swatters.

Sudden, stupid tears stung the back of my eyes.

And then I saw to my total horror that my rucksack had snapped open and my well-thumbed copy of the Nikhil Khoda pocket biography *In Good Nick* was staring him right in the face. He reached for it slowly, held it up, and looked at me, one eyebrow raised. 'Yours?' he inquired smugly.

'Monita's, actually,' I lied quickly, totally mortified, and reached for it, looking anywhere but at him. But then I spotted something on the floor and this thrilling, giddy wave of triumph washed right through me from head to toe. I reached down, and in full slow motion, picked up his fancy phone and held it up for him to see. A smiling, not entirely unattractive image of *me* was the screen saver on it.

'Yours?' I inquired smugly.

He closed his eyes, coming very close (I think) to cursing under his breath. Then opened them again. 'Uh huh,' he muttered.

I nodded triumphantly, going from crushed to cocky in two seconds flat. 'So!' I said, reclaiming my seat with an important air. 'You guys are doing great, congratulations!'

'All thanks to you, of course,' he answered sarcastically, not at all like somebody who was talking to the girl whose picture he'd saved in a very lover-like way on his phone.

I had this sudden urge to snatch his phone back and check if the picture was really of me. But of course that would've looked a little desperate, so I didn't. Instead, I raised my chin and said, 'Well, I seem to be doing more good than harm.'

He shook his head in disbelief. 'You really believe this Zoya Devi stuff! *You really believe you're lucky*! An educated girl like you! It's *amazing!*'

'And you don't?' I asked accusingly.

'Of course, I don't!' he said, sounding genuinely insulted. 'Zoya, you little idiot, luck has nothing to do with my liking you!' He glanced away towards the dancing Aussies, lowered his voice, and added, his eyes urgently appealing, 'You had me in Dhaka, the moment I smelled the gunsmoke in your hair.'

'No, I didn't,' I said instantly, my voice shaking slightly. 'You thought I was *stupid*. You said so!'

He glared at me, fully frustrated, like I was an idiot fielder who'd just let a big one through. 'Well?' I said challengingly.

He shrugged his shoulders and said dryly, 'You know, this may come as a bit of surprise to you, but guys don't always say what they think…'

But I didn't want to hear what he was saying. 'Ya-ya, whatever,' I said, heatedly. 'I've thought about all this okay, you didn't start being nice to me till *after* the IPL and you didn't' – my voice broke a little, how humiliating – 'kiss me till after the Benito's guy ran Rawal over.'

There was a long silence. 'Look, I'm not going to get into a stupid argument about this,' he said finally. 'I simply don't have the time.'

'Oh, I'm really busy too,' I said instantly, just in case he thought I had nothing better to do than hang around and talk to him.

He flashed me a wry smile. 'Aren't you here on an all-expenses-paid holiday?'

'I have an interview with Channel Seven,' I said airily, hitching my bag higher on my shoulder. 'People from all over Australia are going to call me up and ask me questions.'

'About what?' he asked snidely. 'Astrology? Predictions? Or are you holding a séance?'

I didn't say anything. Of course there was no interview. I was being contrary for no good reason again. He seemed to bring that out in me.

He said, 'I see you're still wearing that bracelet.'

My heart gave an absurd jump. 'Oh this,' I said casually, almost as if I'd forgotten it was there. 'Yes, I am.'

He leaned forward, his eyes glinting, 'So, Zoya, did you think about what I said?' he asked. 'Would you still wear my bracelet if I was an account executive at AWB, say?'

I looked up startled. The guy seemed to have this incredible ability to read my mind.

'Well?'

I took a deep breath and decided to be honest. 'Yes, I did think about it,' I admitted steadily. 'And, yes, I *think* I would.'

'No, you wouldn't!' he lashed out, drawing back from me, his voice surprisingly bitter. Then he wrinkled his forehead and switched to a high little voice, 'Because *I've* thought about all this okay (was he actually *copying* me?), and you didn't start being nice to me till *after* I got made captain!'

What kind of crap conversation was this? I pulled off his stupid bracelet and handed it back to him. 'I was only wearing it,' I hissed, 'because I wanted to give it back to you tonight.'

'Oh, so you came here hoping to meet me, then?' he said, grinning obnoxiously and putting his hand out for the bracelet.

'Oh yes,' I said sarcastically, my voice shaking just a little, 'you're *all* I ever think about, day or night, waking or sleeping!'

I dropped his stupid bracelet into his stupid hand and walked away.

'See you at breakfast,' he called after me as the Aussies traipsed back to his table. 'Your *Luckiness*!'

17

Bそ he didn't. See me at breakfast, I mean. Because, late that night, I got wretchedly ill. I tossed and turned all night, red-eyed and feverish. Rinku Chachi insisted the Aussies had poisoned me. '*Soch, beta,*' she said. 'Did you eat and drink anything they gave?'

'Of course I did, Chachi,' I said crossly. 'Don't act so paranoid. Of course they didn't poison me!'

'What about that Reita Sing babe, then?' Mon said from the doorway. She was staying away from me, worried about Armaan catching my bug. 'Maybe she poisoned you, huh, Zo?'

'What is wrong with you people?' I said exasperatedly, massaging my throbbing temples. 'I've caught a viral, that's all. Go to sleep.'

They did go to bed, but the first thing Mon did in the morning was call Dieter Rund and tell him to do something about me. So then Dieter brought over this bald Aussie doctor. They fussed over me, checked me out thoroughly, and then the baldie proclaimed I had some kind of forty-eight-hour flu and would be infectious for the next three days.

Dieter nodded and said, 'Better not come for breakfast tomorrow, Zoya.'

'Okay,' I croaked miserably, crawling back into bed and pulling the covers over my throbbing head. 'Tell the boys best of luck for me.'

My dad called me in the afternoon and clucked on the phone in a most uncharacteristic manner. 'Look after yourself, beta,' he said urgently. 'We need you till the finals.' *Ya right. After that, of course, I could keel over and die for all he cared.* I assured him that I'd look after myself and hung up.

I slept through most of the day and when I woke up Rinku Chachi told me Nikhil had called. He'd sounded concerned, apparently. Well, I sure wasn't going to call him back. *This is your dream, baby,* I thought crabbily, blowing huge quantities of hot snot into my pajama sleeve. *Win tomorrow against Australia and make me redundant if you can!*

Rinku Chachi stayed back to watch the match with me the next day but Mon, eager to escape my flu, took Armaan to the Gabba. We put on the TV bright and early and caught the commentators discussing me:

'So the Zoya Factor seems to be in abeyance today, eh Beeru?' Jay asked brightly.

'That's right,' Beeru nodded. 'Zoya's not well.'

Jay acted all fakely concerned. 'Yes, I believe she has an infectious bug?'

'That's right, but don't let your hopes soar too high, Jay. Besides, the doctors say Zoya will be fine day after tomorrow.'

Jay made a wry face and tried to say something but Beeru cut him off by saying playfully, 'She went pubbing with some of your players a couple of nights back. So...was there any sabotaging you want to tell us about?'

Jay looked pained at this. 'Scurrilous slander,' he said laconically. 'Vicious rumours.'

Beeru laughed. 'Vul, if India win today, Jay, at least you lot can't whine about unfair tactics or Indian black magic.'

Jay smirked good-naturedly. 'We were gonna win this match

anyway,' he said. 'Only thing is, now you have a good excuse for losing.'

Beeru snorted and before he could say anything, Jay smoothly said, 'And here's the pitch report straight from Woolloongabba!' And they cut to the stadium, where the burly looking groundsman was standing with the other anchor, examining the pitch. It was a good pitch, apparently, which would hold up well and not deteriorate and provide a lot of spin, whatever that meant. According to the weather report we could expect warm sunny skies and clear weather, with a maximum temperature of 37 degrees. And then it was time for the toss.

Khoda sauntered in with the chubby-cheeked Aussie captain. He asked for heads and the umpire tossed.

And for the second time during that World Cup, Nikhil Khoda lost the toss.

Hah!

The great Indian Crab Mentality surfaced in my heart, but only half-heartedly. Khoda looked pretty unaffected though, and when the Aussie captain said he wanted to bat first, he told the umpire he'd been looking to field first, anyway. Then they sauntered off and after a short ad break, in which I swallowed my antibiotics and found a whole roll of toilet paper to blow my nose into, the Aussie openers came out to bat.

They hit the ground running. The ground blazed with boundaries in every direction, fours and sixes reigned and the Aussie supporters went nuts cheering. Thind and Zahid tried to stem the flow valiantly but by the time fifteen overs were done the Aussies were 122 for no loss.

'At this run rate they'll close at almost 500,' Rinku Chachi said despondently, looking up from her phone calculator. 'Oh Zoya, beta, get well soon!'

I nodded irritably. My head was splitting, my eyes were watering and I think the flu had somehow affected my heart's functioning – I found I actually sort of almost wanted India to win. Without me. Really. I'd become noble overnight. I said crossly, 'Oh, don't be silly, Chachi. Nikhil *sambhal lega*. He'll do something. There's a long way to go yet, you know!'

On the field Nikhil was scowling and getting his boys into a huddle, his eyes blazing. The commentators, Jay and Beeru, were of course thrilled with the competitive cricket on display and insisted that it was all because I wasn't there.

'That's the trouble with depending on lucky charms, Beeru,' Jay said, a little pompously. 'You lose faith in yourself. This hardly looks like the same side that decimated West Indies four days ago. It's pathetic.'

'I think you're right, my friend,' Beeru said sombrely. 'The Indians are looking sadly at sea. Their ship is pitching and rolling and Nikhil Khoda seems to have lost his compass.'

'You're very nautical today, Beeru. What's up?' Jay asked.

Beeru sighed. 'I've just got a sinking feeling, that's all,' he said.

Get lost, Beeru, I thought, blowing my nose so hard that my eyes started to water. *You don't know your ass from a hole in a sambar vada. The boys will pull it together. They will. They will.*

And surprisingly enough, they did. Right after the break for drinks, Khoda shifted the field around and put hairy-baby Vikram Goyal in and he proved to be awesome. He contained the Aussies brilliantly and then Zahid took two wickets in quick succession. Balaji came in for a short but effective spell and then Harry did some hardcore unsubtle bowling and picked up a couple of wickets too. Suddenly, the Aussies were 181 for five in thirty overs. Pretty soon it got so bad the Aussie crowd started leaving, but it could've just been because prime sunbathing time was over.

I abruptly stopped feeling noble and started feeling awful that India may actually win without me. The speed with which I was switching sides was making me giddy.

Meanwhile Jay and Beeru were doing some quick backtracking:

'Yes, well, I did think they wouldn't be able to maintain that pace for long...' Jay said shamelessly.

Rinku Chachi snorted. 'Look at how they are licking up after spitting!' she said. 'I'm going to the loo, beta.'

The Aussies were all out for 223, their lowest in this World Cup, and the ad break had begun.

We ordered lunch and sat down in front of the telly again fifteen minutes later.

The panel with Jay and Beeru was back and Beeru was gloating shamelessly. 'What happened, Jay?' he crowed. 'What was that fall-down effect we just saw, eh?'

Jay put up a spirited defence but his heart wasn't in it. 'Lots of cricket left in the game, mate,' he said doggedly. 'That pitch is turning something wicked. Wait and watch.'

So we all watched as Harry and Shivnath strutted out cockily and took their place on the pitch. They got off to a solid start, piling up runs steadily. There was no hurry, of course, the required run rate was an easy 4.1 and getting lower with every delivery bowled.

They kept cutting to Khoda in the players' balcony and I couldn't understand why he was scowling so awfully, waving a red plastic stick with his hands. With a pang of regret I recognized the back-scratcher-cum-fly-swatter we'd bought together. Wes looked pretty worried next to him.

'Good performance by India today,' said Jay grudgingly as the camera zoomed in on Nikhil till we could see the stubble on his jaw in gorgeous detail. 'Young Nick Khoda found his compass again, what do you say, Beeru?'

'Or else he's steering by the stars, Jay,' said Beeru. 'He keeps looking at the sky all the time!'

Then a runner came on to the field with water for Harry and he clearly said something to him.

'Now what could that be about?' Jay said.

And Beeru responded, 'I think he's telling them to step up the run rate because he's worried about rain...'

The camera cut to Khoda and sure enough he was frowning up at the sky. With good reason. Grey clouds loomed over the Gabba.

'Oh no,' Rinku Chachi groaned and grabbed her phone calculator. 'Oh no! *Hai Ram!*'

'What?' I asked blankly. 'We're going to win, aren't we?'

And then she told me that if it started raining now and the match had to be stopped after fifteen overs, they'd count it as a whole match. 'It's that bakwaas Duckworth-Lewis system,' she told me. 'When a match is interrupted by rain, they'll compare our score at fifteen or twenty-five or thirty-five overs and *their* score at fifteen, twenty-five or thirty-five overs, and award the match to whoever was doing better at that point. And that, most probably, will be –'

'– Australia,' I said. My heart sank to my toes and then bobbed up again slowly.

They're going to lose, a little crab voice in my head whispered gleefully. *You're safe.* Basically, Harry and Shivee had to take us to 122 in 15 overs. But it was going to be tough.

'Besides, it may not rain after all, you know,' Rinku Chachi said. 'Nikhil is only anticipating every possibility. Or maybe it will rain just a little and they'll continue play after a while...'

But, then, when they were 99 for thirteen overs, there was a flash of lightning and fat drops of rain started to fall. They kept playing, however. Jay told the viewers that the raindrops looked bigger on TV than they actually were, as the camera lens magnified them. In fact, it was really just a tiny drizzle. But the Aussie captain was going for the jugular. He was splurging all ten overs of the Punjab Kings XI star, Kevin 'Butch' Astle, on this bit of the game. The boys struggled to take it up to 117 in fourteen overs, 121 in fifteen and 130 in sixteen. Then the rain stopped, a bit of sunshine peeped through, and we all relaxed a bit. The required run rate, if a whole match was played, was only two point something.

'Maybe India will get lucky after all!' Beeru sounded exultant, but he spoke too soon. Because the cosmos, as Lingnath Baba would say, has its own sublime, immutable, incomprehensible logic. As Butch started his run-up for the first delivery of his last over, the rain lashed down with a vengeance. Huge fat drops practically obscured the players from our view as they made a dash for the pavilion. On the players' balcony, Nikhil Khoda threw down the back-scratcher-cum-fly-swatter and stalked into the dressing room, his face like thunder.

Meanwhile, Jay and Beeru went on to say, 'What bad luck! Brisbane never has rain at this time of the year. What bad luck, what bad luck, what bad luck...'

I should've been there for breakfast, I castigated myself self-importantly, quite enjoying the feeling of having been proved indispensable, again. *I should've worn a plastic sack or something and just gone.*

Then the anchor, reporting live from the field, grabbed

Nikhil in the pavilion and shoved a mike in his face. 'Do you think you had bad luck today because of the Zoya Factor?' he yelled above the sounds of lashing rain.

Nikhil shook his head. 'No,' he said steadily. 'We failed to anticipate the weather collapse early enough, that's all.'

That hit me so hard in my smug little gut, I almost threw up. The sense of not being needed, of not being missed was dreadful. *How could he anticipate a freak cloudburst?* I thought savagely. *How can he talk about me so dismissively? Doesn't he care about me at all?*

I got up blunderingly, grabbed my wad of tissues and rushed out to the balcony to cry in the rain.

'*Fuck*worth-bloody-Lewis!' said Rinku Chachi with feeling.

The anticlimax was depressing. We'd all been hoping India would win this match and be clear till the semis so we could all relax for the next week. But that was not to be. The balding doc came to see me again in the evening and declared me well on the path to recovery. Then, around ten o' clock at night, when Rinku Chachi went into the loo for a long shower, I had the most unexpected guest.

I got a call from Reception. 'Ma'am, there's a gentleman to see you.'

Nikhil!

'I can't see anybody,' I said, 'I'm infectious, but please give him the phone.'

'Ma'am, he says he wants to come up and see you in person.'

'Huh? Okay...' I said, hesitantly. 'Send him up.'

Maybe it wasn't Nikhil. Maybe Lokey was there to inform me that the Sheraan-wali offer had gone up in smoke.

But it was neither.

Clad in three delicious shades of saffron, tinkling gently with various charms and amulets, his hairy halo aglow, Swami Lingnath Baba stood in the doorway, smiling benignly. 'Can we enter?' he asked, pinning me with his hypnotic eyes.

'Uh...sure,' I said. The fever had left me a little weak and the strong waft of incense emanating from him dissolved whatever little opposition I might have put up. I sat down on the sofa and looked at him blankly. 'Uh...should you not be at your ashram in Tundla?' I asked.

He made a graceful sweeping gesture with one hand.

'The world is a small place...' he said, weighing every word. Then he made a sudden forward movement and I jumped back, startled. 'You are still indisposed, Devi?' he asked as he grabbed my wrist, only to take my pulse, I realized after a moment with relief.

His hand felt cool and dry. *No need to panic...yet*, I thought. 'Yes,' I told him. 'But the doctor says I should be well enough for the next match.'

Lingnath nodded. 'That is well. Your gracious hand should *always* be hovering in blessing above the heads of our team.'

My gracious hand was twitching to slap him at that moment. I controlled the impulse and said dismissively, if not completely truthfully, 'No, no, I don't believe in this superstitious nonsense.'

'No?' Lingnath raised both eyebrows in gentle surprise.

'Even when today, the heavens themselves wept because you broke your breakfast appointment?'

'It rained, okay?' I said, blowing my nose. 'The heavens did not *weep!* And, for your information, the Aussie sportscasters have been calling them "showers of blessing". Now I've been advised total bedrest you know, so...'

'Of course, of course,' said Lingnath, getting to his feet gently and reaching into the deep pocket of his saffron choga.

'We had come only to give you some medicine to make you well.'

I looked at him in horrid fascination, fully expecting him to produce some crumpled little paper parcel full of human ash, or dried cow dung, or something. Instead, he pulled out a crisp silver strip of multivitamin tablets from his pocket and handed it to me. 'From Dieter,' he said. 'He was bringing them but we offered to deliver them ourselves.'

'Thank you,' I said shortly.

'We wished to see you in person...' He patted me on my head.

'I'm flattered,' I said.

'So that we could beseech you to stay vigilant in your post as the celestial guardian who will lead our team to victory.'

Vigilant celestial guardian? He made me feel like an antiperspirant. 'Okay,' I said blankly.

He waggled his ringed fingers before me. 'Forces of darkness are gathering around you,' he said sonorously. 'Pressure is building. I see much conflict ahead. Stand strong, Devi!'

'Okay, cool, I will,' I assured him. Then I asked 'Uh... Baba...?'

'Yes yes, speak,' he said, encouraging me on.

'Somebody told me that if I give all my good luck to the team, I'll be left with only bad luck in my personal life,' I said in a rush. (I couldn't believe I was sharing my fears with a god-man.)

He gave a hacking little laugh, took a deep breath, made mystical snatching hand gestures in the air and said splendidly: 'Balance is what keeps the cosmos in motion, Devi.'

The next morning a letter was delivered to me. I opened the letter and sneaked into the loo to read it:

Zoya,

     As you won't take my calls, and may infect me with the flu if I drop in uninvited, I've decided the only way to get through to you is to write. How are you? Dieter tells me you'll be well in a couple of days, definitely well enough to make the breakfast before the Pakistan match, for which I'm really thankful. But what I really want to know is, are you well enough to see me today? If your doctor okays it, can you meet me at your hotel gym at ten o' clock tonight? That shouldn't be too strenuous.

     Message me if you can't make it.

     Nikhil

The doc said I wasn't infectious any more and told me to just keep taking the multivits Dieter had sent me, as they'd keep my immunity up. 'But be very careful with your health now, Zoya,' he warned. 'You're a precious commodity at the moment, eh?'

Ya, ya, whatever. I stole a look at Rinku Chachi and asked him casually, 'I was thinking I might walk the treadmill in the evenings and do a light workout now and then...'

'Sounds good,' he nodded. 'Just be careful not to overexert yourself and give me a call if you feel at all sick, you hear?'

I promised him I would, and when he left, I peeped into Mon's room to borrow suitable sporty attire.

'What's with you?' she asked bluntly, lighting a cigarette. 'Exercise *aur kya kya?*'

I laughed and plonked down on her bed. 'Monita, you are my best friend in the whole world,' I said dreamily.

'Zoya,' she said, 'I'm very touched that you want to enact this princess-in-her-palace-amongst-her-confidantes scene with me, but it won't work if you don't *confide*. What's up with you, brat?'

I shook my head. 'Nothing! What's up with you? I've been ignoring you and the Monster so much lately.'

'You've been sick,' she pointed out, flicking ash into a matchbox. 'I'm fine. I talk to Aman daily, he doesn't seem to be missing me in the slightest, which is breaking my heart a little, I'll admit.'

'And Anand?' I asked, thinking of her extremely-hot-in-a-fair-sanitized-banker-sort-of-way husband. 'Did you tell him about our girls' night out?'

She laughed a gurgling, deep-throated laugh. 'Yes. He was furious when he got his credit card statement for the month. He wanted to know why I was trying to turn the balance of payments between India and Australia upside down.'

'D'you miss him?' I asked, turning over onto my stomach, cupping my chin in my hand and looking at her intently.

She pushed some hair off my forehead. 'Yes,' she said simply. 'Of course I do.'

'So...'

'So, why one month away from him? Well, the financial year has come to an end so he's super busy and the kindest thing I could do was just keep out of his way. I'm bonding so much with Armaan though, he's been neglected so much because of work and his little brother, the poor baby...'

The poor baby was having a rocking time in the loo. We could hear him from the bed, splashing around and shouting, 'Shark! Shark! *Ha Ha! Khooni* Shark,' to the Barbies-in-bikinis he kept in the bathtub.

'But what's with the gymming?' Mon asked me. 'What's up with you?'

So I told her the whole sequence of events – Zoravar warning me against celebrity cricketer types, my conversation with Nikhil, and the fact that he'd now written me a note and wanted to meet me tonight. She pushed away the note I'd been trying to show her and looked at me in disbelief.

'Is *that* why you two haven't been talking?' she asked, in total disgust. She scanned the note briefly and chucked it aside. 'Zoya, you're one dumb choot.'

'Why?' I asked belligerently.

'I thought Nikhil was smarter but I have to say that he's one dumb choot too!' Mon leapt off the bed and starting pacing up and down the room, making an abrupt about-turn when she reached a wall. 'This whole concept of breaking people up into bits and pieces is totally chootiya-matic! "You love me because I'm *lucky*." "You love me because I'm a *captain*." It's such self-indulgent crap! It's like me saying, "Oh no, Anand only loves me because my boobs are so big! Hmmm...now would he have loved me so much if they were smaller? Oh! Oh! Not knowing will drive me insane! I will have to kill myself!"' She arched her wrist against her forehead in the classic tragedy queen pose of the fifties and glared at me.

I blinked.

But there was more to come.

'Look, being captain is part of who he is. And being lucky is part of who you are. Just leave it at that.' Mon stubbed out her cigarette with one shaking hand and said, 'The guy cares about you, period. I was watching his face when you were bitchy in the restaurant and it crumpled like Aman's did when he scrambled onto my lap and realized I was serious about weaning him. Why would he react like that if he's just after your' – she made a large vague gesture in the air – 'Luck?'

'But maybe he's just saying that now,' I said, backing away as I spoke. 'Maybe he'll change his tune when the World Cup's over.'

'Fair enough,' Monita said, sitting down on the bed again. 'I'm not saying that isn't a possibility. But look, you have to go out on a limb a bit here. Don't you think he's worth it?'

'No one's worth my self-respect,' I muttered.

Mon sighed. 'You're just saying that because you've been hurt before. But that doesn't mean you should harden your heart, Zoya.'

Hurt before? Hello, that was the understatement of the century. I'd felt like a piece of used toilet paper by the time my second boyfriend had finished with me.

Mon said urgently, slapping me on the elbow, 'Listen, if you don't stand by him now, when he needs you the most, he may hold that against you later.'

I looked up, dismayed. I hadn't thought of that.

Mon said, very seriously, no hint of laughter in her eyes even though her words were pretty corny, 'His feelings for you will be tested later. But yours for him are being tested right now.'

'Oh please!' I said. 'That's just a twisted version of "sleep with me now to prove how much you love me and then I'll marry you afterwards".'

Mon shrugged. 'What's wrong with that?' she said. 'That happened with Anand and me, you know.'

Oh thanks, Monita. Now I feel like a totally prudish Karol Bagh type. 'But what about his countless conquests?' I demanded.

Mon shrugged impatiently, 'What, you want to end up with some loser "virgin type"?' she snapped. 'And, anyway, it could be worse. Imagine if you were up against one serious girlfriend rather than a gaggle he doesn't really care about?'

I shook my head in disbelief. Didn't she get it? I was obviously just another girl in the gaggle to him. Even if it wasn't my luck

he was after, maybe he was just in it for sheer variety. As in, *I'm
so tired of beautiful babes. Lemme date someone plain and see
what that feels like.*

Mon said doggedly, 'You're *not* one of a gaggle. You're the
special someone he's been waiting for all his life.'

'You're mad,' I told her frankly.

'I'm a romantic,' she said. 'You should be too.'

'Okay, okay,' I said, plucking my letter out of her hands. 'So
you recommend I stop splitting hairs and swing into support-
mode as far as Nikhil Khoda is concerned, and hope for him
not to change his tune in case we lose or in case we win and he
finds he doesn't need me any more?'

It was a hard speech to keep track of, but Monita stayed
with me. 'That's right,' she said, nodding firmly. 'In agony-
aunt-speak, Zo, you're not going to know whether he needs
you *because* he loves you or he loves you *because* he needs you
till after this shindig is over. That's not too long to wait, is it?
Hey, at least you won't have to get a double mastectomy to
find out if his love is true! Just trust in him and hope for the
best.'

I nodded, smoothed out the note and read it again. 'It's
pretty businesslike, isn't it?' I asked nervously, shaking it in front
of her face.

Mon shrugged. 'He wants to meet you. Just take it from
there.'

'So...I should kiss him, right?' I asked, just to be clear on
this vital point.

Mon made an extravagant sweeping gesture with her hands.
'By all means.'

'What else should I do?' I asked eagerly.

'Anyth –' Her face crumpled suddenly. 'Oh shit, I'm supposed to be your chaperone! Oh God, your dad! Zo, don't you dare do more than kiss him, okay?'

That night I had a bad attack of oh-my-God-I-look-ugly-in-whatever-I-wear, changed my clothes a million times and didn't get down to the gym till twenty past ten. It took me a while to find, and a sign saying that the gym timings were from 8 a.m. to 8 p.m. almost put me off, but then I saw that the door was ajar. I pushed it open and stuck my head in.

Nikhil was sitting at some strange-looking machine, doing some strange-looking exercises. He saw me in the mirror and kind of went 'hi' without smiling, so I walked in slowly and peered down at him. 'What are you doing?' I asked curiously.

'What does it look like?' he said irritably, panting a little between repetitions. 'I figured if you weren't coming at least I wouldn't miss my workout.' He released his grip on the contraption with a slight groan and all these silver coloured weights slid smoothly down to the base. He got up from the machine, wiped the back of his neck with a towel and headed purposefully for another strange-looking machine, without even looking at me.

I trailed behind him, not quite knowing what to do. *Sports quota type,* I thought resentfully. He looked like he might bite my head off if I tried to apologize.

Nikhil sat on the contraption, and started curling his legs up backward, from the knee. Huge stacks of silver coloured weights moved smoothly up and down again.

'I've come from across town, Zoya,' he said exasperatedly, a little later. 'You *live* here.'

Instead of just apologizing like a normal person, I was contrary enough to mutter, 'It's harder to be on time when you're close by. You keep thinking *ki* you've got time, it's right here, it'll just take a minute and then you get late. And then when I reached I got confused because the sign outside said this place is closed.'

He stopped pumping iron long enough to give me a sour look. 'I got special permission to keep it open late,' he said briefly. 'So I could meet you.'

'Oh.'

He shook his head at me and moved onto a third machine.

'So...how long will you take to finish now?' I asked, trailing behind him again.

'Seventy-five minutes,' he said briefly. 'You could go back up to your room if you like.'

Of course I didn't want to go up to my room. I was all primed for our big reconciliation. 'It's okay,' I said, settling down on the padded sound-and-shock-absorbing floor. 'I'll wait.'

He nodded curtly and went back to his workout.

I looked around the gym curiously. It was all gleaming steel-and-matte black, just like the set we'd used for a Diet *Zing!* still shoot last year. There were some body-building magazines lying around, so I flipped through them, looking at ads for bulk-building steroids featuring booby guys in tiny chaddis with *humongous* muscles all over their bodies. *They look so gross, Nikhil looks way better than any of them*, I thought, looking at him sideways through my lashes so he wouldn't notice. He was scowling at the TV screen above him, oblivious to my gaze, so I rolled onto my stomach, cupped my chin in my hands, and ogled him shamelessly.

The cool thing about Nikhil Khoda, I mused as I ran my eyes over his lean, toffee-coloured torso in its clinging white ganji, *is that he doesn't try*. He looked around then, so I yawned quickly,

turned my back on him deliberately and pretended to read. I
didn't turn around again till I heard all the stacked weights slide
down to the base of the machine with a clatter, a good fifty
minutes later.

He looked across the room at me and said, still sounding
pretty pissed off, 'I'll shower and be with you in five minutes,
okay?'

'Okay,' I said equally coolly, even though I was quaking
inside.

I wandered around the gym, then sat down on a complicated-
looking cycle and frowned at myself in the glass. *He must want
to make up, otherwise why'd he call me here? It couldn't be
anything else, could it? Could it?*

I was still on the cycle when he came out, dressed in his
usual grey tracks, his hair sleek and gleaming, his expression
unreadable. I raised my chin and met his eyes in the mirror as
he sauntered over.

'So,' I said a little too loudly, 'what did you want to talk to me
about?' It came out sounding a little cockier than I'd intended
but the long wait in the gym had made me jumpy.

Any hopes I'd had of a romantic reconciliation and mad
passionate love-making amongst all the kinky steel machines
went clean out of the window when he said, 'Have you *seen* that
agarbatti script Lokey's mailed for you?'

'What?' Then realization dawned on me. 'Oh. *That.*'

So that was what he wanted to talk to me about. Tauji's
Sheraan-wali ad.

'Yes, that,' Nikhil said. 'Whatever happened to "Cricket is so
uncool and I don't want any mileage out of it"?'

He was playing back what I'd said to him in my hotel room
in Dhaka, I realized. Damn, he really did remember everything
I'd ever said to him.

He sounded like he hated me. And to think I'd rushed down here, tail wagging eagerly, thinking he wanted to smell the gun smoke in my hair. I tossed my head. 'I changed my mind,' I said nonchalantly. 'Anyway, who are you to talk? *You* endorse a million brands yourself, why shouldn't I?'

'Because it's being irresponsible,' he said. 'And untrue. Because it makes my team out to be eleven extras who just got lucky.'

'Sounds like a pretty authentic portrayal to me,' I said coolly, getting off the cycle so I could make a quick exit after delivering my knockout punch, which of course was: 'Hey, bad luck about the match today, by the way.'

He grabbed my arm then. 'You watch it,' he said warningly. 'Don't push me, Zoya, you don't want me to stop being your friend.'

'Well, you definitely aren't being very friendly!' I said, fighting back tears. 'You're cold and horrid all the time and honestly, all I want to do is help. If I do have something that gives you the edge, and it seems like I do, why are you being so proud about admitting that it's helping you to win?'

'Because I want to win fair and square,' he answered without hesitation, his eyes blazing. 'Not like this. Not because of some' – he flung his arms in the air – 'Voodoo goddess.'

'Oh, tell the truth,' I said nastily. 'It's not about fair play at all, it's just that you want to take all the credit.'

'Yes,' he snapped. 'I *want* all the credit. Because it's mine. It belongs to me and to all the boys, who've been sweating it out in seedy small-town stadiums ever since they were old enough to grasp a bat or ball, ever since they were old enough to dream.'

Oh great, he was in Nike-ad mode again. Honestly, he made it sound like all of them played for the love of India alone – not for pot-loads of money.

He was still hanging onto my arm, glaring at me, and all the disappointment of my stupid dashed hopes rushed to my head. 'So, I'm just to be a dirty little secret, then, is that it?' I flung rudely at him, thinking desperately that maybe if I were obnoxious enough this would build to that moment where, in any decent romantic movie, the guy grabs the girl with both arms and lays a strong masterful kiss upon her mouth. 'I've got to help you win and keep quiet about it?'

'No,' he said steadily. 'Ideally I would prefer it if you stopped coming to breakfast altogether. But, of course, both the team and the country will have a heart attack if you do. I'm just asking you to behave responsibly about the situation you find yourself in, that's all.'

I made a frustrated little noise in my throat at this typical Nikhil Khoda speech and, wrenching my arm out of his grasp, pushed my way out through the health club door.

Lingnath Baba had not been bullshitting. The forces of darkness were gathering. The mandatory articles pressing for re-examining the Duckworth-Lewis system made an appearance in the papers the next morning, of course, but they were pushed into relative obscurity by lengthy articles talking about how India had lost because their Lucky Charm took a day off, and how I was proving to be vital in this World Cup. The lunatic fringe of the Australian media, meanwhile, was baying for my blood with harsh headlines: 'It's Not Cricket', 'Go Home, Zoya – Level the Playing Field', 'Mighty Indians Hide Behind Girl'.

'You should make a scrapbook, Zoya,' said Rinku Chachi as she sifted through the papers complacently and sipped her coffee. 'So many pictures of you. And you are looking so pretty too!'

I looked up at her dementedly, my hair in my eyes. I'd woken up with a throbbing headache, thanks to Nikhil Khoda, and now I was faced with this. 'Chachi, don't you get it? It's bad press! They hate me, okay?'

She shrugged, 'Sticks and stones, Zoya beta,' she said soothingly. 'If the dogs are barking let them bark, what goes of yours if they get a sore throat?'

I shook my head in exasperation. She just didn't get it, did she?

'Besides,' she continued calmly, smoothing my hair back from my forehead, 'in India you are a heroine. Why don't you see what some Indian papers are saying about you, *hain*?'

Now *that* wasn't a bad idea! I skipped over to Mon's room and logged onto crickindiya.com on her laptop. A big fat picture of me smiled back at me from the home page. Pleasantly surprised, I clicked on an icon that said 'Zoya Solanki – Karishma or Coincidence?' and found thirty pages of comments!

- 'Of course Zoya Devi is a karishma and should be recognized as such. She has turned the fortunes of the country around. People who do not believe are fools, who would not believe in Bhagwan Krishna himself if he appeared, with a sudharshan chakra on his finger and the three worlds inside his mouth.'

- 'Ganesha statues don't really drink the milk, Mahim water is not really sweet, and Zoya Solanki is not a karishma but a coincidence. Instead of worshipping Zoya, we should be thanking Nikhil Khoda who's got the useless Indian team to finally perform.'

- 'Jogpal Lohia has prepared an army of eunuchs. A hijron ki baraat. They are all useless without this girl. They should all put on bangles and sit at home, rolling chapatis.'

• 'The blood of Robin Rawal, best batsman in India is on this so-called Zoya Devi's hands. Ban her.'

• 'There is no such thing as a coincidence. Zoyamata ki jai.'

• 'It was a black day for Indian cricket when Hharviinder Singh discovered Zoya's so-called luckiness. Our new team, never very strong to begin with, has now been weakened at its very core.'

• 'Aarti of Zoya Devi performed daily every morning and evening. For Zoya Devi amulet, saamagri and autographed photograph visit my website at www.Zoyadevikachamat kaariballa.com. All are welcome.'

• 'Zoya is nothing but the latest in a long line of Rajasthani girls who have been exploited by the male-oriented society since time immemorial. Her life is doomed to end in tragedy.'

• 'Jogpal Lohia is a cunning fox. He is preparing to make this poor girl a scapegoat if we lose the World Cup.'

• 'These things happen. My mother has a large mole on her right cheek. Whenever she massages it gently, India hits a boundary. It is the nazarbattoo, the black mark that repels the evil eye for all of India. My friend has a lucky pajama. Whenever he makes his drawstring loose, India loses a wicket. He sits tight and does not go to bathroom for whole day and then India wins the match. Jogpal Lohia should invite my friend and my mother to the World Cup.'

• 'What a joke. Atal Bihari Vajpayee was born on the twenty-fifth of December. Does that make him Jesus Christ?'

• 'Lakhs of rupees of taxpayers' money is being spent on entertaining this girl and all her family in Australia. That money could have been better spent on opening cricket academies for promising youngsters in Indian hinterland.'

• 'This whole thing is a match-fixing scam. The bookies are hyping up the Zoya Factor so that people will bet on India, then they will give our team money to lose and make a fortune.'

• 'Very soon Nikhil Khoda will be sacked and this girl – who cannot tell batsman from Batman – will become captain. Wah wah, mera Bhaarat mahaan. It happens only in India!'

• 'Nothing can be done for this country.'

It was like dipping your glass into a matka for a drink of cold water and pulling it out full of a million squirming snakelings instead. And these were just the first few pages. The ranting and raving and haranguing went on page after page after page. I kept scanning through them, looking for even *one* positive reasonable comment but I couldn't find any. It's not just Nikhil Khoda, I thought dementedly. Everybody hates me. Correction. Everybody hates me except the lunatics who *worship* me.

Lucky on the field. Unlucky off the field. Lingnath Baba was right. Balance is what kept the cosmos in motion, after all.

The boys gave me a rousing reception when I made an appearance at breakfast the next day. Zahid leapt up, pulled out a chair for me and dropped down on the one next to it, smilingly. 'It's too good to see you, Zoyaji,' he said sincerely. Everybody else chorused the same general emotion. Observing all of them carefully as I ate some fruit, I decided they really meant it. They didn't look like they hated me because I was responsible for them being called 'hijras' and 'credulous morons' on the World

Wide Web. Obviously, they were smart enough to avoid the comments pages on websites like crickindiya.com.

My heart rose to my mouth as Nikhil Khoda sauntered in and took his usual place at the top of the table. I took a deep steadying breath, held on hard to the edge of the table and risked a casual glance Khoda-ways. He was shovelling chunks of pineapple onto his plate as usual. He didn't look like he had read any of those vicious comments. Or, maybe, he just didn't give a damn about stuff like that. Nor did he look like the encounter in the gym was giving him sleepless nights.

Not me. I, of course, was feeling like something out of a Jogpal Lohia ballad. *I am a timid tremulous deer*, I thought dementedly, *wandering hither and thither, oh slay me with your lotus-eyes, my navy-blue hunter!*

I think he sensed I was looking at him, because he looked up just then and met my eyes quizzically. I flushed and got back to the slimy papaya slice on my plate.

'What's up, Zoya?' Hairy asked. 'Not feeling fully strong yet?'

'No, I'm fine…' I said. Then I asked, 'Hair…uh Harry, tell me, d'you read the newspapers nowadays?'

Hairy (*very* hairy, actually, he'd taken a vow not to shave till the World Cup was over) looked at me thoughtfully. 'Bhai, I *toh* don't read them, Zoya,' he said finally, one leg jittering under the table so hard the plates clattered up and down, up and down. 'But Shivee reads them every day.'

'*Mein bhi nahi padta*,' Zahid volunteered. 'I never read *anything* they write about me, unless Hardin-sir asks me to. It spoils your concentration.'

'What saala concentration?' said Shivee. (He had shaved his head the day we got into the Super 8; he was eschewing vanity, he'd told me solemnly.) 'If you're a mature, what everybody is saying won't affect your concentration.'

'So what are they saying, this everybody?' Zahid asked him belligerently.

Shivee started to answer but I broke in, 'Let's not go into all that now. I think Nikhil's ready to go.'

18

'It's India–Pakistan today!' Mon said dreamily as she threw an orange dupatta over her white kameez and green salwar. 'Drama, Tragedy, Emotion…twin siblings with bleeding umbilical cords, seeking closure, in love and death….Ahhhh…' She placed a blue bindi on her forehead and added, 'It's like *Deewar*, only better, because there's no Nirupa Roy.'

'*Arrey*, Monita, you are looking very decent,' Rinku Chachi pronounced as she bounced into Mon's room in her RINKU 10 tee shirt. '*Hain na*, Zoya?'

I nodded yes, while Mon looked at Chachi like she couldn't decide whether to be flattered or insulted. 'Thanks, Rinku,' she said finally, turning to daub large quantities of orange and white face paint on Armaan's cheeks before clamping a jauntily angled Men in Blue cap on his head. 'Let's go, guys,' she said, standing back to survey her handiwork critically. 'I don't want to miss a moment of this.'

We'd flown back to Melbourne for this match. Security had been beefed up at the MCG and the stadium, which can seat up to one lakh people, was sold out. The members' enclosure was packed. A whole contingent of Indian page-3 celebrities had flown in for this last leg of the World Cup and they'd bagged all the best seats. The air was redolent with their tinkling laughter and expensive perfumes. Mon marched purposefully past some lesser Khans and stopped before a gaggle of Bollywood starlets. 'Do you mind?' she said sweetly. 'These are *Zoya's* seats.'

It was the most embarrassing moment of my life! I wanted the earth to swallow me up. No, I wanted the earth to swallow *her* up, the silly lid.

The starlets got all gushy and excited. 'Hey, look, Zoya!' they yelled to the lesser Khans who rushed up to me in a whirl of stubble and sunglasses and started introducing themselves. The girls moved quite willingly to make place for us. The only person who found this exciting was Armaan who was thrilled to have all this firm cool female flesh pressing against him suddenly. He dropped and picked his Beyblade to his heart's content, *and* got to see the whole match ensconced happily in the godi of a hot little starlet who wanted to show her date how maternal she was, really, in spite of her D&G mini-skirted exterior.

We had all settled down and the commentators had just announced that the captains were coming out for the toss when I got this massive attack of nerves. I was suddenly absolutely sure something awful was going to happen. I just knew it somehow. It was divine retribution for having been nasty to Nikhil. Regardless of what he had said to me that evening, the truth of the matter was that he had reached out to me after an awful day that had ended in defeat and what he had got in return was a whole lot of attitude. It was hardly the unconditional support he'd told me he had been looking for.

I concealed my unease as well as I could as we watched the burly, round-shouldered Paki captain push back his dark green cap, scratch his beard and reckon he'd take heads. Khoda shrugged and the umpire flipped the coin up in the air. It seemed to take forever to land today, and my heart beat so loudly I expected people to turn around and go *shush* at me but they didn't.

'Tails it is,' the umpire announced finally and Nikhil said he'd field first and they both strolled back to the pavilion together.

Mon stole a look at me. 'What?' I asked irritably.

'Nothing,' she said. 'You wanna let go of my arm?'

I uncurled my fingers from her wrist. There were huge red welts right around it. 'Shit, sorry, Mon,' I said.

'Quit worrying, Zoya,' she said, hugging me. 'You can't do anything now, just sit back and enjoy the game.'

I nodded and sat back waiting for the bomb to explode.

The stadium looked like a massive inverted hemisphere of the earth itself, part blue and part green. There were continents of Pakistani supporters in dark green, suspended in a rippling ocean of light blue Indians, all screaming their lungs out.

The crowd was heckling the fielders in the outfield shamelessly, hissing and hooting. Thind was foolish enough to do a couple of side bends and squats to stretch his muscles and had to endure a Mexican wave of dark-green figures copying him one after the other – bending, squatting, bending again, and then letting out a huge farty raspberry at the end of the second squat. The cheering began every time an Indian bowler began his run up, paused reverentially as the batsman thwacked the ball away and rose to a deafening roar as the ball raced across the pitch and anywhere close to the boundary.

'They're cheering singles like they are sixes!' Rinku Chachi yelled to me over the din. 'What will they do when they *really* hit a six?'

We knew soon enough. Their fancy-boy opener hit a mighty

six and the crowd combusted. The drumming, the synchronized clapping and war-cry-like chanting felt like we were on a battlefield.

'Amazing how they don't get intimidated,' Mon said, peering out at Nikhil on the field. He was chewing gum and squinting in the sun looking as if he were waiting for a bus.

Must be seeing only thee eye of thee cupboard, I thought slightly hysterically and got up to get myself a drink, deciding that the only way to get through this match without becoming a gibbering wreck was to get systematically sloshed. So I piled on the Victoria Bitter and totally surrendered to the excitement on the field. I cheered and whooped and screamed like a crazed person. Luckily, I was wearing a body suit over my shorts or I'd have probably ripped off my shirt and whirled it over my head.

At one point Mon had to pull me down and hush me because I'd stood up and started yelling: '*Allah-hoo-Akbar*' at the top of my voice.

'Zoya, what are you *doing*? They'll think you're making *fun*,' she hissed in my ear so I covered my mouth with my hands, slightly bewildered. I'd just been trying to show some sporting spirit. Then I took it upon myself to teach the names of the fielding positions to the starlet closest to me. I pulled out a ball point pen and started drawing a neatly labelled cricket pitch on the bare back of the gay designer dude sitting in front of me. He turned around and gave me a smacking kiss on the mouth and said that he was a huge fan of mine. Obviously, I was not the only drunk person in the stands.

When the umpire rejected Balaji's appeal I leapt to my feet and showed him both my middle fingers and the camera crew caught me doing it and beamed my image on the giant stadium screens...

The Bollywood starlets were looking at me in delicate horror, even as they whipped out their cellphones and started taking videos of Zoya Devi smashed out of her skull.

And that's when a totally mortified Rinku Chachi dragged me out onto the steps and hissed, 'Stop it, Zoya! If you have no shame for yourself, have some shame for your papa's sake!'

That rebuke should've sobered me up, I suppose, but I don't know if it did.

Anyway, I allowed her to take me to the loo where I threw up huge quantities of undigested beer, washed my face and combed out my dishevelled hair. Then she made me drink a whole bottle of Aquafina and led me back to my seat through the row of starlets with a grim smile plastered on her face, muttering under her breath, 'Behave yourself now or I'll break both your legs.'

During all this commotion, Pakistan had been hammering away steadily, their bearded, gargantuan captain leading from the front as usual. They finished at 330 for seven.

Of course I had a raging headache by the time the Indians came out to bat. The cheers were totally deafening now, the so-called classy people in the members' enclosure were behaving no better than the rowdies in Bay 13 of the MCG, which is famous for its disorderly conduct. I pressed a chilled can of Zing! to my throbbing forehead and wished I'd stayed at the hotel after all.

The boys seemed to be doing okay, sticking to the required run rate and appearing quite relaxed. The Pakistanis looked tense though; their *poishun* was not very good at the moment. They still had to win two more matches if they wanted to make the semis and they only had three left to play. Their wicketkeeper, a wiry little guy with loads of attitude, kept dancing from foot to foot and goading the bowlers, in a voice that was beginning to sound just a little bit hysterical. And that's when the first little incident happened.

Shivee suddenly turned around and glared at the wicketkeeper murderously.

The crowd was immediately caught up in the action. 'And there seems to be bit of sledging being alleged there if I'm not mistaken,' the commentator said. 'Shivnath's looking upset…'

'I don't really think that could've happened, Beeru,' Jay said confidently. 'The mikes would've picked it up.'

Whatever it was, it got smoothed over quickly and play resumed. The commentators remarked that this was probably one rare occasion when the ICC had appointed both non-Hindi/Urdu-speaking umpires in an India–Pakistan match.

'Umpire Patil is of Indian origin, but he's born and brought up in England,' Beeru informed us. 'He claims to be Hindi-speaking but honestly, his Hindi is no better than yours, Jay.'

I took this to mean that the wicketkeeper could keep spouting mother-sister *ka* abuses to the batsmen and the dudes in the Fly Emirates shirts would never know.

The openers gave us a good start nonetheless and when Laakhi and Khoda finally came on we were 133 for two in seventeen overs, which wasn't bad at all. I finally allowed myself to relax; even my headache eased a bit.

It helped that the starlet next to me was a sighing sticky little bundle, seriously in lust with Khoda. She grabbed my arm the moment he strolled out, swinging his bat and squinting in the sunshine, acknowledging the roar of the crowd with a quick grin.

'He is so hot!' she sighed, squeezing my arm hard. 'He looks like a gladiator, like a king, like God.'

Mon gave her an old-fashioned look. 'Only God looks like God,' she said mildly.

'Oh, I know,' gushed the starlet. 'But he's totally the hottest guy on the team, don't you think?'

'Oh, d'you think so?' I burped politely. 'Zahid's pretty hot.'

The starlet dismissed Zahid with a wave of her hand. 'Zahid's just a boy,' she said, like she chewed and spat out boys like him for brunch. 'Nikhil's a *man*. See how strong his jaw is? And he looks so intense – like he'd let you flirt with other guys all evening and then' – she sighed – 'and then take you home and make violent, passionate love to you and show you who the boss is.'

Mon and I stared at each other, absolutely gobsmacked. We were both reeling under this vision of Nikhil as a bodice-ripping, sari-utaaro demon lover. 'Uh,' Mon coughed. 'Yes...he does look like...a...er *man*. What do you think, Zoya?'

The starlet turned to look at me eagerly. 'Don't you think he's a VPL type? You know, a Violent Passionate Lover?'

'Oh, I don't know,' I said, rather viciously, I must admit. 'Doesn't VPL stand for Visible Panty Line? I think I can see *his* through those horrible blue track pants, actually.'

The starlet let out a half-outraged scream of laughter at this. And right away Mon giggled as Nikhil ran down the pitch with his bat out, 'A VPL with a big *bat*.'

This got everybody giggling and then the bare-backed designer dude cleared his throat authoritatively. 'Sorry to break your hearts, dearies,' he said cosily, 'but I happen to know for a fact that most cricketers don't *have* willies. All they've got is *willows*.'

And so then all of us got into this discussion about whether all batsmen were compensating for something. And while we were all giggling over this, it happened again. Nikhil suddenly stopped play by walking up to the umpire and saying something to him.

'What's happening out there, Beeru?' Jay said. 'It's not like Nick Khoda to disrupt the game like this.'

'You're right, Jay,' Beeru said. 'You know, I have half a notion it's sledging again.'

The mikes couldn't pick up the conversation at all, but the umpire seemed to be wagging his finger, while the Pakistani wicketkeeper made open-handed shrugging gestures, seemingly protesting his innocence. The crowd-monster hissed and booed. Play resumed and the mood lightened when Nikhil – his jaw set and that familiar Boost-ad-gleam in his eyes – flicked the very next delivery away for an arrogant four. The crowd went berserk. Cries of *India! India!* rent the air.

The next delivery was no better and Khoda and Laakhi ended up making seventeen runs in that particular over. The crowd erupted, cheering ecstatically. The lesser Khans broke into a wild jig. One of them yelled, 'Death to Paki scum,' and had to be gagged and sat upon.

'Well, that seems to have backfired on Pakistan somewhat, don't you think, Beeru?'

'Absolutely, these two are mature players, Jay. Such tactics would only goad them to lift their game…'

The Pakistan captain seemed to think the same. He clapped his hands, gathered his boys around him, and gave them a tongue-lashing. Meanwhile, Laakhi yawned and spat. At the other end, Nikhil Khoda leaned on his bat, panting slightly with a fuck-you grin on his face. They did manage to get Laakhi out, finally, but not before he'd made 64 runs.

Zahid came in to bat then and that's when things got ugly.

The Paki wicketkeeper was definitely up to something. He was a tiny guy, but cocky. Apparently, he had a history of being obnoxious.

'That guy's a class act,' I heard one of the lesser Khans say to his buddies. 'I've studied him over the years, dude. He makes an *art* out of figuring out people's insecurities and baiting them when they come out to play. *Pitega ek din.*'

Well, he'd definitely said something that had enraged Zahid. He was looking positively murderous. I remembered what he'd told me about using the crowd's hostility to fuel his performance and I hoped that was what he'd do now.

During the break the umpires called in both skippers and said that any more sledging would cause them to dock runs from the total of the side that was misbehaving. Everybody nodded in a most civilized way and the game resumed. India was at 263, just 68 runs away from an assured place in the semis. The match rolled on, Nikhil and Zahid piled up runs steadily with ease. The Pakis looked desperate. Their pretty-boy bowlers flicked their stylishly cut hair out of their eyes nervously, spat on the ball and rubbed it against their thighs compulsively, hurling it like a lit bomb upon the pitch again and again – it proved ineffectual.

'Yes, the match definitely seems to be slipping away from Pakistan now. Jay, what d'you say?'

'Well, I have to agree with you there, Beeru. A score of 331 seemed like a mountain of a total this morning, but India have made it look like a molehill.'

'Vul, traditionally India–Pakistan matches are very high-scoring, and this has proved to be no exception. And there's the 300 coming up now, Jay, unless I'm very much mistaken.'

He wasn't. Khoda had eased it away for a four through the

slips and India were 302 for three. He got run out a little after that. He'd whacked the ball away and charged down the pitch even as Zahid yelled at him to stay put above the roar of the crowd. Khoda turned around, his bat out, but one of the pretty-boy bowlers got the stumps with a direct hit. There was a terrible cracking sound as the middle stump broke cleanly into two. The Pakis leaped up into the air and the blazing look went out of Nikhil's eyes. He stopped to talk to Zahid on the way back, and seemed to be telling him something intensely. Zahid nodded, looking somewhat sullen, and Khoda slapped him on the back encouragingly and walked back to the pavilion. He got a standing ovation, but I honestly didn't think he noticed. He'd faced 103 deliveries and made 124 runs.

Navneet Singh was the next man in. He looked very unsure, but that was okay. All he had to do was rotate the batting and let Zahid do his thing. It must have been *déjà vu* for Zahid because we were quickly approaching the same situation that he'd faced in Auckland.

Beeru and Jay were quick to remind us of this. They both started speculating if Zahid could do it this time.

'In cricket, it's not often that you get a chance to redeem yourself so wholly, and so soon, Beeru,' Jay said. 'Young Pathan has been given that chance today and I, for one, want to see him do it.'

'Yes, vul, his captain has full faith in him,' Beeru said. 'The knee-jerk reaction after the Auckland showing would have been to place him lower down the order. Khoda's moved him up two places instead.'

'Oh, Pathan's shaping up to be quite an all-rounder,' Jay said. 'That's the wonder of the World Cup, isn't it, Beeru? A whole new crop of talent is discovered through it every four yea – ' he broke off abruptly, then said, his manner completely altered – 'Now what in the world was *that* about?'

Zahid had turned upon the weasely wicketkeeper, and was glaring at him.

The wicketkeeper met his gaze calmly smirking slightly, then turned away and spat casually on the grass behind him. But Zahid kept glowering at him, and so he turned around and shrugged innocently. Then, just as the crowd-monster threatened to slip its leash and charge the pitch, Zahid abruptly turned his back on the wicketkeeper again.

'Bit of an altercation there, Beeru, don't you think? Pathan's shaking his head, telling Umpire Patil that nothing's been said after all.'

And then, when India was at 327, there it was. The final ball.

A scene immortalized in a million cheesy ads along the subcontinent. The hoarse, passionate chanting, the clutching of taveezes, the genuflections. The looks towards heaven with teary, supplicating eyes. The collective holding of a billion breaths. And you felt the thrill every single time.

The pretty-boy bowler licked his lips, launched into his final run-up and hurled the ball. And as the crowd-monster bayed for blood screaming '*Zahid, Zahid, Zahid*' – Zahid Pathan got onto the front foot, his eyes mere slits in his grim young face. He hoisted his bat and thwacked the tiny white ball away with absolutely everything he had. It soared above our heads, above the pavilion roof, and vanished forever.

The crowd-monster roared. It threw back its massive, million-eyed head and laughed manically. It did an ungainly, over-the-top jig. It lay back on its back, kicked its legs into the air and screamed in delight, *INDIYA! INDIYA!*

The relief was indescribable.

We were all hugging each other and looking at the TV, where Zahid was doing a wild dance, swinging his bat about and making strange thrusting movements with his hips.

'Somebody should put that poor boy out of his misery,' one of the starlets whispered and they all started to giggle and make plans about which pub to hit tonight in order to meet Zahid and turn him from a *bud* into a *flower*.

And then, suddenly, it happened.

Zahid's swinging bat made impact with something.

Something skinny and brown and surly-looking. Dressed in green. The Pakistani wicketkeeper to be exact. He'd been walking back to the pavilion too, taking off his helmet, and Zahid's exultantly swinging bat had somehow caught him smack in the face, making a grotesque crunching noise. It felled him instantly.

The commentators suddenly became silent as everybody on the field dropped to the ground to see if the wicketkeeper was okay. The first person to grab his pulse, to urge that something be done, to shout for an ambulance, was an extremely concerned-looking Zahid himself.

The Times of India
'ZAHID'S OOOPS', 'INDIA'S HOUR OF SHAME'
by Shanta Kalra in Melbourne

Spectators around the world were treated to a sublime display of cricket today. There were so many high points in this humdinger of a match. The Pakistani captain's incredible knock, the one-handed running backward catch that got Luckshmun Singh Teja out when he looked set for a big total, Nikhil Khoda's sixteenth ton in One-day cricket and, of course, Zahid Pathan's heroic, match-winning six off the last ball. Unfortunately, today's match will be remembered for none of these. If this date does go down in cricketing history, it will be remembered as the day a demigod behaved like a dastardly dog.

Right after taking India into the semi-finals of the ICC World Cup 2011 with a display of brilliant, aggressive, temperamentally sound cricket, Zahid Pathan (19) unwrote his own place in history by 'accidentally' injuring Naved Khan, the Pakistani wicketkeeper.

While strutting back to the pavilion, a wildly whooping Zahid's willow somehow managed to find a sweet spot in the face of Pak wicketkeeper, Naved Khan, who was walking behind him, leaving him bleeding and almost definitely out of the reckoning for Pakistan's next One-dayer, against the West Indies.

Zahid was all concern and his contrition seemed sincere enough, but anybody who'd witnessed the sledging on the field today would agree that the whole incident smelled strongly of Mickey Mouse.

Definitely the Pakistani skipper and management seemed to think so.

'Arrey, who does he think he's fooling?' said a visibly upset team manager Shahmeya Dilbar. 'He did it on purpose... He waited till our keeper took off his helmet so he could do the maximum damage. We are going to lodge an official complaint and get him a lifelong ban from cricket!'

IBCC chief Jogpal Lohia vehemently denied the allegation that Zahid's 'attack' was premeditated. 'What happened with Naved was unfortunate, but it was an unfortunate accident. See the footage. He did not mean to do it!'

In fact, he went so far as to say that if there was going to be any complaining to be done to the ICC, he would be the one doing it. 'The sledging going on right through the match was disgraceful,' he said. 'The ICC, in its wisdom, had chosen to appoint two non-Hindi/Urdu-speaking umpires, which in my opinion was a gross oversight. Our players lodged two complaints, both of which were more or less disregarded.'

A high-level ICC enquiry – both into the alleged sledging and the alleged attack – is on the cards.

'The sledging definitely happened. As far as Zahid's reaction goes, it was unfortunate,' said a tight-lipped Nikhil Khoda, Indian skipper. 'I'm just extremely thankful the incident didn't escalate from there, with a crowd of a hundred thousand inflamed fans watching, there could have been a break-out of large-scale violence. People could've been killed.'

Speculation was rife last evening here in Melbourne, however, that the alleged sledging had been taunts about Zahid not being a 'true' Muslim, because he's an Indian. But, more persistent were the rumours that the jibes had been about the Indian team's dependency on Zoya Solanki, the so-called Goddess-of-the-Game.

The Zoya Factor, in fact, is quickly becoming massively controversial here in Australia, with the boards of three Super 8 qualifying countries going so far as to lodge official complaints with the ICC about India's 'unfair' advantage.

'Balls,' said Sanks rudely, his eyes glued to the TV on which the Pakistan captain was giving the martyred, my-key-player-has-been-grievously-injured-this-vicious-action-may-cost-my-team-the-World-Cup ones. He'd flown in early that morning to catch the semis and the finals. 'Your team was never gonna win anyway, fucker!' He was sitting in Monita's room, clad in a hideous Hawaiian shirt and Bermudas. Seriously, Sanks in holiday mode was even worse than Sanks in the office. His moustache bristled horridly as he swivelled his bulging eyes my way and barked, 'Must've been something to do with you, I'll bet!'

I counted to ten under my breath slowly and then said, 'A lot of people are saying he taunted him about not being a real Muslim, Sanks,' and thought, *If I do Tauji's ad I will never have to see Sanks again.* 'It's got nothing to do with me.'

He tugged at his moustache in a superior kind of way. 'It's all connected, Zoya,' he said like he was talking to an imbecile. 'That wicketkeeper must have told him, you're not a real Musalmaan, you're a blooming Devi-bhakt, a Goddess-worshipper, shame on you!'

'Oh, please,' Mon said. 'Maybe he just said you're a flatulent jerk and I'm tired of smelling your stink-making behind the wickets.'

'Or maybe he's gay and just told Zahid he liked the view,' offered Rinku Chachi brightly from the next room.

'Whatever,' I sighed. 'We'll never know, shall we?'

Mon's eyes twinkled naughtily. 'I know who'll know,' she said. 'Someone who's been getting very close to our Pathan lately – Ritu.'

Immediately, they started making all these giggly plans to invite Ritu to our rooms for a drink and pump her for information. Somehow they all seemed to be blissfully unaware of the fact that I had hit an all-time low. This latest fiasco was going to make Nikhil dislike me further. He was going to blame me for Zahid having lost his temper. I just knew it.

He was never ever going to speak to me again.

The next day didn't start well. First, I opened the newspaper to find this really nasty article about me. A wild-haired Durga type caricature of me glowered out at the world from the sports page. It had eight arms, seven of which clutched the squirming captains of the other Super 8 qualifying countries in a death grip. The eighth tenderly spooned breakfast cereal into a bibbed and bonneted Khoda's cutely dribbling mouth.

Below the caricature was a two-thousand-word write-up calling me a bloodthirsty Goddess who could only be appeased by violence, citing Rawal's busted arm and the Paki keeper's busted nose as cases in point. It hinted darkly at worse things to come, if India continued to break their pre-match bread with the 'Witch of the Pitch'.

I shuddered and turned the page to find myself faced with another article called 'Goddess For Sale'. It said that Zoya Singh Solanki, the Indian lucky charm, was the latest thing on the endorsement market and that she would push any product – chewing gum, underwear, colas, air conditioners – if the price was right. It said her agent, Lokendar Chugh, was in talks with at least fifteen corporates, all of whom wanted to sign her on if she brought home the World Cup. 'Move aside, Nikhil Khoda,' the article concluded, 'the homecoming prizes are all for the Goddess!'

I lay back weakly in bed and reached for the phone to dial my so-called agent's number. Fortunately, I had to listen to the latest Himesh Reshammiya number for only about three seconds before he snapped it up. 'Joyaji!' he said enthusiastically. 'How are you?'

I told him in no uncertain terms how I was. And infuriatingly, instead of cowering down and grovelling, he started yelling back at me! He said he was only being a good dedicated agent, that nothing he'd told the journalist was a lie, that everybody from Coca Cola to Sahara wanted to sign me on, and he didn't see why I was getting in the way of his making a decent living for the both of us.

I told him I didn't want to take any credit away from the boys.

'Of course you won't, Joyaji! I am not your agent only! Nikhil, Laakhi, openers are all handled by myself. All will get their due! There are many, many corporate houses in India. Enough for all of us. Let us, *zor lagake*, just win this World Cup and life will become an eternal five-star buffet for all of us! The only person whose stock will fall is Kapil Dev!'

'Did you say *Coke* back then, Lokey?' I asked despite myself.

'Ya, then what?' he said cockily. 'They have sent script and everything. You don't know, you are sitting in Sydney, but you have become Number One craze in India. *Arrey*, what Standing you have got in thee Society, Joyaji! Please be practical, don't get emotional. God is being gracious to you. *Arrey*, thee RJP has even been inquiring your age, if you are really over twenty-one they will give you Lok Sabha ticket from Ayodhya Ram mandir.'

'Okay, okay,' I told him uneasily. 'I get your point, but Lokey, I'm supposed to be a Goddess, how can I advertise products?'

'*Tchcha*. Only rich marketing people thinks like this, Joyaji,' he said. 'Poor common people don't. They are more broad-minded. They understand *ki* you also have to live. You will only have to give some small portion – very publicly of course – to charity, that's all.'

'Okay, Lokey, but let's talk about this only after India wins, okay? What's the point of getting all excited if we lose? And please don't speak to the press about it any more.'

I hung up, feeling cheerful. Coke wanted me. Not that I would ever endorse them, but it was nice to know. I was going to be rich. And good too! I was going to be good like Bill and Melinda Gates. I would make a difference, go to orphanages and stuff, become a good example to young people everywhere. Then my eyes fell on the caricature on the sports page again, and my mood plummeted. I could only imagine what Nikhil must have felt like when he saw it – him being fed on my knee. Must have hit his twin-tower ego like a couple of fully fuelled airliners.

An evil part of me sat back and cackled.

It was quite a funny cartoon, actually.

The ICC decision came in three days later. Zahid and Naved would both have to forfeit match fees for the India–Pakistan match. In addition, Zahid had to face a one ODI match ban, which effectively meant he wouldn't be playing in the semis. The Indians picked up on the fact that Naved had to face no such ban. They claimed that India was being victimized because the entire cricket-playing world was so jealous of their 'lucky charm'.

There was an important West Indies versus England match that day, but all the panel discussions on television focused on Zahid, Naved and me. All of us got into Mon's room and started watching the action unfold on a show called 'Australia Decides' where the topic for the day was 'India's Advantage – Fair or Unfair'. The people on the panel consisted of a prissy-looking anchor, a representative of the Australian Orthodox Church, Lingnath Baba, a junior ICC official, a senior Aussie ex-cricketer, Jogpal Lohia and a mixed audience of about two hundred people.

They kicked off the discussion with the usual intro, a mention of my name and my 'unblemished' track record, followed by some some chubby-cheeked pictures of me. Then they talked about the wretched Benito's Pizza incident, and ended by hinting that I had somehow caused the brawl between Naved Khan and Zahid Pathan.

Then they started taking calls. The first caller was Stuart from Yarrawonga. He wanted to know what the *Laws of Cricket* were regarding this issue.

The ICC guy cleared his throat and said that the laws of cricket had nothing to say on this issue. The situation was a complete first in the history of cricket.

Then this very passionate old Sri Lankan gentleman called in to say that the whole thing was a classic example of racial discrimination. He said that in all probability India was going to be the only non-white team to make it to the semis and that the other three teams – Australia, England and South Africa – were ganging up against India. He said, 'Again and again we are faced with incidents that clearly lay bare the Black–White rift that exists in the cricketing world. I am sure that a white lucky charm would have been greeted as a bit of a good joke by the very same gentlemen who are muttering about voodoo, hocus-pocus and unfair advantages in hushed tones right now.' He banged the phone down without waiting for a reply from the panel.

The anchor looked a little rattled. He turned towards Jogpal and said, 'Sir! As the IBCC chief, are your views the same as that of Mr Krishnawardhane who just called from Julong?'

Jogpal stroked his beard meditatively and said, 'I salute Mr Krishnawardhane for his passion and thank him for his support, but no, I don't necessarily agree with his point of view. I'm sure that the cricketing world is a united one, and all the teams have enough faith in their talent not to worry about a harmless little girl from New Delhi.'

The senior Aussie ex-cricketer leaned in and said, 'Mr Lohia, your harmless little girl almost caused an international incident! A *war* could have broken out on the Indo–Pak border yesterday!'

'No, no,' said Jogpal soothingly. 'The Indo–Pak match incident was because of high spirits only. Zoya is nothing, nothing at all, the real thing is that Wes – your own countryman – has done wonders with the team!'

The ICC official jumped in to say, 'Then surely you wouldn't mind if we request that Zoya not be there for the last two matches?'

Jogpal thrust his beard forward belligerently. 'Why*ji*? Of course I mind! Do I get into your kitchen and tell you how to slice your potatoes?' he demanded. 'Do I tell your good wife where to place the TV and the two-seater sofa? Then how can you tell Nikhil Khoda what to do in his own house, eh?'

Ragged cheering broke out from the Indians in the audience. '*Yaah, you tell him, Jogpal*' and '*Zoya Mata ki Jai!*' Jogpal sat back in his seat, looking gratified.

The anchor said hurriedly, 'We have a lady caller from Richmond. Please speak up.'

The caller said that she had read the papers today and learned that the Indian Goddess was for sale and was ready to endorse products for money if the price was right. She wanted to know what Lingnath Baba had to say to this.

Everybody turned to Lingnath who said meditatively, 'These are all gossip reports. We have looked into the eyes of Zoya Devi and seen that her heart is pure. Even if she is accepting money, we are sure it will be donated to a good cause.'

There was a murmur of appreciation from the audience at this but the Aussie ex-cricketer leaned forward and said, 'Even if she donates all the money to the lepers of Calcutta, she will still be doing more harm than good to the game!' He paused, organized his thoughts a little, then said: 'Look, either she's got some hocus-pocus going on, in which case she's no better than a performance-enhancing steroid and should be banned, or it's all coincidence in which case *you*' – he pointed at Jogpal – 'should have no objection to her missing the last two team breakfasts.'

Ragged cheering broke out again, this time from the Aussies in the crowd. Jogpal glared as he waited for them to shut up. 'Fine, so even if she does have some special…um…powers, there's nothing in the *Laws of Cricket* that disallows it. She's a national resource, that's all! The Saudis have oil, the Africans have rhythm, the English have…um, interesting teeth, and we have Zoya! Legally, you people don't have a leg to stand on.'

The prissy-looking anchor said hurriedly, 'We have another caller.'

The next caller turned out to be some old Brit fossil who droned on about how fair play should prevail above all else. He said he'd heard what Jogpal had said and felt that while the *Laws of Cricket* had left a loophole for the likes of Zoya Devi – the spirit of the game was vehemently against her.

Jogpal snorted and pawed the ground militantly right through the caller's speech. 'Begging your pardon, *Uncle*,' he said so forcefully that tiny spit bubbles formed in the corners of his mouth, 'but I think it's about time we exorcized this wretched *spirit of the game*. It's too bloody pompous and too bloody British a spirit for a game that's played at its best in the dusty streets of Jamaica, Ranchi and Lahore. I vote we call in a capable ghostbuster and finish it off for good!'

The ICC official cut in contemptuously, 'Well, I wouldn't go so far as *that*, Mr Lohia. The spirit of cricket is what makes the game unique. But yes, of course, as you said, these are modern times, and that is why your team's dependence on something as archaic as a lucky charm is so oddly repugnant.'

Jogpal's eyes bulged dangerously but before he could speak, the anchor coughed politely and started to wrap up the show. 'Well, that was a very passionate and interesting debate,' he said brightly. 'The votes are in, by the way, and 83 per cent of Australians have voted to disallow Zoya Solanki from the Indian team breakfasts. Not a surprising verdict at all when we consider the fact that most pundits are predicting that the World Cup final, in all probability, will be played between these two nations.'

Jogpal interjected rudely to say, 'Well, 100 per cent Indians vote that Zoya stays! And there are many many more Indians than Australians. So there you have it.'

The anchor thanked all those on the panel with the air of a man who'd earned his salary for the day. He looked right into the camera and said, 'Goodnight,' with huge relief.

The moment the debate on the TV ended, it restarted all over again in the hotel suite.

Sanks kicked it off in his best pontificating manner by observing: 'Basically, Zoya, you are caught between two Indias. The let's-put-a-man-on-Mars one and the don't-go-into-the-kitchen-if-you-have-your-period one.'

And they all took it from there. Mon, Armaan, Ritu and Sanks were in the 'don't go into the kitchen' camp, telling me I should stay. I was definitely lucky for India; it had been proved beyond doubt, repeatedly. They said I should make large sums of money from endorsements and give a little slice of it to charity.

Anand (Mon's hubby, who had also joined us in Australia),

Vishaal and Rinku Chachi were in the 'Mars' camp. They wanted me to give a press conference, announce that I was throwing in the towel and let India win or lose according to her own fate. They said there were more things in life than just money.

Everybody had their own hidden agenda. Mon didn't want me to stop now that I'd come so far; Ritu wanted her Zahid to have every support in winning the World Cup; Sanks because the money was good; Anand because he was a fair-play Nikhil-Khoda fan; Vishaal because he wanted his Nike ad to run and Rinku Chachi because I'd told her what Eppa had said about being lucky in cricket, unlucky in life.

I heard them all out and said, as sweetly as I could, 'Thank you. I am going to bed now.'

'But are you going for the breakfast tomorrow?' they asked eagerly.

'I don't know,' I said. 'I have some phone calls to make.' I walked back into my room, feeling completely fed up, pulled out my phone, scrolled down to N. Khoda and sent him a message before I could lose my nerve. *Should I come for breakfast tomorrow or not?*

The answer took a long time coming. Rinku Chachi got into bed, I wandered around the room, showered, changed my clothes and turned off the lights, my heart beating madly. I had just clambered into bed after drying my hair when I finally heard the phone beep. I lunged for it. *Why are you asking me?*

He sounded so distant and cold. I put the phone on silent and glared furiously down at the screen, wondering what I should say. *Just tell me yes or no,* I punched finally, in a businesslike way, my fingers flying over the buttons in almost complete darkness. *I won't come if you don't want me to.*

There was another long pause. I braced myself. I was pretty sure how he was going to respond. But the answer, when it finally came, was out of syllabus. *I miss you*, it said irrelevantly, glowing gently in the dark and lighting up my world.

I blinked back stupid tears and answered before I could stop myself, *I miss you too.*

Another long pause and then my phone glowed again. *Do you still think I'm pretending to like you because you're lucky?* he asked.

Maybe, I texted back, wiping snot inelegantly as I punched the buttons. *But frankly I don't care any more.*

He took such a long time to answer that I thought I'd made him mad at me again. I'd started to tap out a panicky *Are you still there?* when the reply finally came. *You're at the Hilton right? See you by the pool in 15 minutes.*

Ten minutes later, I sneaked past Rinku Chachi's gently snoring form and headed for the fancy landscaped pool in my baggy pajamas. There was a pretty green grotto with a burbling artificial waterfall next to it. A statue of a simpering mermaid sat on the rocks, looking down sadly into the water. I stood beside her, feeling a little stupid.

Footsteps sounded behind me and I tensed but for some incomprehensible reason I pretended I didn't know he was there. I waited for him to say hi so I could turn around casually and greet him in return. But he didn't say hi. He just slid his arms around my waist and pulled me to him. I didn't say anything either. Just leaned back into him. He held me even tighter, sinking his rough chin into my shoulder, nuzzling my ear. Then he slowly turned me around. 'Hello, you very rude person,' he said huskily.

'Hi,' I said. 'What did you want to talk to me about?'

He said, quite rudely really, 'Who said I wanted to *talk* to you?' He lifted me up and lowered me onto the grass in one smooth move. Then he tugged at my baggy pajama top and calmly started kissing my exposed shoulder.

I gasped, grabbed two thick handfuls of his hair and yanked up his face, so I could look into his playful Boost-brown eyes. 'Hello, that is an extremely sexist thing to say.'

'I know,' he said, pushing my hair away from my forehead with one roughly gentle hand, and looking down at me. 'But you'll just have to lump it, won't you?'

I opened my mouth in protest but he placed a finger on my lips and looked down at me, the smile quite gone from his face. His eyes glistened in the darkness. I could feel his hands trembling, just a little. And then, very deliberately, he lowered his head to kiss me.

Wham. It was like all of me rose up and surged to my lips, as if my life source was where his mouth was, as if my soul was on my lips and he was kissing it.

It took me some time to realize that in spite of his cocky opening speech, and in spite of the total seclusion of the poolside, he didn't seem to be in any hurry. One large warm hand had slid under my shirt and settled tantalizingly right over my madly thumping heart but made no attempt at exploring the rest of me. Instead, I realized, feeling pretty insulted, it seemed to be *patting* me, the way you would pat a baby to sleep.

'Why,' I finally asked in a low outraged voice, 'are you trying to put me to sleep?'

His hand stilled. He hauled himself up on one elbow and said, not quite looking at me, 'Look, it's all a little more complicated than it looks, and in spite of all your big talk you're such a little girl...'

'If you would care to move your hand to either side, just a little, you would be provided with *substantial* proof that I am quite a *big* girl after all,' I said, feeling mortified.

He laughed softly and shook his head, sliding his hand way up, so that his dark brown fingers appeared through the neckline of my shirt and then way down so I could feel them disturbingly warm against my navel.

He said, his voice just a little unsteady, 'Hey, you've got goosebumps, are you cold?'

But I'd just about had it with the polite conversation.

As his hand slid smoothly up again, I shifted it a little and after that there was no more talk at all. For a long time. Then he said, 'You know…' and stopped.

'What?' I asked.

He said, 'Don't laugh, okay?'

'Okay,' I said obligingly.

'Sometimes I think that maybe I'm wrong and everybody else is right…'

'*Matlab?*'

He shrugged. '*Matlab*, maybe you're really some kind of a…I don't know…Goddess?'

'Bullshit!' I exclaimed, quite pleased with this new and exciting possibility.

He laughed, looking a little embarrassed. 'Really,' he said lightly. 'In fact if I narrow my eyes a little, like *this*,' he squinted a little and tilted his head to one side, 'I can almost see your halo and your trident and your eight extra arms.'

'Do I look celestially divine?' I asked, throwing my shoulders back and shaking my head so my hair swirled around in a Goddess-like way.

'No, baba,' he laughed and kissed my chin. 'You look…' he

paused, 'strong. You make me feel…' he hesitated, then shrugged again and said, 'well, I guess the word is humble.' He added ruefully, 'Close your mouth, Zoya.'

I closed it obediently, still slightly dazed, as he raised one dark hand to my cheek. 'So, what did you want to talk to me about?' he asked quietly.

'Who said,' I said cockily, 'that I wanted to *talk* to you?' And I lowered my head and kissed his laughing mouth.

A little while later, he said, 'There's a five-day gap between the semi and the final…'

'Really?' I said, stroking his crisp, dark hair absent-mindedly. 'Good for you.'

'So, can you have dinner with me after the match tomorrow?'

'Okay,' I said dreamily. 'Where?'

'In my suite,' he said.

I rolled off his chest, sat up straight and asked, 'Why? I mean, why in your suite?'

He sat up, pushing his hair back from his forehead, his teeth flashing white as he grinned down at me in the dark. 'So we can watch Cartoon Network together.'

'Yeah right,' I said, pushing him away lightly. 'And I bet you'll even let me hold the remote.'

He looked at me, completely taken aback, and then started laughing – guffawing actually.

I glared at him, wondering how it was that I had this uncanny ability to reduce the most romantic of situations into a complete farce.

There was a long pause where he kept grinning down at me and I kept uprooting blades of grass, fully determined not to look him in the eye. Finally he said he had to go, which frankly was almost a bit of a relief.

As we got to our feet I asked him, 'But what about tomorrow morning?'

'*Haan*, tomorrow morning. I'll see you at breakfast.'

So I went for breakfast the next day. The whole gang woke up to see me off. Mon's entire family, Sanks, Ritu, Chachi, Vishaal, everybody. They watched me as I pottered around, brushing my teeth, putting kaajal in my eyes. I expected them to whip out a bowl of curd and sugar and start feeding it to me for luck.

'Will you guys stop looking at me?' I snapped finally.

Sanks beetled his brows. 'I've paid good money for this trip, Zoya,' he said in his nice, mild voice. 'I haven't done it to see India lose, you hear?'

I turned around and glared at him, 'Sanks, I don't play for the country, okay? If you have any last-minute speeches to make, please call up your precious Men in Blue and make it to them.'

'But you are the good luck charm!' Ritu said earnestly. 'It's all happening because of you, you know that.'

'What about Zahid?' I asked her. 'Isn't he contributing anything?'

It was a dumb thing to say because of course she opened her eyes very wide and said, 'But he isn't playing today, Zoya!'

I stomped my foot in frustration and rushed out of the room, too stressed to take it any more. As I headed out, I heard Chachi say understandingly, 'She's very nervous. So much responsibility, you know.'

God, if they were beginning to wear *me* down with their faith in me, the pressure on Nikhil must be enormous.

The team was gathered around the table when I reached. I took my usual place between Hairy and Shivnath and reached for the fruit platter.

'Hi,' they said in unison, very subdued.

'Hi,' I said and grinned across the table at Zahid, who was eating with the team, even though he wasn't playing.

'Hey, Rambo,' I said lightly and he gave me a weak grin.

'Hi, Zoya,' he said.

I asked him, in a low voice, as I reached for the fruit platter, 'They're letting you play the final *na*, Zahid?'

He nodded and whispered in return, 'Only if they manage to win today without me.'

I giggled and he said, 'Don't *laugh*, Zoya. Skipper is still angry at me.'

I nodded solemnly and sneaked a quick look to the top of the table where Khoda was listening quietly to a very animated Thind.

Hairy said, 'You know, we always thought they discuss strategy and all up there at the top of the table...'

'Don't they?' I asked him.

He shook his head. 'No, actually I think he's telling him what happened in yesterday's episode of *Celebrity Big Brother*.'

I giggled again. A little too loudly. The top of the table all turned to look at me. Zahid got so scared he got up, muttered something about getting some hot toast and scurried off.

'What's so funny?' Khoda asked quizzically, spearing a pineapple chunk from the usual mountain of fruit on his plate.

'Nothing,' I said, hurriedly. Shivnath and Hairy shook their heads too.

Nikhil said nothing further, just glared at all of us suspiciously till we bowed our heads. Then he pulled out his phone and frowned. Laakhi kept talking to him, and he kept nodding curtly. My phone beeped in a bit. I fished it out and looked down at it.

You look like you should be in bed, Zoya.

It was Nikhil! I looked across at him, startled, but he didn't meet my eyes. He kept listening to Laakhi, very seriously. Of course I couldn't message him back, because then Hairy and Shivnath would figure out what was going on. So I just put my phone on silent and tried to look casual. And then there was another message.

In bed, in your baggy grey pajama bottoms, and nothing else.

I went bright pink and pressed the delete button as quickly as I could.

But then another message came. *My bed.*

Red as the watermelon slice on my plate, I hastily covered my phone with a napkin, but not before it said reprovingly, *You're blushing! A 'big' girl like you.*

I glared at Nikhil across the table but he just flashed me an unrepentant grin. Picking up my phone, I made a big production of switching it off.

There was one last message which I saw in the car driving back to the hotel:

Sorry, but I couldn't resist. It's suite 302, at the Conrad. Right after the match. You'll be there, won't you? Don't want to sound dramatic, but if you're not, it may actually kill me. All my love N.

19

The SCG was absolutely packed.

There were wave upon wave of England supporters dressed in red and dark blue with red triple crosses fluttering everywhere, on tee shirts, banners and hats. The light-blue Indian contingent seemed to have swelled too. Maybe it was because – as Mr Krishnawardane had said yesterday – all the coloured races were cheering for India. We'd got lucky with the semis and drawn England, which was easily the least-favoured team of the four teams that had qualified. The other semi, to be held at the MCG three days later, could have easily been the final with Australia playing South Africa.

Our large contingent consisted of Mon and family, Sanks (hideous in Bermudas and binoculars), Ritu, Vishaal, Chachi (in her 'RINKU 10' tee shirt) and me. We'd bought these huge saffron, pre-tied, saafa-style turbans and perched them on our heads, got our first round of beer and *Zing!* and made ourselves comfy in the front row of the members' enclosure.

When Nikhil and the English captain strolled out for the toss a little while later they were greeted with deafening applause. The goras in the crowd leapt to their feet as the two captains shook hands and started singing their national anthem. So of course the moment Nikhil won the toss, we Indians got to our feet and retaliated with, '*Nikhil Khoda datt gaya, Angrezon ka phhat gaya!*'

Nikhil decided he'd put the Brits in to bat first and the commentators started their usual job of taking apart that decision, pondering its wisdom, or lack of it:

'Especially when India will be missing Zahid Pathan today, who must be regretting his impulsive action bitterly, don't you think?' Jay was saying.

'Absolutely, Jay,' Beeru said with great gusto. 'Tell me, are you in the mood to wager a fiver on anybody today, then?'

'Is that a pound, an Aussie dollar or a rupee we're talking about here?' Jay said.

'Vul, it's a rupee if you win and a quid if I win,' said Beeru wittily.

A little pause and then Jay said slowly, 'My money's on England, mate.'

'Misplaced patriotism, Jay!' crowed Beeru. 'I'll trouble you for that fiver before the day is out, see if I don't!'

They prattled on, giving us a full brief on the pitch, the weather, the temperature, everything. Then, finally, the Indians fanned out into fielding positions, two dark-blue figures walked onto the crease, the Fly Emirates dudes handed out the ball, and the match began.

The cheering rose to a crescendo and the first delivery of the semi-final of the ICC World Cup 2011 ended tamely with a wide.

Oh great. Nice start, boys, I thought and then a voice behind me said, '*Oye*, Zoya, move up, I want to sit with you.'

I looked around and saw Zahid, grinning widely, in a bright orange 'Chak De India' tee shirt. 'Sure, okay,' I said doubtfully and shifted up as Armaan beamed up at Zahid. He had totally become his favourite cricketer ever since he drew Pakistani blood on TV the other day. 'Should you be sitting with us, Zahid?' I asked warily.

He nodded happily. 'Why not?' he asked. 'I'll go and sit with the team when our batting starts. Right now only Hardin-sir, manager and Dieter are there, and they're still very angry with me. I don't want to sit with them.'

Zahid dropped down beside me, his long legs dangling, and peered through the railing at Harry, fielding five feet away from us. 'Harry-sir,' he called out cheekily. *'Theek se khelna!* Play properly, okay?'

Harry ignored him, looking grimly ahead. I wondered if he was hassled till I saw that behind his back his left hand was waggling its middle finger in Zahid's face! And then I noticed with a sinking heart that our faces were on the TV screen. 'Oh no,' I murmured, as I heard Jay's voice say: '...And there they are, the two most controversial figures in cricket today. Making a bit of a picnic of it. What d'you say, eh, Beeru?'

'Yes, vul, Young Pathan certainly looks very festive in that turban, Jay!'

I stared out at the field blankly, like I hadn't noticed the camera was on me, thinking *oh great, my dad will freak.*

Uneasy about being broadcast into every home in KB, I jumped to my feet, and announced that I needed a drink. Armaan said he wanted one too so the two of us trotted off. Looking over my shoulder, I saw that Zahid had slid up two places and was now sitting right next to Ritu, looking very cosy indeed. *Wanted to sit with me* indeed, who did he think he was kidding?

When the two of us returned, with more beer and *Zing!*, we found our seat had been taken by an ash-blonde bombshell in a long coat and dark glasses. Vishaal was busy trying to chat her up. 'So, what side are you supporting today?' he was asking her, which was either super-dumb or very witty of him as she had two bright, red-white and-blue Union Jacks painted on both her cheeks.

She laughed and said, 'England. Obviously!'

Vishaal laughed too and introduced me. 'Zoya, this is Gabrielle. Gabrielle, Zoya.'

I shook hands with Gabrielle politely.

'So who's your favourite player, Gabby?' asked Vishaal. Gabby wrinkled her brow. 'Him,' she said reverentially, pointing to one of the Brit openers, playing without a helmet, so that we could all see his bizarre skunk-like hairdo.

'Oh, him,' Vishaal nodded unenthusiastically, adding very casually, 'Are you here with friends?'

She shook her head, tucking a stray wisp of blonde hair behind her ear. 'No, no, I'm all alone,' she said.

'Not any more,' Vishaal said gallantly and she blushed a delicate rose pink, looking shyly at him from under her lashes.

Great, I thought miserably, *sab ki* setting *ho rahi hai.* Vishaal and Gabby, Zahid and Ritu, Mon and her hubby. Even Sanks was cosying up with Rinku Chachi. And Armaan was busy teaching little Aman a song. They were hopping up and down the steps nearby and little lisping snatches of *hand-grenades-and-people-with-AIDS* wafted up to me in the gentle breeze.

I watched the English side pile up their total at an un-alarming pace and reread Nikhil's last sms. The words – *All my love, N* – sent such a surge of happiness through me that I felt almost dizzy. He was a mere speck in the distance, a blue blur fielding at short square leg, way down in the middle of the field, but they kept showing him on the TV screen every now and then. He was looking all grim and focused, scowling in the sunlight, his eyes scanning the field constantly.

All eyes on thee cupboard, I thought dreamily. *But tonight I'll have your full attention, Nikhil Khoda.*

The match rolled on, slowly and uneventfully. Jay and Beeru tried to liven it up by talking about the celebrity types who'd come to watch it. They pointed out Russell Crowe and the governor of New South Wales and any number of Bollywood stars and sparred at length about who was going to win the five-buck wager.

Thind finally struck in the fourteenth over, and the stadium exploded with chants of 'Indiya! Indiya!' One of the openers departed to be replaced by the seriously hot English captain. Gabby stopped talking to Vishaal and started concentrating on the game.

Nikhil gave Vikram Goyal the ball, and the run rate, which was low in any case, now dipped to an all-time low.

'This is Goyal's USP, isn't it, Beeru?' Jay said as the camera followed Vikram's queer, lopsided, run-up down the pitch. 'He doesn't often get wickets, but he sure can bring the scoring to a crashing halt. Handy with the bat too, I believe.'

'Yes, vul, he's very young too, only seventeen, Jay, and he's in a hurry. He's definitely not going to let us miss Zahid Pathan today, that's for sure. And why not? When there's a fire in your belly you'd be a fool to consult a gastro…'

Jay didn't reply and I didn't blame him. I mean what possible answer can you give to a remark like that? The hot-looking English skipper seemed to have Vikram's number though, because he blasted his third delivery away for an awesome six over the covers.

Beeru changed tracks smoothly and shamelessly started talking about how inexperienced Vikram was. 'That ball was looking like an alcoholic, it was so high!' he rhapsodized. 'A clumsy delivery from young Vikram Goyal that was shown absolutely no mercy by the English skipper. And India is sorely missing Zahid Pathan here today at the Sydney Cricket Ground!'

The rest of the over was a total disaster. When it ended England were 93 for 1 in 17 overs and the run rate had jumped to well over five.

Zahid's face had turned ashen. He'd been chatting happily with Ritu, but now he hurried over to me, lifted Armaan onto his lap and settled down right next to me, groping for my hand. 'What?' I snapped at him nastily, moving my hand away.

'Nothing,' he said meekly. 'Cheer, no, for India!'

I turned around to give him a piece of my mind, but he was looking so stricken that I didn't have the heart to do so. I realized that he was in exactly the same boat as I was.

If India lost he, too, was going to think it was all his fault.

'Lots of cricket still to be played yet, Zahid,' I told him comfortingly. 'And why are you looking so sad, anyway? I thought you didn't like Goyal?'

'Zoya, what are you saying?' he said, genuinely hassled. 'He's wearing the blue uniform! We are all in this together.'

Armaan, feeling the tension, had stuck one grubby forefinger into his mouth. 'Are we going to lose again, Zahid?' he asked in a doctor-tell-me-the-worst-I-can-deal-with-it kind of way.

'Arrey, of course not, mere sher!' Zahid said heartily. Armaan sighed and turned to his two-year-old brother.

'We're going to lose, Aman.'

'Okay,' Aman said stoically.

The energy levels were definitely low. All round us English supporters were waving their flags, yelling and stamping and taking off their shirts.

Vishaal's Gabrielle was on her feet, whooping every time Balaji's ball rose to make contact with her idol's bat.

It went on like this for what seemed like forever. Their score climbed steadily and the run rate stayed well above five right through the slog overs.

Vishaal passed me to go get a couple of beers for Gabby and himself and mouthed, *I think I'm in love*, as he went past.

I leapt to my feet and followed him. 'Really?'

He turned and grinned. 'Really! *Wham!* It was like a thunderbolt. She's a simple girl from a small Irish town, you know. Very conservative. Educated by the nuns. I mean, look at the way she's dressed, it's way more modest than what even *you've* got on!'

I glanced down at my shorts and ganji and said, 'Yeah, wow, well good for you, Vishaal.'

He grinned, pushing his hair back from his brow boyishly, 'Yeah, true love, finally, huh? You know, suddenly even the Nike film getting bombed doesn't seem so bad...'

I nodded sympathetically. Then Zahid yelled for me and I hurried back to my seat. 'What *is* it, Zahid?' I said testily.

'*Concentrate*, Zoya!' he said. 'The game is slipping away from us.'

God alone knows what he expected me to do. I sat down and looked out at the field, trying not to absorb the stress he was radiating. Beeru and Jay were doing some serious analyses:

'England's really intent on taking that trophy home this time, Beeru.'

'Yes, we're definitely seeing some very superior batting today, Jay. India are doing their best, I can't fault them really, but England look all set to end with much more than 300 in their kitty and as the groundsmen said earlier today, the pitch is going to deteriorate towards the evening.'

'So, was putting them in to bat such a good decision on Nick Khoda's part?'

Beeru said Khoda was playing to his team's strengths and that the Indians had chased well right through this World Cup.

Then Jay started going on about how Nikhil hadn't lost a single toss right through this tournament, and Beeru corrected him to say that he had actually, twice, and then Jay went on to add, 'Never after breakfasting with Zoya.'

And then they got into that whole damn dreary debate again.

Jay said that if India won today too, then Australia (or South Africa, whoever won the other semi) was going to raise a huge stink about India's voodoo doll, and the unfair advantage of the Zoya Factor.

Beeru told him that it was appalling that an educated man like himself was talking like this, and Jay said that if he (Beeru) was so educated surely he wouldn't mind if Zoya was 'rested' for the final. Beeru started to say something in return but just then Jay said (way too triumphantly for a neutral commentator) *that looks like a big one, yes it is!'* and as Zahid cursed loudly beside me, we saw Vikram Goyal's delivery soaring way over Nikhil's outflung arms and on through the boundary.

The skunk-haired heart-throb got a standing ovation; he'd definitely arrived at his century in style.

Vishaal, on his return from the snacks counter laden with beers and crisps, looked hassled to see his new English friend Gabrielle jumping in her seat, whooping madly. He slid in next to her, treading over Sanks's toes, grinning a good sportsman-spirit type of grin and started trying to hand her a beer, but she pushed him away and got to her feet. Then, chanting 'God Save the Queen' in a high, unsteady voice, she ripped open her long canvas overcoat to reveal that she was stark naked underneath, and leaping lithely over the railing, sped across the outfield, weaving her way past a startled Laakhi, and headed straight for the skunk-haired opener.

The crowd roared its approval, and a million cameras flashed as she streaked past the Fly Emirates guy and closed in on the skunk-head.

He had his bat up in the air, acknowledging the roar his century had evoked and hadn't quite realized that the crowd wasn't cheering just him any more. As Vishaal's Gabby grabbed his arm and spun him around, his eyes widened in total shock and the next moment she was laying the wettest smooch ever on his sunblock-slathered lips. By the way, she'd pulled off the ultimate matching-matching coup. She was sporting a skunk-style hair-do too, but not on her head…

'The lady seems to be feeling the heat, Beeru,' Jay said suavely as a couple of security guards hot-footed onto the pitch, bearing a big blanket.

'Er…yes,' said Beeru in a stunned sort of voice, sounding shocked to the core of his middle-class mind. But then he rallied valiantly, 'Vul!' he said, sounding more urbane by the second. 'Vul, vul, yes! It's a' – he was obviously trying to think of something super-witty to say, you could practically hear the wheels of his mind whirring – 'it's a display of naked emotion all right,' he proclaimed finally.

Vishaal, of course, had heard none of this. He was still standing exactly where Gabby had left him, his eyes twin pools of regret, clutching her discarded trenchcoat to his broken heart…

They closed at 331 for 6, and the mood amongst the India supporters got pretty grim. Zahid said he'd go sit with the team and insisted I tag along with him. 'Just come and say hi to everyone, Zoya,' he said when I protested that this was against the ICC rules.

We walked out of the main pavilion and down to the dressing rooms. People kept waving to us. It was strange the way everybody in light-blue shirts was looking at me – with a desperate look in their eyes, like they expected me to wave a wand and pull off a miracle or something. I kept my eyes glued to the floor till we entered a long, echoing corridor, hit a big wooden door and Zahid said, with fake heartiness, 'Here we are!'

I could hear a low murmur of conversation from inside and suddenly felt like I couldn't possibly go in. There had to be a limit to this whole stupid charade. I shook my head, 'No way, Zahid,' I said. 'I can't.'

He shoved his hands into the small of my back and tried to propel me forward, the way he had when he'd talked me into bungee jumping. 'C'mon, c'mon.'

But this was way more serious than that.

I pushed him away, turned around and started to hurry back to the main pavilion. He called out my name a couple of times but he didn't follow me. I must have taken a wrong turn somewhere because the corridor seemed never-ending. I'd just started to panic when I rounded a corner and practically collided into somebody. Pulling back a little, I registered that it was that chubby baby-with-pubic-hair, Vikram Goyal.

'Zoyaji,' he said surprised.

'Uh, hi, Vikram,' I said relieved. '*Kaise ho?*'

He looked at me, a little blankly. Then, of course, I realized it had been a dumb thing to ask; he'd had a terrible first half. The English attack had broken the back of his bowling. How insensitive of me to go *kaise ho?* to him.

I started to say something soothing, but then the blank, bewildered look left his eyes to be replaced by a fully attentive, rather cunning one. 'Please wish me luck,' he said, his just-broken voice wobbling unpleasantly.

'Best of luck,' I said brightly.

He shook his head slowly. 'Not like that,' he said. *'Theek se.* Properly.'

'Best of *luck?'* I ventured, ending the sentence on a high instead of a low, as I edged away from him, hoping a variation in cadence would satisfy him.

But of course it didn't.

Instead he mumbled, *'Jaise kal* skipper *ko kiya tha.'* Then he lifted two pudgy, clammy hands, placed them on either side of my ears, swooped down, and mashed his little-pink-orifice-amongst-a-thicket-of-pubes-mouth down on mine.

It was completely sick-making. Not just physically – though that was horrible enough, I mean, I could taste his entire lunch, and it had obviously been a six-course meal, onions, mutton, Pan-Parag being the top notes over a basic bouquet of sour, stale sweat – it was the way he just *assumed* he could do this. That I was some kind of team amenity, like a bottle of Gatorade or a pain-relief spray or an ice pack. *Luck levels dipping, boys? Just smooch some Zoya.* It made me so to-the-pit-of-my-stomach mad. I could have killed him.

I pushed him away as violently as I could and he flopped backward, his fleshy little mouth forming a little 'O' of surprise. 'I hope you get out for *duck,* asshole,' I snarled at him, and he backed away from me hurriedly, looking – I was pleased to see – rather *scared* of me. I shook back my dishevelled hair, lifted my hand, made a jabbing evil-eye gesture at him, and dashed away from there, rubbing my mouth furiously with the back of my hand.

I was still seething when I emerged onto the ground. My chest felt tight with anger, my cheeks were hot. I stomped my way out of the stands, made my way to the main gate, and phoned the driver. The phone rang several times; the driver was obviously engrossed in the match.

Around me, the cricket carnival raged on. The entire stadium seemed to be cheering for England – even the Aussies seemed to have their hearts set on an Australia–England final, and couldn't seem to wait to get us Indians out of there.

Frankly, neither could I.

The encounter with Vikram Goyal's eager plump tongue had put me off the light-blue uniform big time. How was Zahid any different from Vikram? Or Harry? Or Shivnath for that matter? *How was Nikhil Khoda any different?* I rubbed my hand across my mouth so hard it hurt.

My cheeks burned with humiliation as I realized that I'd been kidding myself all along. All the wooing, the cute text messages, the poolside meetings, they were probably all fake. Obviously, they all talked about me in their stupid locker room, like it was team strategy or something. *Woo that chubby-cheeked girl with the lucky streak, it's for your country after all, where's your patriotism, keep your eye on the cupboard.*

And I'd fallen for it!

This movie was so going to end with a supermodel making a guest appearance in the last shot. Nikhil would kiss her, hand her the World Cup trophy and drive away with her in a fancy car.

I would probably end up with Vishaal, all my luckiness sucked out of me, and would have to listen to him carp about his wretched Nike ad for the rest of my life.

I blew my nose gloomily and looked around, hoping nobody would look my way. I needn't have worried. Everyone was intent on what was happening down there on the pitch – the match was neck-to-neck. A glance at the display screen informed me that our run rate was steady, hovering around the required 6.06, which was pretty good. If you wanted India to win, that is.

Oh God, I was so sick of cricket! I felt suddenly, violently, homesick. What was I doing here? I didn't even like this game, I used to have a life, a good one, one I was perfectly satisfied with. What did I really hope to achieve out of this whole idiotic circus?

Almost like an answer to that question, the stadium started chanting Nikhil's name. Fighting an urge to cover my ears, I blundered out of the stadium and got into the car, which had just pulled up in front of me, commentary blaring from its radio. I ignored the puzzled look the driver gave me and I told him to take me back to the hotel. As we swung out of the exit gate, a loud groan sounded behind us.

Vikram Goyal had just got out for duck.

Cape Times Page 26

A file photo of Nikhil Khoda acknowledging his sixteenth one-day ton in Johannesburg

MAYBE BABY?

Evalene Adams, the stunning, blonde South African model and actor from the hit TV series *Hospital,* was blessed with a sturdy little bundle of joy, christened William Nicholas Adams, late last night. Both mum and bubba are doing well. Nobody's seen the birth certificate yet, but the local press is making much of the fact that baby William was born almost nine months to the day since the Indian cricket team toured South Africa last year. Ms Adams was sighted with the players quite often during the tour and that, coupled with the fact that the baby's middle name sounds a lot like that of the Indian skipper, Nikhil Khoda,

has got most people nodding knowingly, even though Ms
Adams has neither confirmed nor denied the rumours.

'Evalene's over the moon,' is all her publicist would tell
the media. 'A boy after two girls has made her family
complete. She's ecstatic but exhausted as the labour was
six hours long.'

The doctors wanted to administer an epidural but
reportedly Ms Adams, a yoga and wellness enthusiast,
insisted on having a completely natural delivery.

Baby William weighs in a lusty nine pounds and,
according to the nurses in the maternity ward, seems to
be an alert and unusually muscular baby.

Ms Adam's two daughters have been fathered by Black
Sunday frontmen Davy Keiths and soccer star Mohammad
Montana respectively. She is known for her 'exotic' men-
friends.

Her publicist said Ms Adams and baby Will's father
have no plans to marry.

I found the article slipped under my door when I got back into
my room. Somehow, my brain, miraculously unaffected by the
pummelling my emotions were receiving, sat back and did the
math. And the answer was this.

Nikhil was just using me.

All the pieces fell into place as I stared down at that article.
Hadn't that guy, Jagdish or whatever, in the nightclub in
Melbourne, been telling Zahid something about how his skipper
was a fool, going around having babies for free with random
babes? I think he'd even mentioned a name, but I'd just assumed
he'd been talking about some *other* captain, an earlier one...

Now, of course, I realized it had to be Nikhil. I heard those
six damning words again.

'*Jaise kal* skipper *ko kiya tha.*'

Screwing the newspaper up into a ball, I made up my mind.

All this time the Men in Blue had been using *me*; now it was time for me to use *them*.

Sheraan-wali Agarbatti wasn't going to be the only ad I would sign. Oh no, I would sign everything I could lay my hands on – Coke, soap, air conditioners, whatever. I was going to be as savvy and cynical as the man who'd told me with the love-light in his lying eyes: *If you don't come tonight, it may kill me, Zoya.*

Just then my phone rang.

It was Lokey.

'Joyaji, congratulations!' he shouted, as if I'd personally hit the winning six that won the match. Hey, maybe I had. Then he started harassing me to shoot Tauji's ad right away. He said we had five days before the final and that the set was standing ready at Eagle Studios in Film City, Delhi, and that there was a round-trip, first-class ticket booked for me.

'We can sign the contract tonight, Joyaji,' he yelled above the din in the stadium. 'The money will be wire-transferred into your account by tomorrow morning. Tauji wants *his* ad to be the first one viewers see after Khoda lifts the World Cup.'

'Okay,' I said, suddenly weak with longing at the thought of being home again. 'Come over then, let's do it.'

I'd showered and managed to pack most of my stuff for Delhi when Chachi and gang trooped in about forty minutes later, full of the match and how awesome the last hour of play had been.

Mon's husband was in good humour. 'Superb,' he kept saying. 'Fan-tas-tic, amazing. One could hardly believe it was India out there!'

They all wanted to go out and celebrate.

'...Because, who knows if we'll win the final,' Monita said matter-of-factly and they insisted I come too.

But I played it very smart. 'I have a team meeting now,' I said solemnly, not mentioning a word of my plans to travel. And they bought it. They all nodded, like they knew I had important 'Goddess-business' to attend to and hurtled out again, a scant fifteen minutes later, leaving me in peace.

My phone started ringing then. It was Nikhil, of course, finally back in his suite after the team celebrations in the Indian dressing room. I ignored him. He started messaging me, but I deleted the messages unread and then, finally, the landline started.

I picked it up on the fifth ring, my heart slamming against my ribs and the concierge told me that a Mr Chugh was there to see me. Thankful for the distraction, I went down and met Lokey in the coffee shop. He was in this real big hurry; he said he had lots of other deals all on the boil at the same time. He waved some papers in front of my face and I signed wherever he told me to. Then he hurried off, talking on his phone, and I made my way back to my room and tumbled into bed, quite worn out.

'INDIA STORMS INTO WORLD CUP FINAL' screamed the sports headlines in *The Age* the next day. There was a picture of Nikhil running to embrace Balaji as the English skipper walked away in the background. There was pure elation on both their faces, Khoda's arms were outflung and there was a wild, exultant look in his eyes. Just looking at him made my heart throb with regret. *You could've been with him last night,* a voice in my head said. *He would've claimed you like a 'prize' as Ritu would say. It would've been heaven on earth.*

Thank God I'd been spared *that*, I thought and turned the page.

I sighed when I saw a picture of Vishaal's Gabby, streaking across the pitch with her vital bits pixilated. 'Unlucky Streak?' read the headline. It all seemed so long ago.

There was another, smaller article on the same page. 'Zoya Hexed Me, Claims Goyal' – I frowned and zoomed in on it. It was very short, kind of like they'd got the news minutes before printing the paper:

> When questioned on his dismal performance at the SCG yesterday, conceding eighty-seven runs in eight overs, no wickets and zero with the bat, India's youngest player, Vikram Goyal, said, 'It wasn't nerves. I was fully confident. It was Zoya, she hexed me so I would not be able to perform.' We then asked him why Zoya would do such a thing. Vikram said rather obscurely that Zoya disliked him for 'personal' reasons and invited us to question Zahid Pathan on the issue.
>
> If Vikram's claim is true, then Zoya's displeasure is indeed a terrible thing to incur if you're serious about a career in cricket. Whatever the reason, judging from his performance alone, it seems Vikram may be rested for the final next week. Meanwhile, the Zoya Factor seems to be growing more and more controversial by the minute. (ATP Features)

What a jerk! He'd been playing lousily before he'd groped me in the passage. And what a snivelly, loser-like thing to do, to make excuses for his pathetic performance instead of just admitting he'd panicked or been outplayed or whatever. As expected, the media was playing it up.

My phone started ringing right then. I didn't recognize the

number so I didn't pick it up. *Must be some journo types*, I thought, feeling harassed. *How soon can I get out of this country?*

Mon and Anand came in and wanted to discuss the Vikram issue, but the concierge called just then and said Nikhil was here to see me.

I took a deep breath, fluffed out my hair and went down to meet him. He was in the lobby, looking a lot like the way he'd done in Dhaka when he'd blasted me under the big Bong tree – sleep-deprived and heavy-eyed – not at all like his picture in the paper this morning.

'Zoya,' he said, very curt.

'Still alive, I see,' I said snidely.

He got all tight-lipped and started walking towards the coffee shop without bothering to see if I'd follow. I had half an urge to turn around and scurry for the lift, but then I squared my shoulders and followed him.

So this was not going to be a romantic session by the poolside. Fine. Suited me. He walked up to a table for two and pulled out a chair for me in mock politeness. I sat, and he walked around the table and sat down too. I fidgeted with the fancy cutlery and met his eyes incuriously.

He said, very deliberately, 'Would you care to tell me what you've been up to with Goyal?'

'Oh, are we fighting again?' I asked, acting all surprised. 'I thought we'd made up.'

He sighed. 'Please, Zoya, just tell me, okay?'

I shrugged and looked away. 'There's nothing to tell,' I said tonelessly.

He frowned. 'There must be *something*.'

'Nothing,' I repeated.

'You're saying he's making up the whole thing?' Nikhil

asked in this really neutral voice that somehow completely got my goat. He sounded like he was the presiding officer at a courtmartial or something.

'I'm not saying *anything*,' I glared at him and got to my feet. 'I don't have to justify myself to *you*.'

He raised his eyebrows. 'How about to your fans?' he said mildly. 'Or should I say *devotees*? Want to tell them why you've turned against your own team?'

'It's not my team,' I said, a little thickly. 'It's yours. No one gives a damn about me.'

He looked puzzled at that, like he was wondering where I was coming from, then he said, 'I just want to know what happened that's all.'

I didn't want to tell him. I didn't quite know why. Well, partly it was because I cringed at the idea of sounding like some outraged blushing damsel, flinging accusations and going: *Ho ji*, Vikram *ne meri izzat pe haath dala*; partly because the whole wretched incident had all become entangled in my head with Nikhil's feelings for the South African mother of his offspring; and partly, I thought guiltily, because I had meant what I'd said to Vikram yesterday. I'd wanted him to play badly. I'd definitely spooked him out, that's for sure. He'd totally flinched when I'd made that stabbing, witch's-curse gesture at him.

So I just shrugged. 'It's true. I did hex him.'

'Why?' Nikhil asked.

'Because he made me angry,' I said with vague grandness. 'He displeased the Goddess, okay?' And then, as he opened his mouth to speak, I threatened, 'And don't *you* make me angry because then I may curse you too!'

Nikhil just sat there looking at me, his eyes completely unreadable as I kept scowling at him, my hand drawn back into my witch-fingered jabbing stance. And then a corner of his mouth twitched. As I watched, fully mortified, this really wide smirky grin spread across his face. 'I'm shivering with fright,' he drawled.

'So funny,' I said unwittily, dropping my hexing hand and crossing both arms across my chest. 'And now that I've cheered you up, I'll take your leave. I have to pack.'

He stopped smirking then and shot out one hand to grab my wrist. 'Oh, didn't you pack last night?' he said, leaning in, his tone suddenly silky. 'I thought maybe that's what kept you away.'

Of course this was the moment to tell him that his new fatherhood was what had kept me away. That, coupled with the sickening conviction that he, like his entire team, was chasing me because I made them win.

But I said nothing.

He looked at me in silence for a bit, then sat back and asked, doing a great imitation of being genuinely mystified, '*Why?*'

I said nothing. Just sat there, hoping I was looking dignified and not, you know, just brattish.

He went on, 'I thought you were teasing me first, hiding somewhere. I opened all the cupboards, looked in the loo, out on the balcony... I called your number a million times. *Why* didn't you pick up the phone, Zoya?'

I shook my head, irritated with myself for warming to the urgency in his voice. Instead I forced myself to think, *Serves you right you cocky, two-faced, Khodathing! What do you think I am, some kind of doggie who hides under your bed and comes out when called?*

He kept looking at me, willing me to speak, and who knows what I might have blurted out, had a young voice not broken in just then, 'Nikhil-sir? Dilip Prakash, *Sports News*. Can we get your reaction to the Australian captain's statement?'

Nikhil frowned, let go my hand, and turned to look at the two young eager beavers with close-cropped haircuts who seemed to have materialized out of nowhere. 'Guys, this is a private conversation,' he said, sounding totally exasperated. 'Please! I'll chat with you later.'

'Fine sir, sorry sir,' the first one said, not moving an inch, 'but perhaps you're not aware of this latest development...'

The second one addressed me. 'What do *you* think of the statement, Ma'am?'

Nikhil moved forward and grabbed my arm at that, preparing to get all chivalrous and protect me from the paparazzi, but I didn't need his help. 'Buzz off, buddy, or I'll hex you,' I hissed and the two young journos backed away hurriedly, swiftly retreating to a nearby table where they made a couple of furtive calls, with both eyes peeled on me.

Nikhil said resignedly, 'We'd better leave. They'll be descending here in hordes.'

'Okay,' I said. 'See you then.'

And I walked out of the coffee shop without even saying goodbye.

Chachi and I checked out by eight o'clock that evening. The flight was at midnight but I wanted to get to the airport early. So did Chachi, but that was because she wanted to shop. Her big issue, when I'd told her we were leaving the same day, had been: 'Presents! Zoya! We can't go home empty-handed!'

As she'd done nothing but shop ever since we'd got here, I'd been a bit taken aback, but she claimed there were still a million things left to buy. I told her we'd be back in Melbourne in four days' time, but she said she had to shop anyway. 'Chocolates,' she muttered to herself. 'Opals, transparent, detachable bra straps…'

I had called Dad earlier and told him to come to the airport the next morning. He'd sounded pretty surprised but hadn't asked any questions. Just said cryptically, 'Good, I want to talk to you.'

I'd told Mon I'd see her soon and she'd said, 'I know you want to go home, Zoya, and I know the money's good, but I'm not at all sure you should be doing this dodgy ad. Have you seen the script?'

I admitted I hadn't and she'd insisted, 'Ask for a script narration before you get on that flight.'

I'd shaken my head resolutely. All I could see before me was the garden at Tera Numbar. I just *had* to get back there and drink adrak ki chai and listen to my dad rant on about Gajju and Yogu Chachas' latest peccadilloes.

'Okay,' she'd sighed. 'If it sucks, ask for changes, okay? Don't let them walk all over you. And make sure Lokey's at the shoot.'

I'd promised her I would.

Then Vishaal came bursting in to give me a big hug and to extract a promise that I would definitely be back for the final. 'These flights are all fucked up, man,' he said. 'If there's a problem, just call up Vijay Mallya or someone and ask them to put you on a private jet! They'll have to do it if they're patriotic, dude.'

I laughed. 'Don't worry, Vishaal,' I said. 'I'll be back. But I must say, for someone who made that famous Nike ad, you've become pretty superstitious…'

'Don't mention that ad,' Vishaal said fiercely, 'my eyes had not been opened then. Now I'm like your Devotee Number One, Zoya.'

And then he said, all in a rush, 'It was I who tore up your New Zealand visa, you know.'

What?

He went on hurriedly, without looking me in the eye. 'I was hoping they could win without you. I thought if they did, maybe my ad would finally see the light of the day... Sorry, I didn't know you were a Goddess then.'

I just stared at him, uncomprehendingly, as he shoved my bags into the elevator and mouthed a last sorry as the lift door closed on his face.

I was standing in the lobby, waiting for the car and wondering if *anybody* was who he seemed to be, when a voice behind me went, 'Where d'you think you're going?'

It was Nikhil. I quickly closed my eyes because if I couldn't see him, he wasn't really there, right?

Then he said, 'Actually, don't bother to tell me. I know already.'

I opened my eyes warily. 'You do?'

He nodded, 'Sure. You're going home to shoot that agarbatti ad, for which you will be paid the grand sum of fifty lakh rupees. You're going home to sign a bunch of contracts to endorse products ranging from HB pencils to small-sized cars. You're going home to talk to the Youth Congress about getting a ticket for the state elections...'

I raised my chin. 'You're wrong,' I said.

'Oh?' he asked.

'It's the RJP, actually.'

Khoda's mouth tightened into a thin line. 'Zoya.'

'Don't you *Zoya* me,' I said. 'I've had enough of your goody-goody speeches, when all the time you've been sucking up to me to win matches.'

He said, very slowly, like he was talking to an idiot. 'For the hundredth time, I don't need *you* to win matches!'

'Really?' I said, breathing hard. 'When's the last time you won a match without me, huh?'

'You're irrelevant,' he said bluntly. 'I don't need you.'

'You're incompetent,' I shot back. 'You're nothing but a loser without me, that's why you want me to stay.'

He said, in this really irritating, patronizing way, 'You know, you have some serious self-esteem issues...'

I said, 'And you have a baby boy...'

His expression changed. 'Where did you hear that?'

'Never mind,' I said tersely. 'I know it's true so don't bother to deny it.'

He gave a short laugh. 'Oh, I won't,' he said, his eyes glittering. 'Especially since you've been romancing Zahid behind my back and attempting to sabotage his rival Vikram. And *you're* the one rushing home to rake in the moolah, preying on the religious beliefs of a credulous nation...'

I stared at him in complete incomprehension. What was he talking about? And where did he get that vocabulary? I mean, *preying on the religious beliefs of a credulous nation?* It was bad, even by his pompous Nike-ad standards. *Wow*, I said to myself, *I am so well rid of this two-faced, opportunistic bastard!*

I hitched my red rucksack higher and turned to go, wondering where my shopaholic aunt had wandered off to. 'See you Friday?' Khoda called after me, his tone betraying...what? Sarcasm? Guilt? Panic, that I wouldn't be back in time and he'd lose? I turned around and looked at him.

There was definitely a question in his Boost-brown eyes.

GREED OF THE GODDESS

By Andrea Mehta-Meyer,
(The author is a Wicca Witch of
Indo-Dutch descent)
The Straits Times, Inflight copy

The archetypical Goddess, says ancient Indian lore, was created by the Gods to vanquish demons that the gods themselves could not defeat. The She-mother was a drunken, wide-hipped, bow-twanging, battle-loving warrior with rolling red eyes and a lust for blood. A million manifestations of herself emerged from her large swinging belly and battled with the demons, defeating them effortlessly. And no matter how thick the fray, she always kept one of her eight arms free to quaff a tankard or two of kick-ass celestial nectar along the way.

When it was all over, the Gods would scurry in with bowed hands, step fastidiously over the devastation and the spilt blood, interrupt her as she played happily with the severed heads of the demons, thank her and beseech softly, 'Now return to your abode, Goddess, return to your dwelling place. Remain there in slumber till we summon you again.' The Goddess usually returned. She had no great love for the Gods, they were almost mortal in their petty concerns. She had no taste for their little lives, full of mincing, hair-splitting rules about good and evil, dharma and adharma, right and wrong. The Goddess preferred to take a broader view of things. So she would return to her home in the mountains and stay there till they came bleating to her for help again.

But what would happen if the Goddess started feeling mutinous? What would happen if she decided to step out of her 'God-given' role a little and started to do things that were, uh, just not cricket?

Zoya Singh Solanki is a creation of Jogpal Lohia, Nikhil Khoda and Weston Hardin. They are the Godly Triad that found a simple little girl with an appealing birth date and an intriguing record and fashioned her into a Goddess capable of vanquishing superior foes, whom they had never before succeeded in vanquishing alone.

Today, Zoya has indeed achieved Goddess-like status. A thousand babies have been named after her, temples have sprung up in her honour, her name is chanted fervently as Indian batsmen take guard on the screens of fourteen-inch television sets across the nation.

And as she blazes a trail through the tenth ICC World Cup, as the event gets christened the Goddess of all Conflicts, and as the Australian captain officially issues a statement of protest of unfair advantage to the ICC, the trio who created her have their groin guards in a twist. Because Zoya Devi does not believe in keeping a low profile.

She has, since she got to Australia, broken arms, caused fist fights, bestowed kisses, hexed performances and, with a lotus-pink tongue, greedily lapped up the credit for every Indian victory and, rumour says, the cream of all cricketing endorsements on the subcontinent.

In Australia, a visibly uncomfortable-looking Nikhil Khoda fielded questions on the issue last night. 'Personally, I don't believe in luck,' he said. This disingenuous remark was greeted with derisive hoots from the Australians in the audience. 'Our team is good, they're playing well. Don't you guys have any questions on the game, for heaven's sake?' They didn't. And now, as Zoya Devi, the Raktdantini, the Goddess who likes the taste of blood on her teeth, opens her maw even wider and roars for an even larger share of the juicy cricket pie, the gods are crying foul.

But Zoya Devi is no longer Anybody's Creature.

She's tasted power and loves it. Zoya Devi is on a rampage. The Gods are running for extra cover. I sit here, laugh a deep, guttural belly-laugh and raise an admiring toast to the Goddess.

Zoya Mata ki Jai!

20

Dad came hurrying towards me as soon as I got off the plane, right there on the tarmac at IGI airport. I hugged him in surprise. 'What are you doing *here*, Dad?' I asked. 'How did airport security let you all the way in?'

'They didn't want you to cause a riot,' he said matter-of-factly. 'There's a car waiting for us, right here.' He pointed to a white Ambassador with flashing red sirens. 'They'll send the bags along later.'

The sun was just about breaking through Delhi's winter fog as our car wound its way out of the airport. We passed a huge crowd of reporters and the OB vans of at least six different news channels. Dad cackled, 'Outsmarted them,' with quiet triumph. 'They've been camping here for you all night!' he explained.

'For me?' I said in wonder.

'You're a Grade A celebrity, Zoya.'

Pretty cool, huh? I saw my face on at least a hundred posters on the way home! They'd been put up by the ZDDD – the Zoya Devi Devotee Dal. I saw *Zing!* banners that read 'Zing! Khol, Zoya Bol!' I saw a Zandu Balm poster that said: 'Z for Zandu, Z for Zoya. Lucky Charm *ka* Lucky Balm!' I saw a little chai boy rushing to deliver tea in a tee shirt that had my face on it. It was supercool.

There was a humongous crowd outside our front gate, so Dad got the driver to drive right past it and we sneaked in through the little back gate in G. Singh's part of the house.

G. Singh was waiting there looking teary-eyed. He smothered his wife in a mighty clinch and didn't come up for air for at least three minutes. Then he finally turned to me and said, his wise-turtle face beaming, 'Welcome home, beta.'

I hugged him and then we trooped through the house and down to our bit of it, where Eppa and Meeku waited, shrieking and barking respectively. 'Zoyaaaa!' Eppa exclaimed as Meeku licked my face. 'You are looking so *fair*! So smart! Like a foreigner!'

'Hi, sex bomb,' I said, hugging her bird-like frame fondly as Meeku bounded off to molest Rinku Chachi. 'How are you?'

But the best was still to come. I'd just entered the house when a dark, wiry figure in a blue striped nightsuit came hobbling out on crutches and said, in a ringing voice, 'Gaalu! How are you?'

It was a minor fracture, and a bit of a flesh wound, no big deal, Zoravar claimed. The fallout of a sporadic exchange of fire, right after the Indo–Pak match, which had escalated tensions across the LOC. They'd sent him home to convalesce. Nobody in the family had told me about this because they didn't want to worry me. 'In fact, my buddies said I'd deliberately shot myself in the foot because I wanted to see the World Cup final at home,' Zoravar said, his stubbly, kaaju-face stretched in a grin.

I couldn't believe nobody had told me!

Rinku Chachi had known all along. She and Zoravar had

been having long international chats practically every day, gossiping about me, I bet. Well, I hoped Gajju's BP would go through the roof when he got the bills.

'How are you?' Zoravar asked abruptly as Eppa bustled into the kitchen and started to cook a big lunch. The whole clan was eating with us today.

'Fine,' I said grinning too brightly.

'No, you're not,' he said as he reached for a long red plastic device; my fly-swatter-cum-back-scratcher, I realized with a pang. As I watched in horrid fascination, he inserted it carefully into the gap between his hairy leg and the plaster and dug with gusto, closing his eyes and shuddering with pleasure. I caught a whiff of chloroform and what smelled like stale vase-water in which the roses had been allowed to putrefy.

'What are you doing? Zoravar, you pig!' I cried, totally grossed out.

'Shh...it itches as it heals, Gaalu, it feels *great* when I scratch it, oooh, my mouth has started watering...'

I got up and sat a little further away from him.

'How's the skipper?' he asked, still scratching his leg, his eyes closed.

'Fine,' I said. Then I added grudgingly, 'You were right about him.'

He opened his eyes then, frowning slightly, 'I was? Are you sure?'

I nodded. Then seeing a concerned look cross his face I added hastily, 'But I'm fine. No bones broken.'

'Bad joke,' he said wryly, looking at his own plastered foot. 'D'you wanna tell me the whole story, Gaalu? Get the male perspective?'

'No thanks,' I said, shrugging. 'It's not a big deal.'

'Okay,' he said, still looking concerned. 'But I'm here if you change your mind. *Theek hai?*'

'*Theek hai,*' I said and went in to unpack.

Rinku Chachi ruled at lunch even though Anita Chachi had shown up in a skimpier-than-usual choli, in a desperate attempt to outshine her. But it was a total no-contest. Rinku Chachi dazzled as she held forth on the beauty of Australia, the cuteness of the koala bears she'd cuddled, the sheep she'd sheared, the revolving restaurant in Sydney, the pub crawls in Melbourne and sunset at 'Iyer's' Rock, before smoothly changing gears and talking with great fondness and familiarity about *hamara* Nikhil, and *sharaarti* Zahid and *cute-sa* Harry.

And when Anita Chachi, growing more sullen by the minute, dropped a whole spoon of yellow-dal-tadka on her dupatta, she said large-heartedly, 'No worries, mate,' and totally blew her away. It was awesome.

Anita the hag glowered and glittered and finally said, '*Toh phir* you will definitely be invited to the naamkaran, Bhabhiji!'

'Definitely,' Rinku Chachi said airily. 'Which one of the boys is having a child, Zoya?'

All eyes swivelled on me.

'Nikhil.' I managed to say casually. 'Nikhil.'

Zoravar insisted we sit around a coal fire on the terrace like we used to when we were kids. So Dad and I had to lug up the angeethi, while he followed, hobbling behind us. We settled onto our cosy gaddis and took sneak peeks at the journos crowding the streets below, as they made loud, self-important phone calls. The press throng outside our main gate hadn't lessened all day. They didn't desert their posts at night either and went crazy interviewing anybody they could find. Our dhobi, the electrician, the maali. They were that desperate.

'What a bunch of losers,' I said scornfully.

'They're just doing their jobs,' Dad said mildly.

I scowled and looked away.

Dad said, 'What's the problem with you, Zoya? You seem so hard suddenly.'

'Nothing,' I muttered. 'Just tired.' I sat back on the cushion and looked up sulkily at the starry sky.

Dad said, 'I know you're a celebrity at the moment, but these things don't last. Don't let it change the person you are.'

I rolled my eyes in the dark. 'I know, Dad. I won't. Good night.'

He stood looking down at Zoravar and me for a while, then sighed and said, 'Good night, kids,' and shuffled off slowly downstairs.

The moment he left, Zoravar said, 'Wanna talk?' I shook my head.

'Anita Chachi is a cow,' he said.

'Yes.' I sighed. 'But she didn't make that up. It's all true. I read about it in Sydney.'

He said, very softly, 'I'm sorry, Gaalu.'

I said, 'So am I.'

I'd planned to go with Neelo for the shoot at Eagle Studio the next morning, but Zoravar insisted on tagging along too. He propped himself up on these rather cool steel crutches and hopped into the car, ignoring my protests. Then we sneaked out through the front gate (the journos had discovered the little back entrance early this morning and shifted camp there) in the car that Lokey had sent.

The studio was bustling. Cables and wires lay coiled everywhere, carpenters hammered madly at this big Benares-temple-type structure in the middle of the set, up on the tarafa, the wooden planked platform was suspended from thick jute ropes, lighting assistants rigged up the lights. My heart got a massive jolt when I saw Nikhil standing in the lights in his blue India tee shirt and it took me a full ten minutes to bring it back to normal when I realized it was just a body double with very similar hair and build.

There was a make-up van for me, just like the one Shah Rukh had in Bombay, with ZSS on the door. That perked me up a little as I entered it, nodding graciously at the spot boy who opened the door for me. The three of us had a cup of tea in the van and then Lokey brought the director in to explain what we'd be shooting.

It was PPK. Bearded, hatted, ponytailed – very directorial-looking as always.

'Hi, Zoya,' he grinned. 'Moved up in life, haven't you?'

I laughed, genuinely pleased to see him. 'Hi,' I said.

'Hey, dude,' Neelo said grudgingly. He was not very fond of PPK. They'd shot a bunch of films together and had had 'creative differences'.

'What've you done to your leg, young man?' PPK asked Zoravar.

Zoravar started to explain, but PPK wasn't really interested. He cut him short, saying, 'Because I need some maimed and crippled types in this film, trailing the Goddess, we can cast you if you like!' He smiled this big patronizing smile. 'You wanna be in an ad?'

I said quickly, before Zoravar could react, 'Shall we go through the script?'

PPK took off his hat and sat down. 'Sure,' he said. Then he made a bit of a production of gathering his thoughts – closing his eyes, pressing his thumb and forefinger into his eyelids and everything. Finally, he opened his eyes, took a deep breath and looked at me:

'The film opens on a long shot of a beautiful temple on the banks of the Ganga. It's early morning. We see a figure walk towards the temple. It's Nikhil Khoda, in his blue India uniform, you can tell who it is because his name is written on his shirt. He is then joined by another blue-uniformed figure. It is Laakhi, his vice captain. More and more people join the two batsmen, they are regular Indian cricket fans, from every walk of life. The army of people walks towards the temple gates, which open magically with a triumphant blowing of a traditional Hindu conch shell, a shankh. Inside the temple, Vedic chants sound in the background as Laakhi lights a match which flares up, and with a mystic gesture he holds it out to Nikhil who lights a Sheraan-wali Agarbatti from the flame. The agarbatti flame dies out and smoke rises and wafts over the people's faces as they all bow their heads in worship. We hear the roar of a cricket stadium, a billion voices chanting: *Zoya Zoya Zoya Zoya*... The smoke clears; through it your face, framed in its trademark halo of curls, becomes visible. There is a gleaming trident in your hand, vaguely reminiscent of the three stumps of a cricket wicket. You smile and say, in a hushed, Goddess-like voice, "Pray to the Devi with the Sheraan-wali Agarbatti and your prayers will be answered." And that's pretty much it,' PPK concluded. 'It's a forty-seconder.'

He sat back and looked at us for a reaction.

Zoravar made a strangled little noise in the back of his throat and lurched out of the van, shutting the door loudly behind him.

Neelo said, 'Fuckin' unreal, man.' A long silence followed. 'You're serious?' I asked PPK finally. *That's* the script?'

'Sure,' he nodded. 'That's it. I'd like to add a beatific smiling shot of you, showcasing your divinity, at the end of your dialogue, and cut to an image of the World Cup trophy but yes, that's the lot.'

I looked at Lokey. 'You're Nikhil's agent,' I told him. 'Laakhi's too, I think? What will they say when they see this on TV?'

Lokey shrugged. 'We will have to misspell their names, little bit on thee shirts, PPKji,' he said, 'otherwise it is okay.'

'Is that all you have to say?' I gasped.

He nodded, *'Haan.'*

'But they're *praying* to her, fucker!' Neelo said, revealing unsuspected religious depths. 'That's like...blasphemous.'

Lokey chucked a handful of pistas into his mouth and said patiently, 'Joyaji, it is all good for thee advertising business. Your ad will be seen, thee agarbattis will be sold, thee beedi will sell too. Then Nike and *Zing!* and Nero-Tasha and other sponsors will do more and more ads showcasing their point of view and trying to claim thee World Cup victory as *theirs*. Laakhi and Nikhil will profit from it, they will get much more money than you can even imagine...'

PPK said, 'I'm booked to shoot the Nero-Tasha victory ad one week after the boys get home. Don't worry, Zoya. It'll all work out well.'

I looked at the two of them doubtfully, sitting there like it was all in a day's work, thought about the fifty lakhs in my bank account, and felt a little reassured. Neelo too, I noticed, was already sitting back and endeavouring to wrap his fairly elastic sense of morality around the concept of an unworthy Pappu like me being worshipped as a Goddess. 'Well, you know what they say,' he offered, a little self-consciously. 'Every human being has a spark of the divine in him.'

And then this costume girl traipsed in with my costume and they all had to leave so I could get into it. Wow. I needed sunglasses just to look at it. It was kind of like a Bharatanatyam dancer's costume, with a light-blue divided sari and a low embroidered belt. A shiny, gold-coin-encrusted corset went on top, along with a vast number of gold and bead necklaces and a cardboardy kind of a gold crown for my head. The trident was a flashy blue and silver and a choreographer came in to show me how to hold it.

'Strike a pose like this,' he said, lifting one leg up from the hip and crossing it across the other so he looked like a Nataraj in acid-washed denims and an Eminem tee shirt. 'Toss your mane back. And arch your neck regally – like a queen.' He actually said it. *Mane*.

Of course I've read *Cosmo* magazine and I know that in some rarefied stratospheres the beautiful people call their hair 'mane', their butt 'bootie' and their eyes 'peepers', but I'd never actually met anyone who used the word. The fact that he was asking me to wear an Indian mythological outfit while tossing my mane about kind of took the edge off the moment, though. I nodded and tried to emulate the pose. He poked his bony fingers between my shoulder blades till my chest completely jutted out and said, 'That's it. Be proud! Be powerful! Very good.'

And then he left me with the costume and make-up people to get dressed.

Forty minutes later, I walked out looking like someone from the world-famous-in-Karol-Bagh DCM Mills' production of the Ramleela. They'd pumped my hair so full of goop that every curl stuck out of my head like a frozen bolt of lightning. They'd made my eyes huge and fish-like, my face a dead white mask and my mouth vermilion. Two torpedo missiles protruded from my chest.

The only way I got through the whole process was by chanting *fifty lakhs, fifty lakhs, fifty lakhs* under my breath. But even that was beginning to lose its charm, especially since I'd realized I'd have to pay a huge chunk in taxes. Somehow *thirty-one point five lakhs, thirty-one point five lakhs, thirty-one point five lakhs* didn't have quite the same magical ring.

Zoravar's eyes totally popped when he saw me. 'Wow,' he said finally. 'You in there somewhere, Gaalu?'

Neelo was ruder. 'Look, Asha Parekh made a baby with Tina Turner,' he said. 'Fuck.'

I blinked my extremely stiff eyelashes at them and said, 'I don't have a good feeling about this,' through thickly lipsticked lips.

The shot was still not ready so the spot boys produced three spindly-legged chairs for us and we sat down to wait. The choreographer was lurking in the background looking like he was itching to make me practise the 'Goddess pose'. I hurriedly turned my back on him and almost stabbed myself in the stomach with my trident.

'Namaste, Zoya Devi.'

I looked up warily and beheld a large brown gentleman in a starched white pajama kurta. I brought my hands together into an instinctive namaste and a whole bunch of light bulbs popped in my face. When my eyes finally adjusted to the glare, I realized the large brown gentleman had a posse of photographers lurking behind his large brown shoulders. As they scurried away, the large brown man pulled up a chair and sat down on it, large amounts of him hanging off it from both sides. 'Kuku Prasad, MLA, Bhiwandi,' he said, beaming at me.

'Uh, hello,' I said, as graciously as I could and waited for him to explain himself further. But that seemed to be it. The guy had shot his bolt. He just sat there, beaming. And *gleaming* slightly, as he sweated gently under the studio lights.

Neelo said finally, 'So, Kuku, do you work in film production?'

Kuku laughed, revealing very pink gums. 'No, no, I am here on the party's behalf, to meet Zoya Devi, and her agent Mr Lokendarji. It is about her contesting the upcoming polls, from Ayodhya, on our party's ticket.'

Neelo swivelled around to look at me. 'You're joining politics!' he gasped.

'When were you planning to tell us, Zoya?' Zoravar said in this very quiet voice. But it freaked me out. Because my brother *never* calls me Zoya.

I shrugged evasively. 'It was just an idea,' I muttered. 'Nothing is pukka yet.'

Kuku leaned forward and protested. 'What you're saying, Deviji? High Command has approved your candidature! Everything is pukka! You do not know, you have beaten one freedom fighter, one dowry-victim-with-terrible-burn-scars and one Asian-Games-silver-medallist-who-is-also-a-scheduled-caste for this ticket! Competition was very tough! But don't worry! You are approved! We will seek High Command's blessings first thing tomorrow morning and then file your nomination. Tonight itself, we are doing a press release and printing six lakh posters. That is why the photographers are here!'

Okay, this was news to me. I sucked in my breath and prepared to explode, but Lokey came puffing up just then (which was good, because my exploding would probably have caused my twin torpedo missiles to pop and hit Kuku in his twin Googly eyes and blind him for life, besides leaving me topless).

I said, through gritted teeth, 'What's going on, Lokey?' 'Nothing, Joyaji,' he said, grinning shiftily. 'Mr Kukuji's here to meet you regarding thee possibility of your being interested in contesting thee election, that's all. Zoravarji, please take...' and he tried to placate Zoravar by offering him a handful of pistas.

'*Hain hain*, what-what?' Kuku started to say belligerently, but no one heard the rest of what he had to say, because a huge chanting drowned him out. The sound of a million voices shouting: *Zoya Devi ki Jai! Zoya Devi ki Jai! Zoya Devi ki Jai!*

'It's the soundtrack for the ad,' Neelo said, a little uncertainly. 'I mean, it *has* to be, right?'

'Yeah, of course, it must be,' I said, feeling relieved. For a moment the horrible possibility of a real crowd being out there had come to my mind and frozen my blood solid.

But then Kuku said, 'It is your devotees from your soon-to-be constituency. There are ten truckfuls of them accompanying me.'

Before any one of us could take in the seriousness of this information, the ten truckloads broke through Studio Security and stormed onto the set in a saffron swarm. They charged towards the large POP-and-plyboard temple – fortunately for me they just *assumed* a Goddess would be in her mandir – as PPK's crew swooped down on us and hustled us all into the make-up van. The last sound I heard, before the make-up van door shut behind me, was of PPK giving mother-sister *ka* abuses on his megaphone, then a little yelp, and then there was silence.

Zoravar gave a satisfied little grunt. 'Good scene,' he said. 'If they break his legs he can cast himself in his ad.' Then he

crossed his arms across his chest and levelled his gaze at Kuku.
'You were saying?'

Kuku swallowed hard, 'They are little high-spirited, that's
all... I'm sure if the Devi gives them a darshan...'

I started to say, 'Mr Kukuji, I'm not sure...'

And then the door of the make-up van swung open and two
dishevelled dudes surged in, their Gucci sunglasses glinting
crookedly above their rumpled grey beards. Truly astonished, I
blinked my stiff lashes and said hello to Jogpal Lohia and
Lingnath Baba.

'Hello, hello,' Jogpal said distractedly, looking around the
crowded van. Then he pounced on Kuku with a little cry, his
twin-tunnelled nostrils flaring as he snapped, 'Maderchod,
what're you doing here?'

Neelo said, very austerely, 'Whoa, who's the rude dude,
Zoya?'

I just shook my head, as taken aback as he was. Meanwhile,
Jogpal stuck his hand in Kuku's kurta collar, yanked him up
and booted him out of the van, shutting the door with a decisive
click.Then he turned to Lokey, who was staring at him
completely bug-eyed, and demanded, 'What was that fellow
doing here?'

Lokey backed away hurriedly and came up against the wall
with a bump so hard the whole van shook. Perspiring profusely,
he said, 'He was only here for initial meeting with my client,
Lohiaji. You don't like him, no problem, we will reschedule,
meet him later. But you, Lohiaji, what are you doing here?'

Jogpal said, completely ignoring the question, his voice
shaking with emotion: 'I don't want this innocent child to be
sullied by encounters with such scum-of-the-earth type of
people.'

Then he turned to me, grabbed my non-trident-holding hand in both his own and said effusively, 'Hello, beta, how are you?'

'What are you doing here? I thought you would be in Australia,' I asked, my head in a daze.

'I had a board meeting. And I wanted to take Baba's blessing for our team.' (Lingnath tinkled self-deprecatingly at this.) 'And I wanted to see *you* shoot your first commercial, beta!'

Lokey said smoothly, 'Mr Jogpal is personal friend of Tauji, you know that, no, Joyaji?'

I nodded my goopy head impatiently. I didn't like the way everybody was trying to control me here. It was about time I made it clear to them exactly whose name was on the door of this make-up van. I sat down gingerly, mindful of my protrusions and said, 'Let's take this one at a time, okay? First, it's great you're friends with Tauji, Uncle, because I want you to tell him I don't like this script.'

A minor ripple ran through the ill-assorted group at this statement.

Zoravar grunted his approval, Neelo muttered a low *too fuckin' right*, Lokey made mild protesting noises and Jogpal's eyes popped. Only Lingnath stayed serene. I continued, 'I don't like this costume. I don't like this trident. And finally, Lokey, I'm sorry, but I don't like your Kukuji!'

Jogpal instantly turned belligerently on Lokey and demanded, 'Absolutely! What is all this politics-sholitics, Lokendar?'

Zoravar said, 'Hang on a sec. Let's start from the first item on her list, shall we? Can we do anything about the script?'

Lingnath said smoothly, 'But why, Devi? It is a beautiful script, crafted specially to showcase your divinity.'

That rather startled me, because it was weird, the way he

used exactly the same phrase PPK had used earlier. 'How come you know the script so well?' I asked.

He said, without missing a beat, 'Your interests are very close to my heart, Devi.'

'What about Nikhil's?' I couldn't help demanding. 'This script reduces him and the team to cartoons. You're cool with that?'

'Nikhil is like a son to me,' Jogpal said instantly.

'Then don't you care that the sports media worldwide is laughing at him? At our team?'

Jogpal shifted his bulk a little and shook his hands about dismissively. 'Bete, why are you worried about these white people's campaigning? They are all hypocrites. They are accusing us of voodoo but they are only doing it because they are *scared*, they want to play mind games with our boys.'

'Okay, tell me,' I said. 'Just supposing I don't go back, do you think the outcome of the match will be affected? Seriously? Honestly?'

Jogpal and Lingnath pondered this question for a while, doing a cool sort of a double act where Jogpal's nostrils expanded and contracted in perfect time to Lingnath's ominous tinkling. Outside, my wannabe-constituents were going all out. Ominous thumping sounds filtered through into the make-up van, along with the sound of a shrill thready voice leading the ten truckloads of people in their mindless chant. '*Zoya Devi ki Jai! Zoya Devi ki Jai! Zoya Devi ki Jai!*' Finally Lingnath said, 'Of course the outcome will be affected. You have not seen your astrological chart. Your stars are sublime. Perfect. Unique...'

But I was looking at Jogpal. He said slowly, 'You should have more faith in your God-given powers, Zoya beta.'

I replied, 'And you should have more faith in your team.'

'Yeah, dude,' Neelo piped in. 'As president of the IBCC

shouldn't you be worried that public opinion is going against your boys?'

I was worried Neelo's tone would anger Jogpal, but he just looked at me fondly and said, 'I have to worry about my girl too. I can't leave her to Lokendar here, can I? He is letting her fall into the clutches of corrupt politicians.'

Lokey almost choked on the pistas he'd been chomping absently while waiting for me to get over my conscience pangs and get on with the shoot. While he was coughing and going red in the face, and trying to say that all the high-minded objections were simply because Lingnath supported another political party, Zoravar, who had reached absently for my trident and, much to my disgust, started to dig into his plaster with the back end of it, said matter-of-factly to Jogpal, 'You want total control of her, you mean.'

Jogpal said, pleasantly, 'I want to keep her exclusive to cricket, yes.'

'You know what *I* think?' Zoravar's voice rang out clearly in the crowded little make-up van, even as he continued to dig casually into his stinky plaster. 'I think you're purposely building up Zoya's status so *she* gets all the credit for Nikhil Khoda's World Cup victories. You want to make him into a lame-duck captain so you can slowly ease your convalescing blue-eyed boy Rawal into the captain's post.'

It was like he'd casually pulled out the pin of a hand grenade, and tossed it, smouldering, onto the floor of the make-up van. Suddenly, everything went very still.

Well, if you didn't count Lokey going 'O *behencho*' under his breath.

As I waited for the bomb to burst, I thought, *wait a minute, that actually makes total sense.*

Jogpal was the one who'd picked me and built me up. Nikhil was the one who'd hated to have me foisted on him. Somewhere along the way, Jogpal started making it look like it was all the other way round. Like Nikhil wanted me, and he was just supporting his captain. All his recent interviews, while seeming to defend India in the 'white' media were really subtly undermining both Nikhil's capability and his captaincy.

Rawal was his favourite, always had been, for a million shady reasons none of us would ever know. God knows what kind of dodgy shenanigans the two of them – the three of them, if I counted Lingnath – had planned for Indian cricket in the coming decade. Jogpal had probably never imagined that Nikhil Khoda would manage to lick the loser rag-tag Indian team into shape as a world-beating side. He must've figured that this team would never make it to the Super 8 and when they came home, fully disgraced, the Indians would hate Khoda and then he could chuck him out and get Rawal in as the new captain.

Of course he couldn't do that if Khoda's Eleven emerged as champions, which is why he must have zoomed in on me at the IPL, thinking, here was a way to bring Rawal back as captain – just in case Nikhil did bring home the World Cup! It was *he* who'd put Lokey in touch with Tauji, I recalled now. He probably wrote that cheesy script himself! He wanted to turn Nikhil into a laughing stock. What a snake! And Nikhil thought the world of him!

I turned towards him, ready to speak my mind but winced when I saw his face. Zoravar's bomb was about to burst. I resisted the urge to stuff my fingers into my ears and waited for the detonation.

Jogpal exploded.

He ranted and raved and said he'd been *insulted*, it was an *outrage,* that Zoravar was clearly a deranged lunatic or had been left out in the snow too long. He said I was a thankless little *witch* who had abused his hospitality and a total slut at that, look how I'd been carrying on, unable to leave the Muslim boys alone. He said Nikhil and Rawal were both like sons to him. He said if we dared to go public with these nonsensical allegations, he would sue us so hard we'd be taking chukkars of the criminal courts all our lives. He said, didn't we know how much *Standing* he had in thee *Society?*

When he finally paused for breath I said steadily, 'You can say what you want. I think what my brother says is true.'

Jogpal reared forward and glared at me so manically, I thought his eyeballs would pop and land like two slimy lychees on the floor. He ground his teeth at me, unable to speak, but Lingnath didn't seem to be having any such problems. He leaned towards me, grabbed my gold-coin-encrusted shoulder, fixed me with his horridly hypnotic eyes and hissed: 'Prove it.'

And just then, the door of the van burst open and we were all face-to-face with Kukuji's saffron sena, all pantingly eager to take a dekko at the Devi.

When my 'devotees' saw me, standing there frozen in the doorway of the make-up van, resplendent in my Goddess get-up, an ecstatic, collective groan rippled through their ranks and the chanting started up again, accompanied by the manic tinkling of about fifty little brass bells. *'Zoya Devi ki Jai! Zoya Devi ki Jai!'*

If this was ten truckloads-full, Kuku must have packed them in pretty tight, I thought, blinking down at them through my three-inch-long eyelashes. There seemed to be thousands of them, all wild-eyed and frantic and hysterical-looking. A lot of them looked drunk. Some of them held banners that read:

'*Zoya Devi ka Chamatkaari Balla*'. Some sported bright red tinsel dupattas tied like bandannas across their foreheads. Music blared loudly in the background. I recognized the tune, it was the standard aarti: *Om Jai Jagadisha hare*, but the words were new. The chorus, sung in a sonorous male voice, extolled the virtues of my miraculous bat, or *chamatkaari balla* and rhapsodized about how one whack from it was enough to blow the opposition to bits.

As Lingnath and Jogpal pushed past us, with one last malevolent look, and headed for their cars, the 'devotees' surged towards me, hands reaching out frantically. Zoravar, Neelo and Lokey surrounded me from three sides and tried to reason with the crowd as they waved cricket bats in my face, and begged me to bless them. Some of them had injuries, acquired on the cricket field, which they claimed that they wanted me to cure.

I distinctly heard Zoravar tell one of them, exasperatedly, shaking his crutches about, '*Dekhiye*, I'm her brother. If she can't cure me, how can she cure you?'

Some of them got down onto their knees and were praying to me, their eyes closed, tears streaming down their cheeks, smoking, ruby-tipped, Sheraan-wali Agarbattis held in their hands. The sickly sweet smell of synthetic mogra blossoms filled the air. And all the time, the frantic fervent chanting continued. '*Zoya Devi ki Jai! Zoya Devi ki Jai! Zoya Devi ki Jai! Zoya Devi ki Jai!*'

'*Abbey* Kuku!' Lokey shouted above the din. '*Abbey* Kuku, control your crowds… Where are you?' But Kuku had vanished. So had PPK.

And then a guy with a CREW tag yelled out at us from the temple structure, 'Today's shoot has been cancelled! You ought to –'

But we were never to hear what it was we ought to do. Because, with a crash and a groan and a massive puff of dust, the entire POP-and-plyboard Benares temple collapsed under the onslaught of the fanatical mob, taking large numbers of 'devotees', some production people and a very expensive camera down with it.

'The false temple has been reduced to rubble,' Neelo mused as we rushed to the car, strapped on our seat belts and prepared to flee. 'Kinda symbolic, don't you think?'

'I wouldn't have thought it of you, Zoya!'

Zoravar, Dad and I were sitting in the garden at Tera Numbar. We'd just finished filling him in on the day's happenings. Predictably enough, he was really mad at me for getting mixed up with political types. 'The trouble is,' he said, smoking gently at the nostrils, 'that you children don't have any concept of history. These people have done nothing but create national strife ever since their wretched party came into existence. I can't believe you even agreed to have a meeting with them, Zoya!'

'I wasn't thinking clearly at the time,' I muttered. 'I was very upset.'

'About what?' he asked, genuinely bewildered. 'You went off on a fully-paid holiday, stayed in the fanciest of hotels, you went bungee jumping! You were an effective lucky charm too. They didn't lose a single match with you present... *What* did you have to be upset about?'

'Dad,' Zoravar said soothingly. 'I think she was under a lot of pressure.'

My dad snorted. 'All self-imposed!' he said. 'She started believing she's Durga Mata!' He turned around to glare at me.

'I told you, Zoya. I *told* you when you were leaving, enjoy the attention, but don't let it go to your head!'

'It wasn't like that!' I said, stung to the quick. 'You have no idea. There were so many mean, sniggering articles in the papers every day, I just thought, okay, if I'm going to be called materialistic anyway, I might as well make a little money on the side!'

He shook his head at me. 'You were always scatterbrained,' he said. 'Zoravar was always the sensible one.' We both turned to look at sensible Zoravar who was digging into his plaster with the back of a teaspoon, his eyes closed in ecstasy. Sensing our eyes on him, he looked up, pulled the spoon out of his cast and started stirring his tea with it. '*Tu kucch bhi bol*, Gaalu,' he said. 'That was an inspired moment I had back there, in the make-up van. That Jogpal jumped like a scalded fish. He knew I'd wised up to his plot.'

'You were right,' I said grudgingly. 'I could see it in his eyes.'

Zoravar took a sip of his tea and smacked his lips. 'It's all these strategic warfare courses they send us for,' he said modestly. 'They train you to get inside the enemy's head – to think like him. Of course,' he added, 'the fact that I'm naturally brilliant helps.'

I said waspishly, 'So, what do you recommend I do now?'

He opened his eyes very wide. 'Nothing,' he said. 'I mean, if you *cared* about Nikhil Khoda the smartest thing to do would be to refuse to go to back to Australia. Let him win it on his own, if he can.'

I didn't say anything. My oversmart brother was trying to get a rise out of me in front of dad.

He continued infuriatingly: 'But seeing as you *don't* care, go ahead, do the ad and fly back tomorrow. How does it matter to you that Jogpal is out to shaft Nikhil, as long as you get your money?'

It was a chilly evening. I tucked my hair in a golfing cap, put Meeku on a leash and skulked out to the Ajmal Khan park for a walk.

Crows were cawing in hordes in the neem tree canopies. Old ladies, with set, determined faces and PT shoes under their salwar kameezes, were power-walking briskly in the ladies park. Vendors with big brass pots swathed in red cloth, festooned with fresh mint and bright yellow lemons were selling kulcha-channas to lounging youths on black Hero bicycles. There was the distinctive *thwacckk* sound of bat striking ball from somewhere in the distance. Nearby, some snotty little urchins were trying to fly a kite.

I inhaled the magical mixture of neem blossom, burning leaves and the susu of a hundred stray dogs and smiled to myself.

Whatever else, it was great to be home!

I let Meeku drag me towards his favoured spot for relieving himself – a lantana hedge along the edge of the big, dusty Ramleela maidan. He was taking a long time, sniffing around with great purpose. So I bought a glass full of nimbu pani. A *glass full of jaundice*, Dad called it, and wondered what I should do. I'd told Zoravar and Dad that I didn't give a damn about Nikhil getting shafted, but of course I did. And if I believed what Zoravar said, which I did, especially after the way Jogpal had reacted to it, I would have to believe that Nikhil really didn't give a damn about my luckiness; which of course made me start to hope that he gave a damn about *me*.

What had Monita said? *His feelings for you will be tested*

later, but yours for him are being tested right now. I knew Dad and Zoravar wouldn't push their views down my throat but I got the distinct feeling they'd both be happy if I decided not to go back to Oz for the final.

Eppa too, for that matter. She'd sidled up to me last night and told me in all seriousness that Zoravar had escaped death by a whisker, the very day of the Indo–Pak match. She'd reminded me of my mum's fears for me, that if I expended all my good luck on cricket I'd have only bad luck left for myself.

'You go thyure and makes them vin phynal match, Zoya, and pukka pukka von of us here will...' She drew a hand graphically across her throat and rolled up her eyes.

I sat down on a rusty park bench, and swilled my nimbu pani around in the cloudy glass.

'Excuse me, didi.'

I looked up to see a pair of sweaty ten-year-olds, dishevelled and panting, looking at me expectantly.

'Ball, pliss,' they said.

And then I realized that there was a grimy tennis ball lying at my feet. I picked it up and chucked it to them. The taller one caught it deftly, spat on it and rubbed it against his thigh. The shorter fellow, slightly chubby and missing a couple of teeth, flashed me a grin. 'Thenkyou,' he said. Then, tossing his sweaty brown curls out of his eyes with a movement I'd seen Zahid Pathan make a million times, he sprinted back to the maidan, hauling up his pajamas from the back with one pudgy hand. The taller dude, who was the captain I think, went, *'Ey chal chal,'* and tossed the ball at him.

The little fellow waved his fielders about the ground till he was satisfied with the placement and then did a determined run-up, his eyes all grim and focused, and hurled the ball down the pitch. It tappa khaaoed on the dirt and grit that was the Ajmal Khan park pitch and a young batsman with slickly parted thanda-thanda-cool-cool-Navratan-tel-enriched hair hit out at it with everything he had. The ball rose into the air, coming straight towards my bench again, well above the heads of the tiny fielders and I thought he had hit a six. But Chhota Zahid was running backward, running really fast, his bare feet stamping the ground, ploughing up dirt. He raised both his arms up into the air as he ran, in danger of running into me now, and nearly fell over an empty Frooti Tetra Pak, with which the Ajmal Khan Park is liberally sprinkled. I put a hand in the small of his back to steady him.

He regained balance – just in time to catch the ball smoothly with one hand as the other grabbed his sagging pajamas as they slipped right off, revealing his little brown behind. A cheer arose in the park as he adroitly retrieved both.

Everybody – the gaajar-mooli vendors, their customers, the youths on the bicycles, the power-walking old ladies, the lovers lurking in the bushes and, of course, me – catcalled and clapped for him as he came up, flushed and grinning, slightly cross-eyed and panting, ball in one hand, his pajamas hitched up with the other. 'Thenks didi,' he said, his eyes shining with the joy of victory.

And that's when I had a sudden splendid revelation. If I *was* a Goddess of the game, born at the very moment of India's greatest cricket victory, if my purpose in life was to help them win, if my hand was *supposed* to hover over them in constant benediction, wasn't it part of my job description to keep Indian cricket from harm? By going back to spoon cornflakes and slimy papaya slices into my face with the team before they played the final, all I'd end up doing was erode their faith in their own ability.

Even if they won, they would never be sure of the real reason behind their victory.

But I *wasn't* just a crummy lucky charm. I was specially blest.

A Goddess no less.

Why was I letting mere mortals push me around and take my decisions for me?

I should be looking at the *larger* picture.

By not going back, I'd be foiling a foul plot to discredit the best captain the country'd seen in, like, twenty-seven years.

Sure, I'd be giving up some fame and fortune, I thought, feeling all lofty and noble but I'd go down in history as the person who brought about the downfall of the unholy trinity of Robin shoe-stealer Rawal, Jogpal lump-of-shit Lohia and Lingnath long-turd Baba. No more match fixing! No more shady shenanigans. No more politicking. A new, clean, triumphant era for Indian cricket.

Hah! I'd finally cracked it! *This* was my destiny. *This* is why I was born when I was born! I had been given Great Power and by God, I was going to show Great Responsibility.

Feeling totally at peace with myself for the first time in months, I dialled Nikhil's number.

'Hello,' his deep voice was a little wary.

'I'm not coming back,' I told him.

There was an uncomfortable silence. 'Why?'

I said, 'So you can win this match all on your own, for once.'

'Does your boyfriend know about this? He and his mates might totally collapse...'

Where had he got this notion that Zahid was my boyfriend? And what about the fact that he'd told all his boys about his tryst by the pool with me?

'No, you're the boss, you can give them the good news.'

There was a long pause, then he said, 'Okay, I can't pretend this is not good news.' His voice thawed just a little. 'Are you sure about this? The repercussions are going to be huge. There will be protests and picketing. There may be self-immolations. Vikram's place in Bulandshahar was vandalized after the last match. You guys will need solid security around that house — especially if we lose.'

'We won't lose,' I said.

He didn't reply to that. All he said was, 'I'll speak to the Ministry and organize security for Tera Numbar, okay?'

'Okay,' I said and hung up.

21

The next morning, when I woke up, I saw a hatchet-faced man dressed all in black with a gun slung over his shoulder, sitting on a branch of the guava tree in the compound, staring at me through my bedroom window. When I came out into the inner courtyard, I saw another four gun-toting guys sitting like crows on a wire along the courtyard wall, sipping tea in our second-best crockery.

Rinku Chachi called down to me from her balcony, 'Zoya, *dekha*? Men in Black instead of Men in Blue?'

It was a really chaotic morning. There were twenty-nine commandos prowling about Tera Numbar, getting in the way of all four families. Nikhil must have announced my decision to the media because the phones rang incessantly. I issued a one-line press release: *I want to prove our team can win on its own steam. I know they can do it.* But the journos didn't believe me. They kept calling and badgering me with questions, convinced there was more to the story.

And by noon, that day, there was.

Jogpal Lohia called a press conference before boarding a plane back to Melbourne. It was covered by only about 2953 television channels. He stated that Zoya Singh Solanki, the darling of cricket fans, the lucky charm, the desh-ki-jaan, had come back to India to shoot a tobacco commercial and was demanding a whopping sum of five crores to go back and sit in with the team at the final breakfast. They cut to a picture of me that must have been taken at the shoot. I was doing a pranaam to the camera in my Goddess outfit, with my 'mane' tossed back and my trident staked into the ground. The graphics department of the news channel had animated the picture so that a flurry of thousand-rupee notes showered down on me. Cut to Jogpal wagging his beard sorrowfully. 'Well, we all know cricket can corrupt,' he said. 'In my own experience, I have seen so many young boys being seduced by the lifestyle, the adulation, the hot spotlight. But I had thought a girl divinely blessed by God, born at such an auspicious hour, would be immune to the lure of filthy lucre. Obviously, I was mistaken.' He then appealed to all cricket lovers to persuade Zoya to get on the next flight and fly back to Melbourne to 'save the nation's pride'. He looked directly into the camera with eyes brimming with tears. 'Please persuade her,' he pleaded, his voice quavering. 'Tell her this is not the time for petty greed. Awaken her patriotic spirit!'

Then, having basically incited the entire country to come out on to the streets and terrorize me, he clambered aboard the plane and winged it back to Australia.

I zapped off the TV and sat down with a thump.

Bloody Jogpal. The sarangi-strumming, sadistic *snake*.

I had just made the biggest sacrifice of my life and he'd managed to *totally* warp it. Everybody would believe that I had held out for more money. The whole team would believe it.

Even Nikhil.

Zoravar's voice rang out from a distance. 'You've got to admire his low cunning mind,' he said with grudging admiration. 'What a manoeuvre.'

'But what do we do now?' I said, looking at him, in total

panic. 'Should we call a press conference? Deny this crap he's dishing out? Explain why I'm doing this?'

My dad shook his head. 'Just leave it, Zoya,' he said. 'These are very powerful people.'

Zoravar nodded. 'Dad's right,' he said. 'Nobody's going to believe that your intentions could be so noble. Just drop it for now, Gaalu.'

All hell broke loose outside the house a couple of hours later. A chanting mob, at least a few thousand strong, gathered outside the gates, chanting incessantly, tearing at their clothes, ringing their bells and gnashing their teeth. '*Zoya Devi Waapas Jao! Zoya Devi World Cup Lao! Zoya Devi Waapas Jao! Zoya Devi World Cup Lao!*'

Our guards lounged outside the gate and walked along the top of the garden walls, trampling the madhumalati, polishing the butts of their guns, and scowling darkly at the mob.

'How do you get into these situations, Gaalu?' Zoravar wondered. I bit back the urge to tell him that it was all his fault. If he hadn't had his bloody epiphany in front of Jogpal and Lingnath none of this would've happened. Instead I sighed and said, 'I have no idea.'

We were watching the tamasha on the surveillance monitor the guards had installed inside the house. We'd gone up to the roof first, but the guards had very rudely hissed us away, saying it was an unsafe area. They'd also told my dad that in case India looked as if it were likely to lose tomorrow, we would have to 'evacuate' this 'dwelling structure' by the fortieth over, because then the crowd would get very nasty indeed.

'Having second thoughts, by any chance?' Zoravar asked me as we both sat looking at the maddened masses outside. 'Wanna get a ticket back to Oz? Before they rush in here and lynch us?'

'No way,' I shook my head and stroked a rather traumatized Meeku. 'We just have to put our faith in Nikhil now.'

Zoravar looked at me curiously. 'What did he say?' he asked. 'I mean, when you said you weren't coming back?'

I told him that as far as I could tell he had sounded pretty relieved.

Zoravar said, 'That's good, *na*? It means he likes you, not your luckiness. Strange. But then these sports-quota types aren't very intelligent.'

I shrugged. 'I guess so,' I said absently, too drained to rise to his bait.

We watched the action down below in gloomy silence. The mob was so massive that it had blocked the entire road. The journos and their vans had attracted a lot of aloo-tikki and channa-kulcha wallahs who were rolling their thelas up and down the stretch, briskly peddling their wares. A whole convoy of trucks that should have been driving to Rohtak had parked along the road just to enjoy the moment. The road outside the house looked like a mela. And leading the outraged citizens in the hand-clapping and the breast-beating and the teeth-gnashing was a toli of transvestites, clad in tacky, tinsel-encrusted saris.

Zoravar and I listened to the sounds of the crowd with horrid fascination.

'Hey look,' he said, pointing out one particular 'devotee' on the surveillance monitor. 'Keep your eye on that one, I think he's maybe going to immolate himself!'

'Are you serious?' I gasped, morbidly bloodthirsty. 'Where, where, which one?'

'That one.' He pointed with the fly-swatter-cum-back-scratcher. 'Look! He's all worked up, he's in a religious frenzy, he's turned away from everybody, he's whipping out a bottle of kerosene...'

We watched the would-be immolator excitedly in silence.

'He's whipping out his *pecker*...' I said in a flat voice. 'And he's pissing into the madhumalati.'

Zoravar sighed. 'They don't make devotees like they used to,' he said sadly, and tottered off to go harrass Eppa for something to eat.

The cops showed up a little while later and tear-gassed the mob to disperse it. Then they stood around with their paunches out and told me reproachfully, 'Why don't you just go back to Australia ji? It is not fair that because of your bargaining and haggling we are all endangering our lives...'

Rinku Chachi had to hold me back so I didn't hit them.

'We *need* them,' she whispered urgently, 'Be *nice*, Zoya. Make them some *tea.*'

They slurped up the tea and biscuits but left quickly. I don't think they liked the way the Black Cats, who regarded them as the lowest thing in the men-in-uniform pecking order, were smirking at them.

At least Nikhil hadn't called off the Black Cats, I thought with a pang, maybe that's a sign that he believes in me...

The morning of the final dawned eerily silent. New Rohtak Road was quiet. The truckers had obviously shacked up at some dhaba to catch the match. I was still fully on Aussie time so I woke up at around six a.m., which was okay, because the matches started around seven India time. When I emerged into the courtyard, rubbing my eyes, calling for tea and basically trying to act like my life wasn't in ruins, I found Eppa supervising four Black Cats who were carting our big old TV into the courtyard. 'Kair-phul, kair-phul,' she was yelling bossily. 'Sambhal ke!'

'What's up?' I asked, trying to smile and look bubbly.

'They also vants to vatch the match, Zoya,' Eppa said, jerking her head at the Black Cats who smiled at me bashfully. 'So your daddy has said, phull house vill votch phynal match, here in the aangan only.'

She packed the Black Cats off to go carry the sofas in, and scurried off to stir a massive cauldron of suji ka halwa.

'Indian brakefast, today!' She beamed at me as I followed her into the kitchen. 'Halwa puri. Okay?'

I nodded and hitched myself onto the kitchen counter, trying not to think about the breakfast huddle that would be happening right about this time at the Conrad in Melbourne.

Zoravar emerged just then, and hopping up from behind Eppa, shoved his great horny fist straight into the sizzling halwa cauldron. Eppa shrieked that he would burn himself and so of course he gave us a long lecture on how a soldier's hands were lethal weapons, weathered and toughened, and how he could strangle people with one steely fist anytime he liked. He dropped one hand onto the back of Eppa's scrawny neck, massaged it gently and asked her if she wanted to test that statement. She reminded him dourly that he used to kick and scream for all his single-finger-prick blood tests when he was a kid and that he shouldn't talk so much.

The family trooped in then, Mohindar and Anita in their tracksuits from the Ajmal Khan Park; Rinku Chachi, in her RINKU 10 tee shirt, and G. Singh straight from their bedroom looking deliciously bonded; and Yogu and my dad from the roof where they'd been hanging out with the Black Cats.

'Most of the crowd has left to watch the match,' Dad reported.

'They must have figured that even if you flew there in your own celestial chariot now, you'd never make it in time for breakfast, Zoya,' Yogu added, rolling up a puri and taking a large bite.

'They'll be back if we look like we're losing,' Zoravar warned, grabbing the squishiest sofa and manoeuvring his leg onto a little stool. The Black Cats murmured in agreement as Gajju flicked on the TV.

I felt totally nauseous when I heard the roar of the home crowd. The stadium was a riot of green and gold. Then the camera zoomed to a close-up of Beeru's familiar face under a jaunty light-blue turban, talking to a trio of groundsmen. He turned to the camera, grinned brightly and said, 'Vul, the bears here have produced a Goldilocks of a pitch, Jay! It's neither too bouncy nor too dead. Neither too grassy nor too worn, neither too damp nor too dry. In fact, they've been assuring me, that it is' – he held the mike to the three grinning groundsmen and they chorused into the mike – 'jusssst right!'

Beeru asked, 'Still, what would you do if you won the toss?'

The oldest groundsman lost his grin, pulled at his earlobe, thought about it for a while and then said dourly, 'I'd bat first, mate.'

Beeru started to ask him something further, but suddenly, we lost them. A bewildering flurry of logos flooded the screen in quick succession accompanied by a rushed announcement: 'This-pitch-report-was-bought-to-you-by-Zing! – this is the young nation baby; Navratan hair oil – thanda-thanda-cool-cool; Vodafone – you-and-I-in-a-beautiful-world; Fair-and-Lovely – a-fairer-complexion-in-fourteen-days; Nero-Tasha – desh-ki-dhadkan; Videocon – the-official-appliance-provider-to-the-World-Cup; and Samsung – we-are-in-the-team-too!'

Sony Entertainment Television was obviously raking in the

moolah big time. When the ad break finally got over, some *seven* minutes later, they cut back to the match where the cameras were focused on Miss *Toinnngg* clad, not in her trademark Panghat sari-choli, but in a pink spaghetti top, sporting oversized dark glasses, a sleek ponytail and lashings of lip gloss.

'And that ravishing lovely lady, Jay, unless I'm very much mistaken, is the skipper's sweetheart.'

'Well, yes, Beeru, and while everybody says there's nothing official about the relationship, we *have* been hearing that there's a wedding on the cards soon. Let's hope her presence here doesn't distract him today.'

'Are these people commentators or gossip columnists?' Dad grumbled, shuffling around in his seat, while Rinku Chachi looked at me with large stricken eyes. He glared at the TV and shouted testily, 'Cut to the toss!'

Very obediently, the cameras cut to Nikhil and the chubby-faced little Aussie captain shaking hands at the pitch, their tee shirts fluttering a little in the breeze. When the umpire asked them formally what they had selected, Nikhil crossed his arms across his chest, looked frowningly down at the grass for a bit, then said, 'I'll take heads.'

The Aussie captain shrugged. 'Tails,' he said.

The portly umpire tossed, the coin flipped high up in the air and landed.

'*Tails* it is,' announced the umpire and my heart sank.

The Aussie captain grinned happily and said he'd put the Indians in to field first. Nikhil nodded, his lips tightening a little. Once off the field, the commentator started quizzing him about losing the toss and whether he anticipated more bad luck during the match.

Nikhil told him dismissively that this wretched debate had

gone on for far too long. 'We're focused, we're talented. We're hungry to win. If there's an "X-factor" operating today, it's just a burning need to prove that our side has been winning consistently not because of luck but because of ability.'

The commentator nodded vigorously and they cut to an ad break. I could feel the whole family looking at me out of the corner of their eyes. I couldn't take it any more.

I got up abruptly and said, 'I'm going to my room. Call me when it's over.'

My phone beeped as I lay in bed, head buried under the pillow.

Are you watching?

It was Nikhil.

I rolled over onto my stomach and wondered what to write back, my heart slamming madly against my ribs. I wanted to write, *Do you really think I'm a materialistic bitch?*

I wanted to write, *Why'd you tell Goyal about us?* I wanted to write, *I love you! I love you! I love you!*

So of course I wrote, *Oh hi, aren't you going out to play?*

No, he wrote back.

No? I wondered, looking at the phone screen blankly. What did *that* mean?

And then, another message flashed:

I'm going out to win.

He *hates* me, I decided then and there. He thinks I'm some money-minded *cow* who deserted the team at the penultimate hour. God knows what the *snake* Jogpal had gone back and told him.

I sat in my room and brooded. Every time the family cheered or groaned, I felt physically sick. I did emerge to watch bits and

handled-that-better kind of way. Just looking at them made me feel all murderously, bloodthirstily, tooth-grindingly Raktdantini again.

'C'mon, Khoda,' I muttered, looking at him sitting all padded up and ready to go in the players' balcony. 'Win this thing.'

The mob came back around three in the afternoon.

It created a commotion by our front gate, listening to the commentary on the radios of parked cars. The squawking of the hysterical, over-descriptive radio commentators and the matching-matching grunts and groans of the crowd infiltrated into the aangan, sending Zoravar hobbling to the window to investigate. The Black Cats leapt smoothly to their feet and took up their positions all along the boundary wall.

The Indians needed to make twenty-two runs in two overs. It was doable, of course, but this was Team India we were talking about. These guys had lost every ODI final they'd played, in the last seven years.

The mob's agenda was clear. If it couldn't burst any firecrackers that evening, it was at least going to smear the greedy Goddess's face with gobar. Then, of course, it would trawl the city, drown its sorrow in bad liquor, deface the hoardings of every product the cricketers endorsed, maybe even torch a cola truck or two. Sensing the mood outside, the Black Cats went into a huddle and started fine-tuning their eviction plans. Meanwhile, on the TV screen Khoda and Thind were on the pitch, looking snarly, scowly and fully fuck-you at the roaring Aussie home crowd.

'It's anybody's match still, isn't it, Beeru?' Jay said as the Aussie speedster hurled a wicked-looking delivery at Thind who eased it away casually for a four.

I couldn't hear what Beeru said because Gajju and Yogu whooped and chest-banged so hard they fell about on the sofa and had to drink a glass of water each. Yet another ad break came on then and we watched bemusedly as Hairy and Shivee extolled the virtues of a particular brand of razor with a triple-blade shaving action. And then back to the action, where Nikhil had the strike. He got a single off the delivery and then Bullabullaroo Butch struck on the very next ball and Thind was out and India was down to its last cookie in the jar. They cut to another quick ad break which, ironically, had Thind and Hairy again, dancing some moronic jig for a brand of multi-flavoured, multicoloured, choco-candy, and then it was back to the match.

I wondered who the last man in was and suppressed a major groan when I saw Vikram Goyal's hairy, chubby little form loping onto the pitch. Khoda ran forward to meet him, spoke to him urgently, slapping him on the back so hard he almost buckled over and then, there he was. His pendulous lower lip between his teeth, Vikram Goyal faced the scariest moment of his life.

Zoravar groaned, 'I can't watch.' He hobbled to his feet and went to confer with the Black Cats about whether we should clear out of the house or barricade ourselves behind the stoutest door. Gajju and Yogu sat one behind the other, muttering: 'C'mon, Vikram, C'mon, Vikram,' even as Anita Chachi and Rinku Chachi took up the Gayatri mantra in quavering, desperate voices.

'C'mon, Vikram,' I whispered under my breath. 'I hope you win the World Cup, asshole!'

Vikram practically ran forward to meet the ball, a set look on his chubby baby-with-pubic-hair face, hoicked it up into the air and hit out blindly before taking off for a run. And another. And another. The Aussie fielder at cover sprinted after the ball, picked it up and threw it hard at the stumps. The keeper reached for it but it eluded his gloves and before anybody could react, the ball was off and rolling away. Five runs!

Somebody screamed. Me.

I screamed and yelled and whooped with glee. Now all we needed was three runs off the last two balls.

Vikram almost ruined it for everyone, including himself, by nearly getting out on the next ball. Thankfully he managed to scramble to the other end somehow, collapsing with relief at having managed to successfully hand the strike back to Nikhil.

The bowler took the longest run-up I've ever seen anybody take, even as the fielders closed into a tight circle around the pitch. I closed my eyes...tensing and clenching involuntarily ...and opened them when everybody groaned.

No ball.

Looking a little shaken, Bullabullaroo Butch started his run-up again. Khoda's eyes were mere slits in his dark, grimy face as the ball pitched really high and came on to the bat. He went for it. I closed my eyes again...

And opened them to find he'd hit it away and was running for the last vital run.

He made it. Almost. As he ran in, bat fully out, the wicketkeeper swung the ball at the stumps and knocked the middle one over.

Deathlike silence.

The manic *dhak-dhakking* of a billion brown hearts.

And the portly umpire indicated for the third umpire.

As the entire stadium held its breath, Nikhil Khoda threw down his bat and sprawled onto the grass, panting lightly, looking up at the scoreboard with slit, glinting eyes, his body unnaturally still with a painful tension. I shut my eyes tight.

*God, please let him win. He deserves to win. He'd better.
Please, God. Think how cost-effective it'll be. I mean, why stop at
making a few crummy million souls happy, when you can make a
round billion delirious with joy? Please, God. If India loses, the
mob outside will probably lynch me and why would you want me
to get lynched so young? Please, God. Let Nikhil win because
this country needs a hero not a Goddess.*

I opened my eyes. The light flashed. Not red.

Green.

And all of us exploded into a massive, riotous celebration.

Nikhil's face had that blazing exultant look again as he leapt
up and raced, screaming hoarsely down the pitch to lift Vikram
off his feet. They collapsed onto the grass, laughing crazily. And
then the rest of the gang poured out onto the field – Zahid,
Hairy, Shivee and the rest of the team, Weston Hardin, and
with constipated smiles on their ugly mugs, Jogpal-the-choot
and Robin-the-creep...

Jay ran out with his mike to talk to Nikhil.

'How d'you feel?' he yelled above the din.

Nikhil stopped thumping Zahid madly on the back, grinned
into the camera, looking heartbreakingly handsome, and said,
'Happy.'

It was at that point that Rinku Chachi burst into tears and
ran out of the room. Me, I just sat there, happy for him, suicidal
for myself.

Jay was saying laughingly, 'C'mon! That's not enough! Say
something more!'

Nikhil, with Zahid and Hairy hanging off each arm, thought
a little, then said, 'Uh...I'm very, very happy,' he grinned. 'I
think I already *said* that. So okay, hang on, let me think...' He
paused for a moment, while Jay, the entire team, and one

billion Indians glued to their TVs looked on at him indulgently. Then he looked up at the sky and shouted, 'Thank you!' He took a deep breath and said into the mike, 'The boys have performed brilliantly. It was truly a team effort. Vikram was superb, Laakhi, Zahid, Harry...all of them! The Australians have been brilliant hosts.' (The stadium cheered.) He waved out to the stadium, then looked into the camera and said, 'And I'm glad the viewers got to see a match that was exciting all the way to the last ball.'

Jay nodded. 'That last ball, Nikhil, what was going through your mind at that time?'

Nikhil thought a little, then shrugged again and said, 'Well, it wasn't much of an ask, really. One run off one ball. I've done it hundreds of times before. I just' – he made a graphic gesture with his hand – 'removed the hype from the situation in my head and then it was easy.' He grabbed Vikram, who was lurching past them and said, 'Why don't you ask him something? He's the guy who hit the big one!'

Jay pounced on Vikram then. 'Vikram! That was a magnificent six!'

Vikram looked down, all modest, and said, 'Thank you, sir.'

'You'd had a major setback in the semi, do you feel vindicated?'

Vikram said, looking a little haunted, 'I am glad I managed not to let my country and captain down, that's all.'

'So you've beaten the hex that was put on you, huh?'

Vikram looked uncomfortable and didn't say anything, so Jay turned the mike on Khoda again. 'Nikhil, you have to tell us, what do you say about the Zoya Factor now?'

There was a little silence, all the boys piped down for a bit and looked uneasy. But Nikhil said dryly, 'That's a question you should put to the Australian skipper, Jason.'

Jay said, 'Oh, I most definitely will. But we all want to know what *you* have to say.'

Nikhil said steadily, 'What I've *always* said. That maybe it exists. Maybe it doesn't. But Team India doesn't need her. We can win on our own strengths, if we play with dedication and with belief in ourselves, any time we want.'

I grabbed the remote from Zoravar's hand and zapped off the TV.

An unnatural little silence followed.

Okay, this was it, time to face the family. I didn't know whether my dad and Zoravar had guessed about my feelings for Nikhil, but I did know that Rinku Chachi had the biggest mouth in Karol Bagh. This was so not going to be the best moment of my life. I squared my shoulders and smiled brightly around the room.

But nobody looked at me. The Chachas were busy breaking open some alcohol, Dad was fiddling with some glasses, Rinku and Anita Chachi had vanished, and Zoravar and Eppa were rummaging through a huge cardboard box.

Wow, my large and loud family was being sensitive and all.

I said, in a slightly shaky voice, pushing my hair off my face, 'Eppa, what are you *doing* with that box?'

She looked up, her snappy little eyes bright with tender concern and said, with a break in her usually strident voice, 'Crackers, Zoya Moya! Zoravar and I got for you to light, so you could be a happy.'

I turned to look at my horrible brother, at a total loss for words. He grinned and said, 'Let's light up a blast, Gaalu.'

Zoravar had really gone the whole hog. There were Cock Brand Big Bang Bumper Flowerpots, Chinese Fire Dragons,

8000 Ladi Bombs of Chinatown Celebrations and a whole box
of Pyromania She-Demons.

We staggered out into the garden with the big box between
us and Zoravar sat down on the boundary wall, his plastered leg
dangling before him and watched as I set up a long line of Big
Bang Bumper Flowerpots.

'You gonna light them all together?' he asked, a little uneasily.

'Why not?' I answered with reckless gaiety as I struck a
match and lit a candle, wincing a little at the brightness of the
flare. A throbbing headache had taken possession of me.

As I held a phuljhadi over the flame, all I could hear in an
unrelenting, constant loop were the words: *Team India doesn't
need her.* All I could see before my eyes was a cold, shuttered
face, surrounded by a triumphant band of boys who didn't like
me any more. All I could feel was a sick hollowness at the
thought that somewhere tonight, the Men in Blue were
whooping and cheering and cracking lame jokes, getting
mindlessly drunk and dancing very badly – without me.

*You know what your problem is? You've turned into a male
attention junkie. Unless a knot of world-famous cricketers is
flocking around you, you feel you don't exist.*

But I want to be with him – with all of them! Hey, maybe I
could call him, maybe I could give a press interview explaining
it wasn't about the money, explaining why I wouldn't go back?

Yeah, but to whom? Look over the boundary wall, baby.
The journos, the cameras and the mad mobs...they're all gone!
You're yesterday's news. Didn't you hear the man? Team India
doesn't need the Zoya Factor to win!

The phuljhadi lit up and white hot sparks flew out in every
direction, spluttering wildly. I tossed my hair back and ran with
it to the line of bumper flowerpots, bent low, and one by one,

torched the lot. Magnificent fountains of flames bloomed around me and a fiery rain fell lightly on my skin as I whooped and capered around, but somehow, the pyrotechnics and the smell of barood did nothing for me this once. I felt as cold and as dead as I would've if I'd stayed downstairs and shut myself into the refrigerator.

You had me the moment I smelled the gun smoke in your hair...

Determined to feel something, I ran back to Zoravar and picked up a two litre *Zing!* bottle and shoved a couple of the Chinese Fire Dragons into it. I placed the bottle on the floor and lit another phuljhadi.

Zoravar shouted over the spluttering of sparks as I lit up the Fire Dragons, 'Gaalu, you idiot, be careful!'

'Don't worry,' I shouted as I stepped back nimbly and watched the Fire Dragons zoom up into the sky and explode into a million sparkly bits of ruby red and then go out with a *chimmer*.

Rather like the spectacular way in which my heart has broken, I told myself melodramatically: *Bhadhaam! Kaboom! Dhichkiyaaown!* Nikhil was probably claiming his so-called fiancée like a prize. She was probably simpering, *Nikhil, you played an awesome innings, you brute of a man, you...*

Jogpal's probably buying them *dinner*.

Cho chweet.

Puke puke puke.

'Who the hell cares?' I shouted aloud.

I blinked back my tears, lined up the AK 8000s and lit their long fuses, feeling completely numb. I stood there, the fancy fuse-lighter dangling from one hand, wondering in a detached sort of way why the AK 8000 seemed so *big* today. I didn't remember the ones in Dhaka being so big, or smelling so strong. Tongues of flame flared and rushed up towards the mouths of the dragons on the canisters, hissing softly. And then, suddenly, as I vaguely registered Zoravar leaping up from the boundary wall and rushing towards me, it hit me. The AK 8000s were looking so big because, like an idiotic lovelorn *lid* I'd forgotten to move back after lighting them.

And now, as time stood still and everything moved in dramatic slow motion, I took a step backwards, my hands held up protectively before my eyes. But I'd left it too late. With an incredibly sexy *whoooofft* sound, the AK 8000s exploded. There was a *chimmering* sound and a horrible smell of burning hair.

Oblivion.

'You look like shit.'

I sighed, 'Thanks, Sanks,' and thought, *You don't exactly look like a branch of blooming bougainvillea yourself*. But he did have a point. I won't go into lengthy descriptions, it would be too depressing. Suffice to say that as I'd got out of the auto outside office this morning, the driver had told me: '*Pachaas rupay hue, Bhaisaab.*'

It was a fortnight since the night of the World Cup final. Zoravar's plaster was off and he was due to go back to his unit in Poonch tomorrow, which was good because Dad was really mad at him for letting me run amok on the terrace. 'Her face could've been burnt!' he'd raved and when Zoravar had flippantly said that at least then I would have a legit reason to go in for plastic surgery, he'd almost hit him.

Sanks, who had got back six days ago, had phoned me and, on being told what I'd done to myself, had said irascibly that a drastic haircut was no reason for anybody to pull so much paid leave.

'It's a lesson to you to care more about the little kids in Sivakasi, not to mention the pollution levels in this city,' he'd told me reproachfully. He also told me to quit languishing, to get my sorry ass to office, and to start peddling cola, double quick.

I had dazedly obeyed to find that the world had returned to normal, in the sense that I was back to being a total nobody again. In a way, the loss of my 'mane', as I now thought of it fondly, had been good. At least I wasn't constantly being accosted by sneering citizens going: 'You're Zoya Devi, the greedy Goddess, *na?*' Because, like it or not, that was how I was known. I'd gone down in history as somebody who had priced herself too high and overplayed her hand. In fact, only yesterday I'd overheard people in an office meeting talking about how much to price a premium Kit Kat bar to the client. *'Be careful, don't price it too high and do a Zoya.'* They'd been saying it totally without rancour, but it had hurt.

What hurt even more was that all the players – including my three former acolytes – had totally bought Jogpal's version of the events. None of them had so much as called or messaged me even though they had been received with glorious fanfare three days ago on their return. The president, an ardent cricket fan herself, had broken all official protocol and gone to receive the team at the airport. Their faces were in every newspaper, at every roadside. Even Vishaal's Nike ad, the anti-luck one, was on air now; it must have sold a million pairs of shoes, people loved it, they couldn't get enough of it.

And what hurt the most was that the players were attributing their victory to talent/grit/mental attitude/hard work but definitely not to crummy old luck. *They* were the ones who deserved all the credit. I, if they bothered to talk about me at all, was just a Jogpal protégé, who'd been more or less forced down their throats. They couldn't stop talking about themselves. It seemed like in the course of a single match they'd lost all the innocence and humility that had been their most endearing traits, and set them apart from the overhyped old Indian team that had disgraced itself during the previous World Cup.

I couldn't even bury myself in work. Because guess who was slated to star in the next bunch of *Zing!* commercials? The entire team, that's who. I'd managed to squirm out of the film shoot somehow but the images of the boys, the very same stills Neelo and I had shot in Dhaka, were staring me in the face every day. The Goddess had been replaced by eleven sweaty God-lings. Such is life.

I kept wanting to stand up and shout: *It's just a game. Just a stupid, overrated game. It's not a cure for cancer. Get over it!*

I mean, why couldn't these people just make a nice wholesome Shah Rukh Khan-chases-a-*Zing!*-and-gets-outwitted-by-a-kid/dog/old man, ordinary consumer commercial for a change, anyway? But, of course, I couldn't say anything because people would think I was bitter and grudging and screwed up on top of being greedy. So I just had to grin and bear it.

At least Nikhil wasn't gloating as much as the others. But that wasn't much comfort because all he was doing was appearing in the colour supplements with various babes on his arm. The sight of their simpering face in all the national dailies set my teeth on edge and made me want to puke.

And, of course, there was the baby.

The only consolation I had was that Jogpal was looking more like a cornered rat every day. True to what he'd said in his e-mail, Weston Hardin was insisting on investigating Robin Rawal and the others concerning the Auckland match. And suddenly, now that he'd spearheaded India to a World Cup win, Wes had a lot more people paying attention to what he was saying. Some dodgy-looking characters had been flown in from Sharjah and Dubai to 'assist the CBI in their inquiries'. Their pictures were in the papers, talking shadily into cellphones.

I was sitting in my cubicle and reading one such report

when Mon sauntered up and chucked something on my table –
a dainty gold bracelet, with fat little sheep hanging off it. It lay
there glistening on top of one the artworks I was supposed to be
checking. The words *'Buy a* Zing! *600ml and Get a Kurkure
Red Chilli Chatka Free'* peered through the bracelet.

'Where'd you get that?' I said faintly, my heart starting to
slam against my ribs so painfully I thought it would bruise.

She smiled, and blew a perfect smoke ring right into my
face. 'He gave it to me to give to you,' she said in a smug sing-
song way. 'At the shoot.'

'He *asked* about me?'

She shook her head, frowning a little. 'No, not really,' she
admitted. 'I think he was kind of expecting you to be there, you
know?'

'Did he say *anything?*' I said, trying to sound casual and
failing miserably.

Mon pursed her lips. 'No,' she said. 'He asked about Armaan,
about how the Beyblading was going. That's all.'

I picked up the charm bracelet slowly and turned it over.
There it was, entwined forever on the plumpest sheep's curly
little bum: 'NZ'.

I sighed and slipped it into the pocket of my baggy grey shirt.

There was no way I could wear it.

It so didn't go with my Tihar Jail haircut.

About half an hour after I got home, I was hit with this
massive urge to phone Nikhil. It was the bracelet, of course,
which was to blame. A heavy little mass curled up in the shirt
pocket right over my heart, acting like the Ring of Sauron,
controlling my thoughts and telling me what to do. *Just call and
say hi....Here's the phone, look, now just scroll down to N, and
punch the little black button, go on, just do it....*I chucked both,

the bracelet and my phone, on top of a steel Godrej cupboard, changed into grubby home clothes, and went out into the garden, my hands shaking with resolve.

My dignity was just about all I'd salvaged from my misadventure in Australia. I was so not about to abandon it so late in the game.

In the garden, I found a rusty khurpee right where Dad had left it the night before and crouched down resolutely. Inhaling the scent of rich, upturned earth and gouging out large amounts of bhattua roots from the dahlia beds made me feel a little better. When I found Meeku scratching himself among the verbena blossoms, I felt energetic enough to chuck aside my khurpee, pull him onto my lap and de-tick him thoroughly. As Eppa won't wear the glasses the ophthalmologist advised her and as she watches any number of soaps and gory movies at night, her vision is not exactly twenty-twenty. There were entire colonies of little ticks lurking in his shaggy undercoat that she'd missed completely.

I was working my way down around his collar area and doing a really good job by imagining that every squirming plump tick I was pulling out and squashing to death viciously with a flat stone was really Jogpal Lohia, when a deep hesitant voice above me said, 'Excuse me...Zoravar?'

And I looked up with a feeling of total inevitability and met Nikhil Khoda's Boost-brown eyes.

He gave a startled exclamation and backed off, even as I reared up into a standing position from my squatting stance in the flower bed. In fact, I missed banging the top of my shorn head into his chin by a few millimetres. A couple of tick carcasses did fly up though, and hit him in the eye. Of course Meeku leapt up and started barking madly.

Rubbing his eye vigorously with one hand and fending Meeku off with the other, Nikhil said, 'Whatever happened to your hair?'

'Never mind my hair,' I blustered, totally appalled by the surge of worshipful groupie-ish emotion that had taken possession of me at the sight of him standing tall among the dahlias. 'Whatever do you mean by sneaking up on me like that?'

'Sorry,' he said, and added somewhat confusedly, 'I thought you were your brother.'

'Well, I'm not,' I said crossly. '*That* is my brother.'

Zoravar, having heard the mad barking, had come out to the pillared veranda and was gawping at Khoda with the air of a soldier who was wondering if he should sneak back to his tent and bring out his regulation army rifle.

'Hello,' said Nikhil warily.

'Hello,' replied Zoravar, walking up slowly.

They circled each other like a couple of suspicious street dogs and then, as I said their names, reached out and shook hands gingerly.

'Congratulations,' Zoravar said grudgingly.

'Oh ya…' I chimed in reluctantly. 'You won the World Cup after all.'

Nikhil grinned, folded his arms across his chest and rocked back on his heels cockily. 'Yeah, I did,' he drawled with great satisfaction.

He looked so super-hot saying that! So much so that I had no idea how I managed *not* to throw myself at his superheroic, world-beating chest at that very moment.

Then he turned to me and repeated, 'So what happened to your *hair?*'

Zoravar volunteered information unnecessarily. 'She celebrated your victory a little too enthusiastically.'

Nikhil frowned. 'Meaning?'

So Zoravar told him how my hair had caught fire. He exaggerated the whole episode, of course, running around the lawn dementedly in a witless imitation of me, beating his hands against his head like Nana Patekar. He was so over-the-top. Really. I wanted to tell him that Truly Spiritually Evolved people behave exactly the same in front of kings as they do in front of beggars.

Nikhil finally got a word in. 'Lucky escape.'

I said coldly, 'Can you please not use that word around me?' The two of them laughed.

I asked Khoda pointedly, 'What're you doing here?'

He raised an eyebrow. 'There's a lump of dirt above your lip,' he said.

Zoravar snickered. 'That's her *nose*.'

'*Zoravar*,' I said, through gritted teeth. 'Get lost.'

'Okay,' he said and loped away, stopping halfway up the veranda steps to turn around and shout, in a man-to-man way that made me want to hit him, 'Hey, Nikhil, you want a drink or something?'

'Later, thanks,' Khoda called back and turned around to look at me as I sat there, surreptitiously cleaning the mud off my face. 'You know, this new look of yours will take some getting used to.'

I glowered at him, knowing full well that with all my hair gone, my cheeks looked huger than ever. I had these mad little corkscrew curls all over my head and looked pretty much like a wheatish golliwog. My stupid tee shirt with 'Happy Girl!' written down the front, my grubby cargo shorts revealing unmoisturized legs with dirt-encrusted knees, and sockless and therefore slightly stinky red sneakers didn't help. Besides, I knew that that whole unconcerned attitude of Zoravar's had been an act. He had accelerated rapidly as he made for the house, and I knew that by now he would have gathered the whole clan together and that they would all be watching us and giggling up a storm. I looked towards the house – and all the genteel curtained windows looked like blatantly unblinking eyes to me.

Scowling at Nikhil, I said belligerently, 'Who's telling you to *look* at me?'

He grinned, completely unaffected by this graceless remark and said, 'What were you thinking? That being a Goddess makes you immune to fire?'

'What are *you* thinking?' I retorted instantly. 'That winning a World Cup makes it okay for you to wander around the countryside being rude to people? What are you doing here, anyway? Shouldn't you be in Bombay riding through town on an open bus or something?'

'Are you trying to get rid of me, Zoya?'

I looked up, surprised. His lips were playful, but there was this unsure look in his eyes which, after all these days of waiting for him to call me, was like balm to my broken heart (and, I must admit, to my battered ego). The Raktdantini flexed to life in my veins.

'Maybe,' I said, with a light, soft laugh.

His eyes blazed suddenly, he leaned forward and said, his voice like silk. 'Yes or no?'

I shrugged. '*Uff...no*, okay?' I said crossly.

He folded his arms across his chest. 'Lokey told me what happened at your shoot.'

Okay. So maybe that was good news. And, of course, I

wanted to ask him if he believed what Zoravar and I did, that Jogpal had been out to get him. But I didn't want to talk to him nicely yet. In fact, at that moment, when I looked at him and remembered how even Sonali from *Sonali's Gupshup* had gushed about the Laphroiagh brown of his eyes in yesterday's *Mid-day*, I didn't want to talk to him nicely *ever*.

Words tumbled out of my mouth, anyhow.

'Oh, so now that someone you know well has vouched for me, I'm good enough to be spoken to again? Is that it?'

He said, 'Zoya – '

I put up one hand, 'Hang on, okay? You sent me a stinky sms, you said mean things about me on TV, you have children scattered all over the globe, you don't call me *once* since you get back, and now that your fat friend Lokey has "exonerated me of all charges" you show up here willing to forgive and forget?'

'It isn't like that at all,' he said, urgently. 'Of course Vikram *did* get a guilt attack and tell me what had happened between the two of you....I didn't tell him about us, you know. He happened to see us by the pool that night, that's all.'

I gave a shaky laugh. 'Oh so *now* you like me again because of what Vikram-the-groper said? Is that it? So now supposing tomorrow someone else says –'

'I don't need to be here, you know,' he said, cutting me short. 'And if I remember it correctly, it was *you* who left.'

I sat down abruptly on the garden swing and started swinging, the hinges *chwing-chwonging* madly. He sat down on the swing beside me. 'Zoya, please, what underhand motives could I possibly have *now*?'

'How do I know?' I muttered as I continued to swing. 'You're touring South Africa in ten days' time I hear... Maybe you'll need me there.'

'Shut up,' he said abruptly.

His voice had a nasty edge to it. I shut up.

'You have no idea what it was like, do you? I mean, you called and said you weren't coming, and honestly, I was okay with that. I was sick and tired of being heckled in the media about you and I figured, at least I'll finally know if I can do anything on my own or not. I called a team meeting and told the boys and they all got completely hysterical of course, Harry specially. Wes had to pep-talk him all night. But then Jogpal made that statement to the press, and forgive me, but I believed it. I thought you'd…'

'Gone over to the dark side,' I supplied sulkily.

'Well, yes,' he admitted. 'There were all these pictures of you in some Goddess get-up. I *told* you not to do that stupid ad!'

'Well, I didn't, did I?' I said hotly.

He said, 'Well, anyway, it was all for the best because it made the boys so mad they went out and played their hearts out.'

'So they *did* win because of me,' I couldn't resist pointing out, rather childishly, I'll admit.

He said, 'Zoya, you know as well as I do that if we'd won with you there you'd always have thought me a bit of a loser. And a user too.'

He was right, of course. But then, he mostly always was. It was the most irritating thing about him.

'And what about your little Willie?' I demanded. 'Shouldn't you be thinking about his happiness here?'

He looked at me blankly. 'My little Willie?'

I glared at him in exasperation. 'Your little *William Nicholas.* Your baby boy.'

He said, grinning a little, 'Oh. For a while there I got all excited thinking you were talking dirty to me.'

I didn't laugh. This was important to me. He must have sensed that because he said, very gently, 'Zoya, that baby boy is not *my* baby boy.'

I opened my mouth to argue but he didn't let me: 'And you're just going to have to take my word on that. Like *I'm* taking your word on the fact that you weren't holding out for more money as Jogpal Lohia claimed you were.'

I snorted in a way that reminded even me of my father but I didn't say anything more.

Nikhil said, 'Look, I humoured Jogpal and let him bring you to Australia because I wanted to see more of you. I figured the lucky theory would come a cropper during some match or the other. Then I could tell you I didn't give a damn about your luckiness and that you would be so devastated and so far from home, you'd fall gratefully into my arms.'

'What a romantic little storyline,' I told him. 'Me, the pathetic damsel in distress, you the knight in shining blue.'

'Yes, but then you turned into some kind of rampant Goddess. Everything spun madly out of control.'

'The Gods always think they can control the Raktdantini,' I told him loftily. 'But they can't.'

He choked. 'The *who?*' he asked.

'The Raktdantini,' I told him. 'She, of the bloodstained teeth. She is not a mere tool or a pawn.'

'Uh, okay,' he said.

I shook a finger under his nose, driving the point home: 'She is not Anybody's Creature!' and added, 'Thanks, Eppa,' because Eppa had materialized suddenly at our side, with two mugs of Boost on a tray.

Nikhil started nervously, stood up and said, 'Thank you, thank you...you must be Anita...uh, I mean Eppa.'

She looked him up and down with her beady black eyes and then said kindly, 'You vant to stay for dinner? I vill make *isspecial* Balls Curry and rice. You like Balls Curry?'

'Uh...' Nikhil said uneasily, not looking so world-beating any more as he reeled under the twin onslaught of the Raktdantini and the Balls Curry. 'Sure, why not?'

Eppa nodded approvingly. 'Gud! Now drink yor Boost before malai comzes on top.'

And then she swept indoors magnificently.

Nikhil said, in a stunned sort of voice, 'You were saying?'

'Drink your milk,' I said wickedly.

As he obediently drained the cup, I said, 'Do you know your eyes are exactly the same colour as Boost powder with Advanced Energy Boosters?'

'What?' he said dazedly, then made a valiant attempt at pulling himself together. 'We'd got to the bit where you were saying you were not Anybody's Creature.'

'That's right!' I nodded vigorously, slurping my Boost. 'So I realized that I had a duty to Indian cricket which was bigger than just eating breakfast with you guys before every match.'

'You're doing it again,' he said, smiling a little, and putting his mug down on the grass, where Meeku started licking up the dregs eagerly.

'What?' I asked.

'Making me feel humble,' he replied.

I shrugged uncomfortably even though my cheeks glowed with pleasure. 'Don't be silly,' I said.

He spoke, and the warmth in his voice made my toes curl involuntarily inside my stinky red sneakers. 'That was a really gutsy thing to do, Zoya. Unselfish too. You must have lost out on crores in advertising contracts.'

'I know,' I said sadly. 'Lokey had a fit.'

'Hey,' he said lightly. 'My crores are your crores.'

I gave a shaky laugh, my heart beating madly, 'Yeah, *right*,' I said, putting a hand up to tuck my hair behind my ear and then remembered I didn't have any.

'I'm serious,' he said. 'What do you think I've come here for?'

I said, 'Um...for Balls Curry and rice?'

He said impatiently, 'Be serious. Are you upset about what I said on TV about us not needing you?'

I said carelessly, 'Oh, did you say that? I wasn't watching.'

'Bullshit,' he grinned. 'The entire country was watching. My masterful captaining had all the girls going weak at the knees.'

I almost choked.

He added, rather wryly, 'I hope you've noticed that I took care not to park in your esteemed Gajju Chacha's slot.'

Which made me giggle.

Which made his eyes glitter.

'Now *that*,' he leaned closer and murmured into my ear, 'is a very sexy giggle. In fact, some people may even go so far as to say that is a oh-please-take-me-home-and-turn-me-from-a-*bud*-into-a-*flower* giggle.'

He looked down at me, his eyes teasing. 'Am I right or what?'

I got on to my toes and kissed him – an open, Boost-warm kiss, in the madhumalati-scented garden, as a barely smothered, many-lunged cheer rose from the house behind us.

'You're right,' I admitted happily.

EPILOGUE

SONALI'S GUPSHUP

And so our chocolate browniekins Nikhil Khoda turned out to be a total chhuppa rustam, sweeties…romancing little Zoya under the frangipani trees in Australia, or so a reliable little kukkaburra birdie tells me. Lucky little girl, but let's see how long it lasts. I wouldn't order my shaadi-ka-joda, or whatever it is you Rajasthan rurals wear to get married in, just yet, if I were you, Zoya, because if your horrible new haircut doesn't put off your honhaar hottie, your agent's recent activities certainly will. Yes, my honeycakes, Zoya's agent, Lokendar Chugh, has been hobnobbing with any number of IPL team owners, including two dimpled Bollywood superstars and an overweight business tycoon, all of whom are desperate to get their hands on a lucky charm before the season starts again, no matter how avaricious she may be…

ACKNOWLEDGEMENTS

This book would not have been possible without the encouragement, help and blatant lifting of idiosyncrasies of so many people. Vibha Rishi, who put the thought of a human lucky charm into my head in the first place. Sankar Rajan, whom I miss at work, almost every day. Eppa, my Best Female Friend Forever – well she's *mine* even though she may not deign to think me *hers*.

My long suffering First Readers (*I've written three more pages! Read read read! Whadyuthink, Good? Huh?! Huh?!*) Shalini Beri, Alok Lal, Papa, Nika and (most often) Choku.

The conversation in this book is fully inspired by the moronic one-liners (*who will know?!*) and idiotic what-if scenarios (What if you had to sleep with a really ugly gross person of the opposite gender or a really hot person of the same gender or the Nazis would shoot you dead? Which would you pick? *Whaaaat?* You *pevert*) continually debated by the entire (past and present) gang at JWT, Delhi.

My friend Ritu Khoda, whose surname I borrowed, my friend Swati, whose hair I borrowed, my friend Jo, whose life experiences I borrowed. And Torun, who believed in Zoya, all the way.

Rohit Ohri, who humoured me and gave me leave to write. Puneeta Roy who put me on to Tarun Tejpal and Tarun, who very sweetly recommended me to HarperCollins. Nandita, Karthika and Sunaina, who were kind but firm and *actually took me seriously!*

All the clients whose brands I've worked on, thank you for giving me brilliant opportunities (which I mess up more often than not) every single day.

My little creative team in Delhi: *We're the best!*

Special thanks to Khurram, Manish, Gurdish and Saurabh whose shapely posteriors may or may not grace the cover page, Rohit Chawla and Saurabh Das, long-suffering photographers, Anu Ramaswamy, who designed the rocking cover, and Harjeet 'Bob' Singh, the rock on which JWT is built.

The motley crew-that-grew at 18, RR and has now settled all over the world – I love you all – *East or West, Barbarians are the best!*

Margaret and Niranjan Alva – Mamma, always loving and always worrying. And Dadda – constantly trumpeting my crummy achievements, introducing me to clueless gora VVIPs with, *My daughter-in-law, she wrote Yeh-Dil-Maange-More you know!*

Nicky–Pria, Manu–Jo and Babu–Meera, who are always there for Choku–Anuja.

Revti and Pushpa Raman – Papa, whom I grow to be more like, every day. And Mummy, who was horrified by the language in the book but loyally said, 'It's nice, beta.'

My favourite Usha mausi in whose beautiful home I wrote a major chunk.

Panki, Juicy and Chandra – *Eat dhool, you guys, Choku sabse cool hai!*

Mini, Ruhi and Nandu – *Hum Chauhan sisters hain hi itni beautiful aur talented!*

All my nephews and nieces, especially 'Nikhil' and 'Zoya'.

The Lord Jesus Christ, in whose peace we dwell.

And of course Choku and Nik-Tar-Da, who are everything to me.

EXTRA MATERIAL FROM ANUJA

*H*ere's what was happening in Zoya's life exactly two years
ago

The toad stopped dead in his tracks when he saw me, a look of
utter consternation upon his face.

Didn't see this coming, did you, toad.

'Zoya,' he said slowly, the sing-song Bangalore drawl very
pronounced. (That tended to happen when he got nervous.)
'Hey. How...how *nice* to see you. Didn't you get my mail?'

I cocked my head to one side, innocently. 'What mail?'

His handsome jaw sagged slightly. He looked about the
courtyard (blazing with pink bougainvillea and warm winter
sunshine, by the way) in a harassed manner. I couldn't help
noticing how nicely his aquamarine blue muffler set off the
golden tone of his skin. He was fair for a guy – fairer than me.
And lovely too – in a brooding, manly sort of way. A fair and
lovely toad.

Then he squared his shoulders and looked right at me. 'The
email. From Columbia.'

I smiled brightly, though my palms were clammy. 'You wrote
me *tonnes* of emails from Columbia. Which one d'you mean?'

Silence. I raised my chin then, looking up at him
challengingly.

He met my gaze squarely, his eyes narrowed. We stared at each other like that for almost a full minute, while my heart slammed against my ribs and my stomach churned as busily as a Videocon washing machine in heavy duty mode. *Gwwooon gwwooon gwwooown*

Then he gave a light little laugh. 'You're right,' he admitted. 'I did write you a tonne of letters. It's silly to ask about each one separately. Come 'ere and gimme a hug. I've missed you, babe.'

So of course I ran into his arms and hugged him. He hugged me back. Hard. And when we finally pulled away, his eyes were all soft. His cheeks, flushed. And his heart was slamming hard under my fingers. I could feel it right through his preppy Benetton sweater. I really could.

'Come up to my room?' His voice was low and husky and just the way I used to like it.

'Um, not now,' I said, somewhat breathlessly. Breathless, not because I was so hopelessly turned on. But because I suspected that *he* suspected that I *had* gotten the last mail he'd written me. In which he'd suggested that we should give each other 'space' because, basically,

* he had met somebody hotter
* unlike me, she was totally non-hawji about sex
* I was dumb and he was smart
* I was from Karol Bagh and he was from Golf Links
* I was doing a dopey MBA from Ghaziabad and he was doing a fancy one from New York
* and that he'd only dated a gaalu aalu like me so that my Gajju Chacha – who had been Ayaan's professor, and was this big shot at Delhi University – would recommend him to the folks at Columbia.

He hadn't actually come out and said any of this, of course.

He'd been much more elegant. But, net-net, the message I'd received was *ki yeh jo* world *hai na, isme* two types *ke* people *hotay hain* – users and losers – and that he was the former and I was the latter and that the time had come for a parting of the ways.

(Well, atleast there had been no parting of the thighs. Which is a good thing – or maybe not? Maybe I should use him a bit too, while I'm at it?)

Naturally I was shattered when I received the email. I really liked him. We'd met so romantically – slow-danced that first evening – and sat on the steps and talked till dawn. I'd lost three whole kilos in that first month when he left for the US (a best-ever record for me!) and then spent the last year doodling *Zoya Singh Solanki <3 Ayaan Menon* across my class notes and wondering how our life together would be (A Yawn, my troll-like brother had assured me repeatedly, but he's an ass, what does he know?).

Two (not very attractive, to be honest) guys had asked me out in that year, and I had turned them both down, telling them solemnly that I had a long-distance boyfriend I was serious about. It had been lonely, but it had been romantic.

And then this!

A mail from the US, asking for 'space'. And hello, 'space' mails are just the rokka ceremony of the big break-up mail. I know *that*.

And so I had come up with a low, cunning PLAN.

I would pretend that I hadn't gotten his 'space' mail at all. I would dodge it – like people dodge subpoenas from the courts, in all those legal thrillers. And then, while he was on the back foot and wondering how to dump me while I was being so uncooperative, *I* was going to quickly dump him. And thus avoid all heartbreak. Because heartbreak is ninety per cent just your ego getting kicked in the gut.

Everybody knows that.

Oh God, who am I kidding? This so-called Plan is just a sham! I'm desperately hoping that he'll see me – all freshly-shampooed and exfoliated and lovely – and remember all the good times we had – and fall in love with me all over again – and forget that he had ever met a new girlfriend or written me a space mail. *That's* the real low cunning plan.

And looking into his eyes now, I'm starting to wonder if his kisses still taste sweetly of Hubba Bubba grape and if he's still got that *Hero* CD stashed about someplace. *Hero* is our make-out song. Except that when I close my eyes I sometimes start seeing Enrique in my head instead of Ayaan, which is kinda creepy. Or maybe good? Because it proves that this is not real love? I mean, if it were, would I be seeing Enrique when we lock lips? Surely my One True Love should have the power to drive out the image of random mascara-wearing singers with weird moles from my brain while we're kissing?

This is more like it, Zoya. Hold on to this thought! Ayaan Menon is a toad. You're here to dump him, quick. Now, here's the way to do it. You're going to focus on his flaws – one by one – and gross yourself out completely.

Start with the fact that sometimes his mouth smells, which is probably why he's always chewing Hubba Bubba. No, wait, start with his butt. It's far from ideal. Too high. And it sticks out a bit. Like a shelf. You could stand a Coke can on it. Well, almost. And he wears mommy jeans. And then there's his chest – which is umm, kinda bulbous. *And* he uses Mysore Sandal Soap. Which is just so uncool.

And then there's his...

THE ZOYA FACTOR 453

Shit.

I can't do this.

It's like those diets where you're supposed to gross yourself out by telling your brain that masala dosas look like poopy diapers – all white with a yellow centre – and then you never want to eat them again. They *so* don't work.

I love him. I don't want to break up with him! But I cannot stand around like a deer in the headlights, waiting for him to dump me. I cannot!

'Do you?'

Ayaan was leaning right into my face, looking expectant.

'Huh?' I said stupidly.

'D'you wanna come into the living room atleast? Get some coffee?'

'Yes, please,' I said faintly. 'With lots of sugar.'

He laughed, put his arm around me, hugged me sideways (avoiding boobage? Being platonic?) and started to march me into his house.

'It's good to see you again,' he said, looking right at me. His eyes seemed to shine with sincerity. Or maybe that was just the winter sun bouncing off them?

My heart leapt into my mouth. Was the plan working? Which plan? Damn, I was so confused, I didn't even know what I wanted anymore...

Well, the kisses were just as good as they used to be. When the usual struggle for possession of the top button of my jeans started, I yanked down my sweater, walked out into the fancy living room, and he followed. It always makes me feel inadequate, his living room. It's full of these Tanjore paintings and fancy rugs, and all these genuine paintings with signatures and all. At home, all we have on the walls are a couple of Bhutanese dragon carpets. And they've been hung up only so that my puppy Meeku won't chew on them.

There was a cricket match – running on mute on his fancy flat telly. Our team was losing as usual. Losers.

'Where's everybody?' I asked. 'Your mom and dad?'

'Some family function,' he replied briefly. 'I pleaded jetlag. D'you want some more coffee?'

He got the coffee while I sat on the couch, fiddling with my hair, stealing looks at myself in the hallway mirror. I was looking good. As good as I could get. But as good as *he* could get? Clearly he thought not.

'So listen, you really didn't get my last email?' he asked as he slid the coffee towards me.

I rolled my eyes and shook my head, swinging my hair deliberately from side to side. My hair is super sexy – all corkscrew curly and jet black and down to my waist. It's my best thing.

'No – but what's the big?' I was feeling strangely light-headed. 'Just resend it, na. We'll both sit here and read it together. That'll be fun!'

He went very still.

'Are you *sure*?'

His voice was challenging.

'Abso,' I said coolly.

'Let it be, actually,' he shrugged. 'It isn't that important.'

Which immediately made me seethe inside. Not *important*? The email that broke my heart? *Really?*

He sat down next to me and started to talk. And as he talked, his arm draped casually around the back of my shoulders, his fingers gripping mine, the weirdest thing happened. The masala dosa = poopy diaper, seekh kebab = human turd thingie actually started to work.

I let him talk, and noticed small things about him.

His fingers – bony and hairy. These are the fingers that typed that mean email. Meanfingers.

His aquamarine muffler – chick-ish. And peacocky. He'd pretended his mom picked it out for him, but I bet he bought it himself.

And the stuff coming out of his mouth – always so belittling.

'So what is this AWB you're interviewing with?' he asked. 'Never heard of it.'

'Amos Walter Branson is India's biggest ad agency,' I told him. 'It would be a *huge* deal to get the job.'

Ayaan's forehead creased.

'Will they pay well?'

I mentioned the salary they've offered. It's not insane – but it's not piddly either.

He smiled. A patronizing smile. A patronizing, *toadish* smile. It made me want to slap him.

'What brands do they handle anyway?'

'The best,' I said with more confidence. 'If I get through, I'll get to work on *Zing!* Cola.'

He pursed his lips.

'Don't they do all those flashy, multi-starrer ads?'

'Ya-ya!' I nodded excitely. 'So cool, na?'

He crossed his legs (chick-ish again. Omg, I've been dating a chick!).

'In *our* marketing classes,' he said, emphasizing the 'our' in a way that instantly made me feel all protective about my small-time little MBA school in Ghaziabad, 'they say that celebrity advertising is a double-edged sword, which, if wielded ineptly, can be totally destructive to brand building.'

'So now I'm inept?'

'Zoya!' He spread out his hands, palm raised. 'I didn't say that.'

'Well, I'm *not*,' I told him, nostrils flaring dangerously. 'I have the same genes as my Gajju Chacha, and he's smart enough for you, isn't he?'

Ayaan put down his coffee mug. 'And what is that supposed to mean?'

I didn't say anything. My chest was feeling tight. I felt like I was about to explode. And then I did.

'It means you're an ass. *And* a user. It means I'm tired of you writing me short emails while I write you long ones, it means I'm tired of being made to feel insecure and inadequate, and it means –'

I paused.

'Well?' he asked.

'It means that I dump *you!*' I said it really loud and fast, and sat back, feeling half sick, half smug.

Ayaan blinked. 'What?'

I nodded several times. 'Yeah. I dump you. I dump you *first*.'

'First?' His eyebrows rose. 'Um, I did send you an email, back in December, saying I wanted spac–.'

'Oh shut up,' I said crossly. 'If you couldn't be faithful, at least be graceful. I dumped *you*. Is that clear?'

He nodded. 'Crystal.'

'Good,' I said in a tight little voice.

And then he dropped me home. We didn't talk in the car. There really wasn't anything more to say. I found my dog and got to my room and got into bed and cried.

His mouth did used to smell, I admitted to myself as I blew my nose on my pillow. And he *was* a user. And one day soon I'm going to meet someone truly *fabulous* and *awesome*, who will make me forget I ever knew a toad called Ayaan Menon, and he will be the hero of the movie of my life, and we will live happily ever after.

And then I called Eppa on my phone (she hates when I do that, *this is nott a hotal but a home!*) and asked her to bring me some hot adrak ki chai and a bowl of Bikaner ki bhujia to my bedside.

There's lots to look forward too, actually. In a few days it will be spring and Delhi will be full of flowers. My horrible brother will come home on his annual leave. And I may have good news from that interview at AWB.

I'm only twenty-five years old. And healthy. And I have sexy hair. Life is good.

Anuja Chauhan was born in Meerut and went to school in Meerut, Delhi and Melbourne. She has worked in advertising for over seventeen years and has created many popular ad campaigns for PepsiCo, including 'Nothing Official About It', 'Yeh Dil Maange More', 'Oye Bubbly', 'Darr ke Aage Jeet Hai', and 'Live it Abhi'. She lives outside Bangalore with her husband Niret Alva, their three teenagers, two dogs, two cats and numerous girgits.